IN THE BEDOUIN'S TENT

By the dim light of the paper lantern, Tarzan of the Apes watched the preparations of Tollog, the Bedouin slave trader. He saw the cruel expression. He saw the man approaching slowly, the knife ready in his hand.

With an oath, Tollog struck. The ape-man fended the blow, sending the Bedouin sprawling. But Tollog was instantly up, leaping quickly around Tarzan to strike him from behind. In his efforts to turn, the ape-man lost his balance, his feet being bound together, and he fell prone. Now he was at Tollog's mercy!

A vicious smile bared the yellow teeth of the Bedouin. "Die, Nasrany!" he cried.

Then suddenly the entire tent was snatched and hurled off into the night. A shriek of terror burst from Tollog as he saw, red-eyed and angry, a monstrous head towering above him.

Edgar Rice Burroughs
TARZAN NOVELS

COMPLETE AND UNABRIDGED!

TARZAN, LORD OF THE JUNGLE

Edgar Rice Burroughs

BALLANTINE BOOKS • NEW YORK

CONTENTS

1

Tantor the Elephant

HIS great bulk swaying to and fro as he threw his weight first upon one side and then upon the other. Tantor the elephant lolled in the shade of the father of forests. Almost omnipotent, he, in the realm of his people. Dango, Sheeta, even Numa the mighty were as naught to the pachyderm. For a hundred years he had come and gone up and down the land that had trembled to the comings and the goings of his forebears for countless ages.

In peace he had lived with Dango the hyena, Sheeta the leopard and Numa the lion. Man alone had made war upon him. Man, who holds the unique distinction among created things of making war on all living creatures, even to his own kind. Man, the ruthless; man, the pitiless; man, the most hated living organism that Nature has evolved.

Always during the long hundred years of his life, Tantor had known man. There had been black men, always. Big black warriors with spears and arrows, little black warriors, swart Arabs with crude muskets and white men with powerful express rifles and elephant guns. The white men had been the last to come and were the worst. Yet Tantor did not hate men—not even white men. Hate, vengeance, envy, avarice, lust are a few of the delightful emotions reserved exclusively for Nature's noblest work—the *lower* animals do not know them. Neither do they know fear as man knows it, but rather a certain bold caution that sends the antelope and the zebra, watchful and wary, to the water hole with the lion.

Tantor shared this caution with his fellows and avoided men —especially white men; and so had there been other eyes there that day to see, their possessor might almost have questioned their veracity, or attributed their error to the half-light of the forest as they scanned the figure sprawling prone upon the rough back of the elephant, half dozing in the heat to the swaying of the great body; for, despite the sun-bronzed hide, the figure was quite evidently that of a white man. But there were no other eyes to see and Tantor drowsed in the heat of midday and Tarzan, Lord of the Jungle, dozed upon the back of his mighty friend. A sultry air current moved sluggishly from the north, bringing to the keen nostrils of the ape-man no disquieting perception. Peace lay upon the jungle and the two beasts were content.

In the forest Fahd and Motlog, of the tribe el-Harb, hunted north from the menzil of Shiek Ibn Jad of the Beny Salem fendy el-Guad. With them were black slaves. They advanced warily and in silence upon the fresh spoor of el-fil the elephant, the thoughts of the swart 'Aarab dwelling upon ivory, those of the black slaves upon fresh meat. The 'abd Fejjuan, black Galla slave, sleek, ebon warrior, eater of raw meat, famed hunter, led the others.

Fejjuan, as his comrades, thought of fresh meat, but also he thought of el-Habash, the land from which he had been stolen as a boy. He thought of coming again to the lonely Galla hut of his parents. Perhaps el-Habash was not far off now. For months Ibn Jad had been traveling south and now he had come east for a long distance. El-Habash must be near. When he was sure of that his days of slavery would be over and Ibn Jad would have lost his best Galla slave.

Two marches to the north, in the southern extremity of Abyssinia, stood the round dwelling of the father of Fejjuan, almost on the roughly mapped route that Ibn Jad had planned nearly a year since when he had undertaken this mad adventure upon the advice of a learned Sahar, a magician of repute. But of either the exact location of his father's house or the exact plans of Ibn Jad, Fejjuan was equally ignorant. He but dreamed, and his dreams were flavored with raw meat.

The leaves of the forest drowsed in the heat above the heads of the hunters. Beneath the drowsing leaves of other trees a stone's throw ahead of them Tarzan and Tantor slept, their perceptive faculties momentarily dulled by the soothing influence of fancied security and the somnolence that is a corollary of equatorial midday.

Fejjuan, the Galla slave, halted in his tracks, stopping those behind him by the silent mandate of an upraised hand. Directly before him, seen dimly between the boles and through the foliage, swayed the giant bulk of el-fil. Fejjuan motioned to Fahd, who moved stealthily to the side of the black. The Galla slave pointed through the foliage toward a patch of gray hide. Fahd raised el-Lazzary, his ancient matchlock, to his shoulder. There was a flash of flame, a burst of smoke, a roar and el-fil, unhit, was bolting through the forest.

As Tantor surged forward at the sound of the report Tarzan started to spring to an upright position, and at the same instant the pachyderm passed beneath a low hanging limb which struck the ape-man's head, sweeping him to the ground, where he lay stunned and unconscious.

Terrified, Tantor thought only of escape as he ran north through the forest, leaving in his wake felled trees, trampled or uptorn bushes. Perhaps he did not know that his friend lay helpless and injured, at the mercy of the common enemy, man. Tantor never thought of Tarzan as one of the Tarmangani, for the white man was synonymous with discomfort, pain, annoyance, whereas Tarzan of the Apes meant to him restful companionship, peace, happiness. Of all the jungle beasts, except his own kind, he fraternized with Tarzan only.

"Billah! Thou missed," exclaimed Fejjuan.

"Gluck!" ejaculated Fahd. "Sheytan guided the bullet. But let us see—perhaps el-fil is hit."

"Nay, thou missed."

The two men pushed forward, followed by their fellows, looking for the hoped-for carmine spoor. Fahd suddenly stopped.

"Wellah! What have we here?" he cried. "I fired at el-fil and killed a Nasrany."

The others crowded about. "It is indeed a Christian dog, and naked, too," said Motlog.

"Or some wild man of the forest," suggested another. "Where didst thy bullet strike him, Fahd?"

They stooped and rolled Tarzan over. "There is no mark of bullet upon him."

"Is he dead? Perhaps he, too, hunted el-fil and was slain by the great beast."

"He is not dead," announced Fejjuan, who had kneeled and placed an ear above the ape-man's heart. "He lives and from the mark upon his head I think but temporarily out of his wits from a blow. See, he lies in the path that el-fil made when he ran away—he was struck down in the brute's flight."

"I will finish him," said Fahd, drawing his khusa.

"By Ullah, no! Put back thy knife, Fahd," said Motlog. "Let the sheykh say if he shall be killed. Thou art always too eager for blood."

"It is but a Nasrany," insisted Fahd. "Think thou to carry him back to the menzil?"

"He moves," said Fejjuan. 'Presently he will be able to walk there without help. But perhaps he will not come with us, and look, he hath the size and muscles of a gaint. Wellah! What a man!"

'Bind him," commanded Fahd. So with thongs of camel hide they made the ape-man's two wrists secure together across his belly, nor was the work completed any too soon. They had scarce done when Tarzan opened his eyes and looked them slowly over. He shook his head, like some great lion, and presently his senses cleared. He recognized the 'Aarab instantly for what they were.

"Why are my wrists bound?" he asked them in their own tongue. "Remove the thongs!"

Fahd laughed. "Thinkest thou, Nasrany, that thou art some great sheykh that thou canst order about the Beduw as they were dogs?"

"I am Tarzan," replied the ape-man, as one might say, "I am the sheykh of sheykhs."

"Tarzan!" exclaimed Motlog. He drew Fahd aside. "Of all men," he said, lowering his voice, "that it should be our ill fortune to offend this one! In every village that we have entered in the past two weeks we have heard his name. 'Wait,' they have said, 'until Tarzan, Lord of the Jungle, returns. He will slay you when he learns that you have taken slaves in his country'."

"When I drew my khusa thou shouldst not have stopped my hand, Motlog," complained Fahd; "but it is not too late yet." He placed his hand upon the hilt of his knife.

"Billah, nay!" cried Motlog. "We have taken slaves in this country. They are with us now and some of them will escape. Suppose they carry word to the fendy of this great sheykh that we have slain him? Not one of us will live to return to Beled el-Guad."

"Let us then take him before Ibn Jad that the responsibility may be his," said Fahd.

"Wellah, you speak wisely," replied Motlog. "What the sheykh doeth with this man in the sheykh's business. Come!"

As they returned to where Tarzan stood he eyed them questioningly.

"What have you decided to do with me?" he demanded. "If you are wise you will cut these bonds and lead me to your sheykh. I wish a word with him."

"We are only poor men," said Motlog. "It is not for us to say what shall be done, and so we shall take you to our sheykh who will decide."

The Shiek Ibn Jad of the fendy el-Guad squatted in the open men's compartment of his beyt es-sh'ar, and beside him in the mukaad of his house of hair sat Tollog, his brother, and a young Beduin, Zeyd, who, doubtless, found less attraction in the company of the shiek than in the proximity of the sheik's hareem whose quarters were separated from the mukaad only by a breast high curtain suspended between the waist poles of the beyt, affording thus an occasional glimpse of Ateja, the daughter of Ibn Jad. That it also afforded an occasional glimpse of Hirfa, his wife, raised not the temperature of Zeyd an iota.

As the men talked the two women were busy within their apartment at their housewifely duties. In a great brazen jidda Hirfa was placing mutton to be boiled for the next meal while Ateja fashioned sandals from an old bag of camel leather impregnated with the juice of the dates that it had borne upon many a rahla, and meanwhile they missed naught of the conversation that passed in the mukaad.

"We have come a long way without mishap from our own beled," Ibn Jad was remarking, "and the way has been longer because I wished not to pass through el-Habash lest we be set upon or followed by the people of that country. Now may we turn north again and enter el-Habash close to the spot where the magician foretold we should find the treasure city of Nimmr."

"And thinkest thou to find this fabled city easily, once we are within the boundaries of el-Habash?" asked Tollog, his brother.

"Wellah, yes. It is known to the people of this far south Habash. Fejjuan, himself an Habashy, though he has never been there, heard of it as a boy. We shall take prisoners among them and, by the grace of Ullah, we shall find the means to loose their tongues and have the truth from them."

"By Ullah, I hope it does not prove like the treasure that lies upon the great rock el-Howwara in the plain of Medain Salih," said Zeyd. "An afrit guards it where it lay sealed in a stone tower and they say that should it be removed disaster would befall mankind; for men would turn upon their friends, and even upon their brothers, the sons of their fathers and mothers, and the kings of the world would give battle, one against another."

"Yea," testified Tollog, "I had it from one of the fendy Hazim that a wise Moghreby came by there in his travels and consulting the cabalistic signs in his book of magic discovered that indeed the treasure lay there."

"But none dared take it up," said Zeyd.

"Billah!" exclaimed Ibn Jad. "There be no afrit guarding the treasures of Nimmr. Naught but flesh and blood Habush that may be laid low with ball and powder. The treasure is ours for the taking."

"Ullah grant that it may be as easily found as the treasure of Geryeh," said Zeyd, "which lays a journey north of Tebuk in the ancient ruins of a walled city. There, each Friday, the pieces of money roll out of the ground and run about over the desert until sunset."

"'Once we are come to Nimmr there will be no difficulty finding the treasure," Ibn Jad assured them. "The difficulty will lie in getting out of el-Habash with the treasure and the woman; and if she is as beautiful as the sahar said, the men of Nimmr may protect her even more savagely than they would the treasure."

"Often do magicians lie," said Tollog.

"Who comes?" exclaimed Ibn Jad, looking toward the jungle that hemmed the menzil upon all sides.

"Billah! it is Fahd and Motlog returning from the hunt," said Tollog. "Ullah grant that they bring ivory and meat."

"They return too soon," said Zeyd.

"But they do not come empty handed," and Ibn Jad pointed toward the naked giant that accompanied the returning hunters.

The group surrounding Tarzan approached the sheik's beyt and halted.

Wrapped in his soiled calico thob, his head kerchief drawn across the lower part of his face, Ibn Jad exposed but two villainous eyes to the intent scrutiny of the ape-man which simultaneously included the pock-marked, shifty-eyed visage of Tollog, the shiek's brother, and the not ill-favored countenance of the youthful Zeyd.

"Who is sheykh here?" demanded Tarzan in tones of authority that belied the camel leather thongs about his wrists.

Ibn Jad permitted his thorrib to fall from before his face. "Wellah, I am sheykh," he said, "and by what name art thou known, Nasrany?"

"They call me Tarzan of the Apes, Moslem."

"Tarzan of the Apes," mused Ibn Jad. "I have heard the name."

"Doubtless. It is not unknown to 'Aarab slave raiders. Why, then, came you to my country, knowing I do not permit my people to be taken into slavery?"

"We do not come for slaves," Ibn Jad assured him. "We do but trade in peace for ivory."

"Thou liest in thy beard, Moslem," returned Tarzan, quietly. "I recognize both Manyuema and Galla slaves in thy menzil,

and I know that they are not here of their own choosing.
Then, too, was I not present when your henchmen fired a shot
at el-fil? Is that peaceful trading for ivory? No! it is poaching,
and that Tarzan of the Apes does not permit in his country.
You are raiders and poachers."

"By Ullah! we are honest men," cried Ibn Jad. "Fahd and
Motlog did but hunt for meat. If they shot el-fil it must be
that they mistook him for another beast."

"Enough!" cried Tarzan. "Remove the thongs that bind me
and prepare to return north from whence thou came. Thou
shalt have an escort and bearers to the Soudan. There will I
arrange for."

"We have come a long way and wish only to trade in
peace," insisted Ibn Jad. "We shall pay our bearers for their
labor and take no slaves, nor shall we again fire upon el-fil.
Let us go our way and when we return we will pay you well
for permission to pass through your country."

Tarzan shook his head. "No! you shall go at once. Come,
cut these bonds!"

Ibn Jad's eyes narrowed. "We have offered thee peace and
profits, Nasrany," he said, "but if thou wouldst have war let it
be war. Thou art in our power and remember that dead
enemies are harmless. Think it over." And to Fahd: "Take
him away and bind his feet."

"Be careful, Moslem," warned Tarzan, "the arms of the
ape-man are long—they may reach out even in death and
their fingers encircle your throat."

"Thou shalt have until dark to decide, Nasrany, and thou
mayest know that Ibn Jad will not turn back until he hath
that for which he came."

They took Tarzan then and at a distance from the beyt of
Ibn Jad they pushed him into a small hejra; but once within
this tent it required three men to throw him to the ground
and bind his ankles, even though his wrists were already
bound.

In the beyt of the sheik the Beduins sipped their coffee,
sickish with clove, cinnamon and other spice, the while they
discussed the ill fortune that had befallen them; for, regardless of his bravado, Ibn Jad knew full well that only speed
and most propitious circumstances could now place the seal
of success upon his venture.

"But for Motlog," said Fahd, "we would now have no cause
for worry concerning the Nasrany, for I had my knife ready to
slit the dog's throat when Motlog interfered."

"And had word of his slaying spread broadcast over his

country before another sunset and all his people at our heels," countered Motlog.

"Wellah," said Tollog, the sheik's brother. "I wish Fahd had done the thing he wished. After all how much better off are we if we permit the Nasrany to live? Should we free him we know that he will gather his people and drive us from the country. If we keep him prisoner and an escaped slave carries word of it to his people will they not be upon us even more surely than as though we had slain him?"

"Tollog, thou speakest words of wisdom," said Ibn Jad, nodding appreciatively.

"But wait," said Tollog, "I have within me, unspoken, words of even greater worth." He leaned forward motioning the others closer and lowered his voice. "Should this one whom they call Tarzan escape during the night, or should we set him free, there would be no bad word for an escaped slave to bear to his people."

"Billah!" exclaimed Fahd disgustedly. "There would be no need for an escaped slave to bring word to his people—the Nasrany himself would do that and lead them upon us in person. Bah! the brains of Tollog are as camel's dung."

"Thou hast not heard all that I would say, brother," continued Tollog, ignoring Fahd. "It would only *seem* to the slaves that this man had escaped, for in the morning he would be gone and we would make great lamentation over the matter, or we would say: 'Wellah, it is true that Ibn Jad made peace with the stranger, who departed into the jungle, blessing him'."

"I do not follow thee, brother," said Ibn Jad.

"The Nasrany lies bound in yonder hejra. The night will be dark. A slim knife between his ribs were enough. There be faithful Habush among us who will do our bidding, nor speak of the matter after. They can prepare a trench from the bottom of which a dead Tarzan may not reach out to harm us."

"By Ullah, it is plain that thou art of sheykhly blood, Tollog," exclaimed Ibn Jad. "The wisdom of thy words proclaims it. Thou shalt attend to the whole matter. Then will it be done secretly and well. The blessings of Ullah be upon thee!" and Ibn Jad arose and entered the quarters of his hareem.

2

Comrades of the Wild

ARKNESS fell upon the menzil of Ibn Jad the sheik. Beneath the small flitting tent where his captors had left him, Tarzan still struggled with the bonds that secured his wrists, but the tough camel leather withstood even the might of his giant thews. At times he lay listening to the night noises of the jungle, many of them noises that no other human ear could have heard, and always he interpreted each correctly. He knew when Numa passed and Sheeta the leopard; and then from afar and so faintly that it was but the shadow of a whisper, there came down the wind the trumpeting of a bull elephant.

Without the beyt of Ibn Jad Ateja, the sheik's daughter, loitered, and with her was Zeyd. They stood very close to one another and the man held the maiden's hands in his.

"Tell me, Ateja," he said, "that you love no other than Zeyd."

"How many times must I tell you that?" whispered the girl.

"And you do not love Fahd?" insisted the man.

"Billah, no!" she ejaculated.

"Yet your father gives the impression that one day you will be Fahd's."

"My father wishes me to be of the hareem of Fahd, but I mistrust the man, and I could not belong to one whom I neither loved nor trusted."

"I, too, mistrust Fahd," said Zeyd. "Listen Ateja! I doubt his loyalty to thy father, and not his alone, but another whose name I durst not even whisper. Upon occasions I have seen them muttering together when they thought that there were no others about."

The girl nodded her head. "I know. It is not necessary even to whisper the name to me—and I hate him even as I hate Fahd."

"But he is of thine own kin," the youth reminded her.

"What of that? Is he not also my father's brother? If that bond does not hold him loyal to Ibn Jad, who hath treated

15

him well, why should I pretend loyalty for him? Nay, I think him a traitor to my father, but Ibn Jad seems blind to the fact. We are a long way from our own country and if aught should befall the sheykh, Tollog, being next of blood, would assume the skeykhly duties and honors. I think he hath won Fahd's support by a promise to further his suit for me with Ibn Jad, for I have noticed that Tollog exerts himself to praise Fahd in the hearing of my father."

"And perhaps a division of the spoils of the ghrazzu upon the treasure city," suggested Zeyd.

"It is not unlikely," replied the girl, "and—Ullah! what was that?"

The Beduins seated about the coffee fire leaped to their feet. The black slaves, startled, peered out into the darkness from their rude shelters. Muskets were seized. Silence fell again upon the tense, listening menzil. The weird, uncanny cry that had unnerved them was not repeated.

"Billah!" ejaculated Ibn Jad. "It came from the midst of the menzil, and it was the voice of a beast, where there are only men and a few domestic animals."

Could it have been——?" The speaker stopped as though fearful that the thing he would suggest might indeed be true.

"But he is a man and that was the voice of a beast," insisted Ibn Jad. "It could not have been he."

"But he is a Nasrany," reminded Fahd. "Perhaps he has league with Sheytan."

"And the sound came from the direction where he lies bound in a hejra," observed another.

"Come!" said Ibn Jad. "Let us investigate."

With muskets ready the 'Aarab, lighting the way with paper lanterns, approached the hejra where Tarzan lay. Fearfully the foremost looked within.

"He is here," he reported.

Tarzan, who was sitting in the center of the tent, surveyed the 'Aarab somewhat contemptuously. Ibn Jad pressed forward.

"You heard a cry?" he demanded of the ape-man.

"Yes, I heard it. Camest thou, Sheykh Ibn Jad, to disturb my rest upon so trivial an errand, or camest thou to release me?"

"What manner of cry was it? What did it signify?" asked Ibn Jad.

Tarzan of the Apes smiled grimly. "It was but the call of a beast to one of his kind," he replied. "Does the noble Beduwy tremble thus always when he hears the voices of the jungle people?"

"Gluck!" growled Ibn Jad, "the Beduw fear naught. We thought the sound came from this hejra and we hastened hither believing some jungle beast had crept within the menzil and attacked thee. Tomorrow it is the thought of Ibn Jad to release thee."

"Why not tonight?"

"My people fear thee. They would that when you are released you depart hence immediately."

"I shall. I have no desire to remain in thy lice infested menzil."

"We could not send thee alone into the jungle at night where el-adrea is abroad hunting," protested the sheik.

Tarzan of the Apes smiled again, one of his rare smiles. "Tarzan is more secure in his teeming jungle than are the Beduwy in their desert," he replied. "The jungle night has no terrors for Tarzan."

"Tomorrow," snapped the shiek and then, motioning to his followers, he departed.

Tarzan watched their paper lanterns bobbing across the camp to the sheik's beyt and then he stretched himself at full length and pressed an ear to the ground.

When the inhabitants of the 'Aarab menzil heard the cry of the beast shatter the quiet of the new night it aroused within their breasts a certain vague unrest, but otherwise it was meaningless to them. Yet there was one far off in the jungle who caught the call faintly and understood—a huge beast, the great, gray dreadnaught of the jungle, Tantor the elephant. Again he raised his trunk aloft and trumpeted loudly. His little eyes gleamed redly wicked as, a moment later, he swung off through the forest at a rapid trot.

Slowly silence fell upon the menzil of Sheik Ibn Jad as the 'Aarab and their slaves sought their sleeping mats. Only the sheik and his brother sat smoking in the sheik's beyt—smoking and whispering in low tones.

"Do not let the slaves see you slay the Nasrany, Tollog," cautioned Ibn Jad. "Attend to that yourself first in secrecy and in silence, then quietly arouse two of the slaves. Fejjuan would be as good as another, as he has been among us since childhood and is loyal. He will do well for one."

"Abbas is loyal, too, and strong," suggested Tollog.

"Yea, let him be the second," agreed Ibn Jad. "But it is well that they do not know how the Nasrany came to die. Tell them that you heard a noise in the direction of his hejra and that when you had come to learn the nature of it you found him thus dead."

"You may trust to my discretion, brother," Tollog assured.

"And warn them to secrecy," continued the sheik. "No man but we four must ever know of the death of the Nasrany, nor of his place of burial. In the morning we shall tell the others that he escaped during the night. Leave his cut bonds within the hejra as proof. You understand?"

"By Ullah, fully."

"Good! Now go. The people sleep." The sheik rose and Tollog, also. The former entered the apartment of his hareem and the latter moved silently through the darkness of the night in the direction of the hejra where his victim lay.

Through the jungle came Tantor the elephant and from his path fled gentle beasts and fierce. Even Numa the lion slunk growling to one side as the mighty pachyderm passed.

Into the darkness of the hejra crept Tollog, the sheik's brother; but Tarzan, lying with an ear to the ground, had heard him approaching from the moment that he had left the beyt of Ibn Jad. Tarzan heard other sounds as well and, as he interpreted these others, he interpreted the stealthy approach of Tollog and was convinced when the footsteps turned into the tent where he lay—convinced of the purpose of his visitor. For what purpose but the taking of his life would a Beduin visit Tarzan at this hour of the night?

As Tollog, groping in the dark, entered the tent Tarzan sat erect and again there smote upon the ears of the Beduin the horrid cry that had disturbed the menzil earlier in the evening, but this time it arose in the very hejra in which Tollog stood.

The Beduin halted, aghast. "Ullah!" he cried, stepping back. "What beast is there? Nasrany! Art thou being attacked?"

Others in the camp were awakened, but none ventured forth to investigate. Tarzan smiled and remained silent.

"Nasrany!" repeated Tollog, but there was no reply.

Cautiously, his knife ready in his hand, the Beduin backed from the hejra. He listened but heard no sound from within. Running quickly to his own beyt he made a light in a paper lantern and hastened back to the hejra, and this time he carried his musket and it was at full cock. Peering within, the lantern held above his head, Tollog saw the ape-man sitting upon the ground looking at him. There was no wild beast! Then the Beduin understood.

"Billah! It wast thou, Nasrany, who made the fearful cries."

"Beduwy, thou comest to kill the Nasrany, eh?" demanded Tarzan.

From the jungle came the roar of a lion and the trumpeting of a bull elephant, but the boma was high and sharp with thorns and there were guards and beast fire, so Tollog gave no thought to these familiar noises of the night. He did not answer Tarzan's question but laid aside his musket and drew his khusa, which after all was answer enough.

In the dim light of the paper lantern Tarzan watched these preparations. He saw the cruel expression upon the malevolent face. He saw the man approaching slowly, the knife ready in his hand.

The man was almost upon him now, his eyes glittering in the faint light. To the ears of the ape-man came the sound of a commotion at the far edge of the menzil, followed by an Arab oath. Then Tollog launched a blow at Tarzan's breast. The prisoner swung his bound wrists upward and struck the Beduin's knife arm away, and simultaneously he struggled to his knees.

With an oath, Tollog struck again, and again Tarzan fended the blow, and this time he followed swiftly with a mighty sweep of his arms that struck the Beduin upon the side of the head and sent him sprawling across the hejra; but Tollog was instantly up and at him again, this time with the ferocity of a maddened bull, yet at the same time with far greater cunning, for instead of attempting a direct frontal attack Tollog leaped quickly around Tarzan to strike him from behind.

In his effort to turn upon his knees that he might face his antagonist the ape-man lost his balance, his feet being bound together, and fell prone at Tollog's mercy. A vicious smile bared the yellow teeth of the Beduin.

"Die, Nasrany!" he cried, and then: "Billah! What was that?" as, of a sudden, the entire tent was snatched from above his head and hurled off into the night. He turned quickly and a shriek of terror burst from his lips as he saw, red-eyed and angry, the giant form of el-fil towering above him; and in that very instant a supple trunk encircled his body and Tollog, the sheik's brother, was raised high aloft and hurled off into the darkness as the tent had been.

For an instant Tantor stood looking about, angrily, defiantly, then he reached down and lifted Tarzan from the ground, raised him high above his head, wheeled about and trotted rapidly across the menzil toward the jungle. A frightened sentry fired once and fled. The other sentry lay crushed and dead where Tantor had hurled him when he entered the camp. An instant later Tarzan and Tantor were swallowed by the jungle and the darkness.

The menzil of Sheik Ibn Jad was in an uproar. Armed men hastened hither and thither seeking the cause of the disturbance, looking for an attacking enemy. Some came to the spot where had stood the hejra where the Nasrany had been confined, but Hejra and Nasrany both had disappeared. Nearby, the beyt of one of Ibn Jad's cronies lay flattened. Beneath it were screaming women and a cursing man. On top of it was Tollog, the sheik's brother, his mouth filled with vile Beduin invective, whereas it should have contained only praises of Allah and thanksgiving, for Tollog was indeed a most fortunate man. Had he alighted elsewhere than upon the top of a sturdily pegged beyt he had doubtless been killed or badly injured when Tantor hurled him thus rudely aside.

Ibn Jad, searching for information, arrived just as Tollog was extricating himself from the folds of the tent.

"Billah!" cried the sheik. "What has come to pass? What, O brother, art thou doing upon the beyt of Abd el-Aziz?"

A slave came running to the sheik. "The Nasrany is gone and he hath taken the hejra with him," he cried.

Ibn Jad turned to Tollog. "Canst thou not explain, brother?" he demanded. "Is the Nasrany truly departed?"

"The Nasrany is indeed gone," replied Tollog. "He is in league with Sheytan, who came in the guise of el-fil and carried the Nasrany into the jungle, after throwing me upon the top of the beyt of Abd el-Aziz whom I still hear squealing and cursing beneath as though it had been he who was attacked rather than I."

Ibn Jad shook his head. Of course he knew that Tollog was a liar—that he always had known—yet he could not understand how his brother had come to be upon the top of the beyt of Abed el-Aziz.

"What did the sentries see?" demanded the sheik. "Where were they?"

"They were at their post," spoke up Motlog. "I was just there. One of them is dead, the other fired upon the intruder as it escaped."

"And what said he of it?" demanded Ibn Jad.

"Wellah, he said that el-fil came and entered the menzil, killing Yemeny and rushing to the hejra where the Nasrany lay bound, ripping it aside, throwing Tollog high into the air. Then he seized the prisoner and bore him off into the jungle, and as he passed him Hasan fired."

"And missed," guessed Ibn Jad.

For several moments the sheik stood in thought, then he turned slowly toward his own beyt. "Tomorrow, early, is the rahla," he said; and the word spread quickly that early upon the morrow they would break camp.

Far into the forest Tantor bore Tarzan until they had come to a small clearing well carpeted with grass, and here the elephant deposited his burden gently upon the ground and stood guard above.

"In the morning," said Tarzan, "when Kudu the Sun hunts again through the heavens and there is light by which to see, we shall discover what may be done about removing these bonds, Tantor; but for now let us sleep."

Numa the lion, Dango the hyena, Sheeta the leopard passed near that night, and the scent of the helpless man-thing was strong in their nostrils, but when they saw who stood guard above Tarzan and heard the mutterings of the big bull, they passed on about their business while Tarzan of the Apes slept.

With the coming of dawn all was quickly astir in the menzil of Ibn Jad. Scarce was the meagre breakfast eaten ere the beyt of the sheik was taken down by his women, and at this signal the other houses of hair came tumbling to the ground, and within the hour the 'Aarab were winding north-ward toward el-Habash.

The Beduins and their women were mounted upon the desert ponies that had survived the long journey from the north, while the slaves that they had brought with them from their own country marched afoot at the front and rear of the column in the capacity of askari, and these were armed with muskets. Their bearers were the natives that they had impressed into their service along the way. These carried the impedimenta of the camp and herded the goats and sheep along the trail.

Zeyd rode beside Ateja, the daughter of the sheik, and more often were his eyes upon her profile than upon the trail ahead. Fahd, who rode near Ibn Jad, cast an occasional angry glance in the direction of the two. Tollog, the sheik's brother, saw and grinned.

"Zeyd is a bolder suitor than thou, Fahd," he whispered to the young man.

"He has whispered lies into her ears and she will have none of me," complained Fahd.

"If the sheykh favored thy suit though," suggested Tollog.

"But he does not," snapped Fahd. "A word from you might aid. You promised it."

"Wellah, yes, but my brother is an over-indulgent sire," explained Tollog. "He doth not mislike you, Fahd, but rather he would have his bint happy, and so leaves the selection of her mate to her."

"What is there to do, then?" demanded Fahd.

"If I were sheykh, now," suggested Tollog, "but alas I am not."

"If you were sheykh, what then?"

"My niece would go to the man of my own choosing."

"But you are not sheykh," Fahd reminded him.

Tollog leaned close and whispered in Fahd's ear. "A suitor as bold as Zeyd would find the way to make me sheykh."

Fahd made no reply but only rode on in silence, his head bowed and his brows contracted in thought.

3

The Apes of Toyat

THREE days crawled slowly out of the east and followed one another across the steaming jungle and over the edge of the world beyond. For three days the 'Aarab moved slowly northward toward el-Habash. For three days Tarzan of the Apes lay in the little clearing, bound and helpless, while Tantor the elephant stood guard above him. Once each day the great bull brought the ape-man food and water.

The camel leather thongs held securely and no outside aid appeared to release Tarzan from the ever increasing discomfort and danger of his predicament. He had called to Manu the monkey to come and gnaw the strands apart, but Manu, ever irresponsible, had only promised and forgotten. And so the ape-man lay uncomplaining, as is the way of beasts patiently waiting for release, knowing that it might come in the habiliment of death.

Upon the morning of the fourth day Tantor gave evidences of restlessness. His brief foragings had exhausted the nearby supply of food for himself and his charge. He wanted to move on and take Tarzan with him; but the ape-man was now convinced that to be carried farther into the elephant country would lessen his chances for succor, for he felt that the only one of the jungle people who could release him was Mangani the great ape. Tarzan knew that already he was practically at the outer limits of the Mangani country, yet there was a remote chance that a band of the great anthropoids might pass this way and discover him, while, should Tantor carry him farther north even this meager likelihood of release would be lost forever.

Tantor wanted to be gone. He nudged Tarzan with his trunk and rolled him over. He raised him from the ground.

"Put me down, Tantor," said the ape-man, and the pachyderm obeyed, but he turned and walked away. Tarzan watched him cross the clearing to the trees upon the far side. There Tantor hesitated, stopped, turned. He looked back at Tarzan and trumpeted. He dug up the earth with a great tusk and appeared angry.

"Go and feed," said Tarzan, "and then return. Tomorrow the Mangani may come."

Tantor trumpeted again and, wheeling about, disappeared in the jungle. For a long time the ape-man lay listening to the retreating footfalls of his old friend.

"He is gone," he mused. "I cannot blame him. Perhaps it is as well. What matter whether it be today, tomorrow, or the day after?"

The morning passed. The noonday silence lay upon the jungle. Only the insects were abroad. They annoyed Tarzan as they did the other jungle beasts, but to the poison of their stings he was immune through a lifetime of inoculation.

Suddenly there came a great scampering through the trees. Little Manu and his brothers, his sisters and his cousins came trooping madly through the middle terrace, squealing, chattering and scolding.

"Manu!" called Tarzan. "What comes?"

"The Mangani! The Mangani!" shrieked the monkeys.

"Go and fetch them, Manu!" commanded the ape-man.

"We are afraid."

"Go and call to them from the upper terraces," urged Tarzan. "They cannot reach you there. Tell them that one of their people lies helpless here. Tell them to come and release me."

"We are afraid."

"They cannot reach you in the upper terraces. Go! They will be your friends then."

"They cannot climb to the upper terraces," said an old monkey. "I will go."

The others, halted in their flight, turned and watched the gray-beard as he scampered quickly off amongst the loftiest branches of the great trees, and Tarzan waited.

Presently he heard the deep gutturals of his own people, the great apes, the Mangani. Perhaps there would be those among them who knew him. Perhaps, again, the band may have come from afar and have no knowledge of him, though that he doubted. In them, however, was his only hope. He lay there, listening, waiting. He heard Manu screaming and chattering as he scampered about high above the Mangani, then, of a sudden, silence fell upon the jungle. There was only the sound of insects, buzzing, humming.

The ape-man lay looking in the direction from which had come the sounds of the approaching anthropoids. He knew what was transpiring behind that dense wall of foliage. He knew that presently a pair of fierce eyes would be examining him, surveying the clearing, searching for an enemy, warily probing for a trick or a trap. He knew that the first sight of him might arouse distrust, fear, rage; for what reason had they to love or trust the cruel and merciless Tarmangani?

There lay great danger in the possibility that, seeing him, they might quietly withdraw without showing themselves. That, then, would be the end, for there were no others than the Mangani to whom he might look for rescue. With this in mind he spoke.

"I am a friend," he called to them. "The Tarmangani caught me and bound my wrists and ankles. I cannot move. I cannot defend myself. I cannot get food nor water. Come and remove my bonds."

From just behind the screen of foliage a voice replied, "You are a Tarmangani."

"I am Tarzan of the Apes," replied the ape-man.

"Yes," screamed Manu, "he is Tarzan of the Apes. The Tarmangani and the Gomangani bound him and Tantor brought him here. Four times has Kudu hunted across the sky while Tarzan of the Apes lay bound."

"I know Tarzan," said another voice from behind the foliage and presently the leaves parted and a huge, shaggy ape lumbered into the clearing. Swinging along with knuckles to the ground the brute came close to Tarzan.

"M'walat!" exclaimed the ape-man.

"It is Tarzan of the Apes," said the great ape, but the others did not understand.

"What?" they demanded.

"Whose band is this?" asked Tarzan.

"Toyat is king," replied M'walat.

"Then do not tell them it is really I," whispered Tarzan, "until you have cut these bonds. Toyat hates me. He will kill me if I am defenseless."

"Yes," agreed M'walat.

"Here," said Tarzan, raising his bound wrists. "Bite these bonds in two."

"You are Tarzan of the Apes, the friend of M'walat. M'walat will do as you ask," replied the ape.

Of course, in the meager language of the apes, their conversation did not sound at all like a conversation between men, but was rather a mixture of growls and grunts and gestures which, however, served every purpose that could have been served by the most formal and correct of civilized speech since it carried its messages clearly to the minds of both the Mangani and the Tarmangani, the Great Ape and the Great White Ape.

As the other members of the band pressed forward into the clearing, seeing that M'walat was not harmed, the latter stooped and with powerful teeth severed the camel leather thongs that secured the wrists of the ape-man, and similarly he freed his ankles.

As Tarzan came to his feet the balance of the fierce and shaggy band swung into the clearing. In the lead was Toyat, king ape, and at his heels eight more full grown males with perhaps six or seven females and a number of young. The young and the shes hung back, but the bulls pressed forward to where Tarzan stood with M'walat at his side.

The king ape growled menacingly. "Tarmangani!" he cried. Wheeling in a circle he leaped into the air and came down on all fours; he struck the ground savagely with his clenched fists; he growled and foamed, and leaped again and again. Toyat was working himself to a pitch of rage that would nerve him to attack the Tarmangani, and by these maneuvers he hoped also to arouse the savage fighting spirit of his fellows.

"It is Tarzan of the Apes, friend of the Mangani," said M'walat.

"It is a Tarmangani, enemy of the Mangani," cried Toyat. "They come with great thunder sticks and kill us. They make our shes and our balus dead with a loud noise. Kill the Tarmangani."

"It is Tarzan of the Apes," growled Gayat. "When I was a little balu he saved me from Numa. Tarzan of the Apes is the friend of the Mangani."

"Kill the Tarmangani!" shrieked Toyat, leaping high into the air.

Several of the other bulls were now circling and leaping into the air as Gayat placed himself at Tarzan's side. The ape-man knew them well. He knew that sooner or later one of them would have excited himself to such a pitch of maniacal frenzy that he would leap suddenly upon him. M'walat and Gayat would attack in his defense; several more bulls would launch themselves into the battle and there would ensue a free for all fight from which not all of them would emerge alive, and none without more or less serious injuries; but Tarzan of the Apes did not wish to battle with his friends.

"Stop!" he commanded raising his opened palm to attract attention. "I am Tarzan of the Apes, mighty hunter, mighty fighter; long did I range with the tribe of Kerchak; when Kerchak died I became king ape; many of you know me; all know that I am first a Mangani; that I am friend to all Mangani. Toyat would have you kill me because Toyat hates

Tarzan of the Apes. He hates him not because he is a Tarmangani but because Tarzan once kept Toyat from becoming king. That was many rains ago when some of you were still balus. If Toyat has been a good king Tarzan is glad, but now he is not acting like a good king for he is trying to turn you against your best friend.

"You, Zutho!" he exclaimed, suddenly pointing a finger at a huge bull. "You leap and growl and foam at the mouth. You would sink your fangs into the flesh of Tarzan. Have you forgotten, Zutho, the time that you were sick and the other members of the tribe left you to die? Have you forgotten who brought you food and water? Have you forgotten who it was that kept Sabor the lioness and Sheeta the panther and Dango the hyena from you during those long nights?"

As Tarzan spoke, his tone one of quiet authority, the apes gradually paused to listen to his words. It was a long speech for the jungle folk. The great apes nor the little monkeys long concentrated upon one idea. Already, before he had finished, one of the bulls was overturning a rotted log in search of succulent insects. Zutho was wrinkling his brows in unaccustomed recollection. Presently he spoke.

"Zutho remembers," he said. "He is the friend of Tarzan," and ranged himself beside M'walat. With this the other bulls, except Toyat, appeared to lose interest in the proceedings and either wandered off in search of food or squatted down in the grass.

Toyat still fumed, but as he saw his cause deserted he prosecuted his war dance at a safer distance from Tarzan and his defenders, and it was not long before he, too, was attracted by the more profitable business of bug hunting.

And so Tarzan ranged again with the great apes. And as he loafed lazily through the forest with the shaggy brutes he thought of his foster mother, Kala, the great she-ape, the only mother he had ever known; he recalled with a thrill of pride her savage defense of him against all their natural enemies of the jungle and against the hate and jealousy of old Tublat, her mate, and against the enmity of Kerchak, the terrible old king ape.

As it had been but yesterday since he had seen him, Tarzan's memory projected again upon the screen of recollection the huge bulk and the ferocious features of old Kerchak. What a magnificent beast he had been! To the childish mind of the ape-boy Kerchak had been the personification of savage ferocity and authority, and even today he recalled him with almost a sensation of awe. That he had overthrown and slain this gigantic ruler still seemed to Tarzan almost incredible.

He fought again his battles with Terkoz and with Bolgani the gorilla. He thought of Teeka, whom he had loved, and of Thaka and Tana, and of the little black boy, Tibo, whom he had endeavored to adopt; and so he dreamed through lazy daylight hours while Ibn Jad crept slowly northward toward the leopard city of Nimmr and in another part of the jungle events were transpiring that were to entangle Tarzan in the meshes of a great adventure.

4

Bolgani the Gorilla

A BLACK porter caught his foot in an entangling creeper and stumbled, throwing his load to the ground. Of such trivialities are crises born. This one altered the entire life of James Hunter Blake, young, rich, American, hunting big game for the first time in Africa with his friend Wilbur Stimbol who, having spent three weeks in the jungle two years before, was naturally the leader of the expedition and an infallible authority on all matters pertaining to big game, African jungle, safari, food, weather and Negroes. The further fact that Stimbol was twenty-five years Blade's senior naturally but augmented his claims to omniscience.

These factors did not in themselves constitute the basis for the growing differences between the two men, for Blake was a phlegmatically inclined young man of twenty-five who was rather amused at Stimbol's egotism than otherwise. The first rift had occurred at railhead when, through Stimbol's domineering manner and ill temper, the entire purpose of the expedition had been abandoned by necessity, and what was to have been a quasi scientific motion picture camera study of wild African life had resolved itself into an ordinary big game hunt.

At railhead, while preparations were going on to secure equipment and a safari, Stimbol had so offended and insulted the cameraman that he had left them flat and returned to the coast. Blake was disappointed, but he made up his mind to go on through and get what pictures he could with a still camera. He was not a man who enjoyed killing for the mere sport of taking life, and as originally planned there was to have been no shooting of game except for food and half a dozen trophies that Stimbol particularly wished to add to his collection.

There had since been one or two altercations relative to Stimbol's treatment of the black porters, but these matters, Blake was hopeful, had been ironed out and Stimbol had promised to leave the handling of the safari to Blake and refrain from any further abuse of the men.

They had come into the interior even farther than they had planned, had had the poorest of luck in the matter of game and were about to turn back toward railhead. It seemed now to Blake that after all they were going to pull through without further difficulty and that he and Stimbol would return to America together, to all intent and purpose still friends; but just then a black porter caught his foot in an entangling creeper and stumbled, throwing his load to the ground.

Directly in front of the porter Stimbol and Blake were walking side by side and, as though guided by a malevolent power, the load crashed into Stimbol, hurling him to the ground. Stimbol and the porter scrambled to their feet amidst the laughter of the Negroes who had witnessed the accident. The porter was grinning. Stimbol was flushed with anger.

"You damned clumsy swine!" he cried, and before Blake could interfere or the porter protect himself the angry white man stepped quickly over the fallen load and struck the black a terrific blow in the face that felled him; and as he lay there, Stimbol kicked him in the side. But only once! Before he could repeat the outrage Blake seized him by the shoulder, wheeled him about and struck him precisely as he had struck the black.

Stimbol fell, rolled over on his side and reached for the automatic that hung at his hip, but quick as he was Blake was quicker. "Cut that!" said Blake, crisply, covering Stimbol with a .45. Stimbol's hand dropped from the grip of his gun. "Get up!" ordered Blake, and when the other had risen: "Now listen to me, Stimbol—this is the end. You and I are through. Tomorrow morning we split the safari and equipment, and whichever way you go with your half I'll go in the opposite direction."

Blake had returned his gun to its holster as he spoke, the black had risen and was nursing a bloody nose, the other blacks were looking sullenly. Blake motioned to the porter to pick up his load and presently the safari was again on the move—a sullen safari without laughter or song.

Blake made camp at the first available ground shortly before noon in order that the division of equipment, food and men could be made during the afternoon and the two safaris thus be enabled to make an early start the following morning.

Stimbol, sullen, would give no assistance, but, taking a couple of the askari, the armed natives who act as soldiers for the safari, started out from camp to hunt. He had proceeded scarcely a mile along a mould padded game trail which gave forth no sound in answer to their falling footsteps, when one of the natives in the lead held up his hand in warning as he halted in his tracks.

Stimbol advanced cautiously and the black pointed toward the left, through the foliage. Dimly, Stimbol saw a black mass moving slowly away from them.

"What is it?" he whispered.

"Gorilla," replied the black.

Stimbol raised his rifle and fired at the retreating figure. The black was not surprised that he missed.

"Hell!" ejaculated the white. "Come on, get after him! I've got to have him. Gad! what a trophy he'll make."

The jungle was rather more open than usual and again and again they came within sight of the retreating gorilla. Each time Stimbol fired and each time he missed. Secretly the blacks were amused and pleased. They did not like Stimbol.

At a distance Tarzan of the Apes, hunting with the tribe of Toyat, heard the first shot and immediately took to the trees and was racing in the direction of the sound. He felt sure that the weapon had not been discharged by the Beduins, for he well knew and could differentiate between the reports of their muskets and those made by modern weapons.

Perhaps, he thought, there may be among them such a rifle, because such was not impossible, but more likely it meant white men, and in Tarzan's country it was his business to know what strangers were there and why. Seldom they came even now, though once they had never come. It was those days that Tarzan regretted, for when the white man comes peace and happiness depart.

Racing through the trees, swinging from limb to limb, Tarzan of the Apes unerringly followed the direction of the sound of the succeeding shots; and as he approached more closely the scene of the pursuit of Bolgani the gorilla, he heard the crashing of underbrush and the voices of men.

Bolgani, fleeing with greater haste than caution, his mind and attention occupied by thoughts of escape from the hated Tarmangani and the terrifying thunder stick that roared each time the Tarmangani came within sight of him, abandoned his accustomed wariness and hurried through the jungle forgetful of what few other enemies might beset his path; and so it was that he failed to see Histah the snake draped in sinuous loops along an overhanging branch of a nearby patriarch of the forest.

The huge python, naturally short tempered and irritable, had been disturbed and annoyed by the crashing sounds of pursuit and escape and the roaring voice of the rifle. Ordinarily he would have permitted a full grown bull gorilla to pass unmolested, but in his present state of mind he might have attacked even Tantor himself.

His beady eyes glaring fixedly, he watched the approach of the shaggy Bolgani, and as the gorilla passed beneath the limb to which he clung Histah launched himself upon his prey.

As the great coils, powerful, relentless, silent, encircled Bolgani, he sought to tear the hideous folds from him. Great is the strength of Bolgani, but even greater is that of Histah the snake. A single hideous, almost human scream burst from the lips of Bolgani with the first realization of the disaster that had befallen him, and then he was on the ground tearing futilely at the steadily tightening bands of living steel that would crush the life from him, crush until his bones gave to the tremendous pressure, until only broken pulp remained within a sausage like thing that would slip between the distended jaws of the serpent.

It was upon this sight that Stimbol and Tarzan came simultaneously—Stimbol stumbling awkwardly through the underbrush, Tarzan of the Apes, demi-god of the forest, swinging gracefully through the foliage of the middle terraces.

They arrived simultaneously but Tarzan was the only one of the party whose presence was unsuspected by the others, for, as always, he had moved silently and with the utmost wariness because of the unknown nature of the conditions he might discover.

As he looked down upon the scene below his quick eye and his knowledge of the jungle revealed at a glance the full story of the tragedy that had overtaken Bolgani, and then he saw Stimbol raise his rifle, intent upon bagging two royal specimens with a single shot.

In the heart of Tarzan was no great love for Bolgani the gorilla. Since childhood the shaggy, giant man-beast had been the natural foe of the ape-man. His first mortal combat had been with Bolgani. For years he had feared him, or rather avoided him through caution, for of fear Tarzan was ignorant; and since he had emerged from childhood he had continued to avoid Bolgani for the simple reason that his own people, the great apes, avoided him.

But now when he saw the huge brute beset by two of the natural enemies of both the Mangani and the Bolgani, there flared within his breast a sudden loyalty that burned away the personal prejudices of a lifetime.

He was directly above Stimbol, and with such celerity do the mind and muscles of the ape-man coordinate that even as the American raised his weapon to his shoulder Tarzan had dropped upon his back, felling him to the earth; and before Stimbol could discover what had happened to him, long before he could stumble, cursing, to his feet, Tarzan, who had been unarmed, had snatched the hunter's knife from its scabbard and leaped full upon the writhing, struggling mass of python and gorilla. Stimbol came to his feet ready to kill but what he saw before him temporarily drove the desire for vengeance from his mind.

Naked but for a loin cloth, bronzed, black-haired, a giant white man battled with the dread python; and as Stimbol watched he shuddered as he became aware that the low, beast-like growls he heard came not alone from the savage lips of the gorilla but from the throat of the god-like man-thing that fought for him.

Steel fingers encircled the python just back of its head, while those of the free hand drove Stimbol's hunting knife again and again into the coiling, writhing body of the serpent. With the projection of a new and more menacing enemy into the battle, Histah was forced partially to release his hold upon Bolgani with, at first, the intention of including Tarzan in the same embrace that he might crush them both at once; but soon he discovered that the hairless man-thing constituted a distinct menace to his life that would necessitate his undivided attention, and so he quickly uncoiled from about Bolgani and in a frenzy of rage and pain that whipped his great length into a lashing fury of destruction he sought to encircle the ape-man; but wheresoever his coils approached, the keen knife bit deep into tortured flesh.

Bolgani, the spark of life all but crushed from him, lay gasping upon the ground, unable to come to the aid of his preserver, while Stimbol, goggle-eyed with awe and terror, kept at a safe distance, momentarily forgetful both of his lust for trophies and his bent for revenge.

Thus was Tarzan pitted, single-handed, against one of the mightiest of Nature's creations in a duel to the death, the result of which seemed to the watching American already a foregone conclusion, for what man born of woman could hope, unaided, to escape from the embrace of the deadly coils of a python?

Already Histah had encircled the torso and one leg of the

ape-man, but his powers of constriction, lessened by the frightful wounds he had received, had as yet been unable to crush
his adversary into helplessness, and Tarzan was now con-
centrating his attention and the heavy blade of the hunting
knife upon a single portion of the weakening body in an attempt to cut Histah in two.

Man and serpent were red with blood; and crimson were
the grasses and the brush for yards in all directions as, with a
final effort, Histah closed his giant coils spasmodically about
his victim at the instant that Tarzan with a mighty upward
heavy lunge cut through the vertebrae of the great snake.

Lashing and writhing, the nether portion, headless, flopped
aside while the ape-man, still fighting with what remained,
exerting his superhuman strength to its ultimate utmost, slowly
forced the coils from about his body and cast the dying Histah
from him. Then, without a glance at Stimbol, he turned to
Bolgani.

"You are hurt to death?" he asked in the language of the
great apes.

"No," replied the gorilla. "I am Bolgani! I kill, Tarmangani!"

"I am Tarzan of the Apes," said the ape-man. "I saved
you from Histah."

"You did not come to kill Bolgani?" inquired the gorilla.

"No. Let us be friends."

Bolgani frowned in an effort to concentrate upon this remarkable problem. Presently he spoke. "We will be friends,"
he said. "The Tarmangani behind you will kill us both with
his thunder stick. Let us kill him first." Painfully he staggered
to his feet.

"No," remonstrated Tarzan. "I will send the Tarmangani
away."

"You? He will not go."

"I am Tarzan, Lord of the Jungle," replied the ape-man.
"The word of Tarzan is law in the jungle."

Stimbol, who had been watching, was under the impression
that the man and the beast were growling at one another and
that a new duel impended. Had he guessed the truth and
suspicioned that they considered him a common enemy he
would have felt far less at ease. Now, his rifle regained, he
started toward Tarzan just as the latter turned to address him.

"Stand to one side, young fellow," said Stimbol, "while I
finish that gorilla. After the experience you just had with the
snake, I doubt if you want that fellow to jump you, too." The
American was none too sure of what the attitude of the white

giant might be, for all too fresh in his mind was the startling
and disconcerting manner of the wild man's introduction; but
he felt safe because he held a rifle, while the other was unarmed, and he guessed that the giant might be only too glad
to be saved from the attentions of the gorilla, which, from
Stimbol's imagined knowledge of such beasts, appeared to
him to be quite evidently threatening.

Tarzan halted directly between Bolgani and the hunter and
eyed the latter appraisingly for a moment. "Lower your rifle,"
he said, presently. "You are not going to shoot the gorilla."

"The hell I'm not!" ejaculated Stimbol. "What do you suppose I've been chasing him through the jungle for?"

"Under a misapprehension," replied Tarzan.

"What misapprehension?" demanded Stimbol.

"That you were going to shoot him. You are not."

"Say, young man, do you know who I am?" demanded
Stimbol.

"I am not interested," replied Tarzan coldly.

"Well you'd better be. I'm Wilbur Stimbol of Stimbol &
Company, brokers, New York!" That was a name to conjure
with—in New York. Even in Paris and London it had opened
many a door, bent many a knee. Seldom had it failed the
purpose of this purse-arrogant man.

"What are you doing in my country?" demanded the
ape-man, ignoring Stimbol's egotistical statement of his
identity.

"Your country? Who the hell are you?"

Tarzan turned toward the two blacks who had been standing
a little in the rear of Stimbol and to one side. "I am Tarzan
of the Apes," he said to them in their own dialect. "What is
this man doing in my country? How many are there in his
party—how many white men?"

"Big Bwana," replied one of the men with sincere defer-
ence, "we knew that you were Tarzan of the Apes when we
saw you swing from the trees and slay the great snake. There
is no other in all the jungle who could do that. This white man
is a bad master. There is one other white man with him.
The other is kind. They came to hunt Simba the lion and
other big game. They have had no luck. Tomorrow they turn
back."

"Where is their camp?" demanded Tarzan.

The black who had spoken pointed. "It is not far," he said.

The ape-man turned to Stimbol. "Go back to your camp,"
he said. "I shall come there later this evening and talk with

you and your companion. In the meantime hunt no more except for food in Tarzan's country."

There was something in the voice and manner of the stranger that had finally gone through Stimbol's thick sensibilities and impressed him with a species of awe—a thing he had scarcely ever experienced in the past except in the presence of wealth that was grossly superior to his own. He did not reply. He just stood and watched the bronzed giant turn to the gorilla. He heard them growl at one another for a moment and then, to his vast surprise, he saw them move off through the jungle together, shoulder to shoulder. As the foliage closed about them he removed his helmet and wiped the sweat from his forehead with a silken handkerchief as he stood staring at the green branches that had parted to receive this strangely assorted pair.

Finally he turned to his men with an oath. "A whole day wasted!" he complained. "Who is this fellow? You seemed to know him."

"He is Tarzan," replied one of the blacks.

"Tarzan? Never heard of him," snapped Stimbol.

"All who know the jungle, know Tarzan."

"Humph!" sneered Stimbol. "No lousy wild man is going to tell Wilbur Stimbol where he can hunt and where he can't."

"Master," said the black who had first spoken, "the word of Tarzan is the law of the jungle. Do not offend him."

"I'm not paying you damn fools for advice," snapped Stimbol. "If I say hunt, we hunt, and don't you forget it." But on their return to camp they saw no game, or at least Stimbol saw none. What the blacks saw was their own affair.

5

The Tarmangani

URING Stimbol's absence from camp Blake had been occupied in dividing the food and equipment into two equal parts which were arranged for Stimbol's inspection and approval; but the division of the porters and askari he had left until the other's return, and was writing in his diary when the hunting party entered the camp.

He could see at a glance that Stimbol was in bad humor, but as that was the older man's usual state of temper it caused Blake no particular anxiety, but rather gave him cause for added relief that on the morrow he would be rid of his ill-natured companion for good.

Blake was more concerned, however, by the sullen demeanor of the askari who had accompanied Stimbol for it meant to the younger man that his companion had found some new occasion for bullying, abusing or insulting them, and the difficulty of dividing the safari thus increased. Blake had felt from the moment that he had definitely reached the decision to separate from Stimbol that one of the greatest obstacles they would have to overcome to carry out the plan would be to find sufficient men willing to submit themselves to Stimbol's ideas of discipline, properly to transport his luggage and provisions and guard them and him.

As Stimbol passed and saw the two piles of equipment the frown upon his face deepened. "I see you've got the stuff laid out," he remarked, as he halted before Blake.

'Yes, I wanted you to look it over and see that it is satisfactorily divided before I have it packed."

"I don't want to be bothered with it," replied the other. "I know you wouldn't take any advantage of me on the division."

"Thanks," replied Blake.

"How about the porters?"

"That's not going to be so easy. You know you haven't treated them very well and there will not be many of them anxious to return with you."

"There's where you're dead wrong, Blake. The trouble

with you is that you don't know anything about natives. You're too easy with 'em. They haven't any respect for you, and the man they don't respect they don't like. They know that a fellow who beats 'em is their master, and they know that a master is going to look after them. They wouldn't want to trust themselves on a long trek with you. You divided the junk, now let me handle the men—that's more in my line—and I'll see that you get a square deal and a good, safe bunch, and I'll put the fear of God into 'em so they won't dare be anything but loyal to you."

"Just how do you propose selecting the men?" asked Blake.

"Well, in the first place I'd like you to have those men who may wish to accompany you—I'll grant there are a few—so we'll just have 'em all up, explain that we are separating, and I'll tell all those who wish to return with your safari to step forward, then I'll choose some good men from what are left and make up enough that way to complete your quota— see? That's fair enough, isn't it?"

"It's quite fair," agreed Blake. He was hoping that the plan would work out as easily as Stimbol appeared to believe that it would, but he was far from believing and so he thought it best to suggest an alternative that he was confident would have to be resorted to in the end. "In the event that one of us has difficulty in securing the requisite number of volunteers," he said, "I believe that we can enlist the necessary men by offering a bonus to be paid upon safe arrival at railhead. If I am short of men I shall be willing to do so."

"Not a bad idea if you're afraid you can't hold 'em together after I leave you," said Stimbol. "It will be an added factor of safety for you, too; but as for me my men will live up to their original agreement or there'll be some mighty sick porters in these parts. What say we have 'em up and find out just how much of a job we've got on our hands?" He glanced about until his eyes fell on a head man. "Here, you!" he called. "Come here and make it snappy."

The black approached and stopped before the two white men. "You called me, Bwana?" he asked.

"Gather up every one in camp," directed Stimbol. "Have them up here in five minutes for a palaver—every last man-jack of them."

"Yes, Bwana."

As the head man withdrew Stimbol turned to Blake. "Any stranger in camp today?" he asked.

"No, why?"

"Ran across a wild man while I was hunting," replied Stimbol. "He ordered me out of the jungle. What do you know about that?" and Stimbol laughed.

"A wild man?"

"Yes. Some crazy nut I suppose. The askari seemed to know about him."

"Who is he?"

"Calls himself Tarzan."

Blake elevated his brows. "Ah!" he exclaimed. "You have met Tarzan of the Apes and he has ordered you out of the jungle?"

"You've heard of him?"

"Certainly, and if he ever orders me out of his jungle, I'll go."

"*You* would, but not Wilbur Stimbol."

"Why did he order you out?" asked Blake.

"He just ordered me out, that's all. Wouldn't let me shoot a gorilla I'd been stalking. The fellow saved the gorilla from a python, killed the python, ordered me out of the jungle, said he'd visit us in camp later and walked away with the gorilla like they were old pals. I never saw anything like it, but it doesn't make any difference to me who or what he thinks he is, I know who and what I am and it's going to take more than a half-wit to scare me out of this country till I'm good and ready to go."

"So you think Tarzan of the Apes is a half-wit?"

"I think anyone's a half-wit who'd run about this jungle naked and unarmed."

"You'll find he's not a half-wit, Stimbol; and unless you want to get in more trouble than you ever imagined existed, you'll do just as Tarzan of the Apes tells you to do."

"What do you know about him? Have you ever seen him?"

"No," replied Blake. "But I have heard a lot about him from our men. He's as much a part of this locality as the jungle, or the lions. Very few, if any, of our men have seen him, but he has the same hold upon their imaginations and superstitions as any of their demons, and they are even more fearful of incurring his displeasure. If they think Tarzan has it in for us we're out of luck."

"Well, all I've got to say is that if this monkey-man knows when he's well off he'll not come butting into the affairs of Wilbur Stimbol."

"And he's coming to visit us, is he?" said Blake. "Well, I certainly want to see him. I've heard of little else since we struck his country."

"It's funny I never heard of him," said Stimbol.

"You never talk with the men," Blake reminded him.

"Gad, it seems as though I'm doing nothing but talk to them," grumbled Stimbol.

"I said, talk *with* them."

"I don't chum with porters," sneered Stimbol.

Blake grinned.

"Here are the men," said Stimbol. He turned toward the waiting porters and askari and cleared his throat. "Mr. Blake and I are going to separate," he announced. "Everything has been divided. I am going to hunt a little farther to the west, make a circle toward the south and return to the coast by a new route. I do not know what Mr. Blake's plans are, but he is going to get half the porters and half the askari, and I want to tell you right now that there isn't going to be any funny business about it. Half of you are going with Mr. Blake whether you like it or not."

He paused, impressively, to let the full weight of his pronouncement sink home. "As usual," he continued, "I wish to keep everyone contented and happy, so I'm going to give you who may want to go with Mr. Blake an opportunity to do so. Now listen! The packs over on that side are Mr. Blake's; those on this side are mine. All those who are willing to accompany Mr. Blake go over on that side!"

There was a moment's hesitation upon the part of the men and then some of them moved quietly over among Blake's packs. Others followed as their understandings slowly grasped the meaning of Stimbol's words until all of the men stood upon Blake's side.

Stimbol turned to Blake with a laugh and a shake of his head. "Gad!" he exclaimed. "Did you ever see such a dumb bunch? No one could have explained the thing more simply than I and yet look at 'em! Not one of them understood me!"

"Are you quite sure of that, Stimbol?" inquired Blake.

Stimbol did not immediately grasp the insinuation. When he did he scowled. "Don't be a fool," he snapped. "Of course they misunderstood me." He turned angrily toward the men. "You thick-skulled, black idiots! Can't you understand anything?" he demanded. "I did not say that you all had to go with Mr. Blake—only those who wished to. Now the rest of you—those who wish to accompany me—get back over here on this side with my packs, and step lively!"

No one moved in the direction of Stimbol's packs. The man flushed.

"This is mutiny!" he stormed. "Whoever is at the bottom of this is going to suffer. Come here, you!" He motioned to a head man. "Who put you fellows up to this? Has Mr. Blake been telling you what to do?"

"Don't be a fool, Stimbol," said Blake. "No one has influenced the men and there is no mutiny. The plan was yours. The men have done just what you told them to. If it had not been for your insufferable egotism you would have known precisely what the outcome would be. These black men are human beings. In some respects they are extremely sensitive human beings, and in many ways they are like children. You strike them, you curse them, you insult them and they will fear you and hate you. You have done all these things to them and they do fear you and hate you. You have sowed and now you are reaping. I hope to God that it will teach you a lesson. There is just one way to get your men and that is to offer them a big bonus. Are you willing to do that?"

Stimbol, his self assurance momentarily shaken at last, wilted in the face of the realization that Blake was right. He looked about helplessly for a moment. The blacks, sullen-faced, stood there like dumb beasts, staring at him. In all those eyes there was no single friendly glance. He turned back to Blake. "See what you can do with them," he said.

Blake faced the men. "It will be necessary for half of you to accompany Mr. Stimbol back to the coast," he said. "He will pay double wages to all those who go with him, provided that you serve him loyally. Talk it over among yourselves and send word to us later by your head man. That is all. You may go."

The balance of the afternoon passed, the two white men keeping to their respective tents; the blacks gathered in groups, whispering. Blake and Stimbol no longer messed together, but after the evening meal each appeared with his pipe to await the report of the head men. After half an hour Blake sent his boy to summon them and presently they came and stood before the young man.

"Well, have the men decided who will accompany Mr. Stimbol?" he asked.

"No one will accompany the old bwana," replied their spokesman. "All will go with the young bwana."

"But Mr. Stimbol will pay them well," Blake reminded, "and half of you must go with him."

The black shook his head. "He could not make the pay big enough," he said. "No boy will go with him."

"You agreed to come out with us and return with us," said Blake. "You must fulfil your agreement."

"We agreed to come out with both of you and return with

both of you. There was nothing said about returning separately. We will live up to our agreement and the old bwana may return in safety with the young bwana." There was finality in the tone of the spokesman.

Blake thought for a moment before replying. "You may go," he said. "I will talk with you again in the morning."

The blacks had departed but a moment when the figure of a man appeared suddenly out of the darkness into the light of the camp fire.

"Who the—oh, it's you is it?" exclaimed Stimbol. "Here's the wild man, Blake."

The young American turned and surveyed the figure of the bronze giant who was standing just within the circle of the firelight. He noted the clean cut features, the quiet dignity, the majestic mien and smiled inwardly at recollection of Stimbol's description of this god-like creature—half-wit!

"So you are Tarzan of the Apes!" he said.

Tarzan inclined his head. "And you?" he asked.

"I am Jim Blake of New York," replied the American.

"Hunting of course?"

"With a camera."

"Your companion was using a rifle," Tarzan reminded him.

"I am not responsible for his acts. I cannot control them," replied Blake.

"Nor anyone else," snapped Stimbol.

Tarzan permitted his gaze to move to Stimbol for an instant, but ignored his boast.

"I overheard the conversation between you and the head men," he said, addressing Blake. "Some of your blacks had already told me something about your companion, and twice today I have had an opportunity to form an estimate of my own from personal observation, so I assume that you are separating because you cannot agree. Am I right?"

"Yes," acknowledged Blake.

"And after you separate—what are your plans?"

"I intend to push in a little farther west and then swing——" commenced Stimbol.

"I was speaking to Blake," interrupted Tarzan; "my plans concerning you are already made."

"Well, who the——"

"Silence!" admonished the ape-man. "Go ahead, Blake!"

"We have not had much luck so far," replied Blake, "principally because we never can agree on methods. The result is that I have scarcely a single decent wild animal study. I had planned to go north a way in search of lion pictures. I dislike going back without anything to show for the time and money I have put into the expedition, but now that the men have refused to accompany us separately there is nothing for it but to return to the coast by the shortest route."

"You two don't seem to be taking me into consideration at all," grumbled Stimbol. "I've got as much money and time in this trip as Blake. You forget that I'm here to hunt, and what's more I'm going to hunt and I'm not going straight back to the coast by a damned sight, monkey-man or no monkey-man."

Again Tarzan ignored Stimbol. "Get ready to move out about an hour after sunrise," he said to Blake. "There will be no trouble about dividing the safari. I shall be here to attend to that and give you your final instructions," and as he spoke he turned and disappeared in the darkness.

6

Ara the Lightning

BEFORE dawn the camp was astir and by the appointed hour the packs were made and all was in readiness. The porters loitered, awaiting the word that would start the safari upon its eastward journey toward the coast. Blake and Stimbol smoked in silence. The foliage of a nearby tree moved to the swaying of a branch and Tarzan of the Apes dropped lightly into the camp. Exclamations of surprise broke from the lips of the Negroes—surprise clearly tinged with terror. The ape-man turned toward them and addressed them in their own dialect.

"I am Tarzan of the Apes," he said, "Lord of the Jungle. You have brought white men into my country to kill my people. I am displeased. Those of you who wish to live to return to your villages and your families will listen well and do as Tarzan commands.

"You," he pointed at the chief head man, "shall accompany the younger white man whom I will permit to make pictures in my country where and when he will. Select half the men of the safari to accompany the young bwana."

"And you," he addressed another head man, "take those men that remain and escort the older bwana to railhead in the most direct route and without delay. He is not permitted to hunt and there will be no killing except for food or self-defense. Do not fail me. Remember always that Tarzan watches and Tarzan never forgets."

He turned then to the white men. "Blake," he said, "the arrangements are made. You may leave when you please, with your own safari, and go where you please. The question of hunting is left to your own discretion—you are the guest of Tarzan."

"And you," he addressed Stimbol, "will be taken directly out of the country by the shortest route. You will be permitted to carry firearms for use in self-defense. If you abuse this permission they will be taken away from you. Do not hunt, even for food—your head man will attend to that."

"Now just hold your horses," blustered Stimbol. "If you think I'm going to put up with any such high-handed interference with my rights as an American citizen you're very much mistaken. Why I could buy and sell you and your damned jungle forty times and not know that I'd spent a cent. For God's sake, Blake, tell this poor fool who I am before he gets himself into a lot of trouble."

Tarzan turned to the head man he had selected for Stimbol. "You may up-load and march," he said. "If this white man does not follow you, leave him behind. Take good care of him if he obeys me and deliver him safely at railhead. Obey his orders if they do not conflict with those that I have given you. Go!"

A moment later Stimbol's safari was preparing to depart and, at Tarzan's request, Blake's too was moving out of camp. Stimbol swore and threatened, but his men, sullenly ignoring him, filed off into the jungle toward the east. Tarzan had departed, swinging into the trees and disappearing among the foliage, and at last Stimbol stood alone in the deserted camp.

Thwarted, humiliated, almost frothing with rage he ran after his men, screaming commands and threats that were ignored. Later in the day, sullen and silent, he marched near the head of the long file of porters and askari, convinced at last that the power of the ape-man was greater than his; but in his heart burned resentment and in his mind rioted plans for vengeance—plans that he knew were futile.

Tarzan, wishing to assure himself that his instructions were being carried out, had swung far ahead and was waiting in the crotch of a tree that overhung the trail along which Stimbol must pass. In the distance he could hear the sounds that arose from the marching safari. Along the trail from the opposite direction something was approaching. The ape-man could not see it but he knew what it was. Above the tree tops black clouds rolled low, but no air stirred in the jungle.

Along the trail came a great, shaggy, black man-thing. Tarzan of the Apes hailed it as it came in sight of his arboreal perch.

"Bolgani!" he called in low tones.

The gorilla stopped. He stood erect upon his hind feet and looked about.

"I am Tarzan," said the ape-man.

Bolgani grunted. "I am Bolgani," he replied.

"The Tarmangani comes," warned Tarzan.

"I kill!" growled Bolgani.

"Let the Tarmangani pass," said Tarzan. "He and his people have many thunder sticks. I have sent this Tarmangani out of the jungle. Let him pass. Go a little way from the trail —the stupid Gomangani and the Tarmangani, who is stupider, will pass by without knowing that Tarzan and Bolgani are near."

From the darkening sky distant thunder boomed and the two beasts looked upward toward the broad field of Nature's powers, more savage and destructive than their own.

"Pand the thunder hunts in the sky," remarked the apeman.

"Hunts for Usha the wind," said Bolgani.

"Presently we shall hear Usha fleeing through the trees to escape." Tarzan viewed the lowering, black clouds. "Even Kudu the sun fears Pand, hiding his face when Pand hunts."

Ara the lightning shot through the sky. To the two beasts it was a bolt from Pand's bow and the great drops of rain that commenced to fall shortly after was Meeta, the blood of Usha the wind, pouring from many a wound.

The jungle bent to a great pressure but as yet there was no other noise than the rolling thunder. The trees whipped back and Usha tore through the forest. The darkness increased. The rain fell in great masses. Leaves and branches hurtled through the air, trees crashed amongst their fellows. With deafening roars the elements unleashed their pent anger. The beasts cowered beneath the one awe inspiring power that they acknowledged as supreme.

Tarzan crouched in the crotch of a great tree with his shoulders arched against the beating rain. Just off the trail Bolgani squatted in drenched and bedraggled misery. They waited. There was nothing else that they could do.

Above them the storm broke again with maniacal fury. The thunder crashed with deafening reverberation. There was a blinding flash of light and the branch upon which Tarzan squatted sagged and hurtled to the trail beneath.

Stunned, the ape-man lay where he had fallen, the great branch partially across his body.

As quickly as it had come, the storm departed. Kudu the sun burst through the clouds. Bolgani, dejected and still terrified, remained where he had squatted, motionless and silent. Bolgani had no desire to attract the attention of Pand the thunder.

Soaked with water, cold, furious, Stimbol slopped along the slippery, muddy trail. He did not know that his safari was some little distance behind him, for he had forged ahead during the storm while they had taken refuge beneath the trees.

At a turn in the trail he came suddenly upon a fallen branch that blocked the way. At first he did not see the body of the man lying beneath it, but when he did he recognized it instantly and a new hope sprang to life within his breast. With Tarzan dead he could be free to do as he pleased; but was the ape-man dead?

Stimbol ran forward and, kneeling, placed an ear to the breast of the prostrate figure. An expression of disappointment crossed his face—Tarzan was not dead. The expression upon Stimbol's face changed—a cunning look came into his eyes as he glanced back down the trail. His men were not in sight! He looked quickly about him. He was alone with the unconscious author of his humiliation!

He thought he was alone. He did not see the shaggy figure that had silently arisen as the sound of Stimbol's approach had come to its sensitive ears and was now peering at him through the foliage—peering at him and at the silent figure of the ape-man.

Stimbol drew his hunting knife from its scabbard. He could clip its point into the wild man's heart and run back down the trail. His men would find him waiting for them. Later they would come upon the dead Tarzan, but they would not guess how he had met his end.

The ape-man moved—consciousness was returning. Stimbol realized that he must act quickly, and at the same instant a great hairy arm reached out through the foliage and a mighty hand closed upon his shoulder. With a screaming curse he turned to look into the hideous face of Bolgani. He tried to strike at the shaggy breast of his antagonist with his hunting knife, but the puny weapon was torn from his grasp and hurled into the bushes.

The great yellow fangs were bared against Stimbol's throat as Tarzan opened his eyes.

"Kreeg-ah!" cried the ape-man in warning.

Bolgani paused and looked at his fellow beast.

"Let him go," said Tarzan.

"The Tarmangani would have killed Tarzan," explained the gorilla. "Bolgani stopped him. Bolgani kill!" He growled horribly.

"No!" snapped Tarzan. "Free the Tarmangani!"

The gorilla released his grasp upon Stimbol just as the first of the hunter's men came in sight of them, and as Bolgani saw the blacks and how numerous they were his nervousness and irritability increased.

"Take to the jungle, Bolgani," said Tarzan. "Tarzan will take care of this Tarmangani and the Gomangani."

With a parting growl the gorilla merged with the foliage and the shadows of the jungle as Tarzan of the Apes faced Stimbol and his boys.

"You had a close call then, Stimbol," said the ape-man. "It is fortunate for you that you didn't succeed in killing me. I was here for two reasons. One was to see that you obeyed my instructions and the other to protect you from your men. I did not like the way they eyed you in camp this morning. It would not be a difficult thing to lose you in the jungle, you know, and that would put a period to you as surely as poison or a knife. I felt a certain responsibility for you because you are a white man, but you have just now released me from whatever obligation racial ties may have influenced me to acknowledge.

"I shall not kill you, Stimbol, as your deserve; but from now on you may reach the coast on your own, and you will doubtless discover that one cannot make too many friends in the jungle or afford a single unnecessary enemy." He wheeled upon Stimbol's black boys. "Tarzan of the Apes goes his way. You will not see him again, perhaps. Do your duty by this white man as long as he obeys the word of Tarzan, *but see that he does not hunt!*"

With this final admonition the ape-man swung into the lower branches and was gone.

When Stimbol, after repeatedly questioning his men, discovered that Tarzan had practically assured them that they would see no more of him, he regained much of his former assurance and egotistical bluster. Once more he was the leader of men, shouting at the blacks in a loud tone, cursing them, ridiculing them. He thought that it impressed them with his greatness. He believed that they were simple people whom he could deceive into thinking that he was not afraid of Tarzan, and by flaunting Tarzan's commands win their respect. Now that Tarzan had promised not to return Stimbol felt safer in ignoring his wishes, and so it befell that just before they reached a camping ground Stimbol came upon an antelope and without an instant's hesitation fired and killed it.

It was a sullen camp that Stimbol made that night. The men gathered in groups and whispered. "He has shot an antelope and Tarzan will be angry with us," said one.

"He will punish us," said a head man.

"The bwana is a bad man," said another. "I wish he was dead."

"We may not kill him. Tarzan has said that."

"If we leave him in the jungle he will die."

"Tarzan told us to do our duty."

"He said to do it as long as the bad bwana obeyed the commands of Tarzan."

"He has disobeyed them."

"Then we may leave him."

Stimbol, exhausted by the long march, slept like a log. When he awoke the sun was high. He shouted for his boy. There was no response. Again he shouted and louder, adding an oath. No one came. There was no sound in camp.

"The lazy swine," he grumbled. "They'll step a little livelier when I get out there."

He arose and dressed, but as he was dressing the silence of the camp came to impress him as something almost menacing, so that he hastened to be through and out of the tent. As he stepped into the open the truth was revealed at almost the first quick glance about. Not a human being was in sight and all but one of the packs containing provisions were gone. He had been deserted in the heart of Africa!

His first impulse was to seize his rifle and start after the blacks, but second thought impressed him with the danger of such procedure and convinced him that the last thing he should do would be to place himself again in the power of these men who had demonstrated that they felt no compunction in abandoning him to almost certain death. If they wanted to be rid of him they could easily find even a quicker means if he returned and forced himself upon them again.

There was but a single alternative and that was to find Blake and remain with him. He knew that Blake would not abandon him to death in the jungle.

The blacks had not left him without provisions, nor had they taken his rifle or ammunition, but the difficulty that now confronted Stimbol was largely in the matter of transportation for his food. There was plenty of it to last many days, but he knew that he could not carry it through the jungle together with his rifle and ammunition. To remain where the food was would be equally futile. Blake was returning to the coast by another route; the ape-man had said that he would not follow Stimbol's safari farther; it might be years, therefore, before another human being chanced along this little used game trail.

He knew that he and Blake were now separated by about

two marches and if he travelled light and Blake did not march too rapidly he might hope to overtake him inside a week. Perhaps Blake would find good camera hunting soon and make a permanent camp. In that case Stimbol would find him even more quickly.

He felt better when he had definitely decided upon a plan of action, and after a good breakfast he made up a small pack of provisions, enough to last him a week, filled his belts and pockets with ammunition and started off along the back trail.

It was easy going for the trail of the day before was plain and this was the third time that Stimbol had been over it, so he had no difficulty in reaching the camp at which he and Blake had parted company.

As he entered the little clearing early in the afternoon he determined to keep on and cover as much ground on Blake's trail as he could before dark, but for a few minutes he would rest. As he sat down with his back against the bole of a tree he did not notice a movement of the tops of a clump of jungle grasses a few yards distant, and if he had he would, doubtless, have attached no importance to the matter.

Finishing a cigarette Stimbol arose, rearranged his pack and started off in the direction Blake's men had taken early the preceding morning; but he had covered but a yard or two when he was brought to a sudden halt by an ominous growl that arose from a little clump of jungle grasses close in front of him. Almost simultaneously the fringing grasses parted and there appeared in the opening the head of a great black-maned lion.

With a scream of fear, Stimbol dropped his pack, threw aside his rifle and started on a run for the tree beneath which he had been sitting. The lion, itself somewhat surprised, stood for an instant watching him and then started in pursuit at an easy lope.

Stimbol, casting an affrighted glance rearward, was horrified —the lion seemed so close and the tree so far away. If distance lends enchantment to the view, proximity may also at times have its advantage. In this instance it served to accelerate the speed of the fleeing man to a most surprising degree, and though he was no longer young he clawed his way to the lower branches of the tree with speed, if not with grace, that would have done justice to a trained athlete.

Nor was he an instant too speedy. Numa's raking talons touched his boot and sent him swarming up among the higher branches, where he clung weak and panting looking down into the snarling visage of the carnivore.

For a moment Numa growled up at him and then, with a coughing grunt, turned away and strode majestically in the direction of the clump of grasses from which he had emerged. He stopped to sniff at the pack of provisions Stimbol had discarded and, evidently piqued by the man scent clinging to it, cuffed at it angrily. It rolled to one side and Numa stepped back, eyeing it warily, then, with a growl, he leaped upon it and commenced to maul the insensate thing, ripping and tearing until its contents were scattered about upon the ground. He bit into tins and boxes until scarcely an article remained intact, while Stimbol crouched in the tree and watched the destruction of his provisions, utterly helpless to interfere.

A dozen times he cursed himself for having thrown away his rifle and even more frequently he vowed vengeance. He consoled himself, however, with the realization that Blake could not be far away and that with Blake there were ample provisions which could be augmented by trading and hunting. When the lion left he would descend and follow Blake's trail.

Numa, tired of the contents of the pack, resumed his way toward the long grass, but again his attention was distracted—this time by the thunder stick of the Tarmangani. The lion smelled of the discarded rifle, pawed it and finally picked it up between his jaws. Stimbol looked on, horrified. What if the beast damaged the weapon? He would be left without means of defense or for obtaining food!

"Drop it!" shouted Stimbol. "Drop it!"

Numa, ignoring the ravings of the despised man-thing, strode into his lair, carrying the rifle with him.

That afternoon and night spelled an eternity of terror for Wilbur Stimbol. While daylight lasted the lion remained in the nearby patch of grass effectually deterring the unhappy man from continuing his search for Blake's camp, and after night fell no urge whatever could have induced Stimbol to descend to the paralyzing terrors of the jungle night even had he known that the lion had departed and no sounds had apprised him of the near presence of danger; but sounds did apprise him. From shortly after dark until nearly dawn a perfect bedlam of howls and growls and coughs and grunts and barks arose from directly beneath him as there had been held a convention of all the horrid beasts of the jungle at the foot of the tree that seemed at best an extremely insecure sanctuary.

When morning came the jungle lay silent and peaceful about him and only torn canvas and empty cans bore mute

evidence to the feast of the hyenas that had passed into
jungle history. Numa had departed leaving the remains of the
kill upon which he had lain as the piece de resistance of the
hyenian banquet for which Stimbol had furnished the hors
d'oeuvres.

Stimbol, trembling, descended. Through the jungle, wild-
eyed, startled by every sound, scurried a pitiful figure of
broken, terror stricken old age. Few could have recognized in
it Wilbur Stimbol of Stimbol & Company, brokers, New York.

7

The Cross

THE storm that had overtaken Stimbol's safari wrought even greater havoc with the plans of Jim Blake, altering in the instant of a single blinding flash of lightning the course of his entire life.

Accompanied by a single black, who carried his camera and an extra rifle, Blake had struck out from the direct route of his safari in search of lion pictures, there being every indication that the great carnivores might be found in abundance in the district through which they were passing.

It was his intention to parallel the route of his main body and rejoin it in camp in the afternoon. The boy who accompanied him was intelligent and resourceful, the direction and speed of the marching safari were mutually agreed upon and the responsibility for bringing Blake into camp safely was left entirely to the Negro. Having every confidence in the boy, Blake gave no heed to either time or direction, devoting all his energies to the fascinating occupation of searching for photographic studies.

Shortly after leaving the safari Blake and his companion encountered a herd of seven or eight lions which included a magnificent old male, an old lioness and five or six young, ranging from half to full grown.

At sight of Blake and his companion the lions took off leisurely through rather open forest and the men followed, awaiting patiently the happy coincidence of time, light and grouping that would give the white man such a picture as he desired.

In the mind of the black man was pictured the route of the safari and its relation to the meanderings of the quarry. He knew how far and in what directions he and his companion were being led from their destination. To have returned to the trail of the safari would have been a simple matter to him, but Blake, depending entirely upon the black, gave no heed either to time or direction.

For two hours they clung doggedly to the spoor, encouraged

53

by occasional glimpses of now one, now several members of the regal group, but never was the opportunity afforded for a successful shot. Then the sky became rapidly overcast by black clouds and a few moments later the storm broke in all the terrific fury that only an Equatorial storm can achieve, and an instant later amidst the deafening roar of thunder and a blinding flash of lightning utter disaster engulfed James Hunter Blake.

How long he lay, stunned by the shock of the bolt that had struck but a few feet from him, he did not know. When he opened his eyes the storm had passed and the sun was shining brightly through the leafy canopy of the forest. Still dazed, uncomprehending the cause or extent of the catastrophe, he raised himself slowly upon an elbow and looked about him.

One of the first sights that met his eyes aided materially in the rapid recovery of his senses. Less than a hundred feet from him stood a group of lions, seven of them, solemnly regarding him. The characteristics of individual lions differ as greatly from those of their fellows as do the characteristics of individuals of the human race and, even as a human being, a lion may have his moods as well as his personal idiosyncrasies.

These lions that gravely inspected the man-thing had been spared any considerable experience with the human species; they had seen but few men; they had never been hunted; they were well fed; Blake had done nothing greatly to upset their easily irritated nervous systems. Fortunately for him they were merely curious.

But Blake did not know all this. He knew only that seven lions were standing within a hundred feet of him, that they were not in a cage and that while he had pursued them to obtain photographs, the thing that he most desired at the moment was not his camera but his rifle.

Stealthily, that he might not annoy them, he looked about him for the weapon. To his consternation it was nowhere in sight, nor was his gun bearer with the extra rifle. Where could the boy be? Doubtless, frightened by the lions, he had decamped. Twenty feet away was a most inviting tree. Blake wondered if the lions would charge the moment that he rose to his feet. He tried to remember all that he had heard about lions and he did recall one fact that applies with almost axiomatic verity to all dangerous animals—if you run from them they will pursue you. To reach the tree it would be necessary to walk almost directly toward the lions.

Blake was in a quandary, and then one of the younger

lions moved a few steps nearer! That settled the matter as far as Blake was concerned. for the closer the lions came the shorter his chance of gaining the tree ahead of them in the event that they elected to prevent.

In the midst of a tremendous forest, entirely surrounded by trees, Nature had chosen to strike him down almost in the center of a natural clearing. There was a good tree a hundred feet away and on the opposite side of the clearing from the lions. Blake stole a longing glance at it and then achieved some rapid mental calculations. If he ran for the farther tree the lions would have to cover two hundred feet while he was covering one hundred, while if he chose the nearer tree, they must come eighty feet while he was going twenty. There seemed, therefore, no doubt as to the greater desirability of the nearer tree which ruled favorite by odds of two to one. Against it, however, loomed the mental hazard that running straight into the face of seven lions involved.

Jim Blake was sincerely, genuinely and honestly scared; but unless the lions were psychoanalysts they would never have dreamed the truth as he started nonchalantly and slowly toward them—and the tree. The most difficult feat that he had ever accomplished lay in making his legs behave themselves. They wanted to run. So did his feet and his heart and his brain. Only his will held them in leash.

Those were tense moments for Jim Blake—the first half dozen steps he took with seven great lions watching his approach. He saw that they were becoming nervous. The lioness moved uneasily. The old male growled. A younger male, he who had started forward, lashed his sides with his tail, flattened his head, bared his fangs and stealthily approached.

Blake was almost at the tree when something happened— he never knew what the cause, but inexplicably the lioness turned and bounded away, voicing a low whine, and after her went the other six.

The man leaned against the bole of the tree and fanned himself with his helmet. "Whew!" he breathed, "I hope the next lion I see is in the Central Park Zoo."

But even lions were forgotten in the developments that the next few moments revealed after repeated shouts for the black boy had brought no response and Blake had determined that he must set out in search of him. Nor did he have far to go. On the back track, just inside the clearing, Blake found a few remnants of charred flesh and a blackened and half molten rifle barrel. Of the camera not a vestige remained. The bolt that had bowled Blake over must have squarely struck his gun bearer, killing him instantly, exploding all the ammunition, destroying the camera and ruining the rifle that he had carried.

But what had become of the rifle that had been in Blake's hands? The man searched in all directions, but could not find it and was finally forced to the conclusion that its disappearance could be attributed only to one of those freakish tricks which severe electrical storms so often play upon helpless and futile humanity.

Frankly aware that he was lost and had not the faintest conception of the direction in which lay the proposed camp of his safari, Blake started blindly off on what he devoutly hoped would prove the right route. It was not. His safari was moving northeast. Blake headed north.

For two days he trudged on through dense forest, sleeping at night among the branches of trees. Once his fitful slumbers were disturbed by the swaying of a branch against which he was braced. As he awoke he felt it sag as to the weight of some large animal. He looked and saw two fiery eyes gleaming in the dark. Blake knew it to be a leopard as he drew his automatic and fired point blank. With a hideous scream the great cat sprang or fell to the ground. Blake never knew if he hit it. It did not return and there were no signs of it in the morning.

He found food and water in abundance, and upon the morning of the third day he emerged from the forest at the foot of a range of lofty mountains and for the first time in weeks reveled in an unobstructed view of the blue sky and saw the horizon again and all that lay between himself and it. He had not realized that he had been depressed by the darkness and the crowding pressure of the trees, but now he experienced all the spiritual buoyancy of a released convict long immured from freedom and the light of day. Rescue was no longer problematical, merely a matter of time. He wanted to sing and shout; but he conserved his energies and started toward the mountains. There had been no native villages in the forest and so, he reasoned, as there must be native villages in a well-watered country stocked with game, he would find them upon the mountain slopes.

Topping a rise he saw below him the mouth of a canyon in the bed of which ran a small stream. A village would be built on water.

If he followed the water he would come to the village. Quite easy! He descended to the stream where he was deeply gratified to find that a well-worn path paralleled it. Encouraged by the belief that he would soon encounter natives and believing that he would have no difficulty in enlisting their services in aiding him to relocate his safari, Blake followed the path upward into the canyon.

He had covered something like three miles without having discovered any sign of habitation when, at a turn in the path, he found himself at the foot of a great white cross of enormous proportions. Hewn from limestone, it stood directly in the center of the trail and towered above him fully sixty feet. Checked and weatherworn, it gave an impression of great antiquity, which was further borne out by the remains of an almost obliterated inscription upon the face of its massive base.

Blake examined the carved letters, but could not decipher their message. The characters appeared of early English origin, but he dismissed such a possibility as too ridiculous to entertain. He knew that he could not be far from the southern boundary of Abyssinia and that the Abyssinians are Christians. Thus he explained the presence of the cross; but he could not explain the suggestion of sinister menace that this lonely, ancient symbol of the crucifix held for him. Why was it? What was it?

Standing there, tongueless, hoary with age, it seemed to call upon him to stop, to venture not beyond it into the unknown; it warned him back, but not, seemingly, out of a spirit of kindliness and protection, but rather with arrogance and hate.

With a laugh Blake threw off the mood that had seized him and went on; but as he passed the great white monolith he crossed himself, though he was not a Catholic. He wondered what had impelled him to the unfamiliar act, but he could no more explain it than he could the strange and uncanny suggestion of power and personality that seemed to surround the crumbling cross.

Another turn in the path and the trail narrowed where it passed between two huge boulders that might have fallen from the cliff top towering far above. Cliffs closed in closely now in front and upon two sides. Apparently he was close to the canyon's head and yet there was no slightest indication of a village. Yet where did the trail lead? It had an end and a purpose. He would discover the former and, if possible, the latter.

Still under the depressing influence of the cross, Blake passed between the two boulders; and the instant that he had passed them a man stepped out behind him and another in front. They were Negroes, stalwart, fine-featured fellows, and in themselves nothing to arouse wonder or surprise. Blake had expected to meet Negroes in Africa; but not Negroes wearing elaborately decorated leathern jerkins upon the breasts of which red crosses were emblazoned, close fitting nether garments and sandals held by doeskin thongs, cross gartered half way to their knees; not Negroes wearing close fitting bassinets of leopard skin that fitted their heads closely and reached to below their ears; not Negroes armed with two handed broad swords and elaborately tipped pikes.

Blake was acutely aware of the pike tips as there was one pressing against his belly and another in the small of his back.

"Who be ye?" demanded the Negro that faced Blake.

Had the man addressed him in Greek Blake would have been no more surprised than he was by the incongruity of this archaic form of speech falling from the lips of a twentieth century central African black. He was too dumbfounded for an instant to reply.

"Doubtless the fellow be a Saracen, Paul!" said the black behind Blake, "and understands not what thou sayest—a spy, perchance."

"Nay, Peter Wiggs, as my name be Paul Bodkin he be no infidel—that I know of mine own good eyes."

"Whatsoe'er he be it is for ye to fetch him before the captain of the gate who will question him, Paul Bodkin."

"Natheless there be no hurt in questioning him first, an he will answer."

"Stop thy tongue and take him to the captain," said Peter. "I will abide here and guard the way until thou returnest."

Paul stepped aside and motioned for Blake to precede him. Then he fell in behind and the American did not need to glance back to know that the ornate tip of the pike was ever threateningly ready.

The way lay plain before him and Blake followed the trail toward the cliffs where there presently appeared the black mouth of a tunnel leading straight into the rocky escarpment. Leaning against the sides of a niche just within the entrance were several torches made of reeds or twigs bound tightly together and dipped in pitch. One of these Paul Bodkin selected, took some tinder from a metal box he carried in a pouch at his side, struck a spark to it with flint and steel; and having thus ignited the tinder and lighted the torch he pushed Blake on again with the tip of his pike and the two entered the tunnel, which the American found to be narrow and winding, well suited to defense. Its floor was worn smooth until the stones of which it was composed shone polished in the flaring of the torch. The sides and roof were black with the soot of countless thousands, perhaps, of torch-lighted passages along this strange way that led to—what?

8

The Snake Strikes

UNVERSED in jungle craft, overwhelmed by the enormity of the catastrophe that had engulfed him, his reasoning faculties numbed by terror, Wilbur Stimbol slunk through the jungle, the fleeing quarry of every terror that imagination could conjure. Matted filth caked the tattered remnants of his clothing that scarce covered the filth of his emaciated body. His once graying hair had turned to white, matching the white stubble of a four days' beard.

He followed a broad and well marked trail along which men and horses, sheep and goats had passed within the week, and with the blindness and ignorance of the city dweller he thought that he was on the spoor of Blake's safari. Thus it came that he stumbled, exhausted, into the menzil of the slow moving Ibn Jad.

Fejjuan, the Galla slave, discovered him and took him at once to the sheik's beyt where Ibn Jad, with his brother, Tollog, and several others were squatting in the mukaad sipping coffee.

"By Ullah! What strange creature hast thou captured now, Fejjuan?" demanded the sheik.

"Perhaps a holy man," replied the black, "for he is very poor and without weapons and very dirty—yes, surely he must be a very holy man."

"Who art thou?" demanded Ibn Jad.

"I am lost and starving. Give me food," begged Stimbol. But neither understood the language of the other.

"Another Nasrany," said Fahd, contemptuously. "A Frenjy, perhaps."

"He looks more like one of el-Engleys," remarked Tollog.

"Perhaps he is from Fransa," suggested Ibn Jad. "Speak to him that vile tongue, Fahd, which thou didst come by among the soldiers in Algeria."

"Who are you, stranger?" demanded Fahd, in French.

"I am an American," replied Stimbol, relieved and delighted to have discovered a medium of communication with the Arabs. "I have been lost in the jungle and I am starving."

"He is from the New World and he has been lost and is starving," translated Fahd.

Ibn Jad directed that food be brought, and as the stranger ate they carried on a conversation through Fahd. Stimbol explained that his men had deserted him and that he would pay well to be taken to the coast. The Beduin had no desire to be further hampered by the presence of a weak old man and was inclined to have Stimbol's throat slit as the easiest solution of the problem, but Fahd, who was impressed by the man's boastings of his great wealth, saw the possibilities of a large reward or ransom and prevailed upon the sheik to permit Stimbol to remain among them for a time at least, promising to take him into his own beyt and be responsible for him.

"Ibn Jad would have slain you, Nasrany," said Fahd to Stimbol later, "but Fahd saved you. Remember that when the time comes for distributing the reward and remember, too, that Ibn Jad will be as ready to kill you tomorrow as he was today and that always your life is in the hands of Fahd. What is it worth?"

"I will make you rich," replied Stimbol.

During the days that followed, Fahd and Stimbol became much better acquainted and with returning strength and a feeling of security Stimbol's old boastfulness returned. He succeeded in impressing the young Beduin with his vast wealth and importance, and so lavish were his promises that Fahd soon commenced to see before him a life of luxury, ease and power; but with growing cupidity and ambition developed an increasing fear that someone might wrest his good fortune from him. Ibn Jad being the most logical and powerful competitor for the favors of the Nasrany, Fahd lost no opportunity to impress upon Stimbol that the sheik was still thirsting for his blood; though, as a matter of fact, Ibn Jad was so little concerned over the affairs of Wilbur Stimbol that he would have forgotten his presence entirely were he not occasionally reminded of it by seeing the man upon the march or about the camps.

One thing, however, that Fahd accomplished was to acquaint Stimbol with the fact that there was dissension and treachery in the ranks of the Beduins and this he determined to use to his own advantage should necessity demand.

And ever, though slowly, the 'Aarab drew closer to the fabled Leopard City of Nimmr, and as they marched Zeyd found opportunity to forward his suit for the hand of Ateja the daughter of Sheik Ibn Jad, while Tollog sought by insinuation to advance the claims of Fahd in the eyes of the Sheik. This he did always and only when Fahd might hear as, in reality, his only wish was to impress upon the young traitor the depth of the latter's obligation to him. When Tollog should become sheik he would not care who won the hand of Ateja.

But Fahd was not satisfied with the progress that was being made. Jealousy rode him to distraction until he could not look upon Zeyd without thoughts of murder seizing his mind; at last they obsessed him. He schemed continually to rid himself and the world of his more successful rival. He spied upon him and upon Ateja, and at last a plan unfolded itself with opportunity treading upon its heels.

Fahd had noticed that nightly Zeyd absented himself from the gatherings of the men in the mukaad of the sheik's tent and that when the simple household duties were performed Ateja slipped out into the night. Fahd followed and confirmed what was really too apparent to be dignified by the name of suspicion—Zeyd and Ateja met.

And then one night, Fahd was not at the meeting in the sheik's beyt. Instead he hid near the tent of Zeyd, and when the latter had left to keep his tryst Fahd crept in and seized the matchlock of his rival. It was already loaded and he had but to prime it with powder. Stealthily he crept by back ways through the camp to where Zeyd awaited his light of love and sneaked up behind him.

At a little distance, sitting in his mukaad with his friends beneath the light of paper lanterns, Ibn Jad the sheik was plainly visible to the two young men standing in the outer darkness. Ateja was still in the women's quarters.

Fahd, standing behind Zeyd, raised the ancient matchlock to his shoulder and aimed—very carefully he aimed, but not at Zeyd. No, for the cunning of Fahd was as the cunning of the fox. Had Zeyd been murdered naught could ever convince Ateja that Fahd was not the murderer. Fahd knew that, and he was equally sure that Ateja would have naught of the slayer of her lover.

Beyond Zeyd was Ibn Jad, but Fahd was not aiming at Ibn Jad either. At whom was he aiming? No one. Not yet was the time ripe to slay the sheik. First must they have their hands upon the treasure, the secret of which he alone was supposed to hold.

Fahd aimed at one of the am'dan of the sheik's tent. He aimed with great care and then he pulled the trigger. The prop splintered and broke a foot above the level of Ibn Jad's head, and simultaneously Fahd threw down the musket and leaped upon the startled Zeyd, at the same time crying loudly for help.

Startled by the shot and the cries, men ran from all directions and with them was the sheik. He found Zeyd being held tightly from behind by Fahd.

"What is the meaning of this?" demanded Ibn Jad.

"By Ullah, Ibn Jad, he would have slain thee!" cried Fahd. "I came upon him just in time, and as he fired I leaped upon his back, else he would have killed you."

"He lies!" cried Zeyd. "The shot came from behind me. If any fired upon Ibn Jad it was Fahd himself."

Ateja, wide-eyed, ran to her lover. "Thou didst not do it, Zeyd; tell me that thou didst not do it."

"As Allah is my God and Mohammed his prophet I did not do it," swore Zeyd.

"I would not have thought it of him," said Ibn Jad.

Cunning, Fahd did not mention the matchlock. Shrewdly he guessed that its evidence would be more potent if discovered by another than he, and that it would be discovered he was sure. Nor was he wrong. Tollog found it.

"Here," he exclaimed, "is the weapon."

"Let us examine it beneath the light," said Ibn Jad. "It should dispel our doubts more surely than any lying tongue."

As the party moved in the direction of the sheik's beyt Zeyd experienced the relief of one reprieved from death, for he knew that the testimony of the matchlock would exonerate him. It could not be his. He pressed the hand of Ateja, walking at his side.

Beneath the light of the paper lanterns in the mukaad Ibn Jad held the weapon beneath his gaze as, with craning necks, the others pressed about him. A single glance sufficed. With stern visage the sheik raised his eyes.

"It is Zeyd's," he said.

Ateja gasped and drew away from her lover.

"I did not do it! It is some trick," cried Zeyd.

"Take him away!" commanded Ibn Jad. "See that he is tightly bound."

Ateja rushed to her father and fell upon her knees. "Do not slay him!" she cried. "It could not have been he. I know it was not he."

"Silence, girl!" commanded the sheik sternly. "Go to thy quarters and remain there!"

They took Zeyd to his own beyt and bound him securely, and in the mukaad of the sheik the elders sat in judgment while from behind the curtains of the women's quarters, Ateja listened.

"At dawn, then, he shall be shot!" This was the sentence that Ateja heard passed upon her lover.

Behind his greasy thorrib Fahd smiled a crooked smile. In his black house of hair Zeyd struggled with the bonds that held him, for though he had not heard the sentence he was aware of what his fate would be. In the quarters of the hareem of the Sheik Ibn Jad the sheik's daughter lay sleepless and suffering. Her long lashes were wet with tears but her grief was silent. Wide eyed she waited, listening, and presently her patience was rewarded by the sounds of the deep, regular breathing of Ibn Jad and his wife, Hirfa. They slept.

Ateja stirred. Stealthily she raised the lower edge of the tent cloth beside which lay her sleeping mat and rolled quietly beneath it into the mukaad, now deserted. Groping, she found the matchlock of Zeyd where Ibn Jad had left it. She carried also a bundle wrapped in an old thorrib, the contents of which she had gathered earlier in the evening when Hirfa, occupied with her duties, had been temporarily absent from the women's quarters.

Ateja emerged from the tent of her father and crept cautiously along the single, irregular street formed by the pitched tents of the 'Aarab until she came to the beyt of Zeyd. For a moment she paused at the opening, listening, then she entered softly on sandalled feet.

But Zeyd, sleepless, struggling with his bonds, heard her. "Who comes?" he damanded.

"S-s-sh!" cautioned the girl. "It is I, Ateja." She crept to his side.

"Beloved!" he murmured.

Deftly the girl cut the bonds that held his wrists and ankles. "I have brought thee food and thy musket," she told him. "These and freedom I give thee—the rest thou must do thyself. Thy mare stands tethered with the others. Far is the beled el-Guad, beset with dangers is the way, but night and day will Ateja pray to Allah to guide thee safely. Haste, my loved one!"

Zeyd pressed her tightly to his breast, kissed her and was gone into the night.

9

Sir Richard

THE FLOOR of the tunnel along which Paul Bodkin conducted Blake inclined ever upwards, and again and again it was broken by flights of steps which carried them always to higher levels. To Blake the way seemed interminable. Even the haunting mystery of the long tunnel failed to overcome the monotony of its unchanging walls that slipped silently into the torch's dim ken for a brief instant and as silently back into the Cimmerian oblivion behind to make place for more wall unvaryingly identical.

But, as there ever is to all things, there was an end to the tunnel. Blake first glimpsed it in a little patch of distant daylight ahead, and presently he stepped out into the sunlight and looked out across a wide valley that was tree-dotted and beautiful. He found himself standing upon a wide ledge, or shelf, some hundred feet above the base of the mountain through which the tunnel had been cut. There was a sheer drop before him, and to his right the ledge terminated abruptly at a distance of a hundred feet or less. Then he glanced to the left and his eyes went wide in astonishment.

Across the shelf stood a solid wall of masonry flanked at either side by great, round towers pierced by long, narrow embrasures. In the center of the wall was a lofty gateway which was closed by a massive and handsomely wrought portcullis behind which Blake saw two Negroes standing guard. They were clothed precisely as his captors, but held great battle-axes, the butts of which rested upon the ground.

"What ho, the gate!" shouted Paul Bodkin. "Open to the outer guard and a prisoner!"

Slowly the portcullis rose and Blake and his captor passed beneath. Directly inside the gateway and at the left, built into the hillside, was what was evidently a guardhouse. Before it loitered a score or so of soldiers, uniformed like Paul Bodkin, upon the breast of each the red cross. To a heavy wooden rail gaily caparisoned horses were tethered, their handsome trappings recalling to Blake's memory paintings he had seen of mounted knights of medieval England.

There was so much of unreality in the strangely garbed blacks, the massive barbican that guarded the way, the trappings of the horses, that Blake was no longer capable of surprise when one of the two doors in the guardhouse opened and there stepped out a handsome young man clad in a hauberk of chain mail over which was a light surcoat of rough stuff, dyed purple. Upon the youth's head fitted a leopard skin bassinet from the lower edge of which depended a casmail or gorget of chain mail that entirely surrounded and protected his throat and neck. He was armed only with a heavy sword and a dagger, but against the side of the guardhouse, near the doorway where he paused to look at Blake, leaned a long lance, and near it was a shield with a red cross emblazoned upon its boss.

"Od zounds!" exclaimed the young man. "What has thou there, varlet?"

"A prisoner, an' it pleases thee, noble lord," replied Paul Bodkin, deferentially.

"A Saracen, of a surety," stated the young man.

"Nay, an I may make so bold, Sir Richard," replied Paul —"but me thinks he be no Saracen."

"And why?"

"With mine own eyes I didst see him make the sign before the Cross."

"Fetch him hither, lout!"

Bodkin prodded Blake in the rear with his pike, but the American scarce noticed the offense so occupied was his mind by the light of truth that had so suddenly illuminated it. In the instant he had grasped the solution. He laughed inwardly at himself for his denseness. Now he understood everything—and these fellows thought they could put it over on him, did they? Well, they had come near to doing it, all right.

He stepped quickly toward the young man and halted, upon his lips a faintly sarcastic smile. The other eyed him with haughty arrogance.

"Whence comest thou," he asked, "and what doest thou in the Valley of the Sepulcher, varlet?"

Blake's smile faded—too much was too much. "Cut the comedy, young fellow," he drawled in his slow way. "Where's the director?"

"Director? Forsooth, I know not what thou meanest."

"Yes you don't!" snapped Blake, with fine sarcasm. "But

let me tell you right off the bat that no seven-fifty a day extra can pull anything like that with me!"

"Od's blud, fellow! I ken not the meaning of all the words, but I mislike thy tone. It savors o'er much of insult to fall sweetly upon the ears of Richard Montmorency."

"Be yourself," advised Blake. "If the director isn't handy send for the assistant director, or the camera man—even the continuity writer may have more sense than you seem to have."

"Be myself? And who thinkest thee I would be other than Richard Montmorency, a noble knight of Nimmr."

Blake shook his head in despair, then he turned to the soldiers who were standing about listening to the conversation. He thought some of them would be grinning at the joke that was being played on him, but he saw only solemn, serious faces.

"Look here," he said, addressing Paul Bodkin, "don't any of you know where the director is?"

" 'Director'?" repeated Bodkin, shaking his head. "There be none in Nimmr thus y-clept, nay, nor in all the Valley of the Sepulcher that I wot."

"I'm sorry," said Blake, "the mistake is mine; but if there is no director there must be a keeper. May I see him?"

"Ah, keeper!" cried Bodkin, his face lighting with understanding. "Sir Richard is the keeper."

"My gawd!" exclaimed Blake, turning to the young man. "I beg your pardon, I thought that you were one of the inmates."

"Inmates? Indeed thou speakest a strange tongue and yet withall it hath the flavor of England," replied the young man gravely. "But yon varlet be right—I am indeed this day the Keeper of the Gate."

Blake was commencing to doubt his own sanity, or at least his judgment. Neither the young white man nor any of the Negroes had any of their facial characteristics of mad men. He looked up suddenly at the keeper of the gate.

"I am sorry," he said, flashing one of the frank smiles that was famous amongst his acquaintances. "I have acted like a boor, but I've been under considerable of a nervous strain for a long time, and on top of that I've been lost in the jungle for days without proper or sufficient food.

"I thought that you were trying to play some sort of a joke on me and, well, I wasn't in any mood for jokes when I expected friendship and hospitality instead.

"Tell me, where am I? What country is this?"

"Thou art close upon the city of Nimmr," replied the young man.

"I suppose this is something of a national holiday or something?" suggested Blake.

"I do not understand thee," replied the young man.

"Why, you're all in a pageant or something, aren't you?"

"Od's bodikins! the fellow speaks an outlandish tongue! Pageant?"

"Yes, those costumes."

"What be amiss with this apparel? True, 'tis not of any wondrous newness, but methinks it be at least more fair than thine. At least it well suffices the daily service of a knight."

"You don't mean that you dress like this every day?" demanded Blake.

"And why not? But enough of this. I have no wish to further bandy words with thee. Fetch him within, two of thee. And thou, Bodkin, return to the outer guard!" The young man turned and re-entered the building, while two of the soldiers seized Blake, none too gently, and hustled him within.

He found himself in a high-ceiled room with walls of cut stone and great, hand-hewn beams and rafters blackened with age. Upon the stone floor stood a table behind which, upon a bench, the young man seated himself while Blake was placed facing him with a guard on either hand.

"Thy name," demanded the young man.

"Blake."

"That be all—just Blake?"

"James Hunter Blake."

"What title bearest thou in thine own country?"

"I have no title."

"Ah, thou art not a gentleman, then?"

"I am called one."

"What is thy country?"

"America."

"America! There is no such country, fellow."

"And why not?"

"I never heard of it. What doest thou near the Valley of the Sepulcher? Didst not know 'tis forbidden?"

"I told you I was lost. I didn't know where I was. All I want is to get back to my safari or to the coast."

"That be impossible. We be surrounded by Saracens. For seven hundred and thirty-five years we have been invested by their armies. How come you through the enemies' lines? How passed you through his vast army?"

"There isn't any army."

"Givest thou the lie to Richard Montmorency, varlet? An' thou wert of gentle blood thou shouldst account to me that insult upon the field of honor. Methink'st thou beest some low-born spy sent hither by the Saracen sultan. 'Twould be well an thou confessed all to me, for if I take thee before the Prince he will wrest the truth from thee in ways that are far from pleasant. What say?"

"I have nothing to confess. Take me before the Prince, or whoever your boss is; perhaps he will at least give me food."

"Thou shalt have food here. Never shall it be said that Richard Montmorency turned a hungry man from his doorway Hey! Michel! Michel! Where is the lazy brat? Michel!"

A door opened from an inner apartment to admit a boy, sleepy eyed, digging a grimy fist into one eye. He was clothed in a short tunic, his legs encased in green tights. In his cap was a feather.

"Sleeping again, eh?" demanded Sir Richard. "Thou lazy knave! Fetch bread and meat for this poor wayfarer and be not until the morrow at it!"

Wide-eyed and rather stupidly, the boy stared at Blake. "A Saracen, master?" he asked.

"What boots it?" snapped Sir Richard. "Did not our Lord Jesus feed the multitude, nor ask if there were unbelievers among them? Haste, churl! The stranger be of great hunger."

The youth turned and shuffled from the room, wiping his nose upon his sleeve, and Sir Richard's attention came back to Blake.

"Thou are not ill-favored, fellow," he said. " 'Tis a pity that thou beest not of noble blood, for thy mien appearth not like that of one lowborn."

"I never considered myself lowborn," said Blake, with a grin.

"Thy father, now—was he not at least a sir knight?"

Blake was thinking quickly now. He was far from being able as yet to so much as hazard a guess that might explain his host's archaic costume and language, but he was sure that the man was in earnest, whether sane or not, and were he not sane it seemed doubly wise to humor him.

"Yes, indeed," he replied, "my father is a thirty second degree Mason and a Knight Templar."

"Sblud! I knew it," cried Sir Richard.

"And so am I," added Blake, when he realized the happy effect his statement had produced.

"Ah, I knew it! I knew it!" cried Sir Richard. "Thy bearing proclaimed thy noble blood; but why didst thou seek to deceive me? And so thou are one of the poor Knights of Christ and of the Temple of Solomon who guard the way of the pilgrims to the Holy Land! This explaineth thy poor raiment and glorifies it."

Blake was mystified by the allusion, as the picture always suggested by a reference to Knights Templar was of waving white plumes, gorgeous aprons and glittering swords. He did not know that in the days of their origin they were clothed in any old garments that the charity of others might bequeath them.

At this moment Michel returned bearing a wooden trencher containing cold mutton and several pieces of simnel bread and carrying in one hand a flagon of wine. These he set upon the table before Blake and going to a cupboard fetched two metal goblets into which he decanted a portion of the contents of the flagon.

Sir Richard arose and taking one of the goblets raised it before him on a level with his head.

"Hal, Sir James!" he cried, "and welcome to Nimmr and the Valley of the Sepulcher!"

"Here's looking at you!" replied Blake.

"A quaint saying," remarked Sir Richard. "Methinks the ways of England must be changed since the days of Richard the Lion Hearted when my noble ancestor set forth upon the great crusade in the company of his king. Here's looking at you! Ods bodikins! I must not let that from my memory. Here's looking at you! Just wait thou 'til some fair knight doth drink my health—I shall lay him flat with that!

"But, stay! Here, Michel, fetch yon stool for Sir James, and eat, sir knight. Thou must be passing hungry."

"I'll tell the world I am," replied Blake, feelingly, as he sat down on the stool that Michel brought. There were no knives or forks, but there were fingers and these Blake used to advantage while his host sat smiling happily at him from across the rude table.

"Thou art better than a minstrel for pleasure," cried Sir Richard. "I'll tell the world I am! Ho, ho! Thou wilt be a gift from heaven in the castle of the prince. I'll tell the world I am!"

When Blake had satisfied his hunger, Sir Richard ordered Michel to prepare horses. "We ride down to the castle, Sir James," he explained. "No longer art thou my prisoner, but my friend and guest. That I should have received thee so scurvily shalt ever be to my discredit."

Mounted upon prancing chargers and followed at a respectful distance by Michel, the two rode down the winding mountain road. Sir Richard now carried his shield and lance, a pennon fluttering bravely in the wind from just below the tip of the latter, the sun glancing from the metal of his hauberk, a smile upon his brave face as he chattered with his erstwhile prisoner. To Blake he seemed a gorgeous picture ridden from out the pages of a story book. Yet, belying his martial appearance, there was a childlike simplicity about the man that won Blake's liking from the first, for there was that about him that made it impossible for one to conceive him as the perpetrator of a dishonorable act.

His ready acceptance of Blake's statements about himself bespoke a credulity that seemed incompatible with the high intelligence reflected by his noble countenance, and the American preferred to attribute it to a combination of unsophistication and an innate integrity which could not conceive of perfidy in others.

As the road rounded the shoulder of a hill, Blake saw another barbican barring the way and, beyond, the towers and battlements of an ancient castle. At a command from Sir Richard the warders of the gate opened to them and the three rode through into the ballium. This space between the outer and inner walls appeared unkept and neglected. Several old trees flourished within it and beneath the shade of one of these, close to the outer gateway, lolled several men-at-arms, two of whom were engaged in a game that resembled draughts.

At the foot of the inner wall was a wide moat, the waters of which reflected the gray stones of the wall and the ancient vines that, growing upon its inner side, topped it to form a leaf coping that occasionally hung low upon the outer side.

Directly opposite the barbican was the great gateway in the inner wall and here a drawbridge spanned the moat and a heavy portcullis barred the way into the great court of the castle; but at a word from Sir Richard the gate lifted and, clattering across the drawbridge, they rode within.

Before Blake's astonished eyes loomed a mighty castle of rough hewn stone, while to the right and left, within the great court, spread broad gardens not illy kept, in which were gathered a company of men and women who might have just stepped from Arthur's court.

At sight of Sir Richard and his companion the nearer members of the company regarded Blake with interest and evident surprise. Several called greetings and questions to Sir Richard as the two men dismounted and turned their horses over to Michel.

"Ho, Richard!" cried one. "What bringest thou—a Saracen?"

"Nay," replied Richard. "A fair sir knight who would do his devoir to the prince. Where be he?"

"Yonder," and they pointed toward the far end of the court where a large company was assembled.

"Come, Sir James!" directed Richard, and led him down the courtyard, the knights and ladies following closely, asking questions, commenting with a frankness that brought a flush to Blake's face. The women openly praised his features and his carriage while the men, perhaps prompted by jealousy, made unflattering remarks about his soiled and torn apparel and its, to them, ridiculous cut; and indeed the contrast was great between their gorgeous dalmaticas of villosa or cyclas, their close fitting tights, their colored caps and Blake's drab shirt, whipcord breeches and cordovan boots, now soiled, torn and scratched.

The women were quite as richly dressed as the men, wearing clinging mantles of rich stuff, their hair and shoulders covered with dainty wimples of various colors and often elaborately embroidered.

None of these men, nor any of those in the assemblage they were approaching wore armor, but Blake had seen an armored knight at the outer gateway and another at the inner and he judged that only when engaged in military duties did they wear this heavy and uncomfortable dress.

When they reached the party at the end of the court Sir Richard elbowed his way among them to the center of the group where stood a tall man of imposing appearance, chatting with those about him. As Sir Richard and Blake halted before him the company fell silent.

"My lord prince," said Richard, bowing, "I bring thee Sir James, a worthy Knight Templar who hath come under the protection of God through the lines of the enemy to the gates of Nimmr."

The tall man eyed Blake searchingly and he had not the appearance of great credulity.

"Thou sayest that thou comest from the Temple of Solomon in the Kingdom of Jerusalem?" he demanded.

"Sir Richard must have misunderstood me," replied Blake.

"Then thou art no Knight Templar?"

"Yes, but I am not from Jerusalem."

"Perchance he is one of those doughty sir knights that guard the pilgrims' way to the Holy Land," suggested a young woman standing near the prince.

Blake glanced quickly at the speaker and as their eyes met,

hers fell, but not before he had seen that they were very beautiful eyes set in an equally beautiful, oval face.

"More like it haps he be a Saracen spy sent among us by the sultan," snapped a dark man who stood beside the girl.

The latter raised her eyes to the prince. "He looketh not like a Saracen, my father," she said.

"What knowest thou of the appearance of a Saracen, child?" demanded the prince. "Hast seen so many?" The party laughed and the girl pouted.

"Verily an' I hast seen full as many a Saracen as has Sir Malud or thyself, my lord prince," she snapped, haughtily. "Let Sir Malud describe a Saracen."

The dark young man flushed angrily. "At least," he said, "my lord prince, I knowest an English knight when I seest one, an' if here be an English knight then Sir Malud be a Saracen!"

"Enough," said the prince and then, turning to Blake: "If thou art not from Jerusalem where art thou from?"

"New York," replied the American.

"Ha," whispered Sir Malud to the girl, "didst I not tell you?"

"Tell me what—that he is from New York? Where is that?" she demanded.

"Some stronghold of the infidel," asserted Malud.

"New York?" repeated the prince. "Be that in the Holy Land?"

"It is sometimes called New Jerusalem," explained Blake.

"And thou comest to Nimmr through the lines of the enemy? Tell me, sir knight, had they many men-at-arms? And how were their forces disposed? Be they close upon the Valley of the Sepulcher? Thinkest thou they plan an early attack? Come, tell me all—thou canst be of great service."

"I have come for days through the forest and seen no living man," said Blake. "No enemy surrounds you."

"What?" cried the prince.

"Didst I not tell thee?" demanded Malud. "He is an enemy spy. He wouldst lead us into the belief that we are safe that the forces of the sultan may find us off our guard and take Nimmr and the Valley."

"Ods blud! Methinks thou beest right, Sur Malud," cried the prince. "No enemy indeed! Why else then hast the knights of Nimmr lain here seven and a half centuries if there be no horde of infidels surrounding our stronghold?"

"Search me," said Blake.

"Eh, what?" demanded the prince.

"He hath a quaint manner of speech, my lord prince," explained Richard, "but I do not think him an enemy of England. Myself will vouch for him an' you will take him into your service, my lord prince."

"Wouldst enter my service, sir?" demanded the prince.

Blake glanced at Sir Malud and looked dubious—then his eyes wandered to those of the girl. "I'll tell the world I would!" he said.

10

The Return of Ulala

Numa was hungry. For three days and three nights he had hunted but always the prey had eluded him. Perhaps Numa was growing old. Not so keen were his scent and his vision, not so swift his charges, nor well timed the spring that heretofore had brought down the quarry. So quick the food of Numa that a fraction of a second, a hair's breadth, might mark the difference between a full belly and starvation.

Perhaps Numa was growing old, yet he still was a mighty engine of destruction, and now the pangs of hunger had increased his ferocity many-fold, stimulated his cunning, emboldened him to take great risks that his belly might be filled. It was a nervous, irascible, ferocious Numa that crouched beside the trail. His up-pricked ears, his intent and blazing eyes, his quivering nostrils, the gently moving tail-tip, evidenced his awareness of another presence.

Down the wind to the nostrils of Numa the lion came the man-scent. Four days ago, his belly full, Numa had doubtless slunk away at the first indication of the presence of man, but today is another day and another Numa.

Zeyd, three days upon the back track from the menzil of the sheik Ibn Jad, thought of Ateja, of far Guad, congratulated himself upon the good fortune that had thus far smiled upon his escape and flight. His mare moved slowly along the jungle trail, unurged, for the way was long; and just ahead a beast of prey waited in ambush.

But Numa's were not the only ears to hear, nor his nostrils the only nostrils to scent the coming of the man-thing—another beast crouched near, unknown to Numa.

Overanxious, fearful of being cheated of his meat, Numa made a false move. Down the trail came the mare. She must pass within a yard of Numa, but Numa could not wait. Before she was within the radius of his spring he charged, voicing a horrid roar. Terrified the mare reared and, rearing, tried to turn and bolt. Overbalanced, she toppled backward and fell, and in falling unhorsed Zeyd; but in the instant she was up and flying back along the trail, leaving her master in the path of the charging lion.

Horrified, the man saw the snarling face, the bared fangs almost upon him. Then he saw something else—something equally awe-inspiring—a naked giant who leaped from a swaying branch full upon the back of the great cat. He saw a bronzed arm encircle the neck of the beast of prey as the lion was borne to earth by the weight and impact of the man's body. He saw a heavy knife flashing in the air, striking home again and again as the frenzied lion threw itself about in futile effort to dislodge the thing upon its back. He heard the roars and the growls of el adrea, and mingled with them were growls and snarls that turned his blood cold, for he saw that they came from the lips of the man-beast.

Then Numa went limp and the giant arose and stood above the carcass. He placed one foot upon it and, raising his face toward the heavens, voiced a hideous scream that froze the marrow in the bones of the Beduin—a scream that few men have heard: the victory cry of the bull ape.

It was then that Zeyd recognized his saviour and shuddered again as he saw that it was Tarzan of the Apes. The ape-man looked down at him.

"Thou art from the menzil of Ibn Jad," he said.

"I am but a poor man," replied Zeyd. "I but followed where my sheykh led. Hold it not against Zeyd sheykh of the jungle, that he be in thy beled. Spare my poor life I pray thee and may Allah bless thee."

"I have no wish to harm thee, Beduwy," replied Tarzan. "What wrong hath been done in my country is the fault of Ibn Jad alone. Is he close by?"

"Wellah nay, he be many marches from here."

"Where art thy companions?" demanded the ape-man.

"I have none."

"Thou art alone?"

"Billah, yes."

Tarzan frowned. "Think well Beduwy before lying to Tarzan," he snapped.

"By Ullah, I speak the truth! I am alone."

"And why?"

"Fahd did plot against me to make it appear that I had tried to take the life of Ibn Jad, which, before Allah, is a lie that stinketh to heaven, and I was to be shot; but Ateja, the daughter of the sheykh, cut my bonds in the night and I escaped."

"What is thy name?"

"Zeyd."

"Whither goest thou—to thine own country?"

"Yes, to beled el-Guad, a Beny Salem fendy of el-Harb."

"Thou canst not, alone, survive the perils of the way," Tarzan warned him.

"Of that I be fearful, but death were certain had I not escaped the wrath of Ibn Jad."

For a moment Tarzan was silent in thought. "Great must be the love of Ateja, the daughter of the sheik, and great her belief in you," he said.

"Wellah, yes, great is our love and, too, she knew that I would not slay her father, whom she loves."

Tarzan nodded. "I believe thee and shall help thee. Thou canst not go on alone. I shall take thee to the nearest village and there the chief will furnish you with warriors who will take you to the next village, and thus from village to village you will be escorted to the Soudan."

"May Allah ever watch over and guard thee!" exclaimed Zeyd.

"Tell me," said Tarzan as the two moved along the jungle trail in the direction of the nearest village which lay two marches to the south of them, "tell me what Ibn Jad doth in this country. It is not true that he came for ivory alone. Am I not right?"

"Wellah yes, Sheykh Tarzan," admitted Zeyd. "Ibn Jad came for treasure, but not for ivory."

"What, then?"

"In el-Habash lies the treasure city of Nimmr," explained Zeyd. "This Ibn Jad was told by a learned sahar. So great is the wealth of Nimmr that a thousand camels could carry away not a tenth part of it. It consists of gold and jewels and—a woman."

"A woman?"

"Yes, a woman of such wondrous beauty that in the north she alone would bring a price that would make Ibn Jad rich beyond dreams. Surely thou must have heard of Nimmr."

"Sometimes the Gallas speak of it," said Tarzan, "but always I thought it of no more reality than the other places of their legends. And Ibn Jad undertook this long and dangerous journey on no more than the word of a magician?"

"What could be better than the word of a learned sahar?" demanded Zeyd.

Tarzan of the Apes shrugged.

During the two days that it took them to reach the village Tarzan learned of the white man who had come to the camp of Ibn Jad, but from Zeyd's description of him he was not positive whether it was Blake or Stimbol.

As Tarzan travelled south with Zeyd, Ibn Jad trekked northward into el-Habash, and Fahd plotted with Tollog, and Stimbol plotted with Fahd, while Fejjuan the Galla slave waited patiently for the moment of his delivery from bondage, and Ateja mourned for Zeyd.

"As a boy thou wert raised in this country, Fejjuan," she said one day to the Galla slave. "Tell me, dost thou think Zeyd could make his way alone to el-Guad?"

"Billah, nay," replied the black. "Doubtless he be dead by now."

The girl stifled a sob.

"Fejjuan mourns with thee, Ateja," said the black, "for Zeyd was a kindly man. Would that Allah had spared your lover and taken him who was guilty."

"What do you mean?" asked Ateja. "Knowest thou, Fejjuan, who fired the shot at Ibn Jad, my father? It was not Zeyd! Tell me it was not Zeyd! But thy words tell me that, which I well knew before. Zeyd could not have sought the life of my father!"

"Nor did he," replied Fejjuan.

"Tell me what you know of this thing."

"And you will not tell another who told you?" he asked. "It would go hard with me if one I am thinking of knew that I had seen what I did see."

"I swear by Allah that I wilt not betray you, Fejjuan," cried the girl. "Tell me, what didst thou see?"

"I did not see who fired the shot at thy father, Ateja," replied the black, "but something else I saw before the shot was fired."

"Yes, what was it?"

"I saw Fahd creep into the beyt of Zeyd and come out again bearing Zeyd's matchlock. That I saw."

"I knew it! I knew it!" cried the girl.

"But Ibn Jad will not believe if you tell him."

"I know; but now that I am convinced perhaps I shall find a way to have Fahd's blood for the blood of Zeyd," cried the girl, bitterly.

For days Ibn Jad skirted the mountains behind which he thought lay the fabled city of Nimmr as he searched for an entrance which he hoped to find without having recourse to the natives whose haunts he had sedulously avoided lest through them opposition to his venture might develop.

The country was sparsely settled, which rendered it easy for the 'Aarab to avoid coming into close contact with the natives, though it was impossible that the Gallas were ignorant of their presence. If however the blacks were willing to leave them alone, Ibn Jad had no intention of molesting them unless he found that it would be impossible to carry his project to a successful issue without their assistance, in which event he was equally ready to approach them with false promises or ruthless cruelty, whichever seemed the more likely to better serve his purpose.

As the days passed Ibn Jad waxed increasingly impatient, for, search as he would, he could locate no pass across the mountains, nor any entrance to the fabled valley wherein lay the treasure city of Nimmr.

"Billah!" he exclaimed one day, "there be a City of Nimmr and there be an entrance to it, and, by Allah, I will find it! Summon the Habush, Tollog! From them or through them we shall have a clew in one way or another."

When Tollog had fetched the Galla slaves to the beyt of Ibn Jad, the old sheik questioned them but there was none who had definite knowledge of the trail leading to Nimmr.

"Then, by Allah," exclaimed Ibn Jad, "we shall have it from the native Habush!"

"They be mighty warriors, O brother," cried Tollog, "and we be far within their country. Should we anger them and they set upon us it might fare ill with us."

"We be Bedauwy," said Ibn Jad proudly, "and we be armed with muskets. What could their simple spears and arrows avail against us?"

"But they be many and we be few," insisted Tollog.

"We shall not fight unless we be driven to it," said Ibn Jad. "First we shall seek, by friendly overtures, to win their confidence and cajole the secret from them.

"Fejjuan!" he exclaimed, turning to the great black. "Thou are a Habashy. I have heard thee say that thou well rememberest the days of thy childhood in the hut of thy father and the story of Nimmr was no new story to you. Go, then, and seek out thy people. Make friends with them. Tell them that the great Sheykh Ibn Jad comes among them in friendliness and that he hath gifts for their chiefs. Tell them also that he would visit the city of Nimmr, and if they will lead him there he will reward them well."

"I but await thy commands," said Fejjuan, elated at this opportunity to do what he had long dreamed of doing. "When shall I set forth?"

"Prepare thyself tonight and when dawn comes depart," replied the sheik.

And so it was that Fejjuan, the Galla slave, set forth early the following morning from the menzil of Ibn Jad, sheik of the fendy el-Guad, to search for a village of his own people.

By noon he had come upon a well-worn trail leading toward the west, and this he followed boldly, guessing that he would best disarm suspicion thus than by attempting to approach a Galla village by stealth. Also he well knew that there was little likelihood that he could accomplish the latter in any event. Fejjuan was no fool. He knew that it might be difficult to convince the Gallas that he was of their blood, for there was against him not alone his 'Aarab garments and weapons but the fact that he would be able to speak the Galla tongue but lamely after all these years.

That he was a brave man was evidenced by the fact that he well knew the suspicious and warlike qualities of his people and their inborn hatred of the 'Aarab and yet gladly embraced this opportunity to go amongst them.

How close he had approached a village Fejjuan did not know. There were neither sounds nor odors to enlighten him when there suddenly appeared in the trail ahead of him three husky Galla warriors and behind him he heard others, though he did not turn.

Instantly Fejjuan raised his hands in sign of peace and at the same time he smiled.

"What are you doing in the Galla country?" demanded one of the warriors.

"I am seeking the house of my father," replied Fejjuan.

"The house of your father is not in the country of the Gallas, growled the warrior. "You are one of these who come to rob us of our sons and daughters."

"No," replied Fejjuan. "I am a Galla."

"If you were a Galla you would speak the language of the Gallas better. We understand you, but you do not speak as a Galla speaks."

"That is because I was stolen away when I was a child and have lived among the Bedauwy since, speaking only their tongue."

"What is your name?"

"The Bedauwy call me Fejjuan, but my Galla name was Ulala."

"Do you think he speaks the truth?" demanded one of the blacks of a companion. "When I was a child I had a brother whose name was Ulala."

"Where is he?" asked the other warrior.

"We do not know. Perhaps simba the lion devoured him. Perhaps the desert people took him. Who knows?"

"Perhaps he speaks the truth," said the second warrior. "Perhaps he is your brother. Ask him his father's name."

"What was your father's name?" demanded the first warrior.

"Naliny," replied Fejjuan.

At this reply the Galla warriors became excited and whispered among themselves for several seconds. Then the first warrior turned again to Fejjuan.

"Did you have a brother?" he demanded.

"Yes," replied Fejjuan.

"What was his name?"

"Tabo," answered Fejjuan without hesitation.

The warrior who had questioned him leaped into the air with a wild shout.

"It is Ulala!" he cried. "It is my brother. I am Tabo, Ulala. Do you not remember me?"

"Tabo!" cried Fejjuan. "No, I would not know you, for you were a little boy when I was stolen away and now you are a great warrior. Where are our father and mother? Are they alive? Are they well?"

"They are alive and well, Ulala," replied Tabo. "Today they are in the village of the chief, for there is a great council because of the presence of some desert people in our country. Came you with them?"

"Yes, I am a slave to the desert people," replied Fejjuan. "Is it far to the village of the chief? I would see my mother and my father and, too, I would talk with the chief about the desert people who have come to the country of the Gallas."

"Come, brother!" cried Tabo. "We are not far from the village of the chief. Ah, my brother, that I should see you again whom we thought to be dead all these years! Great will be the joy of our father and mother.

"But, tell me, have the desert people turned you against your own people? You have lived with them many years. Perhaps you have taken a wife among them. Are you sure that you do not love them better than you love those whom you have not seen for many years?"

"I do not love the Bedauwy," replied Fejjuan, "nor have I taken a wife among them. Always in my heart has been the hope of returning to the mountains of my own country, to the house of my father. I love my own people, Tabo. Never again shall I leave them."

"The desert people have been unkind to you—they have treated you with cruelty?" demanded Tabo.

"Nay, on the contrary they have treated me well," replied Fejjuan. "I do not hate them, but neither do I love them. They are not of my own blood. I am a slave among them."

As they talked the party moved along the trail toward the village while two of the warriors ran ahead to carry the glad tidings to the father and mother of the long missing Ulala. And so it was that when they came within sight of the village they were met by a great crowd of laughing, shouting Gallas, and in the forerank were the father and mother of Fejjuan, their eyes blinded by the tears of love and joy that welled at sight of this long gone child.

After the greetings were over, and every man, woman and child in the company must crowd close and touch the returned wanderer, Tabo conducted Fejjuan into the village and the presence of the chief.

Batando was an old man. He had been chief when Ulala was stolen away. He was inclined to be skeptical, fearing a ruse of the desert people, and he asked many questions of Fejjuan concerning matters that he might hold in his memory from the days of his childhood. He asked him about the house of his father and the names of his playmates and other intimate things that an impostor might not know, and when he had done he arose and took Fejjuan in his arms and rubbed his cheek against the cheek of the prodigal.

"You are indeed Ulala," he cried. "Welcome back to the land of your people. Tell me now what the desert people do here. Have they come for slaves?"

"The desert people will always take slaves when they can get them, but Ibn Jad has not come first for slaves, but for treasure."

"Ai! what treasure?" demanded Batando.

"He has heard of the treasure city of Nimmr," replied Fejjuan. "It is a way into the valley where lies Nimmr that he seeks. For this he sent me to find Gallas who would lead him to Nimmr. He will make gifts and he promises rich rewards when he shall have wrested the treasure from Nimmr."

"Are these true words?" asked Batando.

"There is no truth in the beards of the desert dwellers," replied Fejjuan.

"And if he does not find the treasure of Nimmr perhaps he will try to find treasure and slaves in the Galla country to repay the expense of the long journey he has undertaken from the desert country?" asked Batando.

"Batando speaks out of the great wisdom of many years," replied Fejjuan.

"What does he know of Nimmr?" asked the old chief.

"Naught other than what an old medicine man of the 'Aarab told him," replied Fejjuan. "He said to Ibn Jad that great treasure lay hoarded in the City of Nimmr and that there was a beautiful woman who would bring a great price in the far north."

"Nothing more he told him?" demanded Batando. "Did he not tell him of the difficulties of entering the forbidden valley?"

"Nay."

"Then we can guide him to the entrance to the valley," said Batando, smiling slyly.

As Tarzan and Zeyd journeyed toward the village in which the ape-man purposed to enlist an escort for the Arab upon the first stage of his return journey toward his desert home, the Beduin had time to meditate much upon many matters, and having come to trust and respect his savage guide he at last unbosomed himself to Tarzan.

"Great Sheykh of the Jungle," he said one day, "by thy kindness thou hast won the undying loyalty of Zeyd who begs that thou wilt grant him one more favor."

"And what is that?" asked the ape-man.

"Ateja, whom I love, remains here in the savage country in constant danger so long as Fahd be near her. I dare not now return to the menzil of Ibn Jad even could I find it, but later, when the heat of Ibn Jad's anger will have had time to cool, then I might come again among them and convince him of my innocence, and be near Ateja and protect her from Fahd."

"What, then, would you do?" demanded Tarzan.

"I would remain in the village to which you are taking me until Ibn Jad returns this way toward el-Guad. It is the only chance that I have to see Ateja again in this life, as I could not cross the Soudan alone and on foot should you compel me to leave your country now."

"You are right," replied the ape-man. "You shall remain here six months. If Ibn Jad has not returned in that time I shall leave word that you be sent to my home. From there I can find a way to return you in safety to your own country."

"May the blessings of Allah be upon thee!" cried Zeyd.

And when they came at last to the village Tarzan received the promise of the chief to keep Zeyd until Ibn Jad returned.

After he had left the village again the ape-man headed north, for he was concerned over the report that Zeyd had given him of the presence of a European prisoner among the 'Aarab. That Stimbol, whom he had sent eastward toward the coast, should be so far north and west as Zeyd had reported appeared inconceivable, and so it seemed more probable that

84

the prisoner was young Blake, for whom Tarzan had conceived a liking. Of course the prisoner might not be either Stimbol or Blake, but who ever he was Tarzan could not readily brook the idea of a white man being permitted to remain a prisoner of the Beduins.

But Tarzan was in no hurry, for Zeyd had told him that the prisoner was to be held for ransom. He would have a look about for Blake's camp first and then follow up the spoor of the Arabs. His progress, therefore, was leisurely. On the second day he met the apes of Toyat and for two days he hunted with them, renewing his acquaintance with Gayat and Zutho, listening to the gossip of the tribe, often playing with the balus.

Leaving them, he loafed on through the jungle, stopping once for half a day to bait Numa where he lay upon a fresh kill, until the earth trembled to the thunderous roars of the maddened king of beasts as the ape-man taunted and annoyed him.

Sloughed was the thin veneer of civilization that was Lord Greystoke; back to the primitive, back to the savage beast the ape-man reverted as naturally, as simply, as one changes from one suit to another. It was only in his beloved jungle, surrounded by its savage denizens, that Tarzan of the Apes was truly Tarzan, for always in the presence of civilized men there was a certain restraint that was the outcome of that inherent suspicion that creatures of the wild ever feel for man.

Tired of throwing ripe fruit at Numa, Tarzan swung away through the middle terraces of the forest, lay up for the night far away and in the morning, scenting Bara the deer, made a kill and fed. Lazy, he slept again, until the breaking of twigs and the rustle of down tramped grasses awoke him.

He sniffed the air with sensitive nostrils and listened with ears that could hear an ant walk, and then he smiled. Tantor was coming.

For half a day he lolled on the huge back, listening to Manu the Monkey chattering and scolding among the trees. Then he moved on again.

A day or two later he came upon a large band of monkeys. They seemed much excited and at sight of him they all commenced to jabber and chatter.

"Greetings, Manu!" cried the ape-man. "I am Tarzan, Tarzan of the Apes. What happens in the jungle?"

"Gomangani! Gomangani!" cried one.

"Strange Gomangani!" cried another.

"Gomangani with thunder sticks!" chattered a third.

"Where?" asked the ape-man.

"There! There!" they shouted in chorus, pointing toward the northeast.

"Many sleeps away?" asked Tarzan.

"Close! Close!" the monkeys answered.

"There is one Tarmangani with them?"

"No, only Gomangani. With their thunder sticks they kill little Manu and eat him. Bad Gomangani!"

"Tarzan will talk with them," said the ape-man.

"They will kill Tarzan with their thunder sticks and eat him," prophesied a graybeard.

The ape-man laughed and swung off through the trees in the direction Manu had indicated. He had not gone far when the scent spoor of blacks came faintly to his nostrils and this spoor he followed until presently he could hear their voices in the distance.

Silently, warily Tarzan came through the trees, noiseless as the shadows that kept him company, until he stood upon a swaying limb directly above a camp of Negroes.

Instantly Tarzan recognized the safari of the young American, Blake, and a second later he dropped to the ground before the astonished eyes of the blacks. Some of them would have run, but others recognized him.

"It is Big Bwana!" they cried. "It is Tarzan of the Apes!"

"Where is your head man?" demanded Tarzan.

A stalwart Negro approached him. "I am head man," he said.

"Where is your master?"

"He is gone, many days," replied the black.

"Where?"

"We do not know. He hunted with a single askar. There was a great storm. Neither of them ever returned. We searched the jungle for them, but could not find them. We waited in camp where they were to have joined us. They did not come. We did not know what to do. We would not desert the young Bwana, who was kind to us; but we feared that he was dead. We have not provisions to last more than another moon. We decided to return home and tell our story to the friends of the young Bwana."

"You have done well," said Tarzan. "Have you seen a company of the desert people in the jungle?"

"We have not seen them," replied the head man, "but while we were searching for the young Bwana we saw where desert people had camped. It was a fresh camp."

"Where?"

The black pointed. "It was on the trail to the north Galla country in Abyssinia and when they broke camp they went north."

"You may return to your village," said Tarzan, "but first take those things which are the young Bwana's to his friends to keep for him and send a runner to the home of Tarzan with this message: Send one hundred Waziri to Tarzan in the north Galla country. From the water hole of the smooth, round rocks follow the trail of the desert people."

"Yes, Big Bwana, it will be done," said the head man.

"Repeat my message."

The black boy did as he was bidden.

"Good!" said Tarzan. "I go. Kill not Manu the monkey if you can find other food, for Manu is the cousin of Tarzan and of you."

"We understand, Big Bwana."

In the castle of Prince Gobred in the City of Nimmr James Hunter Blake was being schooled in the duties of a Knight of Nimmr. Sir Richard had taken him under his protection and made himself responsible for his training and his conduct.

Prince Gobred, quick to realize Blake's utter ignorance of even the simplest observances of knighthood, was frankly skeptical, and Sir Malud was almost openly antagonistic, but the loyal Sir Richard was a well beloved knight and so he had his way. Perhaps, too, the influence of the Princess Guinalda was not without its effect upon her sire, for first among the treasurers of the Prince of Nimmr ranked his daughter Guinalda; and Guinalda's curiosity and interest had been excited by the romance of the coming of this fair stranger knight to the buried and forgotten city of Nimmr.

Sir Richard had clothed Blake from his own wardrobe until a weaver, a cutter of cloth, a seamstress and an armorer could fashion one for him. Nor did it take long. A week found Sir James clothed, armored and horsed as befitted a Knight of Nimmr, and when he spoke to Sir Richard of payment for all this he found that money was almost unknown among them. There were, Sir Richard told him, a few pieces of coin that their ancestors had brought here seven hundred and thirty five years before, but payment was made by service.

The knights served the prince and he kept them. They protected the laborers and the artisans and in return received what they required from them. The slaves received their food and clothing from the prince or from whichever knight they served. Jewels and precious metals often changed hands in return for goods or service, but each transaction was a matter of barter as there were no standards of value.

They cared little for wealth. The knights valued most highly their honor and their courage upon which there could be no price. The artisan found his reward in the high perfection of his handicraft and in the honors that it brought him.

The valley provided food in plenty for all; the slaves tilled the ground; the freedmen were the artisans, the men-at-arms, the herders of cattle; the knights defended Nimmr against its enemies, competed in tourneys and hunted wild game in the valley and its surrounding mountains.

As the days passed Blake found himself rapidly acquiring a certain proficiency in knightly arts under the wise tutorage of Sir Richard. The use of sword and buckler he found most difficult, notwithstanding the fact that he had been proficient with the foils in his college days, for the knights of Nimmr knew naught of the defensive use of their two edged weapons and seldom used the point for other purpose than the *coup-de-grace*. For them the sword was almost wholly a cutting weapon, the buckler their sole defense; but as Blake practiced with this weapon it dawned upon him that his knowledge of fencing might be put to advantage should the necessity arise, to the end that his awkwardness with the buckler should be outweighed by his nicer defensive handling of his sword and his offensive improved by the judicious use of the point, against which they had developed little or no defense.

The lance he found less difficult, its value being so largely dependent upon the horsemanship of him who wielded it, and that Blake was a splendid horseman was evidenced by his polo rating as an eight goal man.

The ballium, or outer court, which lay between the inner and outer walls of the castle and entirely surrounded it, was, upon the north or valley side, given over entirely to knightly practice and training. Here the ballium was very wide, and against the inner wall was built a wooden grand stand that could be quickly removed in the event of an attack upon the castle.

Jousts and tilts were held here weekly, while the great tourneys that occurred less often were given upon a field outside the castle wall upon the floor of the valley.

Daily many knights and ladies came to watch the practice and training that filled the ballium with life and action and color during the morning hours. Good-natured banter flew back and forth, wagers were laid, and woe betide the contender who was unhorsed during these practice bouts, for the thing that a knight dreaded even more than he dreaded death was ridiculous.

In the formal jousts that were held weekly greater decorum was observed by the audience, but during the daily practice their raillery verged upon brutality.

It was before such an audience as this that Blake received his training, and because he was a novelty the audiences were larger than usual, and because the friends of Sir Malud and the friends of Sir Richard had tacitly acknowledged him as an issue both the applause and the ridicule were loud and boisterous.

Even the Prince came often and Guinalda always was there. It was soon apparent that Prince Gobred leaned slightly to the side of Sir Malud, with the natural result that Malud's party immediately acquired numerous recruits.

The training of the lads who were squires to the knights and who would one day be admitted to the charmed circle of knighthood occupied the earlier hours of the morning. This was followed by practice tilts between knights, during which Sir Richard or one of his friends undertook the training of Blake at the far side of the ballium, and it was during this practice that the American's outstanding horsemanship became apparent, even Gobred being led to applause.

" 'Od's bodikins," he exclaimed, "the man be a part of his charger!"

" 'Twas but chance that saved him from a fall," said Malud.

"Mayhap," agreed Gobred, "but at that me likes the looks of him within a saddle."

"He doeth not too ill with his lance," admitted Malud. "But, 'od's blud! didst ever see a more awkward lout with a buckler? Methinks he hath had more use for a trencher." This sally elicited roars of laughter in which the Princess Guinalda did not join, a fact which Malud, whose eyes were often upon her, was quick to note. "Thou still believest this churl to be a knight, Princess Guinalda?" he demanded.

"Have I said aught?" she asked.

"Thou didst not laugh," he reminded her.

"He is a stranger knight, far from his own country and it seemeth not a knightly nor a gentle thing to ridicule him," she replied. "Therefore I did not laugh, for I was not amused."

Later that day as Blake joined the others in the great court, he ran directly into Malud's party, nor was it at all an accident, as he never made any effort to avoid Malud or his friends and was, seemingly, oblivious to their thinly veiled taunts and insinuations. Malud himself attributed this to the density and ignorance of a yokel, which he insisted Blake to be, but there were others who rather admired Blake for his attitude, seeing in it a studied affront that Malud was too dense to perceive.

Most of the inmates of the grim castle of Nimmr were inclined pleasantly toward the newcomer. He had brought with him an air of freshness and newness that was rather a relief from the hoary atmosphere that had surrounded Nimmr for nearly seven and a half centuries. He had brought them new words and new expressions and new views, which many of them were joyously adopting, and had it not been for the unreasoning antagonism of the influential Sir Malud, Blake had been accepted with open arms.

Sir Richard was far more popular then Malud, but lacked the latter's wealth in horses, arms and retainers and consequently had less influence with Prince Gobred. However there were many independent souls who either followed Sir Richard because they were fond of him or arrived at their own decisions without reference to the dictates of policy, and many of these were staunch friends to Blake.

Not all of those who surrounded Malud this afternoon were antagonistic to the American, but the majority of them laughed when Malud laughed and frowned when he frowned, for in the courts of kings and princes flourished the first order of "yes men."

Blake was greeted by many a smile and nod as he advanced and bowed low before the Princess Guinalda who was one of the company and, being of princely blood, entitled to his first devoirs.

"Thou didst well this morning, Sir James," said the princess, kindly. "It pleases me greatly to see thee ride."

"Methinketh 'twould be a rarer treat to see him serve a side of venison," sneered Malud.

This provoked so much laughter that Malud was encouraged to seek further applause.

"Odzooks!" he cried, "arm him with a trencher and carving knife and he would be at home."

"Speaking of serving," said Blake, "and Sir Malud's mind seems to be more occupied with that than with more knightly things, does any of you know what is necessary quickly to serve fresh pig?"

"Nay, fair sir knight," said Guinalda, "we know not. Prithee tell us.

"Yes, tell us," roared Malud, "thou, indeed, shouldst know."

"You said a mouthful, old scout, I do know!"

"And what be necessary that you may quickly serve fresh pig?" demanded Malud, looking about him and winking.

"A trencher, a carving knife and you, Sir Malud," replied Blake.

It was several seconds before the thrust penetrated their simple minds and it was the Princess Guinalda who first broke into merry laughter and soon all were roaring, while some explained the quip to others.

No, not all were laughing—not Sir Malud. When he grasped the significance of Blake's witticism he first turned very red and then went white, for the great Sir Malud liked not to be the butt of ridicule, which is ever the way of those most prone to turn ridicule upon others.

"Sirrah," he cried, "darest thou affront Malud? 'Od's blud, fellow! Low born varlet! Only thy blood canst atone this affront!"

"Hop to it, old thing!" replied Blake. "Name your poison!"

"I knowest not the meaning of thy silly words," cried Malud, "but I know that an' thou doest not meet me in fair tilt upon the morrow I shalt whip thee across the Valley of the Holy Sepulcher with a barrel starve."

"You're on!" snapped back Blake. "Tomorrow morning in the south ballium with——"

"Thou mayst choose the weapons, sirrah," said Malud.

"Don't call me sirrah, I don't like it," said Blake very quietly, and now he was not smiling. "I want to tell you something, Malud, that may be good for your soul. You are really the only man in Nimmr who didn't want to treat me well and give me a chance, a fair chance, to prove that I am all right."

"You think you are a great knight, but you are not. You have no intelligence, no heart, no chivalry. You are not what we would call in my country a good sport. You have a few horses and a few men-at-arms. That is all you have, for without them you would not have the favor of the Prince, and without his favor you would have no friends.

"You are not so good or great a man in any way as is Sir Richard, who combines all the qualities of chivalry that for centuries have glorified the order of knighthood; nor are you so good a man as I, who, with your own weapons, will best you on the morrow when, in the north ballium, I meet you on horseback with sword and buckler!"

The members of the party, upon seeing Malud's wrath, had gradually fallen away from Blake until, as he concluded his speech, he stood alone a few paces apart from Malud and those who surrounded him. Then it was that one stepped from among those at Malud's side and walked to Blake. It was Guinalda.

"Sir James." she said with a sweet smile, "thou spokest with thy mouth full!" She broke into a merry laugh. "Walk with me in the garden, sir knight," and taking his arm she guided him toward the south end of the eastern court.

"You're wonderful!" was all that Blake could find to say.

"Dost really think I be wonderful?" she demanded. " 'Tis hard to know if men speak the truth to such as I. The truth, as people see it, is spoke more oft to slaves than princes."

"I hope to prove it by my conduct," he said.

They had drawn a short distance away from the others now and the girl suddenly laid her hand impulsively upon his.

"I brought thee away, Sir James, that I might speak with thee alone," she said.

"I do not care what the reason was so long as you did it," he replied, smiling.

"Thou art a stranger among us, unaccustomed to our ways, unversed in knightly practice—so much so that there are many who doubt thy claims to knighthood. Yet thou art a brave man, or else a very simple one, or thou wouldst never have chosen to meet Sir Malud with sword and buckler, for he be skilled with these while thou art clumsy with them.

"Because I thinkest that thou goest to thy death tomorrow I have brought thee aside to speak with thee."

"What can be done about it now?" asked Blake.

"Thou art passing fair with thy lance," she said, "and it is still not too late to change thy selection of weapons. I beg thee to do so."

"You care?" he asked. There can be a world of meaning in two words.

The girl's eyes dropped for an instant and then flashed up to his and there was a touch of hauteur in them. "I am the daughter of the Prince of Nimmr," she said. "I care for the humblest of my father's subjects."

"I guess that will hold you for a while, Sir James," thought Blake, but to the girl he said nothing, only smiled.

Presently she stamped her foot. "Thou hast an impudent smile, sirrah!" she exclaimed angrily. "Meliketh it not. Then thou art too forward with the daughter of a prince."

"I merely asked you if you cared whether I was killed. Even a cat could ask that."

"And I replied. Why then didst thou smile?"

"Because your eyes had answered me before your lips had spoken and I knew that your eyes had told the truth."

Again she stamped her foot angrily. "Thou art indeed a forward boor," she exclaimed. "I shall not remain to be insulted further."

Her head held high she turned and walked haughtily away to rejoin the other party.

Blake stepped quickly after her. "Tomorrow," he whispered, "I meet Sir Malud with sword and buckler. With your favor upon my helm I could overthrow the best sword in Nimmr."

The Princess Guinalda did not deign to acknowledge that she had heard his words as she walked on to join the others clustered about Sir Malud.

12

"Tomorrow Thou Diest!"

THERE WAS a great celebration in the village of Batondo the chief the night that Ulala returned. A goat was killed and many chickens, and there were fruit and cassava bread and native beer in plenty for all. There was music, too, and dancing. With all of which it was morning before they sought their sleeping mats, with the result that it was after noon the following day before Fejjuan had an opportunity to speak of serious matters with Batando.

When finally he sought him out he found the old chief squatting in the shade before his hut, slightly the worse for the orgy of the preceding night.

"I have come to talk with you, Batando," he said, "of the desert people."

Batando grunted. His head ached.

"Yesterday you said that you would lead them to the entrance to the forbidden valley," said Fejjuan. "You mean, then, that you will not fight them?"

"We shall not have to fight them if we lead them to the entrance to the forbidden valley," replied Batando.

"You speak in riddles," said Fejjuan.

"Listen, Ulala," replied the old chief. "In childhood you were stolen from your people and taken from your country. Being young, there were many things you did not know and there are others that you have forgotten.

"It is not difficult to enter the forbidden valley, especially from the north. Every Galla knows how to find the northern pass through the mountains or the tunnel beyond the great cross that marks the southern entrance. There are only these two ways in—every Galla knows them; but every Galla also knows that there is no way out of the forbidden valley."

"What do you mean, Batando?" demanded Fejjuan. "If there are two ways in, there must be two ways out."

"No—there is no way out," insisted the chief. "As far back as goes the memory of man or the tales of our fathers and our fathers' fathers it is known that many men have entered the forbidden valley, and it is also known that no man has ever come out of it."

"And why have they not come out?"

Batando shook his head. "Who knows?" he asked. "We cannot even guess their fate."

"What sort of people inhabit the valley?" asked Fejjuan.

"Not even that is known. No man has seen them and returned to tell. Some say they are the spirits of the dead, others that the valley is peopled by leopards; but no one knows.

"Go therefore, Ulala, and tell the chief of the desert people that we will lead him to the entrance to the valley. If we do this we shall not have to fight him and his people, nor shall we ever again be bothered by them," and Batando laughed at his little joke.

"Will you send guides back with me to lead the Bedauwy to the valley?" asked Fejjuan.

"No," replied the chief. "Tell them we shall come in three days. In the meantime I shall gather together many warriors from other villages, for I do not trust the desert people. Thus we shall conduct them through our country. Explain this to their chief and also that in payment he must release to us all the Galla slaves he has with him—before he enters the valley."

"That Ibn Jad will not do," said Fejjuan.

"Perhaps, when he sees himself surrounded by Galla warriors, he will be glad to do even more," replied Batando.

And so Fejjuan, the Galla slave, returned to his masters and reported all that Batando had told him to report.

Ibn Jad at first refused to give up his slaves, but when Fejjuan had convinced him that under no other terms would Batando lead him to the entrance to the valley, and that his refusal to liberate the slaves would invite the hostile attentions of the Gallas, he finally consented; but in the back of his mind was the thought that before his promise was consummated he might find an opportunity to evade it.

Only one regret had Fejjuan in betraying the Beduins, and that was caused by his liking for Ateja, but being a fatalist he was consoled by the conviction that whatever was to be, would be, regardless of what he might do.

And as Ibn Jad waited and Batando gathered his black warriors from far and near, Tarzan of the Apes came to the water hole of the smooth, round rocks and took up the trail of the Beduins.

Since he had learned from Blake's blacks that the young American was missing and also that they had seen nothing of

Stimbol since the latter had separated from Blake and started for the coast, the ape-man was more convinced than ever that the white prisoner among the Arabs was Blake.

Still he felt no great concern for the man's safety, for if the Beduins had sufficient hopes of reward to spare his life at all he was in no great danger from them. Reasoning thus Tarzan made no pretense of speed as he followed the spoor of Ibn Jad and his people.

Two men sat upon rough benches at opposite sides of a rude table. Between them a cresset of oil with a cotton wick laying in it burned feebly, slightly illuminating the stone flagging of the floor and casting weird shadows of themselves upon the rough stone walls.

Through a narrow window, innocent of glass, the night air blew, driving the flame of the cresset now this way, now that. Upon the table, between the men, lay a square board blocked off into squares, and within some of these were several wooden pieces.

"It is your move, Richard," said one of the men. "You don't appear to be very keen about the game tonight. What's the matter?"

"I be thinking of the morrow, James, and my heart be heavy within me," replied the other.

"And why?" demanded Blake.

"Malud is not the best swordsman in Nimmr," replied Sir Richard, but——" he hesitated.

"I am the worst," Blake finished the sentence for him, laughingly.

Sir Richard looked up and smiled. "Thou wilt always joke, even in the face of death," he said. "Art all the men of this strange country thou tell'st of alike?"

"It is your move, Richard," said Blake.

"Hide not his sword from thine eyes with thy buckler, James," cautioned Richard. "Ever keep thine eyes upon his eyes until thou knowest whereat he striketh, then, with thy buckler ready, thou mayst intercept the blow, for he be over slow and always his eyes proclaim where his blade will fall. Full well I knoweth that for often have I exercised against him."

"And he hasn't killed you," Blake reminded him.

"Ah, we did but practice, but on the morrow it will be different, for Malud engages thee to the death, in mortal combat my friend, to wash away in blood the affront thou didst put upon him."

"He wants to kill me, just for that?" asked Blake. "I'll tell the world he's a touchy little rascal!"

"Were it only that, he might be satisfied merely to draw blood, but there is more that he hath against thee."

"More? What? I've scarcely spoken to him a dozen times," said Blake.

"He be jealous."

"Jealous? Of whom?"

"He would wed the Princess and he hath seen in what manner thou lookest at her," explained Richard.

"Poppycock!" cried Blake, but he flushed.

"Nay, he be not the only one who hath marked it," insisted Richard.

"You're crazy," snapped Blake.

"Often men look thus at the princess, for she be beautiful beyond compare, but——"

"Has he killed them all?" demanded the American.

"No, for the princess didst not look back at *them* in the same manner."

Blake leaned back upon his bench and laughed. "Now I know you're crazy," he cried, "all of you. I'll admit that I think the princess is a mighty sweet kid, but say young fellow, she can't see me a little bit."

"Enough of thy outlandish speech I grasp to gather thy meaning, James, but thou canst not confuse me upon the one subject nor deceive me upon the other. The eyes of the princess seldom leave thee whilst thou art at practice upon the lists and the look in thine when they rest upon her—hast ever seen a hound adoring his master?"

"Run along and sell your papers," admonished Blake.

"For this, Malud wouldst put thee out of the way and it is because I know this that I grieve, for I have learned to like thee over well, my friend."

Blake arose and came around the end of the table. "You're a good old scout, Richard," he said, placing a hand affectionately upon the other's shoulder, "but do not worry—I am not dead yet. I know I seem awkward with the sword, but I have learned much about its possibilities within the past few days and I think that Sir Malud has a surprise awaiting him."

"Thy courage and thy vast assurance should carry thee far, James, but they may not overcome a life-time of practice with the sword, and that is the advantage Malud hath over thee."

"Does Prince Gobred favor Malud's suit?" demanded Blake.

"Why not? Malud is a powerful knight, with a great castle

of his own and many horses and retainers. Besides a dozen knights he hath fully an hundred men-at-arms."

"There are several knights who have their own castles and following are there not?" asked Blake.

"Twenty, perchance," replied Richard.

"And they live close to Gobred's castle?"

"At the edge of the hills, within three leagues upon either hand of Gobred's castle," explained Richard.

"And no others live in all this great valley?" demanded Blake.

"You have heard mention made of Bohun?" asked Richard.

"Yes, often—why?"

"He calls himself king, but never will we refer to him as king. He and his followers dwell upon the opposite side of the valley. They number, perchance, as many as we and we be always at war against them."

"But I've been hearing quite a bit about a great tournament for which the knights are practicing now. I thought that Bohun and his knights were to take part in it."

"They be. Once each year, commencing upon the first Sunday of Lent and extending over a period of three days, there hath been from time immemorial a truce declared between the Fronters and the Backers, during which is held the Great Tourney, one year in the plain before the city of Nimmr and the next year in the plain before the City of the Sepulcher, as they call it."

"Fronters and Backers! What in heck do those mean?" demanded Blake.

"Thou art a knight of Nimmr and know not that?" exclaimed Richard.

"What I know about knighting would rattle around in a peanut shell," admitted Blake.

"Thou shouldst know and I shalt tell thee. Hark thee well, then," said Richard, "for I must need go back to the very beginning." He poured two goblets of wine from a flagon standing on the floor beside him, took a long drink and proceeded with his tale. "Richard I sailed from Sicily in the spring of 1191 with all his great following bound for Acre, where he was to meet the French king, Philip Augustus, and wrest the Holy Land from the power of the Saracen. But Richard tarried upon the way to conquer Cyprus and punish the vile despot who had placed an insult upon Berengaria, whom Richard was to wed.

"When the great company again set their sails for Acre there were many Cyprian maidens hidden away upon the ships by knights who had taken a fancy to their lovely faces, and it so befell that two of these ships, encountering a storm, were blown from their course and wrecked upon the Afric shore.

"One of these companies was commanded by a knight y-clept Bohun and the other by one Gobred and though they marched together they kept separate other than when attacked.

"Thus, searching for Jerusalem, they came upon this valley which the followers of Bohun declared was the Valley of the Holy Sepulcher and that the crusade was over. Their crosses, that they had worn upon their breasts as do all crusaders who have not reached their goal, they removed and placed upon their backs to signify that the crusade was over and that they were returning home.

"Gobred insisted that this was not the Valley of the Holy Sepulcher and that the crusade was not accomplished. He, therefore, and all his followers, retained their crosses upon their breasts and built a city and a strong castle to defend the entrance to the valley that Bohun and his followers might be prevented from returning to England until they had accomplished their mission.

"Bohun crossed the valley and built a city and a castle to prevent Gobred from pushing on in the direction in which the latter knew that the true Sepulcher lay, and for nearly seven and a half centuries the descendants of Bohun have prevented the descendants of Gobred from pushing on and rescuing the Holy Land from the Saracen, while the descendants of Gobred have prevented the descendants of Bohun from returning to England, to the dishonor of knighthood.

"Gobred took the title of prince and Bohun that of king and these titles have been handed down from father to son during the centuries, while the followers of Gobred still wear the cross upon their breasts and are called therefrom, the Fronters, and the followers of Bohun wear theirs upon their backs and are called Backers."

"And you would still push on and liberate the Holy Land?" asked Blake.

"Yes," replied Richard, "and the Backers would return to England; but long since have we realized the futility of either hope since we be surrounded by a vast army of Saracens and our numbers be too few to pit against them.

"Thinkest thou not that we are wise to remain here under such stress?" he demanded.

"Well, you'd certainly surprise 'em if you rode into Jerusalem, or London, either," admitted Blake. "On the whole, Richard, I'd remain right here, if I were you. You see, after seven hundred and thirty-five years most of the home folks may have forgotten you and even the Saracens might not know what it was all about if you came charging into Jerusalem."

"Mayhap you speak wisely, James," said Richard, "and then, too, we be content here, knowing no other country."

For a while both men were silent, in thought. Blake was the first to speak. "This big tourney interests me," he said. "You say it starts the first Sunday in Lent. That's not far away."

"No, not far. Why?"

"I was wondering if you thought I'd be in shape to have a part in it. I'm getting better and better with the lance every day."

Sir Richard looked sadly at him and shook his head. "Tomorrow thou wilt be dead," he said.

"Say! You're a cheerful party," exclaimed Blake.

"I am only truthful, good friend," replied Richard. "It grieveth my heart sorely that it should be true, but true it be—thou canst not prevail over Sir Malud on the morrow. Wouldst that I might take thy place in the lists against him, but that may not be. But I console myself with the thought that thou will comport thyself courageously and die as a good sir knight should, with no stain upon thy escutcheon. Greatly will it solace the Princess Guinalda to know that thou didst die thus."

"You think so?" ventured Blake.

"Verily."

"And if I don't die—will she be put out?"

"Put out! Put out of what?" demanded Richard.

"Will she be sore vexed, then," corrected Blake.

"I should not go so far as to say that," admitted Richard, "but natheless it appears certain that no lady would rejoice to see her promised husband overthrown and killed, and if thou art not slain it may only be because thou hast slain Malud."

"She is his affianced wife?" demanded Blake.

" 'Tis understood, that be all. As yet no formal marriage bans have been proclaimed."

"I'm going to turn in," snapped Blake. "If I've got to be killed tomorrow I ought to get a little sleep tonight."

As he stretched himself upon a rough wool blanket that was spread over a bed of rushes upon the stone floor in one corner of the room and drew another similar blanket over him, he felt less like sleep than he had ever felt before. The knowledge that on the morrow he was to meet a medieval knight in mortal combat naturally gave him considerable concern, but Blake was too self-reliant and too young to seriously harbor the belief that he would be the one to be killed. He knew it was possible but he did not intend to permit the thought to upset him. There was, however, another that did. It upset him very much and, too, it made him angry when he realized that he was concerned about it—about the proposed marriage of Sir Malud of West Castle and Guinalda, Princess of Nimmr.

Could it be that he had been ass enough, he soliloquized, to have fallen in love with this little medieval princess who probably looked upon him as dirt beneath her feet? And what was he going to do about Malud? Suppose he should get the better of the fellow on the morrow? Well, what about it? If he killed him that would make Guinalda unhappy. If he didn't kill him—what? Sir James did not know.

13

In the Beyt of Zeyd

BN JAD waited three days in his menzil but no Galla guides arrived to lead him into the valley as Batando had promised, and so he sent Fejjuan once more to the chief to urge him to hasten, for always in the mind of Ibn Jad was the fear of Tarzan of the Apes and the thought that he might return to thwart and punish him.

He knew he was out of Tarzan's country now, but he also knew that where boundaries were so vague he could not definitely count upon this fact as an assurance of safety from reprisal. His one hope was that Tarzan was awaiting his return through Tarzan's country, and this Ibn Jad had definitely decided not to attempt. Instead he was planning upon moving directly west, passing north of the ape-man's stamping grounds, until he picked up the trail to the north down which he had travelled from the desert country.

In the mukaad of the sheik with Ibn Jad sat Tollog, his brother, and Fahd and Stimbol, besides some other 'Aarab. They were speaking of Batando's delay in sending guides and they were fearful of treachery, for it had long been apparent to them that the old chief was gathering a great army of warriors, and though Fejjuan assured them that they would not be used against the 'Aarab if Ibn Jad resorted to no treachery, yet they were all apprehensive of danger.

Ateja, employed with the duties of the hareem, did not sing nor smile as had been her wont, for her heart was heavy with mourning for her lover. She heard the talk in the mukaad but it did not interest her. Seldom did her eyes glance above the curtain that separated the women's quarters from the mukaad, and when they did the fires of hatred blazed within them as they crossed the countenance of Fahd.

She chanced to be thus glancing when she saw Fahd's eyes, which were directed outward across the menzil, go suddenly wide with astonishment.

"Billah, Ibn Jad!" cried the man. "Look!"

With the others Ateja glanced in the direction Fahd was

staring and with the others she voiced a little gasp of astonishment, though those of the men were rounded into oaths.

Walking straight across the menzil toward the sheik's beyt strode a bronzed giant armed with a spear, arrows and a knife. Upon his back was suspended an oval shield and across one shoulder and his breast was coiled a rope, hand plaited from long fibers.

"Tarzan of the Apes!" ejaculated Ibn Jad. "The curse of Ullah be upon him!"

"He must have brought his black warriors with him and left them hidden in the forest," whispered Tollog. "Not else would he dare enter the menzil of the Beduw."

Ibn Jad was heart sick and he was thinking fast when the ape-man halted directly in the outer opening of the mukaad. Tarzan let his eyes run quickly over the assemblage. They stopped upon Stimbol, finally.

"Where is Blake?" he demanded of the American.

"You ought to know," growled Stimbol.

"Have you seen him since you and he separated?"

"No."

"You are sure of that?" insisted the ape-man.

"Of course I am."

Tarzan turned to Ibn Jad. "You have lied to me. You are not here to trade but to find and sack a city; to take its treasure and steal its women."

"That is a lie!" cried Ibn Jad. "Whoever told thee that, lied."

"I do not think he lied," replied Tarzan. "He seemed an honest youth."

"Who was he?" demanded Ibn Jad.

"His name is Zeyd." Ateja heard and was suddenly galvanized to new interest. "He says all this and more, and I believe him."

"What else did he tell thee, Nasrany?"

"That another stole his musket and sought to slay thee, Ibn Jad, and then put the blame upon him.

"That is a lie, like all he hath told thee!" cried Fahd.

Ibn Jad sat in thought, his brows contracted in a dark scowl, but presently he looked up at Tarzan with a crooked smile. "Doubtless the poor youth thought that he spoke the truth," he said. "Just as he thought that he should slay his sheykh and for the same reason. Always hath his brain been sick, but never before did I think him dangerous.

"He hath deceived thee, Tarzan of the Apes, and that I can prove by all my people as well as by this Nasrany I have befriended, for all will tell thee that I am seeking to obey thee and leave thy country. Why else then should I have travelled north back in the direction of my own beled?"

"If thou wished to obey me why didst thou hold me prisoner and send thy brother to slay me in the night?" asked Tarzan.

"Again thou wrongst Ibn Jad," said the sheik sadly. "My brother came to cut thy bonds and set thee free, but thou set upon him and then came el-fil and carried thee away."

"And what meant thy brother when he raised his knife and cried: 'Die, Nasrany!'" demanded the ape-man. "Sayeth a man thus who cometh to do a kindness?"

"I did but joke," mumbled Tollog.

"I am here again," said Tarzan, "but not to joke. My Waziri are coming. Together we shall see you well on your way toward the desert."

"It is what we wish," said the sheik quickly. "Ask this other Nasrany if it be not true that we are lost and would be but too glad to have thee lead us upon the right way. Here we be beset by Galla warriors. Their chief hath been gathering them for days and momentarily we fear that we shall be attacked. Is that not true, Nasrany?" he turned to Stimbol as he spoke.

"Yes, it is true," said Stimbol.

"It is true that you are going to leave the country," said Tarzan, "and I shall remain to see that you do so. Tomorrow you will start. In the meantime set aside a beyt for me—and let there be no more treachery."

"Thou needst fear nothing," Ibn Jad assured him, then he turned his face toward the women's quarters. "Hirfa! Ateja!" he called. "Make ready the beyt of Zeyd for the sheykh of the jungle."

To one side but at no great distance from the beyt of Ibn Jad the two women raised the black tent for Tarzan, and when the am'dan had been placed and straightened and the tunb el-beyt made fast to the pegs that Ateja drove into the earth Hirfa returned to her household duties, leaving her daughter to stretch the side curtains.

The instant that Hirfa was out of ear shot Ateja ran to Tarzan.

"Oh, Nasrany," she cried, "thou hast seen my Zeyd? He is safe?"

"I left him in a village where the chief will care for him until such time as thy people come upon thy return to the desert country. He is quite safe and well."

"Tell me of him, oh, Nasrany, for my heart hungers for word of him," implored the girl. "How came you upon him? Where was he?"

"His mare had been dragged down by el-adrea who was about to devour your lover. I chanced to be there and slew el-adrea. Then I took Zeyd to the village of a chief who is my friend, for I knew that he could not survive the perils of the jungle should I leave him afoot and alone. It was my thought to send him from the country in safety, but he begged to remain until you returned that way. This I have permitted. In a few weeks you will see your lover."

Tears were falling from Ateja's long, black lashes—tears of joy—as she seized Tarzan's hand and kissed it. "My life is thine, Nasrany," she cried, "for that thou hast given me back my lover."

That night as the Galla slave, Fejjuan, walked through the menzil of his masters he saw Ibn Jad and Tollog sitting in the sheik's mukaad whispering together and Fejjuan, well aware of the inherent turpitude of this precious pair, wondered what might be the nature of their plotting.

Behind the curtain of the hareem Ateja lay huddled upon her sleeping mat, but she did not sleep. Instead she was listening to the whispered conversation of her father and her uncle.

"He must be put out of the way," Ibn Jad insisted.

"But his Waziri are coming," objected Tollog. "If they do not find him here what can we say? They will not believe us, whatever we say. They will set upon us. I have heard that they are terrible men."

"By Ullah!" cried Ibn Jad. "If he stays we are undone. Better risk something than to return empty handed to our own country after all that we have passed through."

"If thou thinkest that I shall again take this business upon myself thou art mistaken, brother," said Tollog. "Once was enough."

"No, not thee; but we must find a way. Is there none among us who might wish more than another to be rid of the Nasrany?" asked Ibn Jad, but to himself as though he were thinking aloud.

"The other Nasrany!" exclaimed Tollog. "He hateth him."

Ibn Jad clapped his hands together. "Thou hast it, brother!"

"But still shall we be held responsible," reminded Tollog.

"What matter if he be out of the way. We can be no worse off than we now are. Suppose Batando came tomorrow with the guides? Then indeed would the jungle sheykh know that we have lied to him, and it might go hard with us. No, we must be rid of him this very night."

"Yes, but how?" asked Tollog.

"Hold! I have a plan. Listen well, O brother!" and Ibn Jad rubbed his palms together and smiled, but he would not have smiled, perhaps had he known that Ateja listened, or had he seen the silent figure crouching in the dark just beyond the outer curtain of his beyt.

"Speak, Ibn Jad," urged Tollog, "tell me thy plan."

"Wellah, it is known by all that the Nasrany Stimbol hates the sheykh of the jungle. With loud tongue he hath proclaimed it many times before all when many were gathered in my mukaad."

"You would send Stimbol to slay Tarzan of the Apes?"

"Thou guessed aright," admitted Ibn Jad.

"But how wilt that relieve us of responsiblity? He wilt have been slain by thy order in thine own menzil," objected Tollog.

"Wait! I shall not command the one Nasrany to slay the other; I shall but suggest it, and when it is done I shall be filled with rage and horror that this murder hath been done in my menzil. And to prove my good faith I shall order that the murderer be put to death in punishment for his crime. Thus we shall be rid of two unbelieving dogs and at the same time be able to convince the Waziri that we were indeed the friends of their sheykh, for we shall mourn him with loud lamentations—when the Waziri shall have arrived."

"Allah be praised for such a brother!" exclaimed Tollog. enraptured.

"Go thou now, at once, and summon the Nasrany Stimbol," directed Ibn Jad. Send him to me alone, and after I have spoken with him and he hath departed upon his errand come thee back to my beyt."

Ateja trembled upon her sleeping mat, while the silent figure crouching outside the sheik's tent arose after Tollog had departed and disappeared in the darkness of the night.

Hastily summoned from the beyt of Fahd, Stimbol, cautioned to stealth by Tollog, moved silently through the darkness to the mukaad of the sheik where he found Ibn Jad awaiting him.

"Sit, Nasrany," invited the Beduin.

"What in hell do you want of me this time of night?" demanded Stimbol.

"I have been talking with Tarzan of the Apes," said Ibn Jad, "and because you are my friend and he is not I have

sent for you to tell you what he plans for you. He has interfered in all my designs and is driving me from the country,
but that is as nothing compared with what he intends for you."

"What in hell is he up to now?" demanded Stimbol. "He's
always butting into some one else's business."

"Thou dost not like him?" asked Ibn Jad.

"Why should I?" and Stimbol applied a vile epithet to
Tarzan.

"Thou wilt like him less when I tell thee," said Ibn Jad.

"Well, tell me."

"He says that thou hast slain thy companion, Blake," explained the sheik, "and for that Tarzan is going to kill thee
on the morrow."

"Eh? What? Kill me?" demanded Stimbol. "Why he can't
do it! What does he think he is—a Roman emperor?"

"Nevertheless he will do as he says," insisted Ibn Jad. "He
is all powerful here. No one questions the acts of this great
jungle sheykh. Tomorrow he will kill thee."

"But—you won't let him, Ibn Jad! Surely, you won't let
him?" Stimbol was already trembling with terror.

Ibn Jad elevated his palms. "What can I do?" he asked.

"You can—you can—why there must be something that
you can do," wailed the frightened man.

"There is naught that any can do—save yourself," whispered the sheik.

"What do you mean?"

"He lies asleep in yon beyt and—thou hast a sharp khusa."

"I have never killed a man," whispered Stimbol.

"Nor hast thou ever been killed," reminded the sheik;
"but tonight thou must kill or tomorrow thou wilt be killed."

"God!" gasped Stimbol.

"It is late," said Ibn Jad, "and I go to my sleeping mat. I
have warned thee—do what thou wilt in the matter," and he
arose as though to enter the women's quarters.

Trembling, Stimbol staggered out into the night. For a
moment he hesitated, then he crouched and crept silently
through the darkness toward the beyt that had been erected
for the ape-man.

But ahead of him ran Ateja to warn the man who had
saved her lover from the fangs of el-adrea. She was almost
at the beyt she had helped to erect for the ape-man when a
figure stepped from another tent and clapping a palm across
her mouth and an arm about her waist held her firmly.

"Where goest thou?" whispered a voice in her ear, a voice
that she recognized at once as belonging to her uncle; but

Tollog did not wait for a reply, he answered for her. "Thou goest to warn the Nasrany because he befriended thy lover! Get thee back to thy father's beyt. If he knew this he would slay thee. Go!" And he gave her a great shove in the direction from which she had come.

There was a nasty smile upon Tollog's lips as he thought how neatly he had foiled the girl, and he thanked Allah that chance had placed him in a position to intercept her before she had been able to ruin them all; and even as Tollog, the brother of the sheik, smiled in his beard a hand reached out of the darkness behind him and seized him by the throat— fingers grasped him and dragged him away.

Trembling, bathed in cold sweat, grasping in tightly clenched fingers the hilt of a keen knife, Wilbur Stimbol crept through the darkness toward the tent of his victim.

Stimbol had been an irritable man, a bully and a coward; but he was no criminal. Every fiber of his being revolted at the thing he contemplated. He did not want to kill, but he was a cornered human rat and he thought that death stared him in the face, leaving open only this one way of escape.

As he entered the beyt of the ape-man he steeled himself to accomplish that for which he had come, and he was indeed a very dangerous, a very formidable man, as he crept to the side of the figure lying in the darkness, wrapped in an old burnous.

14

Sword and Buckler

A S THE sun touched the turrets of the castle of the Prince of Nimmr a youth rolled from between his blankets, rubbed his eyes and stretched. Then he reached over and shook another youth of about his own age who slept beside him.

"Awaken, Edward! Awaken, thou sluggard!" he cried.

Edward rolled over on his back and essayed to say "Eh?" and to yawn at the same time.

"Up, lad!" urged Michel. "Forgottest thou that thy master fares forth to be slain this day?"

Edward sat up, now fully awake. His eyes flashed. "'Tis a lie!" he cried, loyally. "He will cleave Sir Malud from poll to breast plate with a single blow. Livest no sir knight with such mighty thews as hast Sir James. Thou art disloyal, Michel, to Sir Richard's friend who hath been a good and kindly friend to us as well."

Michel patted the other lad upon the shoulder. "Nay, I did but jest, Edward," he said. "My hopes be all for Sir James, and yet——" he paused, "I fear——"

"Fear what?" demanded Edward.

"That Sir James be not well enough versed in the use of sword and buckler to overcome Sir Malud, for even were his strength the strength of ten men it shall avail him naught without the skill to use it."

"Thou shalt see!" maintained Edward, stoutly.

"I see that Sir James hath a loyal squire," said a voice behind them, and turning they saw Sir Richard standing in the doorway, "and may all his friends wish him well this day thus loyally!"

"I fell asleep last night praying to our Lord Jesus to guide his blade through Sir Malud's helm," said Edward.

"Good! Get thee up now and look to thy master's mail and to the trappings of his steed, that he may enter the lists bedight as befits a noble sir knight of Nimmr," instructed Richard, and left them.

It was eleven o'clock of this February morning. The sun shone down into the great north ballium of the castle of Nimmr, glinting from the polished mail of noble knights and from pike and battle-axe of men-at-arms, picking out the gay colors of the robes of the women gathered in the grandstand below the inner wall.

Upon a raised dais at the front and center of the grandstand sat Prince Gobred and his party, and upon either side of them and extending to the far ends of the stand were ranged the noble knights and ladies of Nimmr, while behind them sat men-at-arms who were off duty, then the freedmen and, last of all, the serfs, for under the beneficent rule of the house of Gobred these were accorded many privileges.

At either end of the lists was a tent, gay with pennons and the colors and devices of its owner; one with the green and gold of Sir Malud and the other with the blue and silver of Sir James.

Before each of these tilts stood two men-at-arms, resplendent in new apparel, the metal of their battle-axes gleaming brightly, and here a groom held a restive, richly caparisoned charger, while the squire of each of the contestants busied himself with last-minute preparations for the encounter.

A trumpeter, statuesque, the bell of his trumpet resting upon his hip, waited for the signal to sound the fanfare that would announce the entrance of his master into the lists.

A few yards to the rear a second charger champed upon his bit as he nuzzled the groom that held him in waiting for the knight who would accompany each of the contestants upon the field.

In the blue and silver tilt sat Blake and Sir Richard, the latter issuing instructions and advice, and of the two he was the more nervous. Blake's hauberk, gorget and bassinet were of heavy chain mail, the latter lined inside and covered outside, down to the gorget, with leopard skin, offering fair protection for his head from an ordinary, glancing blow; upon his breast was sewn a large, red cross and from one shoulder depended the streamers of a blue and silver rosette. Hanging from the pole of the tilt, upon a wooden peg, were Blake's sword and buckler.

The grandstand was filled. Prince Gobred glanced up at the sun and spoke to a knight at his side. The latter gave a brief command to a trumpeter stationed at the princely loge and presently, loud and clear, the notes of a trumpet rang in the ballium. Instantly the tilts at either end of the lists were galvanized to activity, while the grandstand seemed to spring to new life as necks were craned first toward the tent of Sir Malud and then toward that of Sir James.

Edward, flushed with excitement, ran into the tilt and seizing Blake's sword passed the girdle about his hips and buckled it in place at his left side, then, with the buckler, he followed his master out of the tilt.

As Blake prepared to mount Edward held his stirrup while the groom sought to quiet the nervous horse. The lad pressed Blake's leg after he had swung into the saddle (no light accomplishment, weighed down as he was by heavy chain mail) and looked up into his face.

"I have prayed for thee, Sir James," he said. "I know that thou wilt prevail."

Blake saw tears in the youth's eyes as he looked down at him and he caught a choking note in his voice. "You're a good boy, Eddie," he said. "I'll promise that you won't have to be ashamed of me."

"Ah, Sir James, how could I? Even in death thou wilt be a noble figure of a knight. An fairer one it hath never been given one to see, methinks," Edward assured him as he handed him his round buckler.

Sir Richard had by now mounted, and at a signal from him that they were ready there was a fanfare from the trumpet at Sir Malud's tilt and that noble sir knight rode forward, followed by a single knight.

Blake's trumpeter now announced his master's entry and the American rode out close along the front of the grandstand, followed by Sir Richard. There was a murmur of applause for each contestant, which increased as they advanced and met before Prince Gobred's loge.

Here the four knights reined in and faced the Prince and each raised the hilt of his sword to his lips and kissed it in salute. As Gobred cautioned them to fight honorably, as true knights, and reminded them of the rules governing the encounter Blake's eyes wandered to the face of Guinalda.

The little princess sat stiffly erect, looking straight before her. She seemed very white, Blake thought, and he wondered if she were ill.

How beautiful, thought Blake, and though she did not once appear to look at him he was not cast down, for neither did she look at Malud.

Again the trumpet sounded and the four knights rode slowly back to opposite ends of the lists and the principals waited for the final signal to engage. Blake disengaged his arm from the leather loop of his buckler and tossed the shield upon the ground.

Edward looked at him aghast. "My Lord knight!" he cried. "Art ill? Art fainting? Didst drop thy buckler?" and he snatched it up and held it aloft to Blake, though he knew full well that his eyes had not deceived him and that his master had cast aside his only protection.

To the horrified Edward there seemed but one explanation and that his loyalty would not permit him to entertain for an instant—that Blake was preparing to dismount and refuse to meet Sir Malud, giving the latter the victory by default and assuring himself of the contempt and ridicule of all Nimmr.

He ran to Richard who had not seen Blake's act. "Sir Richard! Sir Richard!" he cried in a hoarse whisper. "Some terrible affliction hath befallen Sir James!"

"Hey, what?" exclaimed Richard. "What meaneth thou lad?"

"He has cast aside his buckler," cried the youth. "He must be stricken sore ill, for it cannot be that otherwise he would refuse combat."

Richard spurred to Blake's side. "Hast gone mad, man?" he demanded. "Thou canst not refuse the encounter now unless thou wouldst bring dishonor upon thy friends!"

"Where did you get that line?" demanded Blake. "Who said I was going to quit?"

"But thy buckler?" cried Sir Richard.

The trumpet at the Prince's loge rang out peremptorily. Sir Malud spurred forward to a fanfare from his own trumpeter.

"Let her go!" cried Blake to his.

"Thy buckler!" screamed Sir Richard.

"The damned thing was in my way," shouted Blake as he spurred forward to meet the doughty Malud, Richard trailing behind him, as did Malud's second behind that knight.

There was a confident smile upon the lips of Sir Malud and he glanced often at the knights and ladies in the grandstand, but Blake rode with his eyes always upon his antagonist.

Both horses had broken immediately into a gallop, and as they neared one another Malud spurred forward at a run and Blake saw that the man's aim was doubtless to overthrow him at the first impact, or at least to so throw him out of balance as to make it easy for Malud to strike a good blow before he could recover himself.

Malud rode with his sword half raised at his right side,

while Blake's was at guard, a position unknown to the knights of Nimmr, who guarded solely with their bucklers.

The horsemen approached to engage upon each other's left, and as they were about to meet Sir Malud rose in his stirrups and swung his sword hand down, to gain momentum, described a circle with his blade and launched a terrific cut at Blake's head.

It was at that instant that some few in the grandstand realized that Blake bore no buckler.

"His buckler!" Sir James hath no buckler!" "He hath lost his buckler!" rose now from all parts of the stand; and from right beside him, where the two knights met before the log of Gobred, Blake heard a woman scream, but he could not look to see if it were Guinalda.

As they met Blake reined his horse suddenly toward Malud's, so that the two chargers' shoulders struck, and at the same time he cast all his weight in the same direction, whereas Malud, who was standing in his stirrups to deliver his blow, was almost in a state of equilibrium and having his buckler ready for defense was quite helpless insofar as maneuvering his mount was concerned.

Malud, overbalanced, lost the force and changed the direction of his blow, which fell, much to the knight's surprise, upon Blake's blade along which it spent its force and was deflected from its target.

Instantly, his horse well in hand by reason that his left arm was unencumbered by a buckler, Blake reined in and simultaneously cut to the left and rear, his point opening the mail on Malud's left shoulder and biting into the flesh before the latter's horse had carried him out of reach.

A loud shout of approbation arose from the stands for the thing had been neatly done and then Malud's second spurred to the Prince's loge and entered a protest.

"Sir James hath no buckler!" he cried. " 'Tis no fair combat!"

" 'Tis fairer for thy knight than for Sir James," said Gobred.

"We would not take that advantage of him," parried Malud's second, Sir Jarred.

"What sayest thou?" demanded Gobred of Sir Richard who had quickly ridden to Jarred's side. "Is Sir James without a buckler through some accident that befell before he entered the lists?"

"Nay, he cast it aside," replied Richard, "and averred that the 'damned thing' did annoy him; but if Sir Jarred feeleth that, because of this, they be not fairly matched we are willing that Sir Malud, also, should cast aside his buckler."

Gobred smiled. "That be fair," he said.

The two men, concerned with their encounter and not with the argument of their seconds, had engaged once more. Blood was showing upon Malud's shoulder and trickling down his back, staining his skirts and the housing of his charger.

The stand was in an uproar, for many were still shouting aloud about the buckler and others were screaming with delight over the neat manner in which Sir James had drawn his first blood. Wagers were being freely made, and though Sir Malud still ruled favorite in the betting, the odds against Blake were not so great, and while men had no money to wager they had jewels and arms and horses. One enthusiastic adherent of Sir Malud bet three chargers against one that his champion would be victorious and the words were scarce out of his mouth ere he had a dozen takers, whereas before the opening passage at arms offers as high as ten to one had found no takers.

Now the smile was gone from Malud's lips and he glanced no more at the grandstand. There was rage in his eyes as he spurred again toward Blake, who he thought had profited by a lucky accident.

Unhampered by a buckler Blake took full advantage of the nimbleness of the wiry horse he rode and which he had ridden daily since his arrival in Nimmr, so that man and beast were well accustomed to one another.

Again Sir Malud saw his blade glance harmlessly from the sword of his antagonist and then, to his vast surprise, the point of Sir James' blade leaped quickly beneath his buckler and entered his side. It was not a deep wound, but it was painful and again it brought blood.

Angrily Malud struck again, but Blake had reined his charger quickly to the rear and before Malud could gather his reins Blake had struck him again, this time a heavy blow upon the helm.

Half stunned and wholly infuriated Malud wheeled and charged at full tilt, once again determined to ride his adversary down. They met with a crash directly in front of Gobred's loge, there was a quick play of swords that baffled the eyesight of the onlookers and then, to the astonishment of all, most particularly Malud, that noble sir knight's sword flew from his grasp and hurtled to the field, leaving him entirely to the mercy of his foe.

Malud reined in and sat erect, waiting. He knew and

Blake knew that under the rules that governed their encounter
Blake was warranted in running him through unless Malud
sued for mercy, and no one, Blake least of all, expected
this of so proud and haughty a knight.

Sir Malud sat proudly on his charger waiting for Blake to
advance and kill him. Utter silence had fallen upon the stands,
so that the champing of Malud's horse upon its bit was plainly
audible. Blake turned to Sir Jarred.

"Summon a squire, sir knight," he said, "to return Sir
Malud's sword to him."

Again the stands rocked to the applause, but Blake turned
his back upon them and rode to Richard's side to wait until
his adversary was again armed.

"Well, old top," he inquired of Sir Richard, "just how
much a dozen am I offered for bucklers now?"

Richard laughed. "Thou hast been passing fortunate,
James," he replied; "but methinks a good swordsman would
long since have cut thee through."

"I know Malud would have if I had packed that chopping
bowl along on the party," Blake assured him, though it is
doubtful if Sir Richard understood what he was talking
about, as was so often the case when Blake discoursed that
Richard had long since ceased to even speculate as to the
meaning of much that his friend said.

But now Sir Malud was rearmed and riding toward Blake.
He stopped his horse before the American and bowed low. "I
do my devoirs to a noble and generous knight," he said,
graciously.

Blake bowed. "Are you ready sir?" he asked.

Malud nodded.

"On guard, then!" snapped the American.

For a moment the two jockeyed for position. Blake feinted
and Malud raised his buckler before his face to catch the
blow, but as it did not fall he lowered his shield, just as Blake
had known that he would, and as he did so the edge of the
American's weapon fell heavily upon the crown of his bassinet.

Malud's arm dropped at his side, he slumped in his saddle
and then toppled forward and rolled to the ground. Agile, even
in his heavy armor, Blake dismounted and walked to where
his foe lay stretched upon his back almost in front of Gobred's
loge. He placed a foot upon Malud's breast and pressed the
point of his sword against his throat.

The crowd leaned forward to see the coup-de-grace ad-
ministered, but Blake did not drive his point home. He looked
up at Prince Gobred and addressed him.

"Here is a brave knight," he said, "with whom I have no real quarrel. I spare him to your service, Prince, and to those who love him," and his eyes went straight to the eyes of the Princess Guinalda. Then he turned and walked back along the front of the grandstand to his own tilt, while Richard rode behind him, and the knights and the ladies, the men-at-arms, the freedmen and the serfs stood upon their seats and shouted their applause.

Edward was beside himself with joy, as was Michel. The former knelt and embraced Blake's legs, he kissed his hand, and wept, so great were his happiness and his excitement.

"I knew it! I knew it!" he cried. "Didst I not tell thee, Michel, that my own sir knight would overthrow Sir Malud?"

The men-at-arms, the trumpeter and the grooms at Blake's tilt wore grins that stretched from ear to ear. Whereas a few minutes before they had felt ashamed to have been detailed to the losing side, now they were most proud and looked upon Blake as the greatest hero of Nimmr. Great would be their boasting among their fellows as they gathered with their flagons of ale about the rough deal table in their dining hall.

Edward removed Blake's armor and Michel got Richard out of his amidst much babbling upon the part of the youths who could not contain themselves, so doubly great was their joy because so unexpected.

Blake went directly to his quarters and Richard accompanied him, and when the two men were alone Richard placed a hand upon Blake's shoulder.

"Thou hast done a noble and chivalrous thing, my friend," he said, "but I know not that it be a wise one."

"And why?" demanded Blake. "You didn't think I could stick the poor mutt when he was lying there defenseless?"

Richard shook his head. " 'Tis but what he would have done for thee had thy positions been reversed," said he.

"Well, I couldn't do it. We're not taught to believe that it is exactly ethical to hit a fellow when he's down, where I come from," explained Blake.

"Had your quarrel been no deeper than appeared upon the surface thou might well have been thus magnanimous; but Malud be jealous of thee and that jealousy will be by no means lessened by what hath transpired this day. Thou might have been rid of a powerful and dangerous enemy had thou given him the coup-de-grace, as was thy right; but now thou hast raised up a greater enemy since to his jealousy is added hatred and envy against thee for thy prowess over him. Thou didst make him appear like a monkey, James, and that Sir Malud wilt never forgive, and I know the man."

The knights and ladies attached to the castle of Gobred ate together at a great table in the huge hall of the castle. Three hundred people could be accommodated at the single board and it took quite a company of serving men to fill their needs. Whole pigs, roasted, were carried in upon great trenchers and there were legs of mutton and sides of venison and bowls of vegetables, with wine and ale, and at the end immense puddings.

There was much laughter and loud talking, and it all presented a wild and fascinating picture to Sir James Blake as he sat at the lower end of the table far below the salt that night, in his accustomed place as one of the latest neophytes in the noble ranks of the knighthood of Nimmr.

The encounter between himself and Malud was the subject of the moment and many were the compliments bestowed upon him and many the questions as to where and how he had acquired his strange technique of swordsmanship. Although they had seen him accomplish it, yet they still appeared to believe it inconceivable that a man might prevail without a buckler over one who carried this essential article of defense.

Prince Gobred and his family sat, with the higher nobles of Nimmr, at a table slightly raised above the rest of the board and running across its upper end, the whole forming a huge T. When he wished to speak to anyone farther down the table he resorted to the simple expedient of raising his voice, so that if several were so inclined at the same time the room became a bedlam of uproar and confusion.

And as Blake sat at the farthest end of the table it was necessary for one at Gobred's end to scream to attract attention, though when it was discovered that it was the prince who was speaking the rest of the company usually lapsed into silence out of respect for him, unless they were too far gone in drink.

Shortly after the feasters were seated Gobred had arisen and lifted his goblet high in air, and silence had fallen upon the whole company as knights and ladies rose and faced their prince.

"Hal to our King!" cried Gobred. "Hal to our liege lord, Richard of England!"

And in a great chorus rose the answering "Hal!" as the company drank the health of Richard Coeur de Lion seven hundred and twenty-eight years after his death!

Then they drank the health of Gobred and of the Princess

Brynilda, his wife, and of the Princess Guinalda, and each time a voice boomed from just below the dais of the prince: "Here I be looking at thee!" as Sir Richard with a proud smile displayed his newly acquired knowledge.

Again Prince Gobred arose. "Hal!" he cried, "to that worthy sir knight who hath most nobly and chivalrously acquitted himself in the lists this day! Hal to Sir James, Knight Templar and, now, Knight of Nimmr!"

Not even the name of Richard I of England had aroused the enthusiasm that followed the drinking to Sir James. The length of the long hall Blake's eyes travelled straight to where Guinalda stood. He saw her drink to him and he saw that her eyes were regarding him, but the distance was too great and the light of the pitch torches and the oil cressets too dim for him to see whether her glance carried a message of friendship or dislike.

When the noise had partially subsided and the drinkers had retaken their seats Blake arose.

"Prince Gobred," he called the length of the room, "knights and ladies of Nimmr, I give you another toast! To Sir Malud!"

For a moment there was silence, the silence of surprise, and then the company arose and drank the health of the absent Sir Malud.

"Thou art a strange sir knight, with strange words upon thy lips and strange ways, Sir James," shouted Gobred, "but though thou callest a hal 'a toast' and thy friends be 'old top' and 'kid,' yet withal it seemeth that we understand thee and we would know more about thy country and the ways of the noble knights that do abide there.

"Tell us, are they all thus chivalrous and magnanimous to their fallen foes?"

"If they're not they get the raspberry," explained Blake.

" 'Get the raspberry'!" repeated Gobred. " 'Tis some form of punishment, methinks."

"You said it, Prince!"

"Of a surety I said it, Sir James!" snapped Gobred with asperity.

"I mean, Prince, that you hit the nail on the head—you guessed it the first time. You see the raspberry is about the only form of punishment that the Knights of the Squared Circle, or the Knights of the Diamond can understand."

" 'Knights of the Squared Circle'! 'Knights of the Diamond'! Those be knightly orders of which I wot not. Be they doughty knights?"

"Some of them are dotty, but a lot of them are regulars.

Take Sir Dempsey, for instance, a knight of the Squared Circle. He showed 'em all he was a regular knight in defeat, which is much more difficult than being a regular knight in victory."

"Be there other orders of knighthood these days?" demanded Gobred.

"We're lousy with them!"

"What?" cried Gobred.

"We're all knights these days," explained Blake.

"All knights! Be there no serfs nor yeomen? 'Tis incredible!"

"Well, there are some yeomen in the navy, I think; but all the rest of us, pretty much, are knights. You see things have changed a lot since the days of Richard. The people have sort of overthrown the old order of things. They poked a lot of ridicule at knights and wanted to get rid of knighthood, and as soon as they had they all wanted to be knights themselves; so we have Knights Templar now and Knights of Pythias and Knights of Columbus and Knights of Labor and a lot more I can't recall."

"Methinks it must be a fine and noble world," cried Gobred, "for what with so many noble sir knights it would seemeth that they must often contend, one against another—is that not true?"

"Well, they do scrap some," Blake admitted.

15

The Lonely Grave

WITHIN the dark interior of the beyt Stimbol could see nothing. Just before him he heard a man breathing heavily as might one in a troubled sleep. The would-be murderer paused to steady his nerves. Then, on hands and knees, he crept forward inch by inch.

Presently one of his hands touched the prostrate figure of the sleeper. Lightly, cautiously, Stimbol groped until he had definitely discovered the position in which his victim lay. In one hand, ready, he grasped the keen knife. He scarce dared breathe for fear he might awaken the ape-man. He prayed that Tarzan was a sound sleeper, and he prayed that the first blow of his weapon would reach that savage heart.

Now he was ready! He had located the exact spot where he must strike! He raised his knife and struck. His victim shuddered spasmodically. Again and again with savage maniacal force and speed the knife was plunged into the soft flesh. Stimbol felt the warm blood spurt out upon his hand and wrist.

At length, satisfied that his mission had been accomplished, he scurried from the beyt. Now he was trembling so that he could scarcely stand—terrified, revolted by the horrid crime he had committed.

Wild-eyed, haggard, he stumbled to the mukaad of Ibn Jad's beyt and there he collapsed. The sheik stepped from the women's quarters and looked down upon the trembling figure that the dim light of a paper lantern revealed.

"What doest thou here, Nasrany?" he demanded.

"I have done it, Ibn Jad!" muttered Stimbol.

"Done what?" cried the sheik.

"Slain Tarzan of the Apes."

"Ai! Ai!" screamed Ibn Jad. "Tollog! Where art thou? Hirfa! Ateja! Come! Didst hear what the Nasrany sayeth?"

Hirfa and Ateja rushed into the mukaad.

"Didst hear him?" repeated Ibn Jad. "He hath slain my good friend the great sheykh of the Jungle, Motlog! Fahd! Haste!" His voice had been rising until now he was screaming at the top of his lungs and 'Aarab were streaming toward his beyt from all directions.

Stimbol, stunned by what he had done, dumb from surprise and terror at the unexpected attitude of Ibn Jad, crouched speechless in the center of the mukaad.

"Seize him!" cried the sheik to the first man that arrived. "He hath slain Tarzan of the Apes, our great friend, who was to preserve us and lead us from this land of dangers. Now all will be our enemies. The friends of Tarzan will fall upon us and slay us. Allah, bear witness that I be free from guilt in this matter and let Thy wrath and the wrath of the friends of Tarzan fall upon this guilty man!"

By this time the entire population of the menzil was gathered in front of the sheik's beyt, and if they were surprised by his protestations of sudden affection for Tarzan they gave no evidence of it.

"Take him away!" commanded Ibn Jad. "In the morning we shall gather and decide what we must do."

They dragged the terrified Stimbol to Fahd's beyt, where they bound him hand and foot and left him for Fahd to guard. When they had gone the Beduin leaned low over Stimbol, and whispered in his ear.

"Didst really slay the jungle sheykh?" he demanded.

"Ibn Jad forced me to do so and now he turns against me," whispered Stimbol.

"And tomorrow he will have you killed so that he may tell the friends of Tarzan that he hath punished the slayer of Tarzan," said Fahd.

"Save me, Fahd!" begged Stimbol. "Save me and I will give you twenty million francs—I swear it! Once I am safe in the nearest European colony I will get the money for you. Think of it, Fahd—twenty million francs!"

"I am thinking of it, Nasrany," replied the Beduin, "and I think that thou liest. There be not that much money in the world!"

"I swear that I have ten times that amount. If I have lied to you you may kill me. Save me! Save me!"

"Twenty million francs!" murmured Fahd. "Perchance he does not lie! Listen, Nasrany. I do not know that I can save thee, but I shall try, and if I succeed and thou forgettest the twenty million francs I shall kill thee if I have to follow thee across the world—dost understand?"

Ibn Jad called two ignorant slaves to him and commanded them to go to the beyt that had been Zeyd's and carry Tarzan's body to the edge of the menzil where they were to dig a grave and bury it.

With paper lanterns they went to the beyt of death and wrapping the dead man in the old burnous that already covered him they carried him across the menzil and laid him down while they dug a shallow grave; and so, beneath a forest giant in the land that he loved the grave of Tarzan of the Apes was made.

Roughly the slaves rolled the corpse into the hole they had made, shovelled the dirt upon it and left it in its lonely, unmarked tomb.

Early the next morning Ibn Jad called about him the elders of the tribe, and when they were gathered it was noted that Tollog was missing, and though a search was made he could not be found. Fahd suggested that he had gone forth early to hunt.

Ibn Jad explained to them that if they were to escape the wrath of the friends of Tarzan they must take immediate steps to disprove their responsibility for the slaying of the ape-man and that they might only do this and express their good faith by punishing the murderer.

It was not difficult to persuade them to take the life of a Christian and there was only one that demurred. This was Fahd.

"There are two reasons, Ibn Jad, why we should not take the life of this Nasrany," he said.

"By Ullah, there never be any reason why a true believer should not take the life of a Nasrany!" cried one of the old men.

"Listen," admonished Fahd, "to what I have in mind and then I am sure that you will agree that I am right."

"Speak, Fahd," said Ibn Jad.

"This Nasrany is a rich and powerful man in his own beled. If it be possible to spare his life he will command a great ransom—dead he is worth nothing to us. If by chance, the friends of Tarzan do not learn of his death before we are safely out of this accursed land it will have profited us naught to have killed Stimbol and, billah, if we kill him now they may not believe us when we say that he slew Tarzan and we took his life in punishment.

"But if we keep him alive until we are met with the friends of Tarzan, should it so befall that they overtake us, then we may say that we did hold him prisoner that Tarzan's own people might mete out their vengeance to him, which would suit them better."

"Thy words are not without wisdom," admitted Ibn Jad, "but suppose the Nasrany spoke lies concerning us and said that it was we who slew Tarzan? Wouldst they not believe him above us?"

"That be easily prevented," said the old man who had spoken before. "Let us cut his tongue out forthwith that he may not bear false witness against us."

"Wellah, thou hast it!" exclaimed Ibn Jad.

"Billah, nay!" cried Fahd. "The better we treat him the larger will be the reward that he will pay us."

"We can wait until the last moment," said Ibn Jad, "and we see that we are to lose him and our reward, then may we cut out his tongue."

Thus the fate of Wilbur Stimbol was left to the gods, and Ibn Jad, temporarily freed from the menace of Tarzan, turned his attention once more to his plans for entering the valley. With a strong party he went in person and sought a palaver with the Galla chief.

As he approached the village of Batando he passed through the camps of thousands of Galla warriors and realized fully what he had previously sensed but vaguely—that his position was most precarious and that with the best grace possible he must agree to whatever terms the old chief might propose.

Batando received him graciously enough, though with all the majesty of a powerful monarch, and assured him that on the following day he would escort him to the entrance to the valley, but that first he must deliver to Batando all the Galla slaves that were with his party.

"But that will leave us without carriers or servants and will greatly weaken the strength of my party," cried Ibn Jad.

Batando but shrugged his black shoulders.

"Let them remain with us until we have returned from the valley," implored the sheik.

"No Galla man may accompany you," said Batando with finality.

Early the next morning the tent of Ibn Jad was struck in signal that all were to prepare for the rahla, and entirely surrounded by Galla warriors they started toward the rugged mountains where lay the entrance to the valley of Ibn Jad's dreams.

Fejjuan and the other Galla slaves that the 'Aarab had brought with them from beled el-Guad marched with their own people, happy in their new-found freedom. Stimbol, friendless, fearful, utterly cowed, trudged wearily along under guard of two young Beduins, his mind constantly reverting to the horror of the murdered man lying in his lonely grave behind them.

Winding steadily upward along what at times appeared to be an ancient trail and again no trail at all, the 'Aarab and their escort climbed higher and higher into the rugged mountains that rim the Valley of the Sepulcher upon the north. At the close of the second day, after they had made camp beside a rocky mountain brook, Batando came to Ibn Jad and pointed to the entrance to a rocky side ravine that branched from the main canyon directly opposite the camp.

"There," he said, "lies the trail into the valley. Here we leave you and return to our villages. Upon the morrow we go."

When the sun rose the following morning Ibn Jad discovered that the Gallas had departed during the night, but he did not know it was because of the terror they felt for the inhabitants of the mysterious valley from which no Galla ever had returned.

That day Ibn Jad spent in making a secure camp in which to leave the women and children until the warriors had returned from their adventure in the valley or had discovered that they might safely fetch their women, and the next morning, leaving a few old men and boys to protect the camp, he set forth with those who were accounted the fighting men among them, and presently the watchers in the camp saw the last of them disappear in the rocky ravine that lay opposite the menzil.

16

The Great Tourney

KING BOHUN with many knights and squires and serving men had ridden down from his castle above the City of the Sepulcher two days ago to take his way across the valley to the field before the city of Nimmr for the Great Tourney that is held once each year, commencing upon the first Sunday in Lent.

Gay pennons fluttered from a thousand lance tips and gay with color were the housings of the richly caparisoned chargers that proudly bore the Knights of the Sepulcher upon whose backs red crosses were emblazoned to denote that they had completed the pilgrimage to the Holy Land and were returning to home and England.

Their bassinets, unlike those of the Knights of Nimmr, were covered with bullock hide, and the devices upon their bucklers differed, and their colors. But for these and the crosses upon their backs they might have been Gobred's own good knights and true.

Sturdy sumpter beasts, almost as richly trapped as the knight's steeds, bore the marquees and tilts that were to house the knights during the tourney, as well as their personal belongings, their extra arms and their provisions for the three days of the tourney; for custom, over seven centuries old, forbade the Knights of Nimmr and the Knights of the Sepulcher breaking bread together.

The Great Tourney was merely a truce during which they carried on their ancient warfare under special rules which transformed it into a gorgeous pageant and an exhibition of martial prowess which noncombatants might witness in comfort and with impunity. It did not permit friendly intercourse between the two factions as this was not compatible with the seriousness of the event, in which knights of both sides often were killed, or the spirit in which the grand prize was awarded.

This prize as much as any other factor had kept open the breach of seven and a half centuries' duration that separated the Fronters from the Backers, for it consisted of five maidens whom the winners took back with them to their own city and who were never again seen by their friends or relatives.

Though the sorrow was mitigated by the honorable treatment that custom and the laws of knighthood decreed should be accorded these unfortunate maidens, it was still bitter because attached to it was the sting of defeat.

Following the tournament the maidens became the especial charges of Gobred or Bohun, dependent of course upon whether the honors of the tourney had fallen to the Fronters or the Backers, and in due course were given in honorable marriage to knights of the victorious party.

The genesis of the custom, which was now fully seven centuries old, doubtless lay in the wise desire of some ancient Gobred or Bohun to maintain the stock of both factions strong and virile by the regular infusion of new blood, as well, perhaps, as to prevent the inhabitants of the two cities from drifting too far apart in manners, customs and speech.

Many a happy wife of Nimmr had been born in the City of the Sepulcher and seldom was it that the girls themselves repined for long. It was considered an honor to be chosen and there were always many more who volunteered than the requisite number of five that anually made the sacrifice.

The five who constituted the prize offered by the City of the Sepulcher this year rode on white palfreys and were attended by a guard of honor in silver mail. The girls, selected for their beauty to thus honor the city of their birth, were gorgeously attired and weighed down with ornaments of gold and silver and precious stones.

Upon the plain before the city of Nimmr preparations for the tourney had been in progress for many days. The lists were being dragged and rolled with heavy wooden rollers, the ancient stands of stone from which the spectators viewed the spectacle were undergoing their annual repairs and cleansing, a frame superstructure was being raised to support the canopies that would shade the choice seats reserved for the nobility, and staffs for a thousand pennons had been set around the outer margin of the lists—these and a hundred other things were occupying a company of workmen; and in the walled city and in the castle that stood above it the hammers of armorers and smiths rang far into the night forging iron shoes and mail and lance tips.

Blake had been assured that he was to have a part in the Great Tourney and was as keen for it as he had been for the big game of the season during his football days at college. He had been entered in two sword contests—one in which five Knights of Nimmr met five Knights of the Sepulcher and another in which he was pitted against a single antagonist, but his only contest with the lance was to be in the grand finale when a hundred Fronters faced a hundred Backers, since, whereas, before his encounter with Malud he had been considered hopeless with sword and buckler now Prince Gobred looked to him to win many points with these, his lance work being held but mediocre.

King Bohun and his followers were camped in a grove of oaks about a mile north of the lists, nor did the laws governing the Great Tourney permit them to come nearer until the hour appointed for their entrance upon the first day of the spectacle.

Blake, in preparing for the tourney, had followed the custom adopted by many of the knights of wearing distinctive armor and trapping his charger similarly. His chain mail was all of solid black, relieved only by the leopard skin of his bassinet and the blue and silver pennon upon his lance. The housings of his mount were of black, edged with silver and blue, and there were, of course, the prescribed red crosses upon his breast and upon his horse housings.

As he came from his quarters upon the opening morning of the tourney, followed by Edward bearing his lance and buckler, he appeared a somber figure among the resplendently caparisoned knights and the gorgeously dressed women that were gathered in the great court awaiting the word to mount their horses which were being held in the north ballium by the grooms.

That his black mail was distinctive was evidenced by the attention he immediately attracted, and that he had quickly become popular among the knights and ladies of Nimmr was equally apparent by the manner in which they clustered about him, but opinion was divided in the matter of his costume, some holding that it was too dismal and depressing.

Guinalda was there but she remained seated upon a bench where she was conversing with one of the maidens that had been chosen as Nimmr's prize. Blake quickly disengaged himself from those who had crowded about him and crossed the court to where Guinalda sat. At his approach the princess looked up and inclined her head slightly in recognition of his bow and then she resumed her conversation with the maiden.

The rebuff was too obvious to permit of misunderstanding, but Blake was not satisfied to accept it and go his way without an explanation. He could scarce believe, however, that the princess was still vexed merely because he had intimated that he had believed that she took a greater interest in him than she had admitted. There must be some other reason.

He did not turn and walk away, then, although she continued to ignore him, but stood quietly before her waiting patiently until she should again notice him.

Presently he noted that she was becoming nervous as was also the maiden with whom she spoke. There were lapses in their conversation; one of Guinalda's feet was tapping the flagging irritably; a slow flush was creeping upward into her cheeks. The maiden fidgeted, she plucked at the ends of the wimple that lay about her shoulders, she smoothed the rich cyclas of her mantle and finally she arose and bowing before the princess asked if she might go and bid farewell to her mother.

Guinalda bade her begone and then, alone with Blake and no longer able to ignore him, nor caring to, she turned angrily upon him.

"I was right!" she snapped. "Thou art a forward boor. Why standeth thou thus staring at me when I have made it plain that I wouldst not be annoyed by thee? Go!"

"Because——" Blake hesitated, "because I love you."

"Sirrah!" cried Guinalda, springing to her feet. "How darest thou!"

"I would dare anything for you, my princess," replied Blake, "because I love you."

Guinalda looked straight at him for a moment in silence, then her short upper lip curved in a contemptuous sneer.

"Thou liest!" she said. "I have heard what thou hast said concerning me!" and without waiting for a reply she brushed past him and walked away.

Blake hurried after her. "What have I said about you?" he demanded. "I have said nothing that I would not repeat before all Nimmr. Not even have I presumed to tell my best friend, Sir Richard, that I love you. No other ears than yours have heard that."

"I have heard differently," said Guinalda, haughtily, "and I care not to discuss the matter further."

"But——" commenced Blake, but at that instant a trumpet sounded from the north gate leading into the ballium. It was the signal for the knights to mount. Guinalda's page came running to her to summon her to her father's side. Sir Richard appeared and seized Blake by the arm.

"Come, James!" he cried. "We should have been mounted before now for we ride in the forerank of the knights to-day." And so Blake was dragged away from the princess before he could obtain an explanation of her, to him, inexplicable attitude.

The north ballium presented a scene of color and activity, crowded as it was with knights and ladies, pages, squires, grooms, men-at-arms and horses, nor would it accommodate them all, so that the overflow stretched into the east and south balliums and even through the great east gate out upon the road that leads down into the valley.

For half an hour something very like chaos reigned about the castle of the Prince of Nimmr, but eventually perspiring marshals and shouting heralds whipped the cortege into shape as it took its slow and imposing way down the winding mountain road toward the lists.

First rode the marshals and heralds and behind them a score of trumpeters; then came Prince Gobred, riding alone, and following was a great company of knights, their colored pennons streaming in the wind. They rode just before the ladies and behind the ladies was another company of knights, while in the rear marched company after company of men-at-arms, some armed with cross bows, others with pikes and still others again with battle-axes of huge proportions.

Perhaps a hundred knights and men-at-arms all told were left behind to guard the castle and the entrance to the Valley of the Sepulcher, but these would be relieved to witness the second and third days' exercises.

As the Knights of Nimmr wound down to the lists, the Knights of the Sepulcher moved out from their camp among the oaks, and the marshals of the two parties timed their approach so that both entered the lists at the same time.

The ladies of Nimmr dropped out of the procession and took their places in the stand; the five maidens of Nimmr and the five from the City of the Sepulcher were escorted to a dais at one end of the lists, after which the knights lined up in solid ranks, the Knights of Nimmr upon the south side of the lists, the Knights of the Sepulcher upon the north.

Gobred and Bohun rode forward and met in the center of the field, where, in measured and imposing tones, Bohun delivered the ancient challenge prescribed by custom and the laws of the Great Tourney and handed Gobred the gage, the acceptance of which constituted an acceptance of the challenge and marked the official opening of the tourney.

As Gobred and Bohun reined about and faced their own knights these rode out of the lists, those who were not to take part in the encounters of the day seeking places in the stands after turning their chargers over to grooms, while those who were to participate formed again to ride once around the lists, for the double purpose of indicating to their opponents and the spectators the entrants for that day and of viewing the prizes offered by their opponents.

In addition to the maidens there were many minor prizes consisting of jeweled ornaments, suits of mail, lances, swords, bucklers, splendid steeds and the many articles that were valued by knights or that might find favor in the eyes of their ladies.

The Knights of the Sepulcher paraded first, with Bohun at their head, and it was noticeable that the eyes of the king were often upon the women in the stands as he rode past. Bohun was a young man, having but just ascended the throne following the recent death of his father. He was arrogant and tyrannical and it had been common knowledge in Nimmr that for years he had been at the head of a faction that was strong for war with Nimmr, that the city might be reduced and the entire Valley of the Sepulcher brought under the rule of the Bohuns.

His charger prancing, his colors flying, his great company of knights at his back, King Bohun rode along the stands reserved for the people of Nimmr, and when he came to the central loge in which sat Prince Gobred with the Princess Brynilda and Princess Guinalda, his eyes fell upon the face of the daughter of Gobred.

Bohun reined in his charger and stared straight into the face of Guinalda. Gobred flushed angrily, for Bohun's act was a breach of courtesy, and half rose from his seat, but at that moment Bohun, bowing low across his mount's withers, moved on, followed by his knights.

That day the honors went to the Knights of the Sepulcher, for they scored two hundred and twenty seven points against one hundred and six that the Knights of Nimmr were able to procure.

Upon the second day the tourney opened with the riding past of the entrants who, ordinarily, were conducted by a herald, but to the surprise of all, Bohun again led his knights past the stands and again he paused and looked full at the Princess Guinalda.

This day the Knights of Nimmr fared a little better, being for the day but seven points behind their opponents, though the score for the two days stood two hundred and sixty nine to three hundred and ninety seven in favor of the Knights of the Sepulcher.

So the third day opened with the knights from the north

boasting what seemed an insuperable lead of one hundred and twenty eight points and the Knights of Nimmr spurred to greater action by the knowledge that to win the tourney they must score two hundred and thirty two of the remaining three hundred and thirty four points.

Once again, contrary to age old custom, Bohun led his entrants about the lists as they paraded before the opening encounter, and once again he drew rein before the loge of Gobred and his eye rested upon the beautiful face of Guinalda for an instant before he addressed her sire.

"Prince Gobred of Nimmr," he said in his haughty and arrogant voice, "as ye well know my valiant sir knights have bested thine by more than six score points and the Great Tourney be as good as ours already. Yet we would make thee a proposition."

"Speak Bohun! The Great Tourney is yet far from won, but an' ye have any proposition that an honorable prince may consider thou hast my assurance that 'twill be given consideration."

"Thy five maidens are as good as ours," said Bohun, "but give me thy daughter to be queen of the Valley of the Sepulcher and I will grant thee the tourney."

Gobred went white with anger, but when he replied his voice was low and even for he was master of his own emotions, as befitted a princely man.

"Sir Bohun," he said, refusing to accord to his enemy the title of king, "thy words are an offense in the ears of honorable men, implying as they do that the daughter of a Gobred be for sale and that the honor of the knighthood of Nimmr may be bartered for.

"Get thee hence to thine own side of the lists before I set serfs upon ye to drive ye there with staves."

"So that be thine answer, eh?" shouted Bohun. "Then know ye that I shall take the five maidens by the rules of the Great Tourney and thy daughter by force of arms!" With this threat delivered he wheeled his steed and spurred away.

Word of Bohun's proposition and his rebuff spread like wild fire throughout the ranks of the Knights of Nimmr so that those who were to contend this last day of the tourney were keyed to the highest pitch of derring do in the defence of the honor of Nimmr and the protection of the Princess Guinalda. The great lead attained by the Knights of the Sepulcher during the first two days was but an added incentive to greater effort, provoking them, as a spur, to the utmost limits of daring and exertion. There was no need that their marshals should exhort them. The youth and chivalry of Nimmr had heard the challenge and would answer it in the lists!

Blake's sword and buckler encounter with a Knight of the Sepulcher was scheduled for the first event of the day. When the lists were cleared he rode in to a fanfare of trumpets, moving parallel with the south stands while his adversary rode along the front of the north stands, the latter halting before the loge of Bohun as Blake drew rein in front of that of Gobred, where he raised the hilt of his sword to his lips to the Prince, though his eyes were upon Guinalda.

"Conduct thyself as a true knight this day to the glory and honor of Nimmr," charged Gobred, "and may the blessings of Our Lord Jesus be upon thee and thy sword, our well beloved Sir James!"

"To the glory and honor of Nimmr I pledge my sword and my life!" should have been Blake's reply according to the usages of the Great Tourney.

"To the glory and honor of Nimmr and to the protection of my Princess I pledge my sword and my life!" is what he said, and it was evident from the expression on Gobred's face that he was not displeased, while the look of haughty disdain which had been upon Guinalda's face softened.

Slowly she arose and tearing a ribbon from her gown stepped to the front of the loge. "Receive this favor from thy lady, sir knight," she said, "bearing it with honor and to victory in thy encounter."

Blake reined closed to the rail of the loge and bent low while Guinalda pinned the ribbon upon his shoulder. His face was close to hers; he sensed the intoxicating perfume of her hair; he felt her warm breath upon his cheek.

"I love you," he whispered, so low that no other ears than hers could hear.

"Thou art a boor," she replied in a voice as low as his. "It be for the sake of the five maidens that I encourage ye with this favor."

Blake looked straight into her eyes. "I love you, Guinalda," he said, "and—you love me!"

Before she could reply he had wheeled away, the trumpets had sounded, and he was cantering slowly toward the end of the field where the tilts of the Knights of Nimmr stood.

Edward, very much excited, was there and Sir Richard and Michel, with a marshal, heralds, trumpeters, men-at-arms— a martial company to urge him on with encouragement and advice.

Blake cast aside his buckler, nor was there any to reprove him now. Instead they smiled proudly and knowingly, for had they not seen him best Sir Malud without other defense than his horsemanship and his sword?

The trumpets blared again. Blake turned and put spurs to his charger. Straight down the center of the lists he rode. From the opposite end came a Knight of the Sepulcher to meet him!

"Sir James! Sir James!" cried the spectators in the stands upon the south side, while the north stands answered with the name of their champion.

"Who is the black knight?" asked many a man in the north stands of his neighbor.

"He hath no buckler!" cried some. "He be mad!" "Sir Guy wilt cleave him open at the first pass!" "Sir Guy! Sir Guy!"

17

"The Saracens!"

JUST as the second day of the Great Tourney had opened in the Valley of the Sepulcher upon the plains below the city of Nimmr, a band of swart men in soiled thobs and carrying long matchlocks topped the summit of the pass upon the north side of the valley and looked down upon the City of the Sepulcher and the castle of King Bohun.

They had followed upward along what may once have been a trail, but for so long a time had it been unused, or so infrequently had it been used that it was scarce distinguishable from the surrounding brush; but below them now Ibn Jad saw at a short distance a better marked road and, beyond, what appeared to him a fortress. Beyond that again he glimpsed the battlements of Bohun's castle.

What he saw in the foreground was the barbican guarding the approach to the castle and the city, both of which were situated in much the same relative position as were the barbican and castle upon the south side of the valley where Prince Gobred guarded the city of Nimmr and the valley beyond it against the daily expected assault of the Saracens.

Seeking cover, Ibn Jad and his Beduins crept down toward the barbican where an old knight and a few men-at-arms kept perfunctory ward. Hiding in the mountain brush the 'Aarab saw two strangely apparelled blacks hunting just outside the great gateway. They were armed with cross bows and arrows and their prey was rabbits. For years they had seen no stranger come down this ancient road, and for years they had hunted between the gate and the summit of the mountains, though farther than this they were not permitted to wander. Nor had they any great desire to do so, for, though they were descendants of Gallas who lived just beyond this mountain top, they thought that they were Englishmen and that a horde of Saracens awaited to annihilate them should they venture too far afield.

Today they hunted as they had often hunted when they chanced to be placed in the guard at the outer barbican. They moved silently forward, warily awaiting the break of a rabbit. They did not see the dark-faced men in the brush.

Ibn Jad saw that the great gateway was open and that the gate that closed it raised and lowered vertically. It was raised now. Great was the laxity of the old knight and the men-at-arms, but King Bohun was away and there was none to reprove them.

Ibn Jad motioned those nearest him to follow and crept slowly closer to the gateway.

What of the old knight and the other watchers? The former was partaking of a late breakfast just within one of the great towers of the barbican and the latter were taking advantage of the laxity of his discipline to catch a few more winks of sleep as they stretched beneath the shade of some trees within the ballium.

Ibn Jad won to within a few yards of the gateway and waited for the others to reach his side. When they were all there he whispered to them and then trotted on silent sandals toward the gate, his matchlock ready in his hands. Behind him came his fellows. They were all within the ballium before the men-at-arms were aware that there was an enemy this side of Palestine.

With cross bow and battle-axe the men-at-arms sprang to defend the gate. Their cries of "The Saracens! The Saracens!" brought the old sir knight and the hunters running toward the ballium.

Below, at the castle of King Bohun, the men at the gates and the other retainers who had been left while Bohun sallied forth to the Great Tourney heard strange noises from the direction of the outer barbican. The shouts of men floated down to them and strange, sharp sounds that were like thunder and yet unlike it. Such sounds they had never heard before, nor any of their forbears. They rallied at the outer castle gate and the knights with them consulted as to what was best to be done.

Being brave knights there seemed but one thing open for them. If those at the far outer barbican had been attacked they must hasten to their defense. Summoning all but four of the knights and men-at-arms at his disposal the marshal of the castle mounted and rode forth toward the outer gate.

Half way there they were espied by Ibn Jad and his men who, having overcome the poorly armed soldiers at the gate, were advancing down the road toward the castle. At sight of

these reinforcements Ibn Jad hastened to secrete his followers
and himself in the bushes that lined the roadway. So it fell
that the marshal rode by them and did not see them and,
when they had passed, Ibn Jad and his followers came out of
the bushes and continued down the winding mountain road
toward the castle of King Bohun.

The men at the castle gate, now fully upon the alert, stood
ready with the portcullis raised as the marshal instructed them,
so that in the event that those who had ridden out should be
hard pressed upon their return by an enemy at their rear
they could still find sanctuary within the ballium. The plan
was, in such event, to lower the portcullis behind the men of
the Sepulcher and in the faces of the pursuing Saracens, for
that an enemy must be such was a forgone conclusion—had
not they and their ancestors waited for near seven and a half
centuries now for this momentarily expected assault? They
wondered if it really had come at last.

While they discussed the question Ibn Jad watched them
from a concealing clump of bushes a few yards away.

The wily Beduin knew the purpose of that portcullis and he
was trying to plan best how he might enter the enclosure beyond before it could be dropped before his face. At last he
found a plan and smiled. He beckoned three men to come
close and into their ears he whispered that which he had in
mind.

There were four men-at-arms ready to drop the portcullis
at the psychological moment and all four of them stood in
plain sight of Ibn Jad and the three that were beside him.
Carefully, cautiously, noiselessly the four 'Aarab raised their
ancient matchlocks and took careful aim.

"Now!" whispered Ibn Jad and four matchlocks belched
forth flame and black powder and slugs of lead.

The four men-at-arms dropped to the stone flagging and
Ibn Jad and all his followers raced forward and stood within
the ballium of the castle of King Bohun. Before them, across
the ballium, was another gate and a broad moat, but the
drawbridge was lowered, the portcullis raised and the gateway
unguarded.

The marshal and his followers had ridden unhindered into
the ballium of the outer barbican and there they had found
all its defenders lying in their own blood, even to the little
squire of the old knight who should have watched the gate
and did not.

One of the men-at-arms still lived and in his dying breath

he gasped the terrible truth. The Saracens had come at last!

"Where are they?" demanded the marshal.

"Didst thou not see them, sir?" asked the dying man. "They marched down the road toward the castle."

"Impossible!" cried the marshal. "We didst but ride along that very road and saw no one."

"They marched down toward the castle," gasped the man.

The marshal knit his brows. "Were there many?" he demanded.

"There are few," replied the man-at-arms. "It was but the advance guard of the armies of the sultan."

Just then the volley that laid low the four warders at the castle gate crashed upon the ears of the marshal and his men.

" 'Ods blud!" he cried.

"They must have hid themselves in the bush as we passed," exclaimed a knight at the marshal's side, "for of a surety they be there and we be here and there be but one road between.'"

"There be but four men at the castle gate," said the marshal, "and I did bid them keep the 'cullis up til we returned. God pity me! I have given over the Sepulcher to the Saracens. Slay, me, Sir Morley!"

"Nay, man! We need every lance and sword and cross bow that we may command. This be no time to think of taking thy life when thou canst give it to Our Lord Jesus in defense of His Sepulcher against the infidels!"

"Thou art right, Morley," cried the marshal. "Remain you here, then, with six men and hold this gate. I shall return with the others and give battle at the castle!"

But when the marshal came again to the castle gate he found the portcullis down and a dark-faced, bearded Saracen glaring at him through the iron bars. The marshal at once ordered the cross bowmen to shoot the fellow down, but as they raised their weapons to their shoulder there was a loud explosion that almost deafened them and flame leaped from a strange thing that the Saracen held against his shoulder and pointed at them. One of the cross bowmen screamed and lunged forward upon his face and the others turned and fled.

They were brave men in the face of dangers that were natural and to be expected, but in the presence of the supernatural, the weird, the uncanny, they reacted as most men do, and what could have been more weird than death leaping in flame and with a great noise through space to strike their fellow down?

But Sir Bulland, the marshal, was a knight of the Sepulcher.

He might wish to run away fully as much as the simple and lowly men-at-arms, but there was something that held him there that was more potent than fear of death. It is called Honor.

Sir Bulland could not run away and so he sat there on his great horse and challenged the Saracens to mortal combat; challenged them to send their doughtiest sir knight to meet him and thus decide who should hold the gate.

But the 'Aarab already held it. Futhermore they did not understand him. In addition to all this they were without honor as Sir Bulland knew it, and perhaps as any one other than a Beduin knows it, and would but have laughed at his silly suggestion.

One thing they did know—two things they knew—that he was a Nasrany and that he was unarmed. They did not count his great lance and his sword as weapons, for he could not reach them with either. So one of them took careful aim and shot Sir Bulland through his chain mail where it covered his noble and chivalrous heart.

Ibn Had had the run of the castle of King Bohun and he was sure that he had discovered the fabled City of Nimmr that the sahar had told him of. He herded together the women and children and the few men that remained and held them under guard. For a while he was minded to slay them, since they were but Nasrany, but he was so pleased at having found and taken the treasure city that he let them live—for the time at least.

At his command his followers ransacked the castle in search of the treasure. Nor were they disappointed, for the riches of Bohun were great. There was gold in the hills of the Valley of the Sepulcher and there were precious stones to be found there, also. For seven and a half centuries the slaves of the Sepulcher and of Nimmr had been washing gold from the creek beds and salvaging precious stones from the same source. The real value of such was not to the men of the Sepulcher and Nimmr what it would be to men of the outer world. They but esteemed these things as trinkets, yet they liked them and saved them and even bartered for them on occasion, but they did not place them in vaults under lock and key. Why should they in a land where such things were not stolen? Their women and their horses they guarded, but not their gold or their jewels.

And so Ibn Jad gathered a great sack full of treasure, enough to satisfy the wildest imaginings of his cupidity. He gathered all that he could find in the castle of King Bohun, more than he had hoped to find in this fabled city; and then a strange thing happened. Having more wealth than he possibly could use he wanted more. No, not so strange after all, for Ibn Jad was human.

He spent the night with his followers in the castle of King Bohun and during the night he planned, for he had seen a wide valley stretching far away to other mountains and at the base of those mountains he had seen that which appeared to be a city. "Perhaps," thought Ibn Jad, "it is a richer city than this. I shall start on the morrow to see."

18

The Black Knight

D OWN the field thundered the two chargers. Silence fell upon the stands. They were almost met when Sir Guy realized that his adversary bore no shield. But what of that? He had been sent to the lists by his own people—the responsibility was theirs, the advantage Sir Guy's. Had they sent him in without a sword Sir Guy might still have slain him without besmirching his knightly honor, for such were the laws of the Great Tourney.

Yet his discovery had its effect upon the Knight of the Sepulcher as just for an instant it had distracted his attention from the thought that should have been uppermost in his mind—gaining the primary advantage by the skill of his opening attack.

He saw his antagonist's horse swing out just before they met. He stood in his stirrups, as had Sir Malud, to deliver a terrific cut; then Blake threw his horse straight into the shoulder of Sir Guy's. The latter's sword fell and with a loud, clanging noise slipped harmlessly from the blade of the Knight of Nimmr. Guy had raised his buckler to protect his own head and neck and could not see Sir James. Guy's horse stumbled and nearly fell. As it recovered itself Blake's blade slipped beneath the buckler of the Knight of the Sepulcher and its point pierced the gorget of his adversary and passed through his throat.

With a cry that ended in a blood choked gurgle Sir Guy of the Sepulcher toppled backward upon his horse's rump and rolled upon the ground while the south stands went mad with joy.

The laws of the Great Tourney account the knight who is unhorsed as slain, so the coup-de-grace is never given and no knight is killed unnecessarily. The victor rides to the tilt of the vanquished, wheels about and gallops to his own tilt, the full length of the lists, where he waits until a herald of the opposing side fetches the prize to him.

And so it was that as Blake swung from his saddle, sword in hand, and approached the fallen Sir Guy, a gasp arose from the south stands and a roar of angry protest from the north.

Marshals and heralds galloped madly from the tilt of the fallen Backer and, seeing this, Sir Richard, fearing that Blake would be set upon and slain, led a similar party from his end of the field.

Blake approached the fallen knight, who lay upon his back, feebly struggling to arise, and when the spectators looked to see him run Sir Guy through with his sword they saw him instead toss the weapon to the ground and kneel beside the wounded man.

With an arm beneath Sir Guy's shoulders he raised him and held him against his knee while he tore off his helm and gorget, and when the marshals and the heralds and the others drew rein beside him Blake was trying to staunch the flow of blood.

"Quick!" he cried to them, "a chirurgeon! His jugular is not touched, but this flow of blood must be stopped."

Several of the knights dismounted and gathered about, and among them was Sir Richard. A herald of Sir Guy's faction kneeled and took the youth from Blake's arms.

"Come!" said Richard. "Leave the sir knight to his own friends."

Blake arose. He saw how peculiar were the expressions upon the faces of the knights about him, but as he drew away one of them spoke. An older man, who was one of Bohun's marshals.

"Thou art a generous and chivalrous knight," he said to Blake, "and a courageous one too who would thus set at naught the laws of the Great Tourney and the customs of centuries."

Blake faced him squarely. "I do not give a damn for your laws or your customs," he said. "Where I come from a decent man wouldn't let a yellow dog bleed to death without trying to save him, much less a brave and gallant boy like this, and because he fell by my hand, by the customs of my country I should be compelled to aid him."

"Yes," explained Sir Richard, "as otherwise he would be punished with a raspberry."

The winning of the first event of the day was but a forerunner of a series of successes on the part of the Knights of

Nimmr until, at the opening of the last event, the score showed four hundred fifty two points for them against four hundred forty eight for their opponents. A margin of four points, however, was as nothing at this stage of the tourney, as the final event held one hundred points which Fate might allot almost entirely to one side.

This was the most spectacular event of the whole tourney and one which the spectators always looked forward to with the greatest anticipation. Two hundred knights were engaged in it, one hundred Knights of Nimmr against one hundred Knights of the Sepulcher. They formed at opposite ends of the lists and as the trumpets sounded the signal they charged with lances, and thus they fought until all of one side had been unhorsed or had retired from the field because of wounds. Broken lances could be replaced as a polo player may ride out and obtain a fresh mallet when he breaks his. Otherwise there were few rules to govern this concluding number of the Great Tourney, which more nearly approximated a battle scene than any other event of the three days of conflict.

Blake had won his fifteen points for the Knights of Nimmr in the opening event of the day and again with four other comrades, pitted against five mounted swordsmen from the north, he had helped to add still further points to the growing score of the Fronters.

He was entered in the last event largely because the marshals appreciated the value of his horsemanship and felt that it would more than compensate for his inexperience with the lance.

The two hundred mailed knights had paraded for the final event and were forming line at opposite ends of the lists, one hundred Knights of the Sepulcher at one end and one hundred Knights of Nimmr at the other. Their chargers, especially selected for this encounter, were powerful and fleet, chosen for their courage as were the youths who bestrode them.

The knights, with few exceptions, were youths in their twenties, for to youth went the laurels of this great sport of the Middle Ages as they still do in the sports of today. Here and there was a man of middle age, a hardened veteran whose heart and hand had withstood the march of years and whose presence exerted a steadying influence upon the young knights the while it spurred them to their utmost efforts, for these were champions whose deeds were sung by minstrels in the great halls of the castles of Nimmr.

In proud array, with upright lances and fluttering pennons, the sunlight glinting from burnished mail and bit and boss and shining brightly upon the gorgeous housings of their mounts, the two hundred presented a proud and noble spectacle as they awaited the final summons of the trumpet.

Rearing and plunging, eager to be off, many a war horse broke the line as will a thoroughbred at the barrier, while at one side and opposite the center of the lists a herald waited for the moment that both lines should be formed before he gave the signal that would send these iron men hurtling into combat.

Blake found himself well toward the center of the line of Nimmr's knights, beneath him a great black that fretted to be off, before him the flower of the knighthood of the Sepulcher. In his right hand he grasped a heavy, iron-shod lance, the butt of which rested in a boot at his stirrup, and upon his left arm he bore a great shield, nor had he any wish to discard it in the face of all those sturdy, iron-tipped lances.

As he looked down the long length of the lists upon the hundred knights that would presently be racing toward him in solid array with lance points projecting far ahead of their horses, Blake felt that his shield was entirely inadequate and he experienced a certain nervousness that reminded him of similar moments of tense waiting for the referee's whistle during his football days—those seemingly long gone days of another life that he sensed now as a remote and different incarnation.

As last came the signal! He saw the herald raise his sword on high. With the two hundred he gathered his restive charger and couched his lance. The sword fell! From the four corners of the lists trumpets blared; from two hundred throats rose the cri de guerre; four hundred spurs transmitted the awaited signal from man to horse.

The thundering lines bore down the field while a score of heralds raced along the flanks and rear to catch any infraction of the sole regulation that bore upon the final tumultuous collision. Each knight must engage the foe upon his bridle hand, for to couch his lance upon the one to his right was an unknightly act, since thus a single knight might have two lances set upon him at once, against which there could be no defence.

From above the rim of his shield Blake saw the solid front of lances, iron-shod chargers and great shields almost upon him. The speed, the weight, the momentum seemed irresistible and, metaphorically, with deep respect Blake took his hat off to the knights of old.

Now the two lines were about to meet! The spectators sat

in spellbound silence; the riders, grim-jawed, with tight set lips, were voiceless now.

Blake, his lance across his horse's withers, picked the knight racing toward him upon his left hand; for an instant he caught the other's eyes and then each crouched behind his shield as the two lines came together with a deafening crash.

Blake's shield smashed back against his face and body with such terrific force that he was almost carried from his saddle. He felt his own lance strike and splinter and then, half stunned, he was through the iron line, his charger, frantic and uncontrolled, running wildly toward the tilts of Bohun's knights.

With an effort Blake pulled himself together, gathered his reins and finally managed to get his horse under control, and it was not until he had reined him about that he got his first glimpse of the result of the opening encounter. A half dozen chargers were scrambling to their feet and nearly a score more were galloping, riderless, about the lists. A full twenty-five knights lay upon the field and twice that many squires and serving men were running in on foot to succor their masters.

Already several of the knights had again set their lances against an enemy and Blake saw one of the Knights of the Sepulcher bearing down upon him, but he raised his broken spear shaft above his head to indicate that he was momentarily hors de combat and galloped swiftly back to his own end of the lists where Edward was awaiting him with a fresh weapon.

"Thou didst nobly well, beloved master," cried Edward.

"Did I get my man?" asked Blake.

"That thou didst, sir," Edward assured him, beaming with pride and pleasure, "and all be thou breakest thy lance upon his shield thou didst e'en so unhorse him."

Armed anew Blake turned back toward the center of the lists where many individual encounters were taking place. Already several more knights were down and the victors looking for new conquests in which the stands were assisting with hoarse cries and advice, and as Blake rode back into the lists he was espied by many in the north stands occupied by the knights and followers of the Sepulcher.

"The black knight!" they cried. "Here! Here! Sir Wildred! Here is the black knight that overthrew Sir Guy. Have at him, Sir Wildred!"

Sir Wildred, a hundred yards away, couched his lance. "Have at thee, Sir Black Knight!" he shouted.

"You're on!" Blake shouted back, putting spurs to the great black.

Sir Wildred was a large man and he bestrode a raw-boned

oan with the speed of a deer and the heart of a lion. The
pair would have been a match for the best of Nimmr's knighthood.

Perhaps it was as well for Blake's peace of mind that Wildred appeared to him like any other knight and that he did
not know that he was the most sung of all the heroes of the
Sepulcher.

As a matter of fact, any knight looked formidable to Blake,
who was still at a loss to understand how he had unhorsed
his man in the first encounter of this event.

"The bird must have lost both stirrups," is what he had
mentally assured himself when Edward had announced his
victory.

But he couched his lance like a good sir knight and true
and bore down upon the redoubtable Sir Wildred. The Knight
of the Sepulcher was charging diagonally across the field from
the south stands. Beyond him Blake caught a glimpse of a
slim, girlish figure standing in the central loge. He could not
see her eyes, but he knew that they were upon him.

"For my Princess!" he whispered as Sir Wildred loomed
large before him.

Lance smote on shield as the two knights crashed together
with terrific force and Blake felt himself lifted clear of his
saddle and hurled heavily to the ground. He was neither
stunned nor badly hurt and as he sat up a sudden grin
wreathed his face, for there, scarce a lance length from him,
sat Sir Wildred. But Sir Wildred did not smile.

" 'Sdeath!" he cried. "Thou laughest at me, sir-rah?"

"If I look as funny as you do," Blake assured him, "you've
got a laugh coming too."

Sir Wildred knit his brows. "Ods blud!" he exclaimed. "An
thou beest a knight of Nimmr I be a Saracen! Who beest thou?
Thy speech savoreth not of the Valley."

Blake had arisen. "Hurt much?" he asked stepping forward.
"Here, I'll give you a hand up."

"Thou art, of a certainty, a strange sir knight," said Wildred. "I recall now that thou didst offer succor to Sir Guy
when thou hadst fairly vanquished him."

"Well, what's wrong with that?" asked Blake. "I haven't
anything against you. We've had a bully good scrap and are
out of it. Why should we sit here and make faces at one
another?"

Sir Wildred shook his head. "Thou art beyond my compre-
hension," he admitted.

By this time their squires and a couple of serving men had

arrived, but neither of the fallen knights was so badly injured that he could not walk without assistance. As they started for their respective tilts Blake turned and smiled at Wildred.

"So long, old man!" he cried cheerily. "Hope we meet again some day."

Still shaking his head Sir Wildred limped away, followed by the two who had come to assist him.

At his tilt Blake learned that the outcome of the Great Tourney still hung in the balance and it was another half hour before the last of the Knights of Nimmr went down in defeat, leaving two Knights of the Sepulcher victorious upon the field. But this was not enough to overcome the lead of four points that the Fronters had held at the opening of the last event and a moment later the heralds announced that the Knights of Nimmr had won the Great Tourney by the close margin of two points.

Amidst the shouting of the occupants of the stands at the south the Knights of Nimmr who had taken part in the tourney and had won points for the Fronters formed to ride upon the lists and claim the grand prize. Not all were there, as some had been killed or wounded in encounters that had followed their victories, though the toll on both sides had been much smaller than Blake had imagined that it would be. Five men were dead and perhaps twenty too badly injured to ride, the casualties being about equally divided.

As the Knights of Nimmr rode down the field to claim the five maidens from the City of the Sepulcher, Bohun gathered all his knights at his side of the lists as though preparing to ride back to his camp. At the same time a Knight of the Sepulcher, wearing the leopard skin bassinet of Nimmr, entered the stands upon the south side of the field and made his way toward the loge of Prince Gobred.

Bohun watched. The Knights of Nimmr were at the far end of the field engrossed in the ritualistic rites that the laws of the Great Tourney prescribed for the reception of the five maidens.

Close beside Bohun two young knights sat their chargers, their eyes upon their king, and one of them held the bridle of a riderless horse.

Suddenly Bohun raised his hand and spurred across the field followed by his knights. They moved a little toward the end of the field where the Knights of Nimmr were congregated so that the bulk of them were between this end of the field and Gobred's loge.

The young knight who had sat close beside Bohun, and his

companion leading the riderless horse, spurred at a run straight
for the stands of Nimmr and the loge of the Prince. As they
drew in abreast of it a knight leaped into the loge from the
rear, swept Guinalda into his arms, tossed her quickly to the
young knight waiting to receive her, sprang to the edge of the
rail and leaped into the saddle of the spare horse being held in
readiness for him; then they both wheeled and spurred away
before the surprised Gobred or those about him could raise a
hand to stay them. Behind them swept Bohun and the Knights
of the Sepulcher, out toward the camp among the oaks.

Instantly all was pandemonium. A trumpeter in Gobred's
loge sounded the alarm; the prince ran from the stands to the
spot where his horse was being held by a groom; the Knights
of Nimmr, ignorant of what had occurred, not knowing where
to rally or against whom, milled about the lists for a few moments.

Then Gobred came, spurring swiftly before them. "Bohun
has stolen the Princess Guinalda!" he cried. "Knights of
Nimmr—" but before he could say more, or issue orders to
his followers, a black knight on a black charger spurred
roughly through the ranks of surrounding men and was away
after the retreating Knights of the Sepulcher.

19

Lord Tarzan

THERE was a nasty smile upon Tollog's lips as he thought how neatly he had foiled Ateja, who would have warned the Nasrany of the plot to slay him, and he thanked Allah that chance had placed him in a position to intercept her before she had been able to ruin them all. Even as Tollog, the brother of the sheik, smiled in his beard a hand reached out of the darkness behind him and seized him by the throat —fingers grasped him and he was dragged away.

Into the beyt that had been Zeyd's and which had been set up for the Nasrany, Tollog was dragged. He struggled and tried to scream for help, but he was powerless in the grip of steel that held him and choked him.

Inside the beyt a voice whispered in his ear. "Cry out, Tollog," it said, "and I shall have to kill you." Then the grasp upon his throat relaxed, but Tollog did not call for help, for he had recognized the voice that spoke and he knew that it had made no idle threat.

He lay still while the bonds were drawn tight about his wrists and ankles and a gag fastened securely in his mouth. He felt the folds of his burnous drawn across his face and then—silence.

He heard Stimbol creep into the beyt, but he thought that it was still he who had bound him. And thus died Tollog, the brother of Ibn Jad, died as he had planned that Tarzan of the Apes should die.

And, knowing that he would die thus, there was a smile upon the lips of the ape-man as he swung through the forest toward the southeast.

Tarzan's quest was not for Beduins but for Blake. Having assured himself that the white man in the menzil of Ibn Jad was Stimbol and that none knew the whereabouts of the other American, he was hastening back to the locality where Blake's boys had told him their bwana had disappeared, in the hope of picking up his trail and, if unable to assist him, at least to learn what fate had overtaken him.

Tarzan moved swiftly and his uncanny senses of sight and smell aided him greatly in wresting its secrets from the jungle, yet it was three days before he found the spot where Ara the lightning had struck down Blake's gun bearer.

Here he discovered Blake's faint spoor leading toward the north. Tarzan shook his head, for he knew that there was a stretch of uninhabited forest laying between this place and the first Galla villages. Also he knew that if Blake survived hunger and the menace of wild beasts he might only live to fall victim to a Galla spear.

For two days Tarzan followed a spoor that no other human eye might have discerned. On the afternoon of the second day he came upon a great stone cross built directly in the center of an ancient trail. Tarzan saw the cross from the concealment of bushes for he moved as beasts of prey moved, taking advantage of every cover, suspicious of every strange object, always ready for flight or battle as occasion might demand.

So it was that he did not walk blindly into the clutches of the two men-at-arms that guarded the outer way to the City of Nimmr. To his keen ears was borne the sound of their voices long before he saw them.

Even as Sheeta or Numa approach their prey, so Tarzan of the Apes crept through the brush until he lay within a few yards of the men-at-arms. To his vast astonishment he heard them conversing in a quaint form of English that, while understandable to him, seemed yet a foreign tongue. He marvelled at their antiquated costumes and obsolete weapons, and in them he saw an explanation of Blake's disappearance and a suggestion of his fate.

For a time Tarzan lay watching the two with steady, unblinking eyes—it might have been Numa himself, weighing the chances of a sudden charge. He saw that each was armed with a sturdy pike and a sword. They could speak English, after a fashion, therefore, he argued, they might be able to give him word of Blake. But would they receive him in a friendly spirit or would they attempt to set upon and slay him?

He determined that he could never ascertain what their attitude would be by lying hidden among the brush, and so he gathered himself, as Numa does when he is about to spring.

The two blacks were idly gossiping, their minds as far from thoughts of danger as it were possible they could be,

when suddenly without warning Tarzan launched himself full
upon the back of the nearer, hurling him to the ground.
Before the other could gather his wits the ape-man had
dragged his victim into the concealment of the bush from
which he had sprung, while the fellow's companion turned and
fled in the direction of the tunnel.

The man in Tarzan's grasp fought and struggled to be free
but the ape-man held him as easily as he might have held a
child.

"Lie still," he advised, "I shall not harm you."

"Ods blud!" cried the black. "What manner of creature be
thou?"

"One who will not harm you if you will tell him the truth,"
replied Tarzan.

"What wouldst thou know?" demanded the black.

"A white man came this way many weeks ago. Where is
he?"

"Thou speakest of Sir James?" asked the soldier.

"Sir James!" mused Tarzan and then he recollected that
Blake's first name was James. "His name was James," he
replied, "James Blake."

"Verily, 'tis the same," said the soldier.

"You have seen him? Where is he now?"

"He be defending the honor of Our Lord Jesus and the
Knights of Nimmr in the Great Tourney in the lists upon the
plain below the city, and have ye come to wreak dispite upon
our good Sir James thou wilt find many doughty knights and
men-at-arms who will take up the gage in his behalf."

"I am his friend," said Tarzan.

"Then why didst thou leap upon me thus, if thou art a
friend to Sir James?" demanded the man.

"I did not know how you had received him or how you
would receive me."

"A friend of Sir James will be received well in Nimmr," said
the man.

Tarzan took the man's sword from him and permitted him
to rise—his pike he had dropped before being dragged among
the bushes.

"Go before me and lead me to your master," commanded
the ape-man, "and remember that your life will be the forfeit
that you must pay for treachery."

"Do not make me leave the road unguarded against the
Saracens," begged the man. "Soon my companion will return
with others and then I shall beg them to take thee where thou
wilt."

"Very well," agreed the ape-man. They had not waited long before he heard the sound of hastening footsteps and a strange jingling and clanking that might have been caused by the shaking of many chains and the striking against them of objects of metal.

Shortly afterward he was surprised to see a white man clothed in chain mail and carrying a sword and buckler descending the trail at a trot, a dozen pike-men at his back.

"Tell them to halt!" commanded Tarzan, placing the point of the man's sword in the small of his back. "Tell them I would talk with them before they approach too closely."

"Stop, I pray thee!" cried the fellow. "This be a friend of Sir James, but he wilt run me through with my own sword an' ye press him too close. Parley with him, most noble sir knight, for I wouldst live at least to know the result of the Great Tourney."

The knight halted a few paces from Tarzan and looked him up and down from feet to head. "Thou art truly a friend to Sir James?" he demanded.

Tarzan nodded. "I have been seeking him for days."

"And some mishap befell thee and thou lost thy apparel."

The ape-man smiled. "I go thus, in the jungle," he said.

"Art thou a sir knight and from the same country as Sir James?"

"I am an Englishman," replied Tarzan of the Apes.

"An Englishman! Thrice welcome then to Nimmr! I be Sir Bertram and a good friend to Sir James."

"And I am called Tarzan," said the ape-man.

"And thy rank?" inquired Sir Bertram.

Tarzan was mystified by the strange manners and garb of his seemingly friendly inquisitor, but he sensed that whatever the man might be he took himself quite seriously and would be more impressed if he knew that Tarzan was a man of position, and so he answered him truthfully, in his quiet way.

"A Viscount," he said.

"A peer of the realm!" exclaimed Sir Bertram. "Prince Gobred wilt be o'er pleased to greet thee, Lord Tarzan. Come thou with me and I wilt furnish thee with apparel that befits thee."

At the outer barbican Bertram took Tarzan into the quarters reserved for the knight commanding the warders and kept him there while he sent his squire to the castle to fetch raiment and a horse, and while they waited Bertram told Tarzan all that had befallen Blake since his arrival in Nimmr and, too, much of the strange history of this unknown British colony.

When the squire returned with the clothing it was found that it fitted the ape-man well, for Bertram was a large man, and presently Tarzan of the Apes was garbed as a Knight of Nimmr and was riding down toward the castle with Sir Bertram. Here the knight announced him at the gate as the Lord Viscount Tarzan. Once within he introduced him to another knight whom he persuaded to relieve him at the gate while he conducted Tarzan to the lists that he might be presented to Gobred and witness the final scenes of the tourney, were it not concluded before they arrived.

And so it was that Tarzan of the Apes, clad in chain mail, and armed with lance and sword, rode down into the Valley of the Sepulcher just as Bohun put his foul scheme into execution and carried off the Princess Guinalda.

Long before they reached the lists Bertram was aware that something was amiss, for they could see the dust clouds racing rapidly north away from the lists as though one body of knights pursued another. He put spurs to his mount and Tarzan followed suit, and so they came at a stiff run to the lists and there they found all pandemonium.

The women were mounting preparatory to riding back to Nimmr under escort of a few knights that Gobred had sent back to guard them. The men-at-arms were forming themselves into companies, but all was being done in a confused manner since every now and then a great part of the company would rush to the highest part of the stands and peer off toward the north after the clouds of dust that revealed nothing to them.

Sir Bertram accosted one of his fellows. "What hath befallen?" he demanded.

"Bohun hath seized the Princess Guinalda and carried her away," came the astounding reply.

"Zounds!" cried Bertram, reining about. "Wilt ride with me in the service of our princess, Lord Tarzan?"

For answer Tarzan spurred his horse alongside of Bertram's and stirrup to stirrup the two set out across the plain, while far ahead of them Blake drew gradually closer and closer to the fleeing Knights of the Sepulcher. So thick was the cloud of dust they threw up that they were hid from their pursuer even as he was hid from them and so were unaware that Blake was near them.

The American carried no lance nor shield, but his sword clattered and clashed at his side and at his right hip swung his forty-five. Whenever he had been armed, since he entered

Nimmr, he had carried this weapon of another world and another age. To their queries he had answered that it was but a lucky talisman that he carried, but in his heart was the thought that some day it might stand him in better stead than these simple knights and ladies could dream.

He drew that he would never use it except in battle, or as a last resort against overwhelming odds or unfair tactics, but he was glad that he carried it today as it might mean the difference between liberty and captivity for the woman he loved.

Slowly he drew closer to the rearmost Knights of the Sepulcher. Their mounts bred and trained to the utmost endurance and to carry the great weight of man and mail kept to a brisk canter even after the first long spurt of speed that had carried them away from the lists of Nimmr.

The dust rolled up in clouds from iron-shod feet. Through it Blake groped, catching vague glimpses of mounted men just ahead. The black, powerful, fleet, courageous, showed no sign of fatigue. The rider carried his sword in his hand, ready. He was no longer a black knight, but a gray. Bassinet, hauberk, all the rich caparisons of his horse, the horse itself, were gray with dust.

Blake glimpsed a knight toward whom he was slowly drawing closer. This knight was gray! Like a flash Blake realized the value of the camouflage that chance had laid upon him. He might ride among them and they would not suspect that he was not of them!

Instantly he sheathed his sword and pressed forward, but he edged off a little from the knight before he passed him. Urging the black ever a little faster Blake crept up through the ranks of Bohun's knights. Somewhere a knight was carrying double and this knight he sought.

The nearer the head of the column he forged the greater became the danger of discovery, for now the dust was less thick and men could see farther, but yet his own armor, his face, the leopard skin of his bassinet were coated thick with gray and though knights peered intently at him as he passed none recognized him.

Once one hailed him. "Is't thou, Percival?" he demanded.

"Nay," replied Blake and spurred on a trifle faster.

Now, dimly, just ahead, he saw several knights bunched close and once he thought he glimpsed the fluttering garments of a woman in their midst. Pressing on, he drew close behind these and there, surrounded by knights, he saw a woman held before one of the riders.

Drawing his sword he spurred straight between two knights

who rode close behind he who carried Guinalda, and as Blake passed he cut to the right and left and the two knights rolled from their saddles.

At a touch of the spurs the black leaped abreast the young knight that was bearing off the princess. So quickly was the thing accomplished that the knights who rode scarce an arm's length from him had not the time to realize what was occurring and prevent it.

Blake slipped his left arm about the girl and at the same time thrust to the left above his left forearm, driving his blade far into the body of the youthful knight. Then he spurred forward carrying Guinalda from the dead arms as the knight pitched headlong from his saddle.

Blake's sword was wrenched from his grasp, so far had he driven it into the body of the man who dared commit this wrong against the woman Blake loved.

Cries of rage arose about him as knights spurred in pursuit and the black ran free with no guiding hand upon the reins. A huge fellow loomed just at Blake's rear and another was closing in from the other side. The first man swung his sword as he stood in his stirrups and the second was already reaching for Blake with his point.

Strange oaths were on their lips and their countenances were contorted by rage as they strove to have the life of the rash man who had almost thwarted them in their design, but that he could succeed they had not the remotest belief, for he was one against a thousand.

Then something happened the like of which had never been known to them or their progenitors. A blue barreled forty-five flashed from the holster at Blake's hip, there was a loud report and the knight upon Blake's right rear lunged head foremost to the ground. Blake turned in his saddle and shot the knight upon his other side between the eyes.

Terrified, the horses of other knights close by, who might have menaced him, bolted, as did the great black that Blake bestrode; but while the American was trying to replace his weapon in its holster and gather the reins in his right hand he leaned to the left and thus forced the horse slowly around toward the direction he wished him to go, Blake's plan being to cut across the front of the Knights of the Sepulcher and then turn southward toward Nimmr.

He was sure that Gobred and his followers must be close in pursuit, and that it would be but a matter of minutes before he would have Guinalda safe behind a thousand or more knights, any one of whom would lay down his life for her.

But the Knights of the Sepulcher had spread out over a greater front than Blake had anticipated, and now he saw them coming rapidly upon his left and was forced to swerve in a more northerly direction.

Closer and closer they came and once more the American found it necessary to drop his reins and draw his forty-five. One shot sent the horses of the menacing knights rearing and plunging away from the terrifying sound, and it sent the black into a new paroxysm of terror that almost resulted in Blake and the girl being unhorsed.

When the man finally brought the animal again under control the dust cloud that marked the position of the Knights of the Sepulcher was far behind, and close upon Blake's left was a great forest, whose dark depths offered concealment for the moment at least.

Reining quickly within Sir James drew up and gently lowered Guinalda to the ground. Then he dismounted and tied the black to a tree, for Blake was spent after what he had been through this day since his first entry upon the lists, and the black was spent as well.

He slipped the housing and the heavy saddle from the horse's back and took the great bit from his mouth, replacing a portion of the housing to serve as a cooler until the horse should be less heated, nor once did he glance at the princess until he had finished caring for his horse.

Then he turned and faced her. She was standing leaning against a tree, looking at him.

"Thou art brave, sir knight," she said softly, and then added, arrogantly, "but still a boor."

Blake smiled, wanly. He was very tired and had no wish to argue.

"I'm sorry to ask you to do it," he said, ignoring what she had said to him, "but Sir Galahad here will have to be kept moving about a bit until he cools off and I'm too fagged to do it."

The Princess Guinalda looked at him in wide-eyed amazement. "Ye—ye," she stammered, "ye mean that I should lead the beast? I, a princess!"

"I can't do it, Guinalda," replied Blake. "I tell you I'm just about all in, lugging all these skid chains about since sunrise. I guess you'll have to do it."

"Have to! Durst thou command, knave?"

"Snap out if it girl!" advised Blake curtly. "I'm responsible for your safety and it may all depend on this horse. Get busy, and do as I tell you! Lead him back and forth slowly."

There were tears of rage in the eyes of the Princess Guinalda as she prepared to make an angry retort, but there was something in Blake's eyes that silenced her. She looked at him for a long moment and then turned and walked to the black. Untying the rope that tethered him to the tree she led him slowly to and fro, while Blake sat with his back against a great tree and watched out across the plain for the first sign of pursuit.

But there was no pursuit, for the knights of Nimmr had taken the Knights of the Sepulcher and the two forces were engaging in a running fight that was leading them farther and farther away toward the City of the Sepulcher upon the north side of the valley.

Guinalda led the black for half an hour. She led him in silence and in silence Blake sat gazing out across the valley. Presently he turned toward the girl and rose to his feet.

"That'll be good," he said, approaching her. "Thank you. I'll rub him a bit now. I was too exhausted to do it before."

Without a word she turned the black over to him and with dry leaves he rubbed the animal from muzzle to dock. When he had finished he threw the housing over him again and came and sat down beside the girl.

He let his eyes wander to her profile—to her straight nose, her short upper lip, her haughty chin. "She is beautiful," thought Blake, "but selfish, arrogant and cruel." But when she turned her eyes toward him, even though they passed over him as though he had not been there, they seemed to belie all the other evidence against her.

He noticed that her eyes were never quiet. Her glances roved from place to place, but most often into the depths of the wood and upward among the branches of the trees. Once she started and turned suddenly to gaze intently into the forest.

"What is it?" asked Blake.

"Methought something moved within the wood," she said. "Let us be gone."

"It is almost dusk," he replied. "When it is dark we can ride to Nimmr in safety. Some of Bohun's knights may still be searching for you."

"What!" she exclaimed. "Remain here until dark? Knowest thou not where we be?"

"Why, what's wrong with this place?" demanded the man.

She leaned toward him, her eyes wide with terror. "It be the Wood of the Leopards!" she whispered.

"Yes?" he queried casually.

"Here lair the great leopards of Nimmr," she continued, "and after night falls only a camp with many guards and beast fires be safe from them. And even so not always then, for they have been known to leap upon a warder and, dragging him into the wood, devour him within hearing of the camp.

"But," suddenly her eyes responded to a new thought, "I hadst forgot the strange, roaring weapon with which thou slew the knights of Bohun! Of a surety with that thou couldst slay all the leopards of the wood!"

Blake hesitated to undeceive her and add to her alarm. "Perhaps," he said, "it will be as well to start now, for we have a long ride and it will soon be dark."

As he spoke he started toward Sir Galahad. He had almost reached the horse when the animal suddenly raised its head and with up pricked ears and dilated nostrils looked into the gathering shadows of the wood. For an instant Sir Galahad trembled like a leaf and then, with a wild snort, he lay back with all his weight upon the tether, and as it parted with a snap he wheeled and raced out upon the plain.

Blake drew his gun and peered into the wood, but he saw nothing nor could his atrophied sense of smell catch the scent that had come so clearly to the nostrils of Sir Galahad.

Eyes that he could not see were watching him, but they were not the eyes of Sheeta the leopard.

20

"I Love You!"

LORD TARZAN rode with Sir Bertram in the wake of the Knights of Nimmr, nor did they overtake them until after Blake had borne Guinalda out of the battle which had followed immediately the hosts of Gobred had overhauled the Knights of the Sepulcher.

As the two approached, Tarzan saw opposing knights paired off in mortal combat. He saw a Knight of Nimmr go down before an adversary's lance and then the victor espied Tarzan.

"Have at you, sir knight!" cried he of the Sepulcher, and couched his lance and put spurs to his charger.

This was a new experience for the ape-man, a new adventure, a new thrill. He knew as much about jousting as he did about ping-pong, but from childhood he had wielded a spear, and so he smiled as the knight charged upon him.

Lord Tarzan waited, and the Knight of the Sepulcher was disconcerted to see his adversary awaiting him, motionless, his spear not even couched to receive him.

Lord Bertram had reined in his horse to watch the combat and observe how this English peer accounted for himself in battle and he too was perplexed. Was the man mad, or was he fearful of the issue?

As his antagonist approached him, Tarzan rose in his stirrups and carried his lance hand above and behind his head, and when the tip of the other's lance was yet five paces from him the ape-man launched the heavy weapon as he had so often launched his hunting spear and his war spear in the chase and in battle.

It was not Viscount Greystoke who faced the Knight of the Sepulcher; it was not the king of the great apes. It was the chief of the Waziri, and no other arm in the world could cast a war spear as could his.

Forward his spear hand shot, straight as an arrow sped the great lance. It struck the shield of the Knight of the Sepulcher just above the boss and, splitting the heavy wood, drove into the heart of Tarzan's fore, and at the same instant the ape-man reined his horse aside as that of his fallen antagonist thundered past.

Sir Bertram shook his head and spurred to meet an antagonist that had just challenged him. He was not sure that the act of Lord Tarzan had been entirely ethical, but he had to admit that it had been magnificent.

The fortunes of the battle carried Tarzan toward the west. His lance gone, he fought with his sword. Luck and his great strength and wondrous agility carried him through two encounters. By this time the battle had drawn off toward the northeast.

Tarzan had accounted for his second man since he had lost his lance and a Knight of the Sepulcher had slain a Knight of Nimmr. Now these two remained alone upon the field, nor did the other lose a moment in shouting his challenge to the ape-man.

Never in his life had Tarzan seen such fierce, bold men, such gluttons for battle. That they gloried in conflict and in death with a fierce lust that surpassed the maddest fanaticism he had ever witnessed filled Tarzan's breast with admiration. What men! What warriors!

Now the last knight was upon him. Their swords clashed on ready buckler. They wheeled and turned and struck again. They passed and spurred once more to close quarters. Each rose in his stirrups to deliver a terrified cut, each sought to cleave the other's skull.

The blade of the Knight of the Sepulcher glanced from Tarzan's buckler and bit into the skull of the ape-man's charger, but Tarzan's edge smote true.

As his horse went down Tarzan leaped free, his antagonist falling dead at his feet, while the riderless horse of the slain knight galloped swiftly off in the direction in which lay the City of the Sepulcher.

Tarzan looked about him. He was alone upon the field. Far to the north and east he saw the dust of battle. The City of Nimmr lay across the plain toward the south. When the battle was over it was there that Blake would ride and it was Blake whom Tarzan wanted to find. The sun was sinking behind the western hills as Tarzan turned toward Nimmr.

The chain mail that he wore was heavy, hot and uncomfortable, and Tarzan had not gone far before he discarded it. He had his knife and his rope. These he always kept with him, but he left the sword with the armor and with a sigh of relief continued on his way.

Ibn Jad, as he had come across the valley from the City of the Sepulcher toward the city that he had seen upon the opposite side, had been perturbed by the great clouds of dust that had been raised by the Knights of the Sepulcher and the pursuing Nimmrians.

Seeing a forest close upon his right hand he had thought it wiser to seek its concealing shadows until he could learn more concerning that which caused so great a dust cloud, which he saw was rapidly approaching.

Within the forest it was cool and here Ibn Jad and his followers rested.

"Let us remain here," suggested Abd el-Aziz, "until evening, when we may approach the city under cover of darkness."

Ibn Jad approved the plan and so they camped just within the forest and waited. They watched the dust cloud pass and continue on toward the City of the Sepulcher.

"Billah, it is well we did escape that village before yon host returned," said Ibn Jad.

They saw a horseman enter the forest, or pass to the south of it—they could not know which—but they were not interested in single horsemen, or in any horseman, so they did not investigate. He seemed to be either carrying another person upon his horse with him, or some great bundle. At a distance they could not see which.

"Perhaps," said Abd el-Aziz, "we shall find greater treasure in the city to the south."

"And perhaps the beautiful woman of whom the sahar spoke," added Ibn Jad, "for she was not within the city we left this morning."

"There were some there that were beautiful," said Fahd.

"The one I seek is more beautiful than an houri," said Ibn Jad.

When they took up their march again just before dark they moved cautiously just within the edge of the forest. They had covered a mile, perhaps, when those in the lead heard voices ahead. Ibn Jad sent one to investigate.

The man was soon back. His eyes were bright with excitement. "Ibn Jad," he whispered, "thou needst seek no farther—the houri is just ahead!"

Following the suggestion of the scout Ibn Jad, followed by his companions, went deeper into the woods and approached Blake and Guinalda from the west. When Sir Galahad broke loose and Blake drew his forty-five Ibn Jad knew that they could remain in concealment no longer. He called Fahd to him.

"Many of the Nasranys speak the language thou didst learn among the soldiers of the North," he said. "Speak thou therefore to this one in the same tongue, telling him we are friends and that we are lost."

When Fahd saw the Princess Guinalda his eyes narrowed and he trembled almost as might a man with ague. Never in his life had Fahd seen so beautiful a woman, never had he dreamed that an houri might be so lovely.

"Do not fire upon us," he called to Blake from the concealment of some bushes. "We are friends. We are lost."

"Who are you?" demanded Blake, surprised to hear French spoken in the Valley of the Sepulcher.

"We be poor men from the desert country," replied Fahd. "We are lost. Help us to find our way and the blessings of Allah shall be upon thee."

"Come out and let me see you," said Blake. "If you are friendly you need not fear me. I've had all the trouble I'm looking for."

Fahd and Ibn Jad stepped out into view and at sight of them Guinalda voiced a little scream and seized Blake's arm. "The Saracens!" she gasped.

"I guess they're Saracens all right," said Blake, "but you needn't worry—they won't hurt you."

"Not harm a crusader?" she demanded incredulously.

"These fellows never heard of a crusader."

"Melikes not the way they look at me," whispered Guinalda.

"Well, neither do I, but perhaps they mean no harm."

With many smiles the Arabs gathered around the two and through Fahd Ibn Jad repeated his protestations of friendship and his delight at meeting one who could direct him from the valley. He asked many questions about the City of Nimmr; and all the while his followers pressed closer to Blake.

Of a sudden the smiles vanished from their faces as, at a signal from their sheik, four stalwart Beduins leaped upon the American and bore him to the ground, snatching his gun from him, while simultaneously two others seized the Princess Guinalda.

In a moment Blake was securely bound and the 'Aarab were debating what disposition to make of him. Several wanted to slit his throat, but Ibn Jad counseled against it since they were in a valley filled with the man's friends and should the fortunes of war decide to throw some of the Beduins into the hands of the enemy such would fare better if they spared this one's life.

Blake threatened, promised, begged that they give Guinalda

her liberty, but Fahd only laughed at him and spit upon him. For a time it seemed almost certain that they were going to kill Blake, as one of the Beduins stood over him with a keen khusa in his hand, awaiting the word from Ibn Jad.

It was then that Guinalda tore free from those who held her and threw herself upon Blake to shield his body from the blade with her own.

"Thou shalt not slay him!" she cried. "Take my life an' thou must have Christian blood, but spare him."

"They cannot understand you, Guinalda," said Blake. "Perhaps they will not kill me, but that does not matter. You must escape them."

"Oh, they must not kill thee—they shall not! Canst ever forgive me the cruel words I spoke? I did not mean them. My pride was hurt that thou shouldst say of me what Malud told me thou didst say and so I spoke to hurt thee and not from my heart. Canst forgive me?"

"Forgive you? God love you, I could forgive you murder! But what did Malud tell you I had said?"

"Oh, mind not now. I care not what thou said. I tell thee I forgive it! Say to me again thy words that thou didst speak when I pinned my favor upon thy hauberk and I can forgive thee anything."

"What did Malud say?" insisted Blake.

"That thou hadst bragged that thou wouldst win me and then cast my love aside," she whispered.

"The cur! You must know that he lied, Guinalda."

"Say what I have asked and I shall know he lied," she insisted.

"I love you! I love you, Guinalda!" cried Blake.

The Arabs laid heavy hands upon the girl and dragged her to her feet. Ibn Jad and the others still argued about the disposition to be made of Blake.

"By Ullah!" exclaimed the sheik, at last, "we shall leave the Nasrany where he lies and if he dies none can say that the Beduw did slay him.

"Abd el-Aziz," he continued, "let thou take men and continue across the valley to that other city. Come, I shall accompany you a way and we will talk out of hearing of this Nasrany who, perchance, understandeth more of our tongue than he would have us guess."

As they moved away toward the south Guinalda tried to free herself again from the grasp of her captors, but they dragged her with them. Until the last Blake saw her struggling and saw her dear face turned toward him, and as they passed out of sight among the trees she called back through the falling night three words that meant more to him than all the languages of all the world combined: "I love you!"

At a distance from Blake the 'Aarab halted. "I leave thee here, Abd el-Aziz," said Ibn Jad. "Go thou and see if the city appears to be a rich place, and if it be too strongly guarded make no attempt to loot it, but return to the menzil that will be just beyond the northern summit where it now is, or, if we move it, we shall make our trail plain that you may follow us.

"I shall hasten from the valley with this rich treasure that we now have, not the least of which is the woman. Billah! in the north she will fetch the ransom of a dozen sheykh.

"Go, Abd el-Aziz, and may Allah be with thee!"

Ibn Jad turned directly north. His belief that the great body of horsemen he had glimpsed amid the distant dust were returning to the city he had sacked argued against his attempting to leave the valley by the same route that he had entered it, and so he had determined to attempt to scale the steep mountains at a point west of the City of the Sepulcher, avoiding the castle and its defenders entirely.

Blake heard the retreating footsteps of the Beduins die away in the distance. He struggled with his bonds, but the camel leather held securely. Then he lay quiet. How silent, how lonely the great, black wood—the Wood of the Leopards! Blake listened. Momentarily he expected to hear the fall of padded feet, the sound of a great, furred body approaching through the underbrush. The slow minutes dragged. An hour had passed.

The moon rose—a great, swollen, red moon that floated silently up from behind distant mountains. This moon was looking down upon Guinalda as it was on him. He whispered a message to it—a message for his princess. It was the first time that Blake ever had been in love and he almost forgot his bonds and the leopards in recalling those three words that Guinalda had called back at the instant of their separation.

What was that? Blake strained his eyes into the darkness of the shadowy wood. Something was moving! Yes, it was the sound of stealthy, padded feet—the scraping of a furred body against leaves and twigs. The leopard of the wood was coming!

Hark! There must be another in a nearby tree, for he was sure that he could see a shadowy form almost above him.

The moonlight, shining from the low moon near the eastern horizon, crept beneath the trees and lighted the ground upon which Blake lay and beyond him for a dozen yards and more. Presently into this moonlit space stepped a great leopard.

Blake saw the blazing eyes, felt them burning into him like fire. He could not tear his own from the great snarling figure, where they were held in awful fascination.

The carnivore crouched and crept closer. Inch by inch it crept upon him as though with the studied cruelty of premeditated torture. He saw the sinuous tail lashing from side to side. He saw the great fangs bared. He saw the beast flatten against the ground, its muscles tensed. It was about to spring! Helpless, horrified, Blake could not take his eyes from the hideous, snarling face.

He saw it leap suddenly with the lightness and agility of a house cat, and at the same instant he saw something flash through the air. The leopard stopped in mid-leap and was hauled upward into a tree that overhung the spot.

He saw the shadowy form that he had seen before, but now he saw that it was a man and that he was hauling the leopard upward by a rope that had been cast about its neck at the instant that it had risen to leap upon him.

Screaming, pawing with raking talons, Sheeta the leopard was dragged upward. A mighty hand reached out and grasped the great cat by the scruff of the neck and another hand drove a knife blade into the savage heart.

When Sheeta ceased to struggle, and hung quiet, the hand released its grasp and the dead body of the carnivore thudded to the ground beside Blake. Then the god-like figure of an almost naked white man dropped lightly to the leafy mold.

Blake voiced an exclamation of surprised delight. "Tarzan of the Apes!" he cried.

"Blake?" demanded the ape-man, and then: "At last! And I didn't find you much too soon, either."

"I'll tell the world you didn't!" exclaimed Blake.

Tarzan cut the bonds that held the American.

"You've been looking for me?" asked Blake.

"Ever since I learned that you had become separated from your safari."

"By George, that was white of you!"

"Who left you trussed up here?"

"A bunch of Arabs."

Something like a growl escaped the lips of the ape-man. "That villainous old Ibn Jad here?" he demanded incredulously.

"They took a girl who was with me," said Blake. "I do not need to ask you to help me rescue her, I know."

"Which way did they go?" asked Tarzan.

"There." Blake pointed toward the south.

"When?"

"About an hour ago."

"You'd better shed that armor," advised Tarzan, "it makes walking a punishment—I just tried it."

With the ape-man's help Blake got out of his coat of mail and then the two set out upon the plain trail of the Arabs. At the point where Ibn Jad had turned back toward the north they were at a loss to know which of the two spoors to follow, for here the footprints of Guinalda, that the ape-man had been able to pick up from time to time since they left the spot where the girl had been seized, disappeared entirely.

They wondered what had become of them. They could not know that here, when she found that Ibn Jad was going to turn back with her away from Nimmr, she had refused to walk farther. It had been all right as long as they were approaching Nimmr, but she refused absolutely to be a party to her own abduction when it led away from home.

What breeze there was was blowing from the east, nullifying the value of Tarzan's sense of smell so that even the great ape-man could not know in what direction or with which party Guinalda had been carried off.

"The most reasonable assumption," said Tarzan, "is that your princess is with the party that has gone north, for I know that Ibn Jad's menzil must lay in that direction. He did not enter the valley from the south. That I know because I just came in that way myself and Sir Bertram assured me that there are only two entrances—the one through which I came and a pass above the City of the Sepulcher.

"Ibn Jad would want to get the girl out of the valley and into his camp as soon as possible whether he is going to hold her for ransom or take her north to sell her. The party that went south toward Nimmr may have been sent to treat with her people for a ransom; but the chances are that she is not with that party.

"However, it is at best but a matter of conjecture. We must ascertain definitely, and I suggest that you follow the northern spoor, which is, I am certain, the one that will lead to the girl, while I overtake the party to the south.

"I can travel faster than you and if I am right and the girl is with the northern party I'll turn back and overtake you without much loss of time. If you catch up with the other band and find the girl is not with them, you can turn back and join me; but if she is with them you'd better not risk trying to recover her until you have help, for you are unarmed and those Beduins would think no more of cutting your throat than they would of drinking a cup of coffee.

"Now, good-bye and good luck!" And Tarzan of the Apes was off at a trot upon the trail of the party that had gone in the direction of Nimmr, while Blake turned northward to face a dismal journey through the black depths of the Wood of the Leopards.

21

"For Every Jewel a Drop of Blood!"

A LL night Ibn Jad and his party marched northward. Though they were hampered by the refusal of Guinalda to walk, yet they made rapid progress for they were spurred on by their great desire to escape from the valley with their booty before they should be discovered and set upon by the great host of fighting men they were now convinced were quartered in the castle and city they had been fortunate enough to find almost deserted.

Avarice gave them strength and endurance far beyond that which they normally displayed, with the result that dawn found them at the foot of the ragged mountains that Ibn Jad had determined to scale rather than attempt an assault upon the castle which guarded the easy way from the valley.

It was a jaded party that won eventually to the pass just above the outer barbican that guarded the road to the City of the Sepulcher, nor were they discovered by the warders there until the last man of them was safely on the trail leading to the low saddle at the summit of the mountains, beyond which lay the menzil of the Beduins.

The defenders of the barbican made a sortie against them and approached their rear so closely that the knight who commanded saw Guinalda and recognized her, but a volley from the matchlocks of the desert people sent the crudely armed soldiers of Bohun back in retreat, though the brave knight couched his lance and charged again until his hosse was brought down by a bullet and he lay pinned beneath it.

It was afternoon before Ibn Jad with his fagged company staggered into the menzil. Though they dropped in their tracks from sheer exhaustion, he allowed them but an hour of sleep before he gave the signal for the rahla, for the sheik of the fendy el-Guad was filled with an ever increasing fear that the treasure and the woman would be taken away from him before he could reach the sandy wastes of his own barren beled.

The heavy weight of the treasure had been divided into several bundles and these were distributed among his least mistrusted followers, while the custody of the girl captive was placed in the hands of Fahd, whose evil eyes filled the princess with fear and loathing.

Stimbol, who had secretly scoffed at the stories of treasure and the mad tales of a beautiful woman that the 'Aarab expected to find in some fabulous, hidden city, was dumbfounded when he viewed the spoils of the Beduin, and at first was inclined to attribute them to the hallucinations of his fever-racked brain.

Weak, Stimbol staggered feebly along the trail, keeping as close to Fahd as he could, for he knew that of all the company this unscrupulous scoundrel would be most likely to assist him, for to Fahd a live Stimbol meant great wealth; nor was Fahd unmindful of the fact. And now there was another purpose in the evil mind of the Beduin who had conceived for the white girl an infatuation that was driving him to the verge of madness.

With the wealth that Stimbol had promised him Fahd realized that he could afford to possess this lovely houri whom otherwise a poor Beduwy must sell for the great price that she would bring, and so there revolved in the mind of Fahd many schemes whereby he might hope to gain sole possession of both Guinalda and Stimbol; but always there loomed in the path of every plan that he considered the dour figure of his greedy sheykh.

At the foot of the Mountains of the Sepulcher Ibn Jad turned toward the east, thus to avoid passing again through the country of Batando. Beyond the eastern end of the range he would turn south again and later strike west just above the northern limits of the territory that was nominally Tarzan's, for though he knew that the Lord of the Jungle was dead he yet feared the vengeance of his people.

It was late before Ibn Jad made camp. The preparations for the evening meal were hurried. The light from the cooking fire and the paper lanterns in the beyt of the sheik was dim and flickering, yet not so dim but that Ateja saw Fahd drop something into the bowl of food that she had prepared for Ibn Jad and which stood upon the ground between him and his would-be assassin.

As the shiek reached for the receptacle Ateja stepped from the women's quarters and struck it from his hand, but before she could explain her act or charge Fahd with his villainy the culprit, realizing that his perfidy had been discovered, leaped to his feet and seizing his matchlock sprang into the women's quarters where Guinalda had been left under the watchful care of Hirfa and Ateja.

Seizing the girl by the wrist and dragging her after him Fahd broke through the curtains at the rear of the beyt and ran in the direction of his own tent. By this time the mukaad of Ibn Jad was in an uproar. The sheik was demanding an explanation from Ateja and still unaware that Fahd had escaped through the rear of the beyt no one had followed him into the women's quarters.

"He placed *simm* in thy food!" cried Ateja. "I saw him and the proof of it be that he fled when he knew that I had seen."

"Billah," exclaimed Ibn Jad. "The son of a jackal would poison me? Seize him and fetch him to me!"

"He hath fled through the beyt!" cried Hirfa, "and taken the Nasrawia with him."

The Beduins sprang to their feet and took after Fahd, but at his own beyt he stopped them with a bullet and they retreated. In his tent he seized Stimbol who was lying upon a filthy sleeping mat and dragged him to his feet.

"Hasten!" he hissed in the American's ear. "Ibn Jad has ordered that thou be slain! Quick! follow me and I will save thee."

Again Fahd had recourse to the rear curtains of a beyt and as his fellows approached the front in anger but with caution, Fahd, dragging Guinalda and followed by Stimbol, sneaked through the darkness of the menzil and turned toward the west.

It was dusk when James Blake, following the plain trail of Ibn Jad, finally clambered over the last escarpment and stood upon the trail that led through the pass toward the outer world beyond the valley of the Sepulcher.

A hundred yards to his right loomed the gray towers of the barbican, to his left was the trail that led in the direction of his heart's desire, and all about him, concealed in the bushes, were the men-at-arms of King Bohun of the Sepulcher; but this he did not guess, for how could he know that for hours the eyes of the warders had been watching his slow ascent toward the pass trail?

Spent by the long climb following hours of gruelling exertion without food or rest, unarmed, Blake was helpless to resist or to attempt escape when a dozen armed men stepped from the surrounding bushes and encircled him in a band of steel. And so Sir James of Nimmr was seized and haled before King Bohun, and when he was questioned and Bohun found that he was the same black knight that had thwarted his plan to abduct the Princess Guinalda he could scarce contain himself.

Assuring Blake only of the fact that he would be put to death as soon as Bohun could determine upon a fate commensurate with the heinousness of the crime, the king ordered him to be placed in chains, and the American was led away by guards to a black hole beneath the castle, where by the light of flares a smith forged a heavy iron band about one ankle and he was chained to a damp stone wall.

In the light of the flare Blake saw two emaciated, naked creatures similarly chained, and in a far corner glimpsed a skeleton among the bones of which rusted a length of chain and a great anklet. Then silently the guards and the smith departed, taking the flares with them, and James Blake was left in darkness and despair.

Upon the plain, below the City of Nimmr, Tarzan had overtaken the party of Beduins led by Abd el-Aziz, and after assuring himself that the girl was not with them he had turned without revealing himself to them and hurried northward to take up the trail of the other party.

Requiring food and rest he lay up in the Wood of the Leopards during the heat of the day after stalking Horta the boar and making a quick kill. His belly filled, the ape-man found a high flung tree crotch where there was little likelihood of the heavy leopards of Nimmr disturbing his slumbers, and here he slept until the sun was sinking behind the western menzil where Ibn Jad's people had camped during his incursion of the Valley of the Sepulcher.

Some time since, he had lost the spoor of Blake, but that of the girl frequently recurred, and as her rescue now took precedence over other considerations he followed doggedly along the trail of Ibn Jad. For a time he was mystified by the fact that Guinalda's spoor, well marked by the imprints of the tiny sandals of medieval design, did not appear among the footprints of those who left the Beduin menzil.

He lost some time searching about in an effort to discover a clew to the riddle and presently he hit upon the truth, which lay in the fact that Guinalda's light sandals having been badly worn by her journey and far too tight for comfortable walking she had been given a pair belonging to Ateja, and thus it became difficult to differentiate between the spoor of the two girls, who were of equal weight and of a similarity of carriage that rendered their footprints practically identical.

Tarzan therefore contented himself with following the spoor

of the party, and so it was that he passed their first night's camp, where Fahd had stolen Guinalda from the Sheik, without discovering that three of its members had there turned to the west, while the main body of the 'Aarab marched toward the east.

And as Tarzan followed the spoor of Ibn Jad a hundred stalwart Waziri moved northward from the water hole of the smooth, round rocks upon the old trail of the Beduins. With them was Zeyd, who had begged so hard to accompany them when they passed the village where he had been waiting that at last the sub-chief had consented.

When Tarzan overtook the 'Aarab they had already turned south around the eastern end of the Mountains of the Sepulcher. He saw the bags they carried and the evident concern with which Ibn Jad watched and guarded them, and he shrewdly guessed that the wily old thief had indeed found the treasure he had sought; but he saw no evidence of the presence of the Princess, and Stimbol, too, was missing.

Tarzan was furious. He was furious at the thieving Beduins for daring to invade his country and he was furious at himself because he felt that in some way he had been tricked.

Tarzan had his own methods of inflicting punishment upon his enemies and he had, as well, his own grim and grisly sense of humor. When men were doing wrong it pleased him to take advantage of whatever might cause them the greatest suffering and in this he was utterly ruthless with his enemies.

He was confident that the 'Aarab thought him dead and it did not suit his whim to reveal their error to them at this time, but it did accord with his fancy to let them commence to feel the weight of his displeasure and taste the first fruits of their villainy.

Moving silently through the trees Tarzan paralleled the course of the 'Aarab. They were often plainly visible to him; but none saw Tarzan, nor dreamed that savage eyes were watching their every move.

Five men carried the treasure, though its weight was not so great but that one powerful man might have borne it for a short distance. Tarzan watched these men most often, these and the Sheik Ibn Jad.

The trail was wide and the sheik walked beside one of those who bore the treasure. It was very quiet in the jungle. Even the 'Aarab, garrulous among themselves, were quiet, for they were very tired and the day was hot and they were unused to the burdens they were forced to carry since Batando had robbed them of their slaves.

Of a sudden, without warning and with only the swish of its flight through the air to announce it, an arrow passed through the neck of the Beduin who walked beside Ibn Jad.

With a scream the man lunged forward upon his face and the 'Aarab, warned by their sheik, cocked their muskets and prepared to receive an attack, but look where they would they saw no sign of an enemy. They waited, listening, but there was no sound other than the droning of insects and the occasional raucous cry of a bird; but when they moved on again, leaving their fellow dead upon the trail, a hollow voice called to them from a distance.

"For every jewel a drop of blood!" it wailed dismally, for its author knew well the intensely superstitious nature of the desert dwellers and how best to affright them.

It was a shaken column that continued on its way, nor was there any mention of making camp until almost sunset, so anxious were they all to leave behind this gloomy wood and the horrid afrit that inhabited it; but the forest persisted and at length it became necessary to make camp.

Here the camp fires and food relieved the tension upon their overwrought nerves, and their spirits had revived to such an extent that there were again singing and laughter in the menzil of Ibn Jad.

The old sheik himself sat in his mukaad surrounded by the five bags of treasure, one of which he had opened and beneath the light of a lantern was fondling the contents. About him were his cronies, sipping their coffee.

Suddenly something fell heavily upon the ground before the beyt and rolled into the mukaad among them. It was the severed head of a man! Glaring up at them were the dead eyes of their fellow, whose corpse they had left lying in the trail earlier in the day.

Horror struck, spellbound, they sat staring at the gruesome thing when, from out of the dark forest, came the hollow voice again: *"For every jewel a drop of blood!"*

Ibn Jad shook as a man with ague. The men of the camp gathered close together in front of the beyt of the sheik. Each grasped a musket in one hand and searched for his hijab with the other, for each carried several of these amulets, and that in demand this night was the one written against the jin, for certainly none but a jin could have done this thing.

Hirfa stood half within the mukaad staring at the dead face of her fellow while Ateja crouched upon a sleeping mat in the quarters of the women. She did not see the back curtain rise, nor the figure that crept within. It was dark in the quarters of the hareem since little light filtered in from the lanterns in the mukaad.

Ateja felt a hand clapped across her mouth at the same instant that another grasped her by the shoulder. A voice whispered in her ear. "Make no sound! I shall not hurt thee. I am a friend to Zeyd. Tell me the truth and no harm will befall you or him. Where is the woman Ibn Jad brought from the valley?"

He who held her placed his ear close to her lips and removed his hand from them. Ateja trembled like a leaf. She had never seen a jin. She could not see the creature that leaned close to her, but she knew that it was one of those fearsome creatures of the night.

"Answer!" whispered the voice in her ear. "If thou wouldst save Zeyd, speak and speak the truth!"

"Fahd took the woman from our menzil last night," she gasped. "I do not know where they went."

As it came, in silence the presence left the side of the terrified girl. When Hirfa sought her a moment later she found her in a swoon.

22

Bride of the Ape

BLAKE squatted upon the stone floor in the utter darkness of his dungeon. After his jailers had left he had spoken to his fellow prisoners, but only one had replied and his jibbering tones assured the American that the poor wretch had been reduced to stark insanity by the horrors of imprisonment in this foul hole.

The young man, accustomed to freedom, light, activity, already felt the hideousness of his position and wondered how long it would be before he, too, jibbered incoherently at the end of a rusting chain, how long before he, too, was but mildewed bones upon a clammy floor.

In utter darkness and in utter silence there is no time, for there is no means by which one may compute the passage of time. How long Blake crouched in the stifling air of his dank dungeon he could not know. He slept once, but whether he had dozed for an instant or slept the clock around he could not even hazard a guess. And of what moment was it? A second a day, a year meant nothing here. There were only two things that could mean anything to Jim Blake now—freedom or death. He knew that it would not be long before he would welcome the latter.

A sound disturbed the silence of the buried vault. Footsteps were approaching. Blake listened as they came nearer. Presently he discerned a flickering light that grew in intensity until a pine torch illuminated the interior of his prison. At first it blinded his eyes so that he could not see who came, bearing the light, but whoever it was crossed and stopped before him.

Blake looked up, his eyes more accustomed to the unwonted brilliance, and saw two knights standing before him.

"It be he," said one.

"Dost thou not know us, Sir Black Knight?" demanded the other.

Blake looked at them closely. A slow smile lighted his face, as he saw a great bandage wrapped about the neck of the younger man.

174

"I suppose," he said, "here is where I get mine."

"Get thine! What meanest thou?" demanded the older man.

"Well, you two certainly haven't come to pin any medals on me, Sir Wildred," said Blake, with a wry smile.

"Thou speakest in riddles," said Wildred. "We have come to free thee that the young king may not bring disgrace upon the Knights of the Sepulcher by carrying out his wicked will with thee. Sir Guy and I heard that he would burn thee at the stake, and we said to one another that while blood flowed in our bodies we would not let so valorous a knight be thus shamelessly wronged by any tyrant."

As he spoke Wildred stooped and with a great rasp commenced filing upon the iron rivets that held the hinged anklet in place.

"You are going to help me to escape!" exclaimed Blake. "But suppose you are discovered—will not the king punish you?"

"We shall not be discovered," said Wildred, "though I would take that chance for so noble a knight as thee. Sir Guy be upon the outer barbican this night and 'twill be no trick to get thee that far. He can pass thee through and thou canst make thy way down the mountain side and cross to Nimmr. We cannot get thee through the city gates for these be held by two of Bohun's basest creatures, but perchance upon the morrow Sir Guy or I may find the way to ride out upon the plain with a led horse, and that we shall if so it hap that it be possible."

"Tell us a thing that hath filled us with questioning," said Sir Guy.

"I don't follow you," said Blake.

"Thou didst, and mighty prettily too, take the Princess Guinalda from under the very nose of Bohun," continued Guy, "and yet later she was seen in the clutches of the Saracens. How came this to pass?"

"She was seen?" demanded Blake. "Where?"

"Beyond the outer barbican she was and the Saracens carried her away through the pass that leadeth no man knoweth where," said Wildred.

Blake told them of all that had transpired since he had taken Guinalda from Bohun, and by the time he had finished the rivets had been cut and he stood again a free man.

Wildred smuggled him through secret passages to his own quarters and there gave him food and new clothing and a suit of armor, for now that they knew he was riding out over the pass into the strange country they had decided that he could only be permitted to do so properly armored, armed and mounted.

It was midnight when Wildred smuggled Blake through the castle gate and rode with him toward the outer barbican. Here Sir Guy met them and a few minutes later Blake bid these chivalrous enemies good-bye and, mounted on a powerful charger, his own colors flying from his lance tip, rode beneath the portcullis and out upon the starlit road that led to the summit of the Mountains of the Sepulcher.

Toyat, the king ape, picked a succulent beetle from the decaying bark of a fallen tree. About him were the great, savage people of his tribe. It was afternoon and the apes loafed in the shade of great trees beside a little natural clearing in the jungle. They were content and at peace with all the world.

Coming toward them were three people, but the wind blew from the apes toward the people and so neither Toyat nor any of his fellows caught the scent spoor of the Tarmangani. The jungle trail was soft with damp mold, for it had rained the night before, and the feet of the three gave forth no sound that the apes heard. Then, too, the three were moving cautiously for they had not eaten for two days and they were hunting for food.

There was a gray old man, emaciated by fever, tottering along with the aid of a broken tree branch; there was a wicked-eyed Beduin carrying a long musket; and the third was a girl whose strange garments of splendid stuffs were torn and soiled. Her face was streaked with dirt and was drawn and thin, yet still it was a face of almost heavenly beauty. She walked with an effort, and though she sometimes stumbled from weariness never did she lose a certain regalness of carriage, nor lower the haughty elevation of her well moulded chin.

The Beduin was in the lead. It was he who first sighted a young ape playing at the edge of the clearing, farthest from the great bulls of the tribe of Toyat. Here was food! The Beduin raised his ancient weapon and took aim. He pressed the trigger and the ensuing roar mingled with the scream of pain and terror that burst from the wounded balu.

Instantly the great bulls leaped to action. Would they flee the feared and hated thunder stick of the Tarmangani, or would they avenge the hurting of the balu? Who might know? Today they might do the one, tomorrow, under identical circumstances, the other. Today they chose vengeance.

Led by Toyat, growling hideously, the bulls lumbered forward to investigate. It was this sight that met the horrified gaze of the three as they followed up Fahd's shot to learn if at last they were to eat or if they must plod on hopelessly, weakened by the hunger gnawing at their vitals.

Fahd and Stimbol turned and bolted back down the trail, the Arab, in his cowardly haste, pushing Guinalda to one side and hurling her to the ground. The leading bull, seeing the girl, leaped upon her and was about to sink his teeth into her neck when Toyat seized him and dragged him from her, for Toyat had recognized her for what she was. The king ape had once seen another Tarmangani she and had decided that he would like to have one as a wife.

The other ape, a huge bull, seeing that Toyat wanted the prey and angered by the bullying manner of the king, immediately decided to contest Toyat's right to what he had first claimed. Baring his fangs he advanced menacingly toward Toyat who had dragged the girl back into the clearing.

Toyat snarled back at him. "Go away," said Toyat. "This is Toyat's she."

"It is Go-yad's," replied the other, advancing.

Toyat turned back. "I kill!" he screamed.

Go-yad came on and suddenly Toyat seized Guinalda in his hairy arms and fled into the jungle. Behind him, bellowing and screaming, pursued Go-yad.

The Princess Guinalda, wide-eyed with horror, fought to free herself from the hideous, hairy creature that was bearing her off. She had never seen nor even heard of such a thing as a great ape, and she thought them now some hideous, low inhabitant of that outer world that she had always been taught consisted of encircling armies of Saracens and beyond and at a great distance a wonderful country known as England. What else was there she had not even tried to guess, but evidently it was a horrid place peopled by hideous creatures, including dragons.

Toyat had run no great distance when he realized that he could not escape while burdened with the she, and as he had no mind to give her up he turned suddenly and faced the roaring Go-yad. Go-yad did not stop. He came on frothing at the mouth, bristling, snarling—a picture of bestial savagery, power and frenzied rage.

Toyat, relinquishing his hold upon the girl, advanced to meet the charge of his rebellious subject, while Guinalda, weakened by unaccustomed exertion and lace of nourishment, appalled by the hideous circumstances of her plight, sank panting to the ground.

Toyat and Go-yad, immersed in the prospect of battle, were oblivious to all else. Could Guinalda have taken advantage of this temporary forgetfulness of her she might have escaped; but she was too stunned, too exhausted to take advantage of her opportunity. Spellbound, fascinated by the horror of it, she watched these terrifying, primordial man-beasts preparing to do battle for possession of her.

Nor was Guinalda the sole witness of these savage preliminaries. From the concealment of a low bush behind which he lay another watched the scene with steady, interested eyes. Absorbed by their own passion neither Toyat nor Go-yad noted the occasional movement of the outer leaves of the bush behind which this other watcher lay, a movement imparted by the body of the watcher with each breath and with each slightest change of position.

Perhaps the watcher discovered no sporting interest in the impending duel, for just as the two apes were about to engage he arose and stepped into the open—a great black-maned lion, whose yellow coat gleamed golden in the sunlight.

Toyat saw him first and with a growl of rage turned and fled, leaving his adversary and their prize to whatever fate Providence might hold in store for them.

Go-yad, thinking his rival had abandoned the field through fear of him, beat loudly upon his breast and roared forth the victory cry of the bull ape, then, swaggering as became a victor and a champion, he turned to claim the prize.

Between himself and the girl he saw the lion standing, gazing with serious mien straight into his eyes. Go-yad halted. Who would not have? The lion was within springing distance but he was not crouched. Go-yad backed away, snarling, and when the lion made no move to follow, the great ape suddenly turned and lumbered off into the jungle, casting many a backward glance in the direction of the great cat until intervening foliage shut him from his view.

Then the lion turned toward the girl. Poor little Princess! Hopeless, resigned, she lay upon the ground staring, wide-eyed, at this new engine of torture and destruction. The king of beasts surveyed her for a moment and then walked toward her. Guinalda clasped her hands and prayed—not for life, for hope of that she had long since resigned, but for death, speedy and painless.

The tawny beast came close. Guinalda closed her eyes to shut out the fearsome sight. She felt hot breath upon her cheek, its fetid odor assailed her nostrils. The lion sniffed about her. God! why did he not end it? Tortured nerves could endure no more and Guinalda swooned. Merciful surcease of her suffering.

23

Jad-bal-ja

NERVE shaken, the remnants of Ibn Jad's company turned toward the west and hastened by forced marches to escape the hideous forest of the jin. Abd el-Aziz and those who had accompanied him from the Wood of the Leopards toward Nimmr had not rejoined them. Nor ever would they, for upon the plain below the treasure city of the Beduins' dreaming the knights of Gobred had discovered them and, despite the thundering havoc of the ancient matchlocks, the iron Knights of Nimmr had couched their spears against the Saracens and once again the victorious cri de guerre of the Crusaders had rung out after seven centuries of silence to announce a new engagement in the hoary war for the possession of the Holy Land—the war that is without end.

From the north a mailed knight rode down through the forest of Galla land. A blue and silver pennon fluttered from his lance. The housings of his great charger were rich with gold and silver from the treasure vaults of Wildred of the Sepulcher. Wide-eyed Galla warriors viewed this solitary anachronism from afar, and fled.

Tarzan of the Apes, ranging westward, came upon the spoor of Fahd and Stimbol and Guinalda and followed it toward the south.

Northward marched a hundred ebon giants, veterans of a hundred battles—the famed Waziri—and with them came Zeyd, the lover of Ateja. One day they came upon a fresh spoor crossing their line of march diagonally toward the southwest. It was the spoor of Arab sandals, those of two men and a woman, and when the Waziri pointed them out to Zeyd the young Beduin swore that he recognized those of the woman as belonging to Ateja, for who knew better the shape and size of her little foot, or the style of the sandals she fabricated? He begged the Waziri to turn aside for a time and aid him in finding his sweetheart, and while the sub-chief was debating the

question in his mind the sound of something hurrying through
the jungle attracted the attention of every ear.

While they listened a man staggered into view. It was Fahd.
Zeyd recognized him instantly and as immediately became
doubly positive that the footprints of the woman had been
made by Ateja.

Zeyd approached Fahd menacingly. "Where is Ateja?" he
demanded.

"How should I know? I have not seen her for days," replied Fahd, truthfully enough.

"Thou liest!" cried Zeyd, and pointed at the ground. "Here
are her own footprints beside thine!"

A cunning expression came into the eyes of Fahd. Here he
saw an opportunity to cause suffering to the man he hated. He
shrugged his shoulders.

"Wellah, if you know, you know," he said.

"Where is she?" demanded Zeyd.

"She is dead. I would have spared you," answered Fahd.

"Dead?" The suffering in that single word should have
melted a heart of stone—but not Fahd's.

"I stole her from her father's beyt," continued Fahd, wishing to inflict as much torture as possible upon his rival. "For
days and nights she was mine; then a huge ape stole her from
me. By now she must be dead."

But Fahd had gone to far. He had encompassed his own un-
doing. With a scream of rage Zeyd leaped upon him with
drawn khusa, and before the Waziri could interfere or Fahd
defend himself the keen blade had drunk thrice in the heart of
the lying Beduin.

With bent head and dull eyes Zeyd marched on northward
with the Waziri, as, a mile behind them, a wasted old man,
burning with fever, stumbled in the trail and fell. Twice he
tried to regain his feet, only to sink weakly back to earth. A
filthy, ragged bundle of old bones, he lay—sometimes raving
in delirium, sometimes so still that he seemed dead.

Down from the north came Tarzan of the Apes upon the
spoor of Guinalda and the two who had accompanied her.
Knowing well the windings of the trail he took short cuts,
swinging through the branches of the trees, and so it happened
that he missed the Waziri at the point where their trail had
encountered that of Fahd, where Zeyd had slain his rival, and
presently his nostrils picked up the scent of the Mangani in
the distance.

Toward the great apes he made his way swiftly for he

feared that harm might befall the girl should she, by any mis-
chance, fall into the hands of the anthropoids. He arrived
in the clearing where they lazed, a short time after the return of Toyat and Go-yad, who, by now, had abandoned their
quarrel, since the prize had been taken by one stronger than
either of them.

The preliminaries of meeting over and the apes having
recognized and acknowledged Tarzan, he demanded if any
had seen the Tarmangani she who had recently passed through
the jungle.

M'walat pointed at Toyat and Tarzan turned toward the
king.

"You have seen the she?" demanded Tarzan, fearful, for he
did not like the manner of the king ape.

Toyat jerked a thumb toward the south. "Numa," he said
and went on hunting for food, but Tarzan knew what the ape
meant as surely as though he had spoken a hundred words of
explanation.

"Where?" asked Tarzan.

Toyat pointed straight to where he had abandoned Guinalda
to the lion, and the ape-man, moving straight through the
jungle along the line indicated by the king ape, went sadly to
investigate, although he already guessed what he would find.
At least he could drive Numa from his kill and give decent
burial to the unfortunate girl.

Slowly consciousness returned to Guinalda. She did not open
her eyes, but lay very quiet wondering if this was death. She
felt no pain.

Presently a sickly sweet and pungent odor assailed her
nostrils and something moved very close to her, so close that
she felt it against her body, pressing gently, and where it
pressed she felt heat as from another body.

Fearfully she opened her eyes and the horror of her predicament again swept over her for she saw that the lion had
lain down almost against her. His back was toward her, his
noble head was lifted, his black mane almost brushed her face.
He was looking off, intently, toward the north.

Guinalda lay very quiet. Presently she felt, rather than
heard, a low rumbling growl that seemed to have its origin
deep in the cavernous chest of the carnivore.

Something was coming! Even Guinalda sensed that, but it
could not be succor, for what could succor her from this hideous beast?

There was a rustling among the branches of the trees a hundred feet away and suddenly the giant figure of a demigod dropped to the ground. The lion rose and faced the man. The two stood thus, eying one another for a brief moment. Then the man spoke.

"Jad-bal-ja!" he exclaimed, and then: "Come to heel!"

The great, golden lion whined and strode across the open space, stopping before the man. Guinalda saw the beast look up into the face of the demigod and saw the latter stroke the tawny head affectionately, but meanwhile the eyes of the man, or god, or whatever he was, were upon Guinalda and she saw the sudden relief that came to them as Tarzan realized that the girl was unharmed.

Leaving the lion the ape-man crossed to where the princess lay and knelt beside her.

"You are the Princess Guinalda?" he asked.

The girl nodded, wondering how he knew her. As yet she was too stunned to command her own voice.

"Are you hurt?" he asked.

She shook her head.

"Do not be afraid," he assured her in a gentle voice. "I am your friend. You are safe now."

There was something in the way he said it that filled Guinalda with such a sense of safety as all the mailed knights of her father's realm had scarce imparted.

"I am not afraid—any more," she said simply.

"Where are your companions?" he asked.

She told him all that had happened.

"You are well rid of them," said the ape-man, "and we shall not attempt to find them. The jungle will account for them in its own way and in its own good time."

"Who art thou?" asked the girl.

"I am Tarzan."

"How didst thou know my name?" she queried.

"I am a friend of one whom you know as Sir James," he explained. "He and I were searching for you."

"Thou art his friend?" she cried. "Oh, sweet sir, then thou art mine as well!"

The ape-man smiled. "Always!" he said.

"Why did the lion not kill thee, Sir Tarzan?" she demanded, thinking him a simple knight, for in her land there were only these beside the members of her princely house and the pseudo king of the City of the Sepulcher. For in the original company that had been wrecked upon the coast of Africa at the time of the Third Crusade there were only knights, except one bastard son of Henry II, who had been the original Prince Gobred. Never having been in contact with an English king since they parted from Richard at Cyprus no Gobred had assumed the right to issue patents of nobility to his followers, solely the prerogative of the king.

"Why did the lion not kill me?" repeated Tarzan. "Because he is Jad-bal-ja, the Golden Lion, which I raised from cubhood. All his life he has known me only as friend and master. He would not harm me and it was because of his lifelong association with human beings that he did not harm you; though I was fearful when I saw him beside you that he had, for a lion is always a lion!"

"Thou dwellest nearby?" asked the girl.

"Far away," said Tarzan, "But there must be some of my people nearby, else Jad-bal-ja would not be here. I sent for my warriors and doubtless he has accompanied them."

Finding that the girl was hungry Tarzan bade the Golden Lion remain and guard her while he went in search of food.

"Do not fear him," he told her, "and remember that you could not have a protector more competent than he to discourage the approach of enemies."

"And well mayst I believe it," admitted Guinalda.

Tarzan returned with food and then, as the day was not done, he started back toward Nimmr with the rescued girl, carrying her, as she was now too weak to walk; and beside them strode the great, black-maned lion of gold.

During that journey Tarzan learned much of Nimmr and also discovered that Blake's love for his princess was apparently fully reciprocated by the girl, for she seemed never so content as when talking about her Sir James and asking questions concerning his far country and his past life, of which, unfortunately, Tarzan could tell her nothing.

Upon the second day the three came to the great cross and here Tarzan hailed the warders and bade them come and take their princess.

She urged the ape-man to accompany her to the castle and receive the thanks of her father and mother, but he told her that he must leave at once to search for Blake, and at that she ceased her urging.

"An' thou findst him," she said, "tell him that the gates of Nimmr be always open to him and that the Princess Guinalda awaits his return."

Down from the Cross went Tarzan and Jad-bal-ja and before she turned back to enter the tunnel that led to her father's castle the Princess Guinalda stood watching them until a turn in the trail hid them from her view.

"May Our Lord Jesus bless thee, sweet sir knight," she murmured, "and watch o'er thee and fetch thee back once more with my beloved!"

24

Where Trails Met

D OWN through the forest rode Blake searching for some clew to the whereabouts of the Arabs, ranging this way and that, following trails and abandoning them.

Late one day he came suddenly in to a large clearing where once a native village had stood. The jungle had not yet reclaimed it and as he entered it he saw a leopard crouching upon the far side, and before the leopard lay the body of a human being. At first Blake thought the poor creature dead, but presently he saw it attempt to rise and crawl away.

The great cat growled and advanced toward it. Blake shouted and spurred forward, but Sheeta paid no attention to him, evidently having no mind to give up its prey; but as Blake came nearer the cat turned to face him with an angry growl.

The American wondered if his horse would dare the close proximity of the beast of prey, but he need not have feared. Nor would he had he been more fully acquainted with the customs of the Valley of the Sepulcher, where one of the greatest sports of the knights of the two enemy cities is hunting the giant cats with lance alone when they venture from the sanctuary of the Wood of the Leopards.

The charger that Blake bestrode had faced many a savage cat, and larger, too, by far than this one, and so he fell into his charging stride with no show of fear or nervousness and the two thundered down upon Sheeta while the creature that was to have been its prey looked on with wide, astounded eyes.

Within the length of its spring Sheeta rose swiftly to meet the horse and man. He leaped and as he leaped he struck full on the metal tip of the great lance, and the wooden shaft passed through him so far that it was with difficulty that the man forced the carcass from it. When he had done so he turned and rode to the side of the creature lying helpless on the ground.

"My God!" he cried as his eyes rested on the face below him. "Stimbol!"

"Blake!"

The younger man dismounted.

"I'm dying, Blake," whispered Stimbol. "Before I go I want to tell you that I'm sorry. I acted like a cad. I guess I've got what was coming to me."

"Never mind that, Stimbol," said Blake. "You're not dead yet. The first thing is to get you where there are food and water." He stooped and lifted the emaciated form and placed the man in his saddle. "I passed a small native village a few miles back. They all ran when they saw me, but we'll try there for food."

"What are you doing here?" asked Stimbol. "And in the name of King Arthur, where did you get the outfit?"

"I'll tell you about it when we get to the village," said Blake. "It's a long story. I'm looking for a girl that was stolen by the Arabs a few days ago."

"God!" ejaculated Stimbol.

"You know something about her?" demanded Blake.

"I was with the man that stole her," said Stimbol, "or at least who stole her from the other Arabs."

"Where is she?"

"She's dead, Blake!"

"Dead?"

"A bunch of those big anthropoid apes got her. The poor child must have been killed immediately."

Blake was silent for a long time, walking with bowed head as, weighted down by heavy armor, he led the horse along the trail.

"Did the Arabs harm her?" he asked presently.

"No," said Stimbol. "The sheik stole her either for ransom or to sell her in the north, but Fahd stole her for himself. He took me along because I had promised him a lot of money if he'd save me, and I kept him from harming the girl by telling him that he'd never get a cent from me if he did. I felt sorry for the poor child and I made up my mind that I was going to save her if I could."

When Blake and Stimbol approached the village the blacks fled, leaving the white men in full possession of the place. It did not take Blake long to find food for them both.

Making Stimbol as comfortable as possible, Blake found fodder for his horse and presently returned to the old man. He was engaged in narrating his experiences when he was suddenly aware of the approach of many people. He could hear voices and the pad of naked feet. Evidently the villagers were returning.

Blake prepared to meet them with friendly overtures, but

the first glimpse he had of the approaching party gave him a distinct shock, for these were not the frightened villagers he had seen scurrying into the jungle a short time before.

With white plumes waving about their heads a company of stalwart warriors came swinging down the trail. Great oval shields were upon their backs, long war spears in their hands.

"Well," said Blake, "I guess we're in for it. The villagers have sent for their big brothers."

The warriors entered the village and when they saw Blake the halted in evident wonder. One of their number approached him and to Blake's surprise addressed him in fairly good English.

"We are the Waziri of Tarzan," he said. "We search for our chief and master. Have you seen him, Bwana?"

The Waziri! Blake could have hugged them. He had been at his wits end to know what he was to do with Stimbol. Alone he never could have brought the man to civilization, but now he knew that his worries were over.

Had it not been for the grief of Blake and Zeyd, it had been a merry party that made free with the cassava and beer of the villagers that night, for the Waziri were not worrying about their chief.

"Tarzan cannot die," said the sub-chief to Blake, when the latter asked if the other felt any fear as to the safety of his master, and the simple conviction of the quiet words almost succeeded in convincing Blake of their truth.

Along the trail plodded the weary 'Aarab of the Beny Salem fendy, el-Guad. Tired men staggered beneath the weight of half-loads. The women carried even more. Ibn Jad watched the treasure with greedy eyes. An arrow came from no where and pierced the heart of a treasure bearer close before Ibn Jad. A hollow voice sounded from the jungle: *"For every jewel a drop of blood!"*

Terrified, the Beduins hastened on. Who would be next? They wanted to cast aside the treasure, but Ibn Jad, greedy, would not let them. Behind them they caught a glimpse of a great lion. He terrified them because he did not come nearer or go away—he just stalked silently along behind. There were no stragglers.

An hour passed. The lion paced just within sight of the tail end of the column. Never had the head of one of Ibn Jad's columns been so much in demand. Everyone wished to go in the lead.

A scream burst from another treasure carrier. An arrow had passed through his lungs. *"For every jewel a drop of blood!"*

The men threw down the treasure. "We will not carry the accursed thing more!" they cried, and again the voice spoke.

"Take up the treasure, Ibn Jad!" it said. *"Take up the treasure! It is thou who murdered to acquire it. Pick it up, thief and murderer, and carry it thyself!"*

Together the 'Aarab made the treasure into one load and lifted it to Ibn Jad's back. The old sheik staggered beneath the weight.

"I cannot carry it!" he cried aloud. "I am old and I am not strong."

"Thou canst carry it, or—die!" boomed the hollow voice, while the lion stood in the trail behind them, his eyes glaring fixedly at them.

Ibn Jad staggered on beneath the great load. He could not now travel as fast as the others and so he was left behind with only the lion as company; but only for a short time. Ateja saw his predicament and came back to his side, bearing a musket in her hands.

"Fear not," she said, "I am not the son thou didst crave, but yet I shall protect thee even as a son!"

It was almost dusk when the leaders of the Beduin company stumbled upon a village. They were in it and surrounded by a hundred warriors before they realized that they were in the midst of the one tribe of all others they most feared and dreaded—the Waziri of Tarzan.

The sub-chief disarmed them at once.

"Where is Ibn Jad?" demanded Zeyd.

"He cometh!" said one.

They looked back along the trail and presently Zeyd saw two figures approaching. One was a man bent beneath a great load and the other was that of a young girl. What he did not see was the figure of a great lion in the shadows behind them.

Zeyd held his breath because, for an instant, his heart had stopped beating.

"Ateja!" he cried and ran forward to meet her and clasp her in his arms.

Ibn Jad staggered into the village. He took one look at the stern visages of the dread Waziri and sank weakly to the ground, the treasure almost burying him as it fell upon his head and shoulders.

Hirfa voiced a sudden scream as she pointed back along the trail, and as every eye turned in that direction, a great golden lion stepped into the circle of the firelight in the village, and at its side strode Tarzan, Lord of the Jungle.

As Tarzan entered the village Blake came forward and grasped his hand.

"We were too late!" said the American sadly.

"What do you mean?" asked the ape-man.

"The Princess Guinalda is dead!"

"Nonsense!" exclaimed Tarzan. "I left her this morning at the entrance to the City of Nimmr."

A dozen times Tarzan was forced to assure Blake that he was not playing a cruel joke upon him. A dozen times Tarzan had to repeat Guinalda's message: "An' thou findst him tell him that the gates of Nimmr be always open to him and that the Princess Guinalda awaits his return!"

Later in the evening Stimbol, through Blake, begged Tarzan to come to the hut in which he lay.

"Thank God!" exclaimed the old man fervently. "I thought that I had killed you. It has preyed on my mind and now I know that it was not you I believe that I can recover."

"You will be taken care of properly, Stimbol," said the ape-man, "and as soon as you are well enough you will be taken to the coast," then he walked away. He would do his duty by the man who had disobeyed him and tried to kill him, but he would not feign a friendship he did not feel.

The following morning they prepared to leave the village. Ibn Jad and his Arabs, with the exception of Zeyd and Ateja, who had asked to come and serve Tarzan in his home, were being sent to the nearest Galla village under escort of a dozen Waziri. Here they would be turned over to the Galla and doubtless sold into slavery in Abyssinia.

Stimbol was borne in a litter by four stout Waziri as the party prepared to take up its march toward the south and the country of Tarzan. Four others carried the treasure of the City of the Sepulcher.

Blake, dressed again in his iron mail, bestrode his great charger as the column started out of the village and down the trail into the south. Tarzan and the Golden Lion stood beside him. Blake reached down and extended his hand to the ape-man.

"Good-bye, sir!" he said.

"Good-bye?" demanded Tarzan. "Aren't you coming home with us?"

Blake shook his head.

"No," he said, "I'm going back into the middle ages with the woman I love!"

Tarzan and Jad-bal-ja stood in the trail watching as Sir James rode out toward the City of Nimmr, the blue and silver of his pennon fluttering bravely from the iron tip of his great lance.

ABOUT EDGAR RICE BURROUGHS

Edgar Rice Burroughs is one of the world's most popular authors. With no previous experience as an author, he wrote and sold his first novel—*A Princess of Mars*—in 1912. In the ensuing thirty-eight years until his death in 1950, Burroughs wrote 91 books and a host of short stories and articles. Although best known as the creator of the classic *Tarzan of the Apes* and *John Carter of Mars,* his restless imagination knew few bounds. Burroughs' prolific pen ranged from the American West to primitive Africa and on to romantic adventure on the moon, the planets, and even beyond the farthest star.

No one knows how many copies of ERB books have been published throughout the world. It is conservative to say, however, that of the translations into 32 known languages, including Braille, the number must run into the hundreds of millions. When one considers the additional world-wide following of the Tarzan newspaper feature, radio programs, comic magazines, motion pictures and television, Burroughs must have been known and loved by literally a thousand million or more.

THE WARLORD
OF MARS

Edgar Rice Burroughs

BALLANTINE BOOKS • NEW YORK

The Warlord of Mars was first published in All-Story Magazine
as a four-part serial, December 1913 through March 1914.

ISBN 0-345-27059-2

This edition published by arrangement with Edgar Rice Burroughs, Inc.

Manufactured in the United States of America

First U. S. Printing: March 1963
Twelfth U. S. Printing: July 1977

Cover art by Gino D'Achille

CONTENTS

THE WARLORD OF MARS

ON THE RIVER ISS

IN THE shadows of the forest that flanks the crimson plain by the side of the Lost Sea of Korus in the Valley Dor, beneath the hurtling moons of Mars, speeding their meteoric way close above the bosom of the dying planet, I crept stealthily along the trail of a shadowy form that hugged the darker places with a persistency that proclaimed the sinister nature of its errand.

For six long Martian months I had haunted the vicinity of the hateful Temple of the Sun, within whose slow-revolving shaft, far beneath the surface of Mars, my princess lay entombed—but whether alive or dead I knew not. Had Phaidor's slim blade found that beloved heart? Time only would reveal the truth.

Six hundred and eighty-seven Martian days must come and go before the cell's door would again come opposite the tunnel's end where last I had seen my ever-beautiful Dejah Thoris.

Half of them had passed, or would on the morrow, yet vivid in my memory, obliterating every event that had come before or after, there remained the last scene before the gust of smoke blinded my eyes and the narrow slit that had given me sight of the interior of her cell closed between me and the Princess of Helium for a long Martian year.

As if it were yesterday, I still saw the beautiful face of Phaidor, daughter of Matai Shang, distorted with jealous rage and hatred as she sprang forward with raised dagger upon the woman I loved.

I saw the red girl, Thuvia of Ptarth, leap forward to prevent the hideous deed.

The smoke from the burning temple had come then to blot out the tragedy, but in my ears rang the single shriek as the knife fell. Then silence, and when the smoke had cleared, the revolving temple had shut off all sight or sound from the chamber in which the three beautiful women were imprisoned.

Much there had been to occupy my attention since that terrible moment; but never for an instant had the memory of the thing faded, and all the time that I could spare from the numerous duties that had devolved upon me in the reconstruction of the government of the First Born since our victorious fleet and land forces had overwhelmed them, had been spent close to the grim shaft that held the mother of my boy, Carthoris of Helium.

The race of blacks that for ages had worshiped Issus, the false deity of Mars, had been left in a state of chaos by my revealment of her as naught more than a wicked old woman. In their rage they had torn her to pieces.

From the high pinnacle of their egotism the First Born had been plunged to the depths of humiliation. Their deity was gone, and with her the whole false fabric of their religion. Their vaunted navy had fallen in defeat before the superior ships and fighting men of the red men of Helium.

Fierce green warriors from the ocher sea bottoms of outer Mars had ridden their wild thoats across the sacred gardens of the Temple of Issus, and Tars Tarkas, Jeddak of Thark, fiercest of them all, had sat upon the throne of Issus and ruled the First Born while the allies were deciding the conquered nation's fate.

Almost unanimous was the request that I ascend the ancient throne of the black men, even the First Born themselves concurring in it; but I would have none of it. My heart could never be with the race that had heaped indignities upon my princess and my son.

At my suggestion Xodar became Jeddak of the First Born. He had been a dator, or prince, until Issus had degraded him, so that his fitness for the high office bestowed was unquestioned.

The peace of the Valley Dor thus assured, the green warriors dispersed to their desolate sea bottoms, while we of Helium returned to our own country. Here again was a throne offered me, since no word had been received from the missing Jeddak of Helium, Tardos Mors, grandfather of Dejah Thoris, or his son, Mors Kajak, Jed of Helium, her father.

Over a year had elapsed since they had set out to explore the northern hemisphere in search of Carthoris, and at last their disheartened people had accepted as truth the vague rumors of their death that had filtered in from the frozen region of the pole.

Once again I refused a throne, for I would not believe that the mighty Tardos Mors, or his no less redoubtable son, was dead.

"Let one of their own blood rule you until they return," I said to the assembled nobles of Helium, as I addressed them from the Pedestal of Truth beside the Throne of Righteousness in the Temple of Reward, from the very spot where I had stood a year before when Zat Arrras pronounced the sentence of death upon me.

As I spoke I stepped forward and laid my hand upon the shoulder of Carthoris where he stood in the front rank of the circle of nobles about me.

As one, the nobles and the people lifted their voices in a long cheer of approbation. Ten thousand swords sprang on high from as many scabbards, and the glorious fighting men of ancient Helium hailed Carthoris Jeddak of Helium.

His tenure of office was to be for life or until his great-grandfather, or grandfather, should return. Having thus satisfactorily arranged this important duty for Helium, I started the following day for the Valley Dor that I might remain close to the Temple of the Sun until the fateful day that should see the opening of the prison cell where my lost love lay buried.

Hor Vastus and Kantos Kan, with my other noble lieutenants, I left with Carthoris at Helium, that he might have the benefit of their wisdom, bravery, and loyalty in the performance of the arduous duties which had devolved upon him. Only Woola, my Martian hound, accompanied me.

At my heels tonight the faithful beast moved softly in my tracks. As large as a Shetland pony, with hideous head and frightful fangs, he was indeed an awsome spectacle, as he crept after me on his ten short, muscular legs; but to me he was the embodiment of love and loyalty.

The figure ahead was that of the black dator of the First Born, Thurid, whose undying enmity I had earned that time I laid him low with my bare hands in the courtyard of the Temple of Issus, and bound him with his own harness before the noble men and women who had but a moment before been extolling his prowess.

Like many of his fellows, he had apparently accepted the

9

new order of things with good grace, and had sworn fealty to Xodar, his new ruler; but I knew that he hated me, and I was sure that in his heart he envied and hated Xodar, so I had kept a watch upon his comings and goings, to the end that of late I had become convinced that he was occupied with some manner of intrigue.

Several times I had observed him leaving the walled city of the First Born after dark, taking his way out into the cruel and horrible Valley Dor, where no honest business could lead any man.

Tonight he moved quickly along the edge of the forest until well beyond sight or sound of the city, then he turned across the crimson sward toward the shore of the Lost Sea of Korus.

The rays of the nearer moon, swinging low across the valley, touched his jewel-incrusted harness with a thousand changing lights and glanced from the glossy ebony of his smooth hide. Twice he turned his head back toward the forest, after the manner of one who is upon an evil errand, though he must have felt quite safe from pursuit.

I did not dare follow him there beneath the moonlight, since it best suited my plans not to interrupt his—I wished him to reach his destination unsuspecting, that I might learn just where that destination lay and the business that awaited the night prowler there.

So it was that I remained hidden until after Thurid had disappeared over the edge of the steep bank beside the sea a quarter of a mile away. Then, with Woola following, I hastened across the open after the black dator.

The quiet of the tomb lay upon the mysterious valley of death, crouching deep in its warm nest within the sunken area at the south pole of the dying planet. In the far distance the Golden Cliffs raised their mighty barrier faces far into the starlit heavens, the precious metals and scintillating jewels that composed them sparkling in the brilliant light of Mars's two gorgeous moons.

At my back was the forest, pruned and trimmed like the sward to parklike symmetry by the browsing of the ghoulish plant men.

Before me lay the Lost Sea of Korus, while farther on I caught the shimmering ribbon of Iss, the River of Mystery, where it wound out from beneath the Golden Cliffs to empty

10

into Korus, to which for countless ages had been borne the deluded and unhappy Martians of the outer world upon the voluntary pilgrimage to this false heaven.

The plant men, with their blood-sucking hands, and the monstrous white apes that make Dor hideous by day, were hidden in their lairs for the night.

There was no longer a Holy Thern upon the balcony in the Golden Cliffs above the Iss to summon them with weird cry to the victims floating down to their maws upon the cold, broad bosom of ancient Iss.

The navies of Helium and the First Born had cleared the fortresses and the temples of the therns when they had refused to surrender and accept the new order of things that had swept their false religion from long-suffering Mars.

In a few isolated countries they still retained their age-old power; but Matai Shang, their hekkador, Father of Therns, had been driven from his temple. Strenuous had been our endeavors to capture him; but with a few of the faithful he had escaped, and was in hiding—where we knew not.

As I came cautiously to the edge of the low cliff overlooking the Lost Sea of Korus I saw Thurid pushing out upon the bosom of the shimmering water in a small skiff—one of those strangely wrought craft of unthinkable age which the Holy Therns, with their organization of priests and lesser therns, were wont to distribute along the banks of the Iss, that the long journey of their victims might be facilitated.

Drawn up on the beach below me were a score of similar boats, each with its long pole, at one end of which was a pike, at the other a paddle. Thurid was hugging the shore, and as he passed out of sight round a near-by promontory I shoved one of the boats into the water and, calling Woola into it, pushed out from shore.

The pursuit of Thurid carried me along the edge of the sea toward the mouth of the Iss. The farther moon lay close to the horizon, casting a dense shadow beneath the cliffs that fringed the water. Thuria, the nearer moon, had set, nor would it rise again for near four hours, so that I was ensured concealing darkness for that length of time at least.

On and on went the black warrior. Now he was opposite the mouth of the Iss. Without an instant's hesitation he turned up the grim river, paddling hard against the strong current. After him came Woola and I, closer now, for the man was

11

too intent upon forcing his craft up the river to have any eyes for what might be transpiring behind him. He hugged the shore where the current was less strong.

Presently he came to the dark cavernous portal in the face of the Golden Cliffs, through which the river poured. On into the Stygian darkness beyond he urged his craft.

It seemed hopeless to attempt to follow him here where I could not see my hand before my face, and I was almost on the point of giving up the pursuit and drifting back to the mouth of the river, there to await his return, when a sudden bend showed a faint luminosity ahead.

My quarry was plainly visible again, and in the increasing light from the phosphorescent rock that lay embedded in great patches in the roughly arched roof of the cavern I had no difficulty in following him.

It was my first trip upon the bosom of Iss, and the things I saw there will live forever in my memory.

Terrible as they were, they could not have commenced to approximate the horrible conditions which must have obtained before Tars Tarkas, the great green warrior, Xodar, the black dator, and I brought the light of truth to the outer world and stopped the mad rush of millions upon the voluntary pilgrimage to what they believed would end in a beautiful valley of peace and happiness and love.

Even now the low islands which dotted the broad stream were choked with the skeletons and half devoured carcasses of those who, through fear or a sudden awakening to the truth, had halted almost at the completion of their journey.

In the awful stench of these frightful charnel isles haggard maniacs screamed and gibbered and fought among the torn remnants of their grisly feasts; while on those which contained but clean-picked bones they battled with one another, the weaker furnishing sustenance for the stronger; or with clawlike hands clutched at the bloated bodies that drifted down with the current.

Thurid paid not the slightest attention to the screaming things that either menaced or pleaded with him as the mood directed them—evidently he was familiar with the horrid sights that surrounded him. He continued up the river for perhaps a mile; and then, crossing over to the left bank, drew his craft up on a low ledge that lay almost on a level with the water.

I dared not follow across the stream, for he most surely would have seen me. Instead I stopped close to the opposite wall beneath an overhanging mass of rock that cast a dense shadow beneath it. Here I could watch Thurid without danger of discovery.

The black was standing upon the ledge beside his boat, looking up the river, as though he were awaiting one whom he expected from that direction.

As I lay there beneath the dark rocks I noticed that a strong current seemed to flow directly toward the center of the river, so that it was difficult to hold my craft in its position. I edged farther into the shadow that I might find a hold upon the bank; but, though I proceeded several yards, I touched nothing; and then, finding that I would soon reach a point from where I could no longer see the black man, I was compelled to remain where I was, holding my position as best I could by paddling strongly against the current which flowed from beneath the rocky mass behind me.

I could not imagine what might cause this strong lateral flow, for the main channel of the river was plainly visible to me from where I sat, and I could see the rippling junction of it and the mysterious current which had aroused my curiosity.

While I was still speculating upon the phenomenon, my attention was suddenly riveted upon Thurid, who had raised both palms forward above his head in the universal salute of Martians, and a moment later his "Kaor!" the Barsoomian word of greeting, came in low but distinct tones.

I turned my eyes up the river in the direction that his were bent, and presently there came within my limited range of vision a long boat, in which were six men. Five were at the paddles, while the sixth sat in the seat of honor.

The white skins, the flowing yellow wigs which covered their bald pates, and the gorgeous diadems set in circlets of gold about their heads marked them as Holy Therns.

As they drew up beside the ledge upon which Thurid awaited them, he in the bow of the boat arose to step ashore, and then I saw that it was none other than Matai Shang, Father of Therns.

The evident cordiality with which the two men exchanged greetings filled me with wonder, for the black and white

13

men of Barsoom were hereditary enemies—nor ever before had I known of two meeting other than in battle.

Evidently the reverses that had recently overtaken both peoples had resulted in an alliance between these two individuals—at least against the common enemy—and now I saw why Thurid had come so often out into the Valley Dor by night, and that the nature of his conspiring might be such as to strike very close to me or to my friends.

I wished that I might have found a point closer to the two men from which to have heard their conversation; but it was out of the question now to attempt to cross the river, and so I lay quietly watching them, who would have given so much to have known how close I lay to them, and how easily they might have overcome and killed me with their superior force.

Several times Thurid pointed across the river in my direction, but that his gestures had any reference to me I did not for a moment believe. Presently he and Matai Shang entered the latter's boat, which turned out into the river and, swinging round, forged steadily across in my direction.

As they advanced I moved my boat farther and farther in beneath the overhanging wall, but at last it became evident that their craft was holding the same course. The five paddlers sent the larger boat ahead at a speed that taxed my energies to equal.

Every instant I expected to feel my prow crash against solid rock. The light from the river was no longer visible, but ahead I saw the faint tinge of a distant radiance, and still the water before me was open.

At last the truth dawned upon me—I was following a subterranean river which emptied into the Iss at the very point where I had hidden.

The rowers were now quite close to me. The noise of their own paddles drowned the sound of mine, but in another instant the growing light ahead would reveal me to them.

There was no time to be lost. Whatever action I was to take must be taken at once. Swinging the prow of my boat toward the right, I sought the river's rocky side, and there I lay while Matai Shang and Thurid approached up the center of the stream, which was much narrower than the Iss.

As they came nearer I heard the voices of Thurid and the Father of Therns raised in argument.

"I tell you, Thern," the black dator was saying, "that I wish only vengeance upon John Carter, Prince of Helium. I am leading you into no trap. What could I gain by betraying you to those who have ruined my nation and my house?"

"Let us stop here a moment that I may hear your plans," replied the hekkador, "and then we may proceed with a better understanding of our duties and obligations."

To the rowers he issued the command that brought their boat in toward the bank not a dozen paces beyond the spot where I lay.

Had they pulled in below me they must surely have seen me against the faint glow of light ahead, but from where they finally came to rest I was as secure from detection as though miles separated us.

The few words I had already overheard whetted my curiosity, and I was anxious to learn what manner of vengeance Thurid was planning against me. Nor had I long to wait. I listened intently.

"There are no obligations, Father of Therns," continued the First Born. "Thurid, Dator of Issus, has no price. When the thing has been accomplished I shall be glad if you will see to it that I am well received, as is befitting my ancient lineage and noble rank, at some court that is yet loyal to thy ancient faith, for I cannot return to the Valley Dor or elsewhere within the power of the Prince of Helium; but even that I do not demand—it shall be as your own desire in the matter directs."

"It shall be as you wish, Dator," replied Matai Shang; "nor is that all—power and riches shall be yours if you restore my daughter, Phaidor, to me, and place within my power Dejah Thoris, Princess of Helium.

"Ah," he continued with a malicious snarl, "but the Earth man shall suffer for the indignities he has put upon the holy of holies, nor shall any vileness be too vile to inflict upon his princess. Would that it were in my power to force him to witness the humiliation and degradation of the red woman."

"You shall have your way with her before another day has passed, Matai Shang," said Thurid, "if you but say the word."

"I have heard of the Temple of the Sun, Dator," replied Matai Shang, "but never have I heard that its prisoners could be released before the allotted year of their incarceration had elapsed. How, then, may you accomplish the impossible?"

"Access may be had to any cell of the temple at any time," replied Thurid. "Only Issus knew this; nor was it ever Issus' way to divulge more of her secrets than were necessary. By chance, after her death, I came upon an ancient plan of the temple, and there I found, plainly writ, the most minute directions for reaching the cells at any time.

"And more I learned—that many men had gone thither for Issus in the past, always on errands of death and torture to the prisoners; but those who thus learned the secret way were wont to die mysteriously immediately they had returned and made their reports to cruel Issus."

"Let us proceed, then," said Matai Shang at last. "I must trust you, yet at the same time you must trust me, for we are six to your one."

"I do not fear," replied Thurid, "nor need you. Our hatred of the common enemy is sufficient bond to insure our loyalty to each other, and after we have defiled the Princess of Helium there will be still greater reason for the maintenance of our allegiance—unless I greatly mistake the temper of her lord."

Matai Shang spoke to the paddlers. The boat moved on up the tributary.

It was with difficulty that I restrained myself from rushing upon them and slaying the two vile plotters; but quickly I saw the mad rashness of such an act, which would cut down the only man who could lead the way to Dejah Thoris' prison before the long Martian year had swung its interminable circle.

If he should lead Matai Shang to that hollowed spot, then, too, should he lead John Carter, Prince of Helium.

With silent paddle I swung slowly into the wake of the larger craft.

UNDER THE MOUNTAINS

As WE advanced up the river which winds beneath the Golden Cliffs out of the bowels of the Mountains of Otz to mingle its dark waters with the grim and mysterious Iss the faint glow which had appeared before us grew gradually into an all-enveloping radiance.

The river widened until it presented the aspect of a large lake whose vaulted dome, lighted by glowing phosphorescent rock, was splashed with the vivid rays of the diamond, the sapphire, the ruby, and the countless, nameless jewels of Barsoom which lay incrusted in the virgin gold which forms the major portion of these magnificent cliffs.

Beyond the lighted chamber of the lake was darkness—what lay behind the darkness I could not even guess.

To have followed the thern boat across the gleaming water would have been to invite instant detection, and so, though I was loath to permit Thurid to pass even for an instant beyond my sight, I was forced to wait in the shadows until the other boat had passed from my sight at the far extremity of the lake.

Then I paddled out upon the brilliant surface in the direction they had taken.

When, after what seemed an eternity, I reached the shadows at the upper end of the lake I found that the river issued from a low aperture, to pass beneath which it was necessary that I compel Woola to lie flat in the boat, and I, myself, must need bend double before the low roof cleared my head.

Immediately the roof rose again upon the other side, but no longer was the way brilliantly lighted. Instead only a feeble glow emanated from small and scattered patches of phosphorescent rock in wall and roof.

Directly before me the river ran into this smaller chamber through three separate arched openings.

Thurid and the therns were nowhere to be seen—into which of the dark holes had they disappeared? There was no means by which I might know, and so I chose the center opening as being as likely to lead me in the right direction as another.

Here the way was through utter darkness. The stream was narrow—so narrow that in the blackness I was constantly bumping first one rock wall and then another as the river wound hither and thither along its flinty bed.

Far ahead I presently heard a deep and sullen roar which increased in volume as I advanced, and then broke upon my ears with all the intensity of its mad fury as I swung round a sharp curve into a dimly lighted stretch of water.

Directly before me the river thundered down from above in a mighty waterfall that filled the narrow gorge from side to side, rising far above me several hundred feet—as magnificent a spectacle as I ever had seen.

But the roar—the awful, deafening roar of those tumbling waters penned in the rocky, subterranean vault! Had the fall not entirely blocked my further passage and shown me that I had followed the wrong course I believe that I should have fled anyway before the maddening tumult.

Thurid and the therns could not have come this way. By stumbling upon the wrong course I had lost the trail, and they had gained so much ahead of me that now I might not be able to find them before it was too late, if, in fact, I could find them at all.

It had taken several hours to force my way up to the falls against the strong current, and other hours would be required for the descent, although the pace would be much swifter.

With a sigh I turned the prow of my craft down stream, and with mighty strokes hastened with reckless speed through the dark and tortuous channel until once again I came to the chamber into which flowed the three branches of the river.

Two unexplored channels still remained from which to choose; nor was there any means by which I could judge which was the more likely to lead me to the plotters.

Never in my life, that I can recall, have I suffered such an agony of indecision. So much depended upon a correct choice; so much depended upon haste.

The hours that I had already lost might seal the fate of the incomparable Dejah Thoris were she not already dead—to sacrifice other hours, and maybe days in a fruitless exploration of another blind lead would unquestionably prove fatal.

Several times I essayed the right-hand entrance only to turn back as though warned by some strange intuitive sense that this was not the way. At last, convinced by the oft-recurring phenomenon, I cast my all upon the left-hand archway; yet it was with a lingering doubt that I turned a parting look at the sullen waters which rolled, dark and forbidding, from beneath the grim, low archway on the right.

And as I looked there came bobbing out upon the current from the Stygian darkness of the interior the shell of one of the great, succulent fruits of the sorapus tree.

I could scarce restrain a shout of elation as this silent, insensate messenger floated past me, on toward the Iss and Korus, for it told me that journeying Martians were above me on that very stream.

They had eaten of this marvelous fruit which nature concentrates within the hard shell of the sorapus nut, and having eaten had cast the husk overboard. It could have come from no others than the party I sought.

Quickly I abandoned all thought of the left-hand passage, and a moment later had turned into the right. The stream soon widened, and recurring areas of phosphorescent rock lighted my way.

I made good time, but was convinced that I was nearly a day behind those I was tracking. Neither Woola nor I had eaten since the previous day, but in so far as he was concerned it mattered but little, since practically all the animals of the dead sea bottoms of Mars are able to go for incredible periods without nourishment.

Nor did I suffer. The water of the river was sweet and cold, for it was unpolluted by decaying bodies—unlike the Iss —and as for food, why the mere thought that I was nearing my beloved princess raised me above every material want.

As I proceeded, the river became narrower and the current swift and turbulent—so swift in fact that it was with difficulty that I forced my craft upward at all. I could not have been making to exceed a hundred yards an hour when, at a bend, I was confronted by a series of rapids through which the river foamed and boiled at a terrific rate.

My heart sank within me. The sorapus nutshell had proved a false prophet, and, after all, my intuition had been correct —it was the left-hand channel that I should have followed.

Had I been a woman I should have wept. At my right was a great, slow-moving eddy that circled far beneath the cliff's

19

overhanging side, and to rest my tired muscles before turning back I let my boat drift into its embrace.

I was almost prostrated by disappointment. It would mean another half-day's loss of time to retrace my way and take the only passage that yet remained unexplored. What hellish fate had led me to select from three possible avenues the two that were wrong?

As the lazy current of the eddy carried me slowly about the periphery of the watery circle my boat twice touched the rocky side of the river in the dark recess beneath the cliff. A third time it struck, gently as it had before, but the contact resulted in a different sound—the sound of wood scraping upon wood.

In an instant I was on the alert, for there could be no wood within that buried river that had not been man brought. Almost coincidentally with my first apprehension of the noise, my hand shot out across the boat's side, and a second later I felt my fingers gripping the gunwale of another craft.

As though turned to stone I sat in tense and rigid silence, straining my eyes into the utter darkness before me in an effort to discover if the boat were occupied.

It was entirely possible that there might be men on board it who were still ignorant of my presence, for the boat was scraping gently against the rocks upon one side, so that the gentle touch of my boat upon the other easily could have gone unnoticed.

Peer as I would I could not penetrate the darkness, and then I listened intently for the sound of breathing near me; but except for the noise of the rapids, the soft scraping of the boats, and the lapping of the water at their sides I could distinguish no sound. As usual, I thought rapidly.

A rope lay coiled in the bottom of my own craft. Very softly I gathered it up, and making one end fast to the bronze ring in the prow I stepped gingerly into the boat beside me. In one hand I grasped the rope, in the other my keen long-sword.

For a full minute, perhaps, I stood motionless after entering the strange craft. It had rocked a trifle beneath my weight, but it had been the scraping of its side against the side of my own boat that had seemed most likely to alarm its occupants, if there were any.

But there was no answering sound, and a moment later I had felt from stem to stern and found the boat deserted.

Groping with my hands along the face of the rocks to which the craft was moored, I discovered a narrow ledge which I knew must be the avenue taken by those who had come before me. That they could be none other than Thurid and his party I was convinced by the size and build of the boat I had found.

Calling to Woola to follow me I stepped out upon the ledge. The great, savage brute, agile as a cat, crept after me.

As he passed through the boat that had been occupied by Thurid and the therns he emitted a single low growl, and when he came beside me upon the ledge and my hand rested upon his neck I felt his short mane bristling with anger. I think he sensed telepathically the recent presence of an enemy, for I had made no effort to impart to him the nature of our quest or the status of those we tracked.

This omission I now made haste to correct, and, after the manner of green Martians with their beasts, I let him know partially by the weird and uncanny telepathy of Barsoom and partly by word of mouth that we were upon the trail of those who had recently occupied the boat through which we had just passed.

A soft purr, like that of a great cat, indicated that Woola understood, and then, with a word to him to follow, I turned to the right along the ledge, but scarcely had I done so than I felt his mighty fangs tugging at my leathern harness.

As I turned to discover the cause of his act he continued to pull me steadily in the opposite direction, nor would he desist until I had turned about and indicated that I would follow him voluntarily.

Never had I known him to be in error in a matter of tracking, so it was with a feeling of entire security that I moved cautiously in the huge beast's wake. Through Cimmerian darkness he moved along the narrow ledge beside the boiling rapids.

As we advanced, the way led from beneath the overhanging cliffs out into a dim light, and then it was that I saw that the trail had been cut from the living rock, and that it ran up along the river's side beyond the rapids.

For hours we followed the dark and gloomy river farther and farther into the bowels of Mars. From the direction and distance I knew that we must be well beneath the Valley Dor, and possibly beneath the Sea of Omean as well—it could not be much farther now to the Temple of the Sun.

Even as my mind framed the thought Woola halted suddenly before a narrow, arched doorway in the cliff by the trail's side. Quickly he crouched back away from the entrance, at the same time turning his eyes toward me.

Words could not have more plainly told me that danger of some sort lay near by, and so I pressed quietly forward to his side, and passing him looked into the aperture at our right.

Before me was a fair-sized chamber that, from its appointments, I knew must have at one time been a guardroom. There were racks for weapons, and slightly raised platforms for the sleeping silks and furs of the warriors, but now its only occupants were two of the therns who had been of the party with Thurid and Matai Shang.

The men were in earnest conversation, and from their tones it was apparent that they were entirely unaware that they had listeners.

"I tell you," one of them was saying, "I do not trust the black one. There was no necessity for leaving us here to guard the way. Against what, pray, should we guard this long-forgotten, abysmal path? It was but a ruse to divide our numbers.

"He will have Matai Shang leave others elsewhere on some pretext or other, and then at last he will fall upon us with his confederates and slay us all."

"I believe you, Lakor," replied the other, "there can never be aught else than deadly hatred between thern and First Born. And what think you of the ridiculous matter of the light? 'Let the light shine with the intensity of three radium units for fifty tals, and for one xat let it shine with the intensity of one radium unit, and then for twenty-five tals with nine units.' Those were his very words, and to think that wise old Matai Shang should listen to such foolishness."

"Indeed, it is silly," replied Lakor. "It will open nothing other than the way to a quick death for us all. He had to make some answer when Matai Shang asked him flatly what he should do when he came to the Temple of the Sun, and so he made his answer quickly from his imagination—I would wager a hekkador's diadem that he could not now repeat it himself."

"Let us not remain here longer, Lakor," spoke the other thern. "Perchance if we hasten after them we may come in time to rescue Matai Shang, and wreak our own vengeance upon the black dator. What say you?"

"Never in a long life," answered Lakor, "have I disobeyed a single command of the Father of Therns. I shall stay here until I rot if he does not return to bid me elsewhere."

Lakor's companion shook his head.

"You are my superior," he said; "I cannot do other than you sanction, though I still believe that we are foolish to remain."

I, too, thought that they were foolish to remain, for I saw from Woola's actions that the trail led through the room where the two therns held guard. I had no reason to harbor any considerable love for this race of self-deified demons, yet I would have passed them by were it possible without molesting them.

It was worth trying anyway, for a fight might delay us considerably, or even put an end entirely to my search—better men than I have gone down before fighters of meaner ability than that possessed by the fierce thern warriors.

Signaling Woola to heel I stepped suddenly into the room before the two men. At sight of me their long-swords flashed from the harness at their sides, but I raised my hand in a gesture of restraint.

"I seek Thurid, the black dator," I said. "My quarrel is with him, not with you. Let me pass then in peace, for if I mistake not he is as much your enemy as mine, and you can have no cause to protect him."

They lowered their swords and Lakor spoke.

"I know not whom you may be, with the white skin of a thern and the black hair of a red man; but were it only Thurid whose safety were at stake you might pass, and welcome, in so far as we be concerned.

"Tell us who you be, and what mission calls you to this unknown world beneath the Valley Dor, then maybe we can see our way to let you pass upon the errand which we should like to undertake would our orders permit."

I was surprised that neither of them had recognized me, for I thought that I was quite sufficiently well known either by personal experience or reputation to every thern upon Barsoom as to make my identity immediately apparent in any part of the planet. In fact, I was the only white man upon Mars whose hair was black and whose eyes were gray, with the exception of my son, Carthoris.

To reveal my identity might be to precipitate an attack, for every thern upon Barsoom knew that to me they owed the fall of their age-old spiritual supremacy. On the other hand my reputation as a fighting man might be sufficient to pass me by these two were their livers not of the right complexion to welcome a battle to the death.

To be quite candid I did not attempt to delude myself with any such sophistry, since I knew well that upon warlike Mars there are few cowards, and that every man, whether prince, priest, or peasant, glories in deadly strife. And so I gripped my long-sword the tighter as I replied to Lakor.

"I believe that you will see the wisdom of permitting me to pass unmolested," I said, "for it would avail you nothing to die uselessly in the rocky bowels of Barsoom merely to protect a hereditary enemy, such as Thurid, Dator of the First Born.

"That you shall die should you elect to oppose me is evidenced by the moldering corpses of all the many great Barsoomian warriors who have gone down beneath this blade—I am John Carter, Prince of Helium."

For a moment that name seemed to paralyze the two men; but only for a moment, and then the younger of them, with a vile name upon his lips, rushed toward me with ready sword.

He had been standing a little behind his companion, Lakor, during our parley, and now, ere he could engage me, the older man grasped his harness and drew him back.

"Hold!" commanded Lakor. "There will be plenty of time to fight if we find it wise to fight at all. There be good reasons why every thern upon Barsoom should yearn to spill the blood of the blasphemer, the sacrilegist; but let us mix wisdom with our righteous hate. The Prince of Helium is bound upon an errand which we ourselves, but a moment since, were wishing that we might undertake.

"Let him go then and slay the black. When he returns we shall still be here to bar his way to the outer world, and thus we shall have rid ourselves of two enemies, nor have incurred the displeasure of the Father of Therns."

24

As he spoke I could not but note the crafty glint in his evil eyes, and while I saw the apparent logic of his reasoning I felt, subconsciously perhaps, that his words did but veil some sinister intent. The other thern turned toward him in evident surprise, but when Lakor had whispered a few brief words into his ear he, too, drew back and nodded acquiescence to his superior's suggestion.

"Proceed, John Carter," said Lakor; "but know that if Thurid does not lay you low there will be those awaiting your return who will see that you never pass again into the sunlight of the upper world. Go!"

During our conversation Woola had been growling and bristling close to my side. Occasionally he would look up into my face with a low, pleading whine, as though begging for the word that would send him headlong at the bare throats before him. He, too, sensed the villainy behind the smooth words.

Beyond the therns several doorways opened off the guardroom, and toward the one upon the extreme right Lakor motioned.

"That way leads to Thurid," he said.

But when I would have called Woola to follow me there the beast whined and held back, and at last ran quickly to the first opening at the left, where he stood emitting his coughing bark, as though urging me to follow him upon the right way.

I turned a questioning look upon Lakor.

"The brute is seldom wrong," I said, "and while I do not doubt your superior knowledge, Thern, I think that I shall do well to listen to the voice of instinct that is backed by love and loyalty."

As I spoke I smiled grimly that he might know without words that I distrusted him.

"As you will," the fellow replied with a shrug. "In the end it shall be all the same."

I turned and followed Woola into the left-hand passage, and though my back was toward my enemies, my ears were on the alert; yet I heard no sound of pursuit. The passageway was dimly lighted by occasional radium bulbs, the universal lighting medium of Barsoom.

These same lamps may have been doing continuous duty in these subterranean chambers for ages, since they require no attention and are so compounded that they give off but the minutest of their substance in the generation of years of luminosity.

We had proceeded for but a short distance when we commenced to pass the mouths of diverging corridors, but not once did Woola hesitate. It was at the opening to one of these corridors upon my right that I presently heard a sound that spoke more plainly to John Carter, fighting man, than could the words of my mother tongue—it was the clank of metal—the metal of a warrior's harness—and it came from a little distance up the corridor upon my right.

Woola heard it, too, and like a flash he had wheeled and stood facing the threatened danger, his mane all abristle and all his rows of glistening fangs bared by snarling, backdrawn lips. With a gesture I silenced him, and together we drew aside into another corridor a few paces farther on.

Here we waited; nor did we have long to wait, for presently we saw the shadows of two men fall upon the floor of the main corridor athwart the doorway of our hiding place. Very cautiously they were moving now—the accidental clank that had alarmed me was not repeated.

Presently they came opposite our station; nor was I surprised to see that the two were Lakor and his companion of the guardroom.

They walked very softly, and in the right hand of each gleamed a keen long-sword. They halted quite close to the entrance of our retreat, whispering to each other.

"Can it be that we have distanced them already?" said Lakor.

"Either that or the beast has led the man upon a wrong trail," replied the other, "for the way which we took is by far the shorter to this point—for him who knows it. John Carter would have found it a short road to death had he taken it as you suggested to him."

"Yes," said Lakor, "no amount of fighting ability would have saved him from the pivoted flagstone. He surely would have stepped upon it, and by now, if the pit beneath it has a bottom, which Thurid denies, he should have been rapidly approaching it. Curses on that calot of his that warned him toward the safer avenue!"

"There be other dangers ahead of him, though," spoke Lakor's fellow, "which he may not so easily escape—should

26

he succeed in escaping our two good swords. Consider, for example, what chance he will have, coming unexpectedly into the chamber of——"

I would have given much to have heard the balance of that conversation that I might have been warned of the perils that lay ahead, but fate intervened, and just at the very instant of all other instants that I would not have elected to do it, I sneezed.

THE TEMPLE OF THE SUN

THERE was nothing for it now other than to fight; nor did I have any advantage as I sprang, sword in hand, into the corridor before the two therns, for my untimely sneeze had warned them of my presence and they were ready for me.

There were no words, for they would have been a waste of breath. The very presence of the two proclaimed their treachery. That they were following to fall upon me unawares was all too plain, and they, of course, must have known that I understood their plan.

In an instant I was engaged with both, and though I loathe the very name of thern, I must in all fairness admit that they are mighty swordsmen; and these two were no exception, unless it were that they were even more skilled and fearless than the average among their race.

While it lasted it was indeed as joyous a conflict as I ever had experienced. Twice at least I saved my breast from the mortal thrust of piercing steel only by the wondrous agility with which my earthly muscles endow me under the conditions of lesser gravity and air pressure upon Mars.

Yet even so I came near to tasting death that day in the gloomy corridor beneath Mars's southern pole, for Lakor played a trick upon me that in all my experience of fighting upon two planets I never before had witnessed the like of.

The other thern was engaging me at the time, and I was forcing him back—touching him here and there with my point until he was bleeding from a dozen wounds, yet not being able to penetrate his marvelous guard to reach a vulnerable spot for the brief instant that would have been sufficient to send him to his ancestors.

It was then that Lakor quickly unslung a belt from his harness, and as I stepped back to parry a wicked thrust he lashed one end of it about my left ankle so that it wound there for an instant, while he jerked suddenly upon the other end, throwing me heavily upon my back.

Then, like leaping panthers, they were upon me; but they

had reckoned without Woola, and before ever a blade touched me, a roaring embodiment of a thousand demons hurtled above my prostrate form and my loyal Martian calot was upon them.

Imagine, if you can, a huge grizzly with ten legs armed with mighty talons and an enormous froglike mouth splitting his head from ear to ear, exposing three rows of long, white tusks. Then endow this creature of your imagination with the agility and ferocity of a half-starved Bengal tiger and the strength of a span of bulls, and you will have some faint conception of Woola in action.

Before I could call him off he had crushed Lakor into a jelly with a single blow of one mighty paw, and had literally torn the other thern to ribbons; yet when I spoke to him sharply he cowed sheepishly as though he had done a thing to deserve censure and chastisement.

Never had I had the heart to punish Woola during the long years that had passed since that first day upon Mars when the green jed of the Tharks had placed him on guard over me, and I had won his love and loyalty from the cruel and loveless masters of his former life, yet I believe he would have submitted to any cruelty that I might have inflicted upon him, so wondrous was his affection for me.

The diadem in the center of the circlet of gold upon the brow of Lakor proclaimed him a Holy Thern, while his companion, not thus adorned, was a lesser thern, though from his harness I gleaned that he had reached the Ninth Cycle, which is but one below that of the Holy Therns.

As I stood for a moment looking at the gruesome havoc Woola had wrought, there recurred to me the memory of that other occasion upon which I had masqueraded in the wig, diadem, and harness of Sator Throg, the Holy Thern whom Thuvia of Ptarth had slain, and now it occurred to me that it might prove of worth to utilize Lakor's trappings for the same purpose.

A moment later I had torn his yellow wig from his bald pate and transferred it and the circlet, as well as all his harness, to my own person.

Woola did not approve of the metamorphosis. He sniffed at me and growled ominously, but when I spoke to him and patted his huge head he at length became reconciled to the change, and at my command trotted off along the corridor in the direction we had been going when our progress had been interrupted by the therns.

We moved cautiously now, warned by the fragment of conversation I had overheard. I kept abreast of Woola that we might have the benefit of all our eyes for what might appear suddenly ahead to menace us, and well it was that we were forewarned.

At the bottom of a flight of narrow steps the corridor turned sharply back upon itself, immediately making another turn in the original direction, so that at that point it formed a perfect letter S, the top leg of which debouched suddenly into a large chamber, illy lighted, and the floor of which was completely covered by venomous snakes and loathsome reptiles.

To have attempted to cross that floor would have been to court instant death, and for a moment I was almost completely discouraged. Then it occurred to me that Thurid and Matai Shang with their party must have crossed it, and so there was a way.

Had it not been for the fortunate accident by which I overheard even so small a portion of the therns' conversation we should have blundered at least a step or two into that wriggling mass of destruction, and a single step would have been all-sufficient to have sealed our doom.

These were the only reptiles I had ever seen upon Barsoom, but I knew from their similarity to the fossilized remains of supposedly extinct species I had seen in the museums of Helium that they comprised many of the known prehistoric reptilian genera, as well as others undiscovered.

A more hideous aggregation of monsters had never before assailed my vision. It would be futile to attempt to describe them to Earth men, since substance is the only thing which they possess in common with any creature of the past or present with which you are familiar—even their venom is of an unearthly virulence that, by comparison, would make the cobra de capello seem quite as harmless as an angleworm.

As they spied me there was a concerted rush by those nearest the entrance where we stood, but a line of radium bulbs inset along the threshold of their chamber brought them to a sudden halt—evidently they dared not cross that line of light.

I had been quite sure that they would not venture beyond the room in which I had discovered them, though I had not guessed at what deterred them. The simple fact that we had found no reptiles in the corridor through which we had just come was sufficient assurance that they did not venture there.

I drew Woola out of harm's way, and then began a careful survey of as much of the Chamber of Reptiles as I could see from where I stood. As my eyes became accustomed to the dim light of its interior I gradually made out a low gallery at the far end of the apartment from which opened several exits.

Coming as close to the threshold as I dared, I followed this gallery with my eyes, discovering that it circled the room as far as I could see. Then I glanced above me along the upper edge of the entrance to which we had come, and there, to my delight, I saw an end of the gallery not a foot above my head. In an instant I had leaped to it and called Woola after me.

Here there were no reptiles—the way was clear to the opposite side of the hideous chamber—and a moment later Woola and I dropped down to safety in the corridor beyond.

Not ten minutes later we came into a vast circular apartment of white marble, the walls of which were inlaid with gold in the strange hieroglyphics of the First Born.

From the high dome of this mighty apartment a huge circular column extended to the floor, and as I watched I saw that it slowly revolved.

I had reached the base of the Temple of the Sun!

Somewhere above me lay Dejah Thoris, and with her were Phaidor, daughter of Matai Shang, and Thuvia of Ptarth. But how to reach them, now that I had found the only vulnerable spot in their mighty prison, was still a baffling riddle.

Slowly I circled the great shaft, looking for a means of ingress. Part way around I found a tiny radium flash torch, and as I examined it in mild curiosity as to its presence there in this almost inaccessible and unknown spot, I came suddenly upon the insignia of the house of Thurid jewel-inset in its metal case.

I am upon the right trail, I thought, as I slipped the bauble into the pocket-pouch which hung from my harness.

Then I continued my search for the entrance, which I knew must be somewhere about; nor had I long to search, for almost immediately thereafter I came upon a small door so cunningly inlaid in the shaft's base that it might have passed unnoticed by a less keen or careful observer.

There was the door that would lead me within the prison, but where was the means to open it? No button or lock were visible. Again and again I went carefully over every square inch of its surface, but the most that I could find was a tiny pinhole a little above and to the right of the door's center—a pinhole that seemed only an accident of manufacture or an imperfection of material.

Into this minute aperture I attempted to peer, but whether it was but a fraction of an inch deep or passed completely through the door I could not tell—at least no light showed beyond it. I put my ear to it next and listened, but again my efforts brought negligible results.

During these experiments Woola had been standing at my side gazing intently at the door, and as my glance fell upon him it occurred to me to test the correctness of my hypothesis, that this portal had been the means of ingress to the temple used by Thurid, the black dator, and Matai Shang, Father of Therns.

Turning away abruptly, I called to him to follow me. For a moment he hesitated, and then leaped after me, whining and tugging at my harness to draw me back. I walked on, however, some distance from the door before I let him have his way, that I might see precisely what he would do. Then I permitted him to lead me wherever he would.

Straight back to that baffling portal he dragged me, again taking up his position facing the blank stone, gazing straight at its shining surface. For an hour I worked to solve the mystery of the combination that would open the way before me.

Carefully I recalled every circumstance of my pursuit of Thurid, and my conclusion was identical with my original belief—that Thurid had come this way without other assistance than his own knowledge and passed through the door that barred my progress, unaided from within. But how had he accomplished it?

I recalled the incident of the Chamber of Mystery in the Golden Cliffs that time I had freed Thuvia of Ptarth from the dungeon of the therns, and she had taken a slender, needle-like key from the keyring of her dead jailer to open the door leading back into the Chamber of Mystery where Tars Tarkas fought for his life with the great banths. Such a tiny keyhole as now defied me had opened the way to the intricate lock in that other door.

Hastily I dumped the contents of my pocket-pouch upon the ground before me. Could I but find a slender bit of steel I might yet fashion a key that would give me ingress to the temple prison.

As I examined the heterogeneous collection of odds and ends that is always to be found in the pocket-pouch of a Martian warrior my hand fell upon the emblazoned radium flash torch of the black dator.

As I was about to lay the thing aside as of no value in my present predicament my eyes chanced upon a few strange characters roughly and freshly scratched upon the soft gold of the case.

Casual curiosity prompted me to decipher them, but what I read carried no immediate meaning to my mind. There were three sets of characters, one below another:

$$3 \ |\!-\!| \ 50 \ T$$
$$1 \ |\!-\!| \ 1 \ X$$
$$9 \ |\!-\!| \ 25 \ T$$

For only an instant my curiosity was piqued, and then I replaced the torch in my pocket-pouch, but my fingers had not unclasped from it when there rushed to my memory the recollection of the conversation between Lakor and his companion when the lesser thern had quoted the words of Thurid and scoffed at them: "And what think you of the ridiculous matter of the light? Let the light shine with the intensity of three radium units for fifty tals"—ah, there was the first line of characters upon the torch's metal case—3—50 T; "and for one xat let it shine with the intensity of one radium unit"—there was the second line; "and then for twenty-five tals with nine units."

The formula was complete; but—what did it mean?

I thought I knew, and, seizing a powerful magnifying glass from the litter of my pocket-pouch, I applied myself to a careful examination of the marble immediately about the pinhole in the door. I could have cried aloud in exultation when my scrutiny disclosed the almost invisible incrustation of particles of carbonized electrons which are thrown off by these Martian torches.

It was evident that for countless ages radium torches had been applied to this pinhole, and for what purpose there could be but a single answer—the mechanism of the lock was actuated by light rays; and I, John Carter, Prince of Helium, held the combination in my hand—scratched by the hand of my enemy upon his own torch case.

In a cylindrical bracelet of gold about my wrist was my Barsoomian chronometer—a delicate instrument that records the tals and xats and zodes of Martian time, presenting them to view beneath a strong crystal much after the manner of an earthly odometer.

Timing my operations carefully, I held the torch to the small aperture in the door, regulating the intensity of the light by means of the thumb-lever upon the side of the case.

For fifty tals I let three units of light shine full in the pinhole, then one unit for one xat, and for twenty-five tals nine units. Those last twenty-five tals were the longest twenty-five seconds of my life. Would the lock click at the end of those seemingly interminable intervals of time?

Twenty-three! Twenty-four! Twenty-five!

I shut off the light with a snap. For seven tals I waited—there had been no appreciable effect upon the lock's mechanism. Could it be that my theory was entirely wrong?

Hold! Had the nervous strain resulted in a hallucination, or did the door really move? Slowly the solid stone sank noiselessly back into the wall—there was no hallucination here.

Back and back it slid for ten feet until it had disclosed at its right a narrow doorway leading into a dark and narrow corridor that paralleled the outer wall. Scarcely was the entrance uncovered than Woola and I had leaped through —then the door slipped quietly back into place.

Down the corridor at some distance I saw the faint reflection of a light, and toward this we made our way. At the point where the light shone was a sharp turn, and a little distance beyond this a brilliantly lighted chamber.

Here we discovered a spiral stairway leading up from the center of the circular room.

Immediately I knew that we had reached the center of the base of the Temple of the Sun—the spiral runway led upward past the inner walls of the prison cells. Somewhere above me was Dejah Thoris, unless Thurid and Matai Shang had already succeeded in stealing her.

We had scarcely started up the runway when Woola suddenly displayed the wildest excitement. He leaped back and forth, snapping at my legs and harness, until I thought that he was mad, and finally when I pushed him from me and started once more to ascend he grasped my sword arm between his jaws and dragged me back.

No amount of scolding or cuffing would suffice to make him release me, and I was entirely at the mercy of his brute strength unless I cared to use my dagger upon him with my left hand; but, mad or no, I had not the heart to run the sharp blade into that faithful body.

Down into the chamber he dragged me, and across it to the side opposite that at which we had entered. Here was another doorway leading into a corridor which ran directly down a steep incline. Without a moment's hesitation Woola jerked me along this rocky passage.

Presently he stopped and released me, standing between me and the way we had come, looking up into my face as though to ask if I would now follow him voluntarily or if he must still resort to force.

Looking ruefully at the marks of his great teeth upon my bare arm I decided to do as he seemed to wish me to do. After all, his strange instinct might be more dependable than my faulty human judgment.

And well it was that I had been forced to follow him. But a short distance from the circular chamber we came suddenly into a brilliantly lighted labyrinth of crystal glass partitioned passages.

At first I thought it was one vast, unbroken chamber, so clear and transparent were the walls of the winding corridors, but after I had nearly brained myself a couple of times by attempting to pass through solid vitreous walls I went more carefully.

We had proceeded but a few yards along the corridor that had given us entrance to this strange maze when Woola gave mouth to a most frightful roar, at the same time dashing against the clear partition at our left.

35

The resounding echoes of that fearsome cry were still reverberating through the subterranean chambers when I saw the thing that had startled it from the faithful beast.

Far in the distance, dimly through the many thicknesses of intervening crystal, as in a haze that made them seem unreal and ghostly, I discerned the figures of eight people—three females and five men.

At the same instant, evidently startled by Woola's fierce cry, they halted and looked about. Then, of a sudden, one of them, a woman, held her arms out toward me, and even at that great distance I could see that her lips moved—it was Dejah Thoris, my ever beautiful and ever youthful Princess of Helium.

With her were Thuvia of Ptarth, Phaidor, daughter of Matai Shang, and Thurid, and the Father of Therns, and the three lesser therns that had accompanied them.

Thurid shook his fist at me, and then two of the therns grasped Dejah Thoris and Thuvia roughly by their arms and hurried them on. A moment later they had disappeared into a stone corridor beyond the labyrinth of glass.

They say that love is blind; but so great a love as that of Dejah Thoris that knew me even beneath the thern disguise I wore and across the misty vista of that crystal maze must indeed be far from blind.

THE SECRET TOWER

I HAVE no stomach to narrate the monotonous events of the tedious days that Woola and I spent ferreting our way across the labyrinth of glass, through the dark and devious ways beyond that led beneath the Valley Dor and Golden Cliffs to emerge at last upon the flank of the Otz Mountains just above the Valley of Lost Souls—that pitiful purgatory peopled by the poor unfortunates who dare not continue their abandoned pilgrimage to Dor, or return to the various lands of the outer world from whence they came.

Here the trail of Dejah Thoris' abductors led along the mountains' base, across steep and rugged ravines, by the side of appalling precipices, and sometimes out into the valley, where we found fighting aplenty with the members of the various tribes that make up the population of this vale of hopelessness.

But through it all we came at last to where the way led up a narrow gorge that grew steeper and more impracticable at every step until before us loomed a mighty fortress buried beneath the side of an overhanging cliff.

Here was the secret hiding place of Matai Shang, Father of Therns. Here, surrounded by a handful of the faithful, the hekkador of the ancient faith, who had once been served by millions of vassals and dependents, dispensed the spiritual word among the half dozen nations of Barsoom that still clung tenaciously to their false and discredited religion.

Darkness was just falling as we came in sight of the seemingly impregnable walls of this mountain stronghold, and lest we be seen I drew back with Woola behind a jutting granite promontory, into a clump of the hardy, purple scrub that thrives upon the barren sides of Otz.

Here we lay until the quick transition from daylight to darkness had passed. Then I crept out to approach the fortress walls in search of a way within.

Either through carelessness or over-confidence in the supposed inaccessibility of their hiding place, the triple-barred gate stood ajar. Beyond were a handful of guards, laughing and talking over one of their incomprehensible Barsoomian games.

I saw that none of the guardsmen had been of the party that accompanied Thurid and Matai Shang; and so, relying entirely upon my disguise, I walked boldly through the gateway and up to the thern guard.

The men stopped their game and looked up at me, but there was no sign of suspicion. Similarly they looked at Woola, growling at my heel.

"Kaor!" I said in true Martian greeting, and the warriors arose and saluted me. "I have but just found my way hither from the Golden Cliffs," I continued, "and seek audience with the hekkador, Matai Shang, Father of Therns. Where may he be found?"

"Follow me," said one of the guard, and, turning, led me across the outer courtyard toward a second buttressed wall.

Why the apparent ease with which I seemingly deceived them did not rouse my suspicions I know not, unless it was that my mind was still so full of that fleeting glimpse of my beloved princess that there was room in it for naught else. Be that as it may, the fact is that I marched buoyantly behind my guide straight into the jaws of death.

Afterward I learned that thern spies had been aware of my coming for hours before I reached the hidden fortress.

The gate had been purposely left ajar to tempt me on. The guards had been schooled well in their part of the conspiracy; and I, more like a schoolboy than a seasoned warrior, ran headlong into the trap.

At the far side of the outer court a narrow door let into the angle made by one of the buttresses with the wall. Here my guide produced a key and opened the way within; then, stepping back, he motioned me to enter.

"Matai Shang is in the temple court beyond," he said; and as Woola and I passed through, the fellow closed the door quickly upon us.

The nasty laugh that came to my ears through the heavy planking of the door after the lock clicked was my first intimation that all was not as it should be.

I found myself in a small, circular chamber within the buttress. Before me a door opened, presumably, upon the inner court beyond. For a moment I hesitated, all my suspicions now suddenly, though tardily, aroused; then, with a shrug of my shoulders, I opened the door and stepped out into the glare of torches that lighted the inner court.

Directly opposite me a massive tower rose to a height of three hundred feet. It was of the strangely beautiful modern Barsoomian style of architecture, its entire surface hand carved in bold relief with intricate and fanciful designs. Thirty feet above the courtyard and overlooking it was a broad balcony, and there, indeed, was Matai Shang, and with him were Thurid and Phaidor, Thuvia, and Dejah Thoris—the last two heavily ironed. A handful of thern warriors stood just behind the little party.

As I entered the enclosure the eyes of those in the balcony were full upon me.

An ugly smile distorted the cruel lips of Matai Shang. Thurid hurled a taunt at me and placed a familiar hand upon the shoulder of my princess. Like a tigress she turned upon him, striking the beast a heavy blow with the manacles upon her wrist.

He would have struck back had not Matai Shang interfered, and then I saw that the two men were not over-friendly; for the manner of the thern was arrogant and domineering as he made it plain to the First Born that the Princess of Helium was the personal property of the Father of Therns. And Thurid's bearing toward the ancient hekkador savored not at all of liking or respect.

When the altercation in the balcony had subsided Matai Shang turned again to me.

"Earth man," he cried, "you have earned a more ignoble death than now lies within our weakened power to inflict upon you; but that the death you die tonight may be doubly bitter, know you that when you have passed, your widow becomes the wife of Matai Shang, Hekkador of the Holy Therns, for a Martian year.

"At the end of that time, as you know, she shall be discarded, as is the law among us, but not, as is usual, to lead a quiet and honored life as high priestess of some hallowed shrine. Instead, Dejah Thoris, Princess of Helium, shall become the plaything of my lieutenants—perhaps of thy most hated enemy, Thurid, the black dator."

As he ceased speaking he awaited in silence evidently for some outbreak of rage upon my part—something that would have added to the spice of his revenge But I did not give him the satisfaction that he craved.

Instead, I did the one thing of all others that might rouse his anger and increase his hatred of me, for I knew that if I died Dejah Thoris, too, would find a way to die before they could heap further tortures or indignities upon her.

Of all the holy of holies which the thern venerates and worships none is more revered than the yellow wig which covers his bald pate, and next thereto comes the circlet of gold and the great diadem, whose scintillant rays mark the attainment of the Tenth Cycle.

And, knowing this, I removed the wig and circlet from my head, tossing them carelessly upon the flagging of the court. Then I wiped my feet upon the yellow tresses; and as a groan of rage arose from the balcony I spat full upon the holy diadem.

Matai Shang went livid with anger, but upon the lips of Thurid I could see a grim smile of amusement, for to him these things were not holy; so, lest he should derive too much amusement from my act, I cried: "And thus did I with the holies of Issus, Goddess of Life Eternal, ere I threw Issus herself to the mob that once had worshiped her, to be torn to pieces in her own temple."

That put an end to Thurid's grinning, for he had been high in the favor of Issus.

"Let us have an end to this blaspheming!" he cried, turning to the Father of Therns.

Matai Shang rose and, leaning over the edge of the balcony, gave voice to the weird call that I had heard from the lips of the priests upon the tiny balcony upon the face of the Golden Cliffs overlooking the Valley Dor, when, in times past, they called the fearsome white apes and the hideous plant men to the feast of victims floating down the broad bosom of the mysterious Iss toward the silian-infested waters of the Lost Sea of Korus.

"Let loose the death!" he cried, and immediately a dozen doors in the base of the tower swung open, and a dozen grim and terrible banths sprang into the arena.

This was not the first time that I had faced the ferocious Barsoomian lion, but never had I been pitted, single-handed, against a full dozen of them. Even with the assistance of the fierce Woola, there could be but a single outcome to so unequal a struggle.

For a moment the beasts hesitated beneath the brilliant glare of the torches; but presently their eyes, becoming accustomed to the light, fell upon Woola and me, and with bristling manes and deep-throated roars they advanced, lashing their tawny sides with their powerful tails.

In the brief interval of life that was left me I shot a last, parting glance toward my Dejah Thoris. Her beautiful face was set in an expression of horror; and as my eyes met hers she extended both arms toward me as, struggling with the guards who now held her, she endeavored to cast herself from the balcony into the pit beneath, that she might share my death with me. Then, as the banths were about to close upon me, she turned and buried her dear face in her arms.

Suddenly my attention was drawn toward Thuvia of Ptarth. The beautiful girl was leaning far over the edge of the balcony, her eyes bright with excitement.

In another instant the banths would be upon me, but I could not force my gaze from the features of the red girl, for I knew that her expression meant anything but the enjoyment of the grim tragedy that would so soon be enacted below her; there was some deeper, hidden meaning which I sought to solve.

For an instant I thought of relying on my earthly muscles and agility to escape the banths and reach the balcony, which I could easily have done, but I could not bring myself to desert the faithful Woola and leave him to die alone beneath the cruel fangs of the hungry banths; that is not the way upon Barsoom, nor was it ever the way of John Carter.

Then the secret of Thuvia's excitement became apparent as from her lips there issued the purring sound I had heard once before; that time that, within the Golden Cliffs, she called the fierce banths about her and led them as a shepherdess might lead her flock of meek and harmless sheep.

At the first note of that soothing sound the banths halted in their tracks, and every fierce head went high as the beasts sought the origin of the familiar call. Presently they discovered the red girl in the balcony above them, and, turning, roared out their recognition and their greeting.

Guards sprang to drag Thuvia away, but ere they had succeeded she had hurled a volley of commands at the listening brutes, and as one they turned and marched back into their dens.

"You need not fear them now, John Carter!" cried Thuvia, before they could silence her. "Those banths will never harm you now, nor Woola, either."

It was all I cared to know. There was naught to keep me from that balcony now, and with a long, running leap I sprang far aloft until my hands grasped its lowest sill.

In an instant all was wild confusion. Matai Shang shrank back. Thurid sprang forward with drawn sword to cut me down.

Again Dejah Thoris wielded her heavy irons and fought him back. Then Matai Shang grasped her about the waist and dragged her away through a door leading within the tower.

For an instant Thurid hesitated, and then, as though fearing that the Father of Therns would escape him with the Princess of Helium, he, too, dashed from the balcony in their wake.

Phaidor alone retained her presence of mind. Two of the guards she ordered to bear away Thuvia of Ptarth; the others she commanded to remain and prevent me from following. Then she turned toward me.

"John Carter," she cried, "for the last time I offer you the love of Phaidor, daughter of the Holy Hekkador. Accept and your princess shall be returned to the court of her grandfather, and you shall live in peace and happiness. Refuse and the fate that my father has threatened shall fall upon Dejah Thoris.

"You cannot save her now, for by this time they have reached a place where even you may not follow. Refuse and naught can save you; for, though the way to the last stronghold of the Holy Therns was made easy for you, the way hence hath been made impossible. What say you?"

"You knew my answer, Phaidor," I replied, "before ever you spoke. Make way," I cried to the guards, "for John Carter, Prince of Helium, would pass!"

With that I leaped over the low baluster that surrounded the balcony, and with drawn long-sword faced my enemies.

There were three of them; but Phaidor must have guessed what the outcome of the battle would be, for she turned and fled from the balcony the moment she saw that I would have none of her proposition.

The three guardsmen did not wait for my attack. Instead, they rushed me—the three of them simultaneously; and it was that which gave me an advantage, for they fouled one another in the narrow precincts of the balcony, so that the foremost of them stumbled full upon my blade at the first onslaught.

The red stain upon my point roused to its full the old blood-lust of the fighting man that has ever been so strong within my breast, so that my blade flew through the air with a swiftness and deadly accuracy that threw the two remaining therns into wild despair.

When at last the sharp steel found the heart of one of them the other turned to flee, and, guessing that his steps would lead him along the way taken by those I sought, I let him keep ever far enough ahead to think that he was safely escaping my sword.

Through several inner chambers he raced until he came to a spiral runway. Up this he dashed, I in close pursuit. At the upper end we came out into a small chamber, the walls of which were blank except for a single window overlooking the slopes of Otz and the Valley of Lost Souls beyond.

Here the fellow tore frantically at what appeared to be but a piece of the blank wall opposite the single window. In an instant I guessed that it was a secret exit from the room, and so I paused that he might have an opportunity to negotiate it, for I cared nothing to take the life of this poor servitor—all I craved was a clear road in pursuit of Dejah Thoris, my long-lost princess.

But, try as he would, the panel would yield neither to cunning nor force, so that eventually he gave it up and turned to face me.

"Go thy way, Thern," I said to him, pointing toward the entrance to the runway up which we had but just come. "I have no quarrel with you, nor do I crave your life. Go!"

For answer he sprang upon me with his sword, and so suddenly, at that, that I was like to have gone down before his first rush. So there was nothing for it but to give him what he sought, and that as quickly as might be, that I might not be delayed too long in this chamber while Matai Shang and Thurid made way with Dejah Thoris and Thuvia of Ptarth.

The fellow was a clever swordsman—resourceful and extremely tricky. In fact, he seemed never to have heard that there existed such a thing as a code of honor, for he repeatedly outraged a dozen Barsoomian fighting customs that an honorable man would rather die than ignore.

He even went so far as to snatch his holy wig from his head and throw it in my face, so as to blind me for a moment while he thrust at my unprotected breast.

When he thrust, however, I was not there, for I had fought with therns before; and while none had ever resorted to precisely that same expedient, I knew them to be the least honorable and most treacherous fighters upon Mars, and so was ever on the alert for some new and devilish subterfuge when I was engaged with one of their race.

But at length he overdid the thing; for, drawing his shortsword, he hurled it, javenlinwise, at my body, at the same instant rushing upon me with his long-sword. A single sweeping circle of my own blade caught the flying weapon and hurled it clattering against the far wall, and then, as I sidestepped my antagonist's impetuous rush, I let him have my point full in the stomach as he hurtled by.

Clear to the hilt my weapon passed through his body, and with a frightful shriek he sank to the floor, dead.

Halting only for the brief instant that was required to wrench my sword from the carcass of my late antagonist, I sprang across the chamber to the blank wall beyond, through which the thern had attempted to pass. Here I sought for the secret of its lock, but all to no avail.

In despair I tried to force the thing, but the cold, unyielding stone might well have laughed at my futile, puny endeavors. In fact, I could have sworn that I caught the faint suggestion of taunting laughter from beyond the baffling panel.

In disgust I desisted from my useless efforts and stepped to the chamber's single window.

The slopes of Otz and the distant Valley of Lost Souls held nothing to compel my interest then; but, towering far above me, the tower's carved wall riveted my keenest attention.

Somewhere within that massive pile was Dejah Thoris. Above me I could see windows. There, possibly, lay the only way by which I could reach her. The risk was great, but not too great when the fate of a world's most wondrous woman was at stake.

I glanced below. A hundred feet beneath lay jagged granite boulders at the brink of a frightful chasm upon which the tower abutted; and if not upon the boulders, then at the chasm's bottom, lay death, should a foot slip but once, or clutching fingers loose their hold for the fraction of an instant.

But there was no other way and with a shrug, which I must admit was half shudder, I stepped to the window's outer sill and began my perilous ascent.

To my dismay I found that, unlike the ornamentation upon most Heliumetic structures, the edges of the carvings were quite generally rounded, so that at best my every hold was most precarious.

Fifty feet above me commenced a series of projecting cylindrical stones some six inches in diameter. These apparently circled the tower at six-foot intervals, in bands six feet apart; and as each stone cylinder protruded some four or five inches beyond the surface of the other ornamentation, they presented a comparatively easy mode of ascent could I but reach them.

Laboriously I climbed toward them by way of some windows which lay below them, for I hoped that I might find ingress to the tower through one of these, and thence an easier avenue along which to prosecute my search.

At times so slight was my hold upon the rounded surfaces of the carving's edges that a sneeze, a cough, or even a slight gust of wind would have dislodged me and sent me hurtling to the depths below.

But finally I reached a point where my fingers could just clutch the sill of the lowest window, and I was on the point of breathing a sigh of relief when the sound of voices came to me from above through the open window.

"He can never solve the secret of that lock." The voice was Matai Shang's. "Let us proceed to the hangar above that we may be far to the south before he finds another way—should that be possible."

"All things seem possible to that vile calot," replied another voice, which I recognized as Thurid's.

"Then let us haste," said Matai Shang. "But to be doubly sure, I will leave two who shall patrol this runway. Later they may follow us upon another flier—overtaking us at Kaol."

My upstretched fingers never reached the window's sill. At the first sound of the voices I drew back my hand and clung there to my perilous perch, flattened against the perpendicular wall, scarce daring to breathe.

What a horrible position, indeed, in which to be discovered by Thurid! He had but to lean from the window to push me with his sword's point into eternity.

Presently the sound of the voices became fainter, and once again I took up my hazardous ascent, now more difficult, since more circuitous, for I must climb so as to avoid the windows.

Matai Shang's reference to the hangar and the fliers indicated that my destination lay nothing short of the roof of the tower, and toward this seemingly distant goal I set my face.

The most difficult and dangerous part of the journey was accomplished at last, and it was with relief that I felt my fingers close about the lowest of the stone cylinders.

It is true that these projections were too far apart to make the balance of the ascent anything of a sinecure, but I at least had always within my reach a point of safety to which I might cling in case of accident.

Some ten feet below the roof, the wall inclined slightly inward possibly a foot in the last ten feet, and here the climbing was indeed immeasurably easier, so that my fingers soon clutched the eaves.

As I drew my eyes above the level of the tower's top I saw a flier all but ready to rise.

Upon her deck were Matai Shang, Phaidor, Dejah Thoris, Thuvia of Ptarth, and a few thern warriors, while near her was Thurid in the act of clambering aboard.

He was not ten paces from me, facing in the opposite direction; and what cruel freak of fate should have caused him to turn about just as my eyes topped the roof's edge I may not even guess.

But turn he did; and when his eyes met mine his wicked face lighted with a malignant smile as he leaped toward me, where I was hastening to scramble to the secure footing of the roof.

Dejah Thoris must have seen me at the same instant, for

46

she screamed a useless warning just as Thurid's foot, swinging in a mighty kick, landed full in my face.

Like a felled ox, I reeled and tumbled backward over the tower's side.

IF THERE be a fate that is sometimes cruel to me, there surely is a kind and merciful Providence which watches over me.

As I toppled from the tower into the horrid abyss below I counted myself already dead; and Thurid must have done likewise, for he evidently did not even trouble himself to look after me, but must have turned and mounted the waiting flier at once.

Ten feet only I fell, and then a loop of my tough, leathern harness caught upon one of the cylindrical stone projections in the tower's surface—and held. Even when I had ceased to fall I could not believe the miracle that had preserved me from instant death, and for a moment I hung there, cold sweat exuding from every pore of my body.

But when at last I had worked myself back to a firm position I hesitated to ascend, since I could not then know that Thurid was not still awaiting me above.

Presently, however, there came to my ears the whirring of the propellers of a flier, and as each moment the sound grew fainter I realized that the party had proceeded toward the south without assuring themselves as to my fate.

Cautiously I retraced my way to the roof, and I must admit that it was with no pleasant sensation that I raised my eyes once more above its edge; but, to my relief, there was no one in sight, and a moment later I stood safely upon its broad surface.

To reach the hangar and drag forth the only other flier which it contained was the work of but an instant; and just as the two thern warriors whom Matai Shang had left to prevent this very contingency emerged upon the roof from the tower's interior, I rose above them with a taunting laugh.

Then I dived rapidly to the inner court where I had last seen Woola, and to my immense relief found the faithful beast still there.

The twelve great banths lay in the doorways of their lairs, eyeing him and growling ominously, but they had not

48

disobeyed Thuvia's injunction; and I thanked the fate that had made her their keeper within the Golden Cliffs, and endowed her with the kind and sympathetic nature that had won the loyalty and affection of these fierce beasts for her.

Woola leaped in frantic joy when he discovered me; and as the flier touched the pavement of the court for a brief instant he bounded to the deck beside me, and in the bearlike manifestation of his exuberant happiness all but caused me to wreck the vessel against the courtyard's rocky wall.

Amid the angry shouting of thern guardsmen we rose high above the last fortress of the Holy Therns, and then raced straight toward the northeast and Kaol, the destination which I had heard from the lips of Matai Shang.

Far ahead, a tiny speck in the distance, I made out another flier late in the afternoon. It could be none other than that which bore my lost love and my enemies.

I had gained considerably on the craft by night; and then, knowing that they must have sighted me and would show no lights after dark, I set my destination compass upon her —that wonderful little Martian mechanism which, once attuned to the object of destination, points away toward it, irrespective of every change in its location.

All that night we raced through the Barsoomian void, passing over low hills and dead sea bottoms; above long-deserted cities and populous centers of red Martian habitation upon the ribbon-like lines of cultivated land which border the globe-encircling waterways, which Earth men call the canals of Mars.

Dawn showed that I had gained appreciably upon the flier ahead of me. It was a larger craft than mine, and not so swift; but even so, it had covered an immense distance since the flight began.

The change in vegetation below showed me that we were rapidly nearing the equator. I was now near enough to my quarry to have used my bow gun; but, though I could see that Dejah Thoris was not on deck, I feared to fire upon the craft which bore her.

Thurid was deterred by no such scruples; and though it must have been difficult for him to believe that it was really I who followed them, he could not very well doubt the witness of his own eyes; and so he trained their stern gun

49

upon me with his own hands, and an instant later an explosive radium projectile whizzed perilously close above my deck.

The black's next shot was more accurate, striking my flier full upon the prow and exploding with the instant of contact, ripping wide open the bow buoyancy tanks and disabling the engine.

So quickly did my bow drop after the shot that I scarce had time to lash Woola to the deck and buckle my own harness to a gunwale ring before the craft was hanging stern up and making her last long drop to ground.

Her stern buoyancy tanks prevented her dropping with great rapidity; but Thurid was firing rapidly now in an attempt to burst these also, that I might be dashed to death in the swift fall that would instantly follow a successful shot.

Shot after shot tore past or into us, but by a miracle neither Woola nor I was hit, nor were the after tanks punctured. This good fortune could not last indefinitely, and, assured that Thurid would not again leave me alive, I awaited the bursting of the next shell that hit; and then, throwing my hands above my head, I let go my hold and crumpled, limp and inert, dangling in my harness like a corpse.

The ruse worked, and Thurid fired no more at us. Presently I heard the diminishing sound of whirring propellers, and realized that again I was safe.

Slowly the stricken flier sank to the ground, and when I had freed myself and Woola from the entangling wreckage I found that we were upon the verge of a natural forest—so rare a thing upon the bosom of dying Mars that, outside of the forest in the Valley Dor beside the Lost Sea of Korus, I never before had seen its like upon the planet.

From books and travelers I had learned something of the little-known land of Kaol, which lies along the equator almost halfway round the planet to the east of Helium.

It comprises a sunken area of extreme tropical heat, and is inhabited by a nation of red men varying but little in manners, customs, and appearance from the balance of the red men of Barsoom.

I knew that they were among those of the outer world who still clung tenaciously to the discredited religion of the Holy Therns, and that Matai Shang would find a ready welcome and safe refuge among them; while John Carter could look for nothing better than an ignoble death at their hands.

The isolation of the Kaolians is rendered almost complete by the fact that no waterway connects their land with that of any other nation, nor have they any need of a waterway since the low, swampy land which comprises the entire area of their domain self-waters their abundant tropical crops.

For great distances in all directions rugged hills and arid stretches of dead sea bottom discourage intercourse with them, and since there is practically no such thing as foreign commerce upon warlike Barsoom, where each nation is sufficient to itself, really little has been known relative to the court of the Jeddak of Kaol and the numerous strange, but interesting, people over whom he rules.

Occasional hunting parties have traveled to this out-of-the-way corner of the globe, but the hostility of the natives has usually brought disaster upon them, so that even the sport of hunting the strange and savage creatures which haunt the jungle fastnesses of Kaol has of later years proved insufficient lure even to the most intrepid warriors.

It was upon the verge of the land of the Kaols that I now knew myself to be, but in what direction to search for Dejah Thoris, or how far into the heart of the great forest I might have to penetrate I had not the faintest idea.

But not so Woola.

Scarcely had I disentangled him than he raised his head high in air and commenced circling about at the edge of the forest. Presently he halted, and, turning to see if I were following, set off straight into the maze of trees in the direction we had been going before Thurid's shot had put an end to our flier.

As best I could, I stumbled after him down a steep declivity beginning at the forest's edge.

Immense trees reared their mighty heads far above us, their broad fronds completely shutting off the slightest glimpse of the sky. It was easy to see why the Kaolians needed no navy; their cities, hidden in the midst of this towering forest, must be entirely invisible from above, nor could a landing be made by any but the smallest fliers, and then only with the greatest risk of accident.

How Thurid and Matai Shang were to land I could not

imagine, though later I was to learn that to the level of the forest top there rises in each city of Kaol a slender watchtower which guards the Kaolians by day and by night against the secret approach of a hostile fleet. To one of these the hekkador of the Holy Therns had no difficulty in approaching, and by its means the party was safely lowered to the ground.

As Woola and I approached the bottom of the declivity the ground became soft and mushy, so that it was with the greatest difficulty that we made any headway whatever.

Slender purple grasses topped with red and yellow fernlike fronds grew rankly all about us to the height of several feet above my head.

Myriad creepers hung festooned in graceful loops from tree to tree, and among them were several varieties of the Martian "man-flower," whose blooms have eyes and hands with which to see and seize the insects which form their diet.

The repulsive calot tree was, too, much in evidence. It is a carnivorous plant of about the bigness of a large sagebrush such as dots our western plains. Each branch ends in a set of strong jaws, which have been known to drag down and devour large and formidable beasts of prey.

Both Woola and I had several narrow escapes from these greedy, arboreous monsters.

Occasional areas of firm sod gave us intervals of rest from the arduous labor of traversing this gorgeous, twilight swamp, and it was upon one of these that I finally decided to make camp for the night which my chronometer warned me would soon be upon us.

Many varieties of fruit grew in abundance about us; and as Martian calots are omnivorous, Woola had no difficulty in making a square meal after I had brought down the viands for him. Then, having eaten, too, I lay down with my back to that of my faithful hound, and dropped into a deep and dreamless sleep.

The forest was shrouded in impenetrable darkness when a low growl from Woola awakened me. All about us I could hear the stealthy movement of great, padded feet, and now and then the wicked gleam of green eyes upon us. Arising, I drew my long-sword and waited.

Suddenly a deep-toned, horried roar burst from some savage throat almost at my side. What a fool I had been not to have found safer lodgings for myself and Woola among the branches of one of the countless trees that surrounded us!

By daylight it would have been comparatively easy to have hoisted Woola aloft in one manner or another, but now it was too late. There was nothing for it but to stand our ground and take our medicine, though, from the hideous racket which now assailed our ears, and for which that first roar had seemed to be the signal, I judged that we must be in the midst of hundreds, perhaps thousands, of the fierce, man-eating denizens of the Kaolian jungle.

All the balance of the night they kept up their infernal din, but why they did not attack us I could not guess, nor am I sure to this day, unless it is that none of them ever venture upon the patches of scarlet sward which dot the swamp.

When morning broke they were still there, walking about as in a circle, but always just beyond the edge of the sward. A more terrifying aggregation of fierce and blood-thirsty monsters it would be difficult to imagine.

Singly and in pairs they commenced wandering off into the jungle shortly after sunrise, and when the last of them had departed Woola and I resumed our journey.

Occasionally we caught glimpses of horrid beasts all during the day; but, fortunately, we were never far from a sward island, and when they saw us their pursuit always ended at the verge of the solid sod.

Toward noon we stumbled upon a well-constructed road running in the general direction we had been pursuing. Everything about this highway marked it as the work of skilled engineers, and I was confident, from the indications of antiquity which it bore, as well as from the very evident signs of its being still in everyday use, that it must lead to one of the principal cities of Kaol.

Just as we entered it from one side a huge monster emerged from the jungle upon the other, and at sight of us charged madly in our direction.

Imagine, if you can, a bald-faced hornet of your earthly experience grown to the size of a prize Hereford bull, and you will have some faint conception of the ferocious appearance and awesome formidability of the winged monster that bore down upon me.

Frightful jaws in front and mighty, poisoned sting behind made my relatively puny long-sword seem a pitiful weapon of defense indeed. Nor could I hope to escape the lightning-like movements or hide from those myriad facet eyes which covered three-fourths of the hideous head, permitting the creature to see in all directions at one and the same time.

Even my powerful and ferocious Woola was as helpless as a kitten before that frightful thing. But to flee were useless, even had it ever been to my liking to turn my back upon a danger; so I stood my ground, Woola snarling at my side, my only hope to die as I had always lived—fighting.

The creature was upon us now, and at the instant there seemed to me a single slight chance for victory. If I could but remove the terrible menace of certain death hidden in the poison sacs that fed the sting the struggle would be less unequal.

At the thought I called to Woola to leap upon the creature's head and hang there, and as his mighty jaws closed upon that fiendish face, and glistening fangs buried themselves in the bone and cartilage and lower part of one of the huge eyes, I dived beneath the great body as the creature rose, dragging Woola from the ground, that it might bring its sting beneath and pierce the body of the thing hanging to its head.

To put myself in the path of that poison-laden lance was to court instant death, but it was the only way; and as the thing shot lightning-like toward me I swung my long-sword in a terrific cut that severed the deadly member close to the gorgeously marked body.

Then, like a battering-ram, one of the powerful hind legs caught me full in the chest and hurled me, half stunned and wholly winded, clear across the broad highway and into the underbrush of the jungle that fringes it.

Fortunately, I passed between the boles of trees; had I struck one of them I should have been badly injured, if not killed, so swiftly had I been catapulted by that enormous hind leg.

Dazed though I was, I stumbled to my feet and staggered back to Woola's assistance, to find his savage antagonist circling ten feet above the ground, beating madly at the clinging calot with all six powerful legs.

Even during my sudden flight through the air I had not once released my grip upon my long-sword, and now I ran beneath the two battling monsters, jabbing the winged terror repeatedly with its sharp point.

The thing might easily have risen out of my reach, but evidently it knew as little concerning retreat in the face of danger as either Woola or I, for it dropped quickly toward me, and before I could escape had grasped my shoulder between its powerful jaws.

Time and again the now useless stub of its giant sting struck futilely against my body, but the blows alone were almost as effective as the kick of a horse; so that when I say futilely, I refer only to the natural function of the disabled member—eventually the thing would have hammered me to a pulp.

Nor was it far from accomplishing this when an interruption occurred that put an end forever to its hostilities.

From where I hung a few feet above the road I could see along the highway a few hundred yards to where it turned toward the east, and just as I had about given up all hope of escaping the perilous position in which I now was I saw a red warrior come into view from around the bend.

He was mounted on a splendid thoat, one of the smaller species used by red men, and in his hand was a wondrous long, light lance.

His mount was walking sedately when I first perceived them, but the instant that the red man's eyes fell upon us a word to the thoat brought the animal at full charge down upon us. The long lance of the warrior dipped toward us, and as thoat and rider hurtled beneath, the point passed through the body of our antagonist.

With a convulsive shudder the thing stiffened, the jaws relaxed, dropping me to the ground, and then, careening once in mid air, the creature plunged headforemost to the road, full upon Woola, who still clung tenaciously to its gory head.

By the time I had regained my feet the red man had turned and ridden back to us. Woola, finding his enemy inert and lifeless, released his hold at my command and wriggled from beneath the body that had covered him, and together we faced the warrior looking down upon us.

I started to thank the stranger for his timely assistance, but he cut me off peremptorily.

"Who are you," he asked, "who dare enter the land of Kaol and hunt in the royal forest of the jeddak?"

Then, as he noted my white skin through the coating of grime and blood that covered me, his eyes went wide and in an altered tone he whispered: "Can it be that you are a Holy Thern?"

I might have deceived the fellow for a time, as I had deceived others, but I had cast away the yellow wig and the holy diadem in the presence of Matai Shang, and I knew that it would not be long ere my new aquaintance discovered that I was no thern at all.

"I am not a thern," I replied, and then, flinging caution to the winds, I said: "I am John Carter, Prince of Helium, whose name may not be entirely unknown to you."

If his eyes had gone wide when he thought that I was a Holy Thern, they fairly popped now that he knew that I was John Carter. I grasped my long-sword more firmly as I spoke the words which I was sure would precipitate an attack, but to my surprise they precipitated nothing of the kind.

"John Carter, Prince of Helium," he repeated slowly, as though he could not quite grasp the truth of the statement. "John Carter, the mightiest warrior of Barsoom!"

And then he dismounted and placed his hand upon my shoulder after the manner of most friendly greeting upon Mars.

"It is my duty, and it should be my pleasure, to kill you, John Carter," he said, "but always in my heart of hearts have I admired your prowess and believed in your sincerity the while I have questioned and disbelieved the therns and their religion.

"It would mean my instant death were my heresy to be suspected in the court of Kulan Tith, but if I may serve you, Prince, you have but to command Torkar Bar, Dwar of the Kaolian Road."

Truth and honesty were writ large upon the warrior's noble countenance, so that I could not but have trusted him, enemy though he should have been. His title of Captain of the Kaolian Road explained his timely presence in the heart of the savage forest, for every highway upon Barsoom is patrolled by doughty warriors of the noble class, nor is there any service more honorable than this lonely and dangerous duty in the less frequented sections of the domains of the red men of Barsoom.

"Torkar Bar has already placed a great debt of gratitude

upon my shoulders," I replied, pointing to the carcass of the creature from whose heart he was dragging his long spear.

The red man smiled.

"It was fortunate that I came when I did," he said. "Only this poisoned spear pricking the very heart of a sith can kill it quickly enough to save its prey. In this section of Kaol we are all armed with a long sith spear, whose point is smeared with the poison of the creature it is intended to kill; no other virus acts so quickly upon the beast as its own.

"Look," he continued, drawing his dagger and making an incision in the carcass a foot above the root of the sting, from which he presently drew forth two sacs, each of which held fully a gallon of the deadly liquid.

"Thus we maintain our supply, though were it not for certain commercial uses to which the virus is put it would scarcely be necessary to add to our present store, since the sith is almost extinct.

"Only occasionally do we now run upon one. Of old, however, Kaol was overrun with the frightful monsters that often came in herds of twenty or thirty, darting down from above into our cities and carrying away women, children, and even warriors."

As he spoke I had been wondering just how much I might safely tell this man of the mission which brought me to his land, but his next words anticipated the broaching of the subject on my part, and rendered me thankful that I had not spoken too soon.

"And now as to yourself, John Carter," he said, "I shall not ask your business here, nor do I wish to hear it. I have eyes and ears and ordinary intelligence, and yesterday morning I saw the party that came to the city of Kaol from the north in a small flier. But one thing I ask of you, and that is: the word of John Carter that he contemplates no overt act against either the nation of Kaol or its jeddak."

"You have my word as to that, Torkar Bar," I replied.

"My way leads along the Kaolian road, away from the city of Kaol," he continued. "I have seen no one—John Carter least of all. Nor have you seen Torkar Bar, nor ever heard of him. You understand?"

"Perfectly," I replied.

He laid his hand upon my shoulder.

"This road leads directly into the city of Kaol," he said. "I wish you fortune," and vaulting to the back of his thoat he trotted away without even a backward glance.

It was after dark when Woola and I spied through the mighty forest the great wall which surrounds the city of Kaol.

We had traversed the entire way without mishap or adventure, and though the few we had met had eyed the great calot wonderingly, none had pierced the red pigment with which I had smoothly smeared every square inch of my body.

But to traverse the surrounding country, and to enter the guarded city of Kulan Tith, Jeddak of Kaol, were two very different things. No man enters a Martian city without giving a very detailed and satisfactory account of himself, nor did I delude myself with the belief that I could for a moment impose upon the acumen of the officers of the guard to whom I should be taken the moment I applied at any one of the gates.

My only hope seemed to lie in entering the city surreptitiously under cover of the darkness, and once in, trust to my own wits to hide myself in some crowded quarter where detection would be less liable to occur.

With this idea in view I circled the great wall, keeping within the fringe of the forest, which is cut away for a short distance from the wall all about the city, that no enemy may utilize the trees as a means of ingress.

Several times I attempted to scale the barrier at different points, but not even my earthly muscles could overcome that cleverly constructed rampart. To a height of thirty feet the face of the wall slanted outward, and then for almost an equal distance it was perpendicular, above which it slanted in again for some fifteen feet to the crest.

And smooth! Polished glass could not be more so. Finally I had to admit that at last I had discovered a Barsoomian fortification which I could not negotiate.

Discouraged, I withdrew into the forest beside a broad highway which entered the city from the east, and with Woola beside me lay down to sleep.

A HERO IN KAOL

It was daylight when I was awakened by the sound of stealthy movement near by.

As I opened my eyes Woola, too, moved and, coming up to his haunches, stared through the intervening brush toward the road, each hair upon his neck stiffly erect.

At first I could see nothing, but presently I caught a glimpse of a bit of smooth and glossy green moving among the scarlet and purple and yellow of the vegetation.

Motioning Woola to remain quietly where he was, I crept forward to investigate, and from behind the bole of a great tree I saw a long line of the hideous green warriors of the dead sea bottoms hiding in the dense jungle beside the road.

As far as I could see, the silent line of destruction and death stretched away from the city of Kaol. There could be but one explanation. The green men were expecting an exodus of a body of red troops from the nearest city gate, and they were lying there in ambush to leap upon them.

I owed no fealty to the Jeddak of Kaol, but he was of the same race of noble red men as my own princess, and I would not stand supinely by and see his warriors butchered by the cruel and heartless demons of the waste places of Barsoom.

Cautiously I retraced my steps to where I had left Woola, and warning him to silence, signaled him to follow me. Making a considerable detour to avoid the chance of falling into the hands of the green men, I came at last to the great wall.

A hundred yards to my right was the gate from which the troops were evidently expected to issue, but to reach it I must pass the flank of the green warriors within easy sight of them, and, fearing that my plan to warn the Kaolians might thus be thwarted, I decided upon hastening toward the left, where another gate a mile away would give me ingress to the city.

I knew that the word I brought would prove a splendid passport to Kaol, and I must admit that my caution was due more to my ardent desire to make my way into the city than to avoid a brush with the green men. As much as I enjoy a fight, I cannot always indulge myself, and just now I had more weighty matters to occupy my time than spilling the blood of strange warriors.

Could I but win beyond the city's wall, there might be opportunity in the confusion and excitement which were sure to follow my announcement of an invading force of green warriors to find my way within the palace of the jeddak, where I was sure Matai Shang and his party would be quartered.

But scarcely had I taken a hundred steps in the direction of the farther gate when the sound of marching troops, the clank of metal, and the squealing of thoats just within the city apprised me of the fact that the Kaolians were already moving toward the other gate.

There was no time to be lost. In another moment the gate would be opened and the head of the column pass out upon the death-bordered highway.

Turning back toward the fateful gate, I ran rapidly along the edge of the clearing, taking the ground in the mighty leaps that had first made me famous upon Barsoom. Thirty, fifty, a hundred feet at a bound are nothing for the muscles of an athletic Earth man upon Mars.

As I passed the flank of the waiting green men they saw my eyes turned upon them, and in an instant, knowing that all secrecy was at an end, those nearest me sprang to their feet in an effort to cut me off before I could reach the gate.

At the same instant the mighty portal swung wide and the head of the Kaolian column emerged. A dozen green warriors had succeeded in reaching a point between me and the gate, but they had but little idea who it was they had elected to detain.

I did not slacken my speed an iota as I dashed among them, and as they fell before my blade I could not but recall the happy memory of those other battles when Tars Tarkas, Jeddak of Thark, mightiest of Martian green men, had stood shoulder to shoulder with me through long, hot Martian days, as together we hewed down our enemies until the pile of corpses about us rose higher than a tall man's head.

When several pressed me too closely, there before the carved gateway of Kaol, I leaped above their heads, and fashioning my tactics after those of the hideous plant men of Dor, struck down upon my enemies' heads as I passed above them.

From the city the red warriors were rushing toward us, and from the jungle the savage horde of green men were coming to meet them. In a moment I was in the very center of as fierce and bloody a battle as I had ever passed through.

These Kaolians are most noble fighters, nor are the green men of the equator one whit less warlike than their cold, cruel cousins of the temperate zone. There were many times when either side might have withdrawn without dishonor and thus ended hostilities, but from the mad abandon with which each invariably renewed hostilities I soon came to believe that what need not have been more than a trifling skirmish would end only with the complete extermination of one force or the other.

With the joy of battle once roused within me, I took keen delight in the fray, and that my fighting was noted by the Kaolians was often evidenced by the shouts of applause directed at me.

If I sometimes seem to take too great pride in my fighting ability, it must be remembered that fighting is my vocation. If your vocation be shoeing horses, or painting pictures, and you can do one or the other better than your fellows, then you are a fool if you are not proud of your ability. And so I am very proud that upon two planets no greater fighter has ever lived than John Carter, Prince of Helium.

And I outdid myself that day to impress the fact upon the natives of Kaol, for I wished to win a way into their hearts—and their city. Nor was I to be disappointed in my desire.

All day we fought, until the road was red with blood and clogged with corpses. Back and forth along the slippery highway the tide of battle surged, but never once was the gateway to Kaol really in danger.

There were breathing spells when I had a chance to converse with the red men beside whom I fought, and once the jeddak, Kulan Tith himself, laid his hand upon my shoulder and asked my name.

"I am Dotar Sojat," I replied, recalling a name given me by the Tharks many years before, from the surnames of the first two of their warriors I had killed, which is the custom among them.

"You are a mighty warrior, Dotar Sojat," he replied, "and when this day is done I shall speak with you again in the great audience chamber."

And then the fight surged upon us once more and we were separated, but my heart's desire was attained, and it was with renewed vigor and a joyous soul that I laid about me with my long-sword until the last of the green men had had enough and had withdrawn toward their distant sea bottom.

Not until the battle was over did I learn why the red troops had sallied forth that day. It seemed that Kulan Tith was expecting a visit from a mighty jeddak of the north—a powerful and the only ally of the Kaolians, and it had been his wish to meet his guest a full day's journey from Kaol.

But now the march of the welcoming host was delayed until the following morning, when the troops again set out from Kaol. I had not been bidden to the presence of Kulan Tith after the battle, but he had sent an officer to find me and escort me to comfortable quarters in that part of the palace set aside for the officers of the royal guard.

There, with Woola, I had spent a comfortable night, and rose much refreshed after the arduous labors of the past few days. Woola had fought with me through the battle of the previous day, true to the instincts and training of a Martian war dog, great numbers of which are often to be found with the savage green hordes of the dead sea bottoms.

Neither of us had come through the conflict unscathed, but the marvelous, healing salves of Barsoom had sufficed, overnight, to make us as good as new.

I breakfasted with a number of the Kaolian officers, whom I found as courteous and delightful hosts as even the nobles of Helium, who are renowned for their ease of manners and excellence of breeding. The meal was scarcely concluded when a messenger arrived from Kulan Tith summoning me before him.

As I entered the royal presence the jeddak rose, and stepping from the dais which supported his magnificent throne, came forward to meet me—a mark of distinction that is seldom accorded to other than a visiting ruler.

"Kaor, Dotar Sojat!" he greeted me. "I have summoned you to receive the grateful thanks of the people of Kaol, for had it not been for your heroic bravery in daring fate to warn us of the ambuscade we must surely have fallen into the well-

their giant thoats; but when compared to the relatively small red man and his breed of thoats they assume Brobdingnagian proportions that are truly appalling.

The beasts were hung with jeweled trappings and saddle-pads of gay silk, embroidered in fanciful designs with strings of diamonds, pearls, rubies, emeralds, and the countless un-named jewels of Mars, while from each chariot rose a dozen standards from which streamers, flags, and pennons fluttered in the breeze.

Just in front of the chariots the visiting jeddak rode alone upon a pure white thoat—another unusual sight upon Barsoom—and after them came interminable ranks of mounted spearmen, riflemen, and swordsmen. It was indeed a most imposing sight.

Except for the clanking of accouterments and the occasional squeal of an angry thoat or the low guttural of a zitidar, the passage of the cavalcade was almost noiseless, for neither thoat nor zitidar is a hoofed animal, and the broad tires of the chariots are of an elastic composition, which gives forth no sound.

Now and then the gay laughter of a woman or the chatter of children could be heard, for the red Martians are a social, pleasure-loving people—in direct antithesis to the cold and morbid race of green men.

The forms and ceremonials connected with the meeting of the two jeddaks consumed an hour, and then we turned and retraced our way toward the city of Kaol, which the head of the column reached just before dark, though it must have been nearly morning before the rear guard passed through the gateway.

Fortunately, I was well up toward the head of the column, and after the great banquet, which I attended with the officers of the royal guard, I was free to seek repose. There was so much activity and bustle about the palace all during the night with the constant arrival of the noble officers of the visiting jeddak's retinue that I dared not attempt to prosecute a search for Dejah Thoris, and so, as soon as it was seemly for me to do so, I returned to my quarters.

As I passed along the corridors between the banquet hall and the apartments that had been allotted me, I had a sudden feeling that I was under surveillance, and, turning quickly in my tracks, caught a glimpse of a figure which darted into an open doorway the instant I wheeled about.

Though I ran quickly back to the spot where the shadower had disappeared I could find no trace of him, yet in the brief glimpse that I had caught I could have sworn that I had seen a white face surmounted by a mass of yellow hair.

The incident gave me considerable food for speculation, since if I were right in the conclusion induced by the cursory glimpse I had had of the spy, then Matai Shang and Thurid must suspect my identity, and if that were true not even the service I had rendered Kulan Tith could save me from his religious fantacisim.

But never did vague conjecture or fruitless fears for the future lie with sufficient weight upon my mind to keep me from my rest, and so tonight I threw myself upon my sleeping silks and furs and passed at once into dreamless slumber.

Calots are not permitted within the walls of the palace proper, and so I had had to relegate poor Woola to quarters in the stables where the royal thoats are kept. He had comfortable even luxurious apartments, but I would have given much to have had him with me; and if he had been, the thing which happened that night would not have come to pass.

I could not have slept over a quarter of an hour when I was suddenly awakened by the passing of some cold and clammy thing across my forehead. Instantly I sprang to my feet, clutching in the direction I thought the presence lay. For an instant my hand touched against human flesh, and then, as I lunged headforemost through the darkness to seize my nocturnal visitor, my foot became entangled in my sleeping silks and I fell sprawling to the floor.

By the time I had resumed my feet and found the button which controlled the light my caller had disappeared. Careful search of the room revealed nothing to explain either the identity or business of the person who had thus secretly sought me in the dead of night.

That the purpose might be theft I could not believe, since thieves are practically unknown upon Barsoom. Assassination, however, is rampant, but even this could not have been the motive of my stealthy friend, for he might easily have killed me had he desired.

I had about given up fruitless conjecture and was on the point of returning to sleep when a dozen Kaolian guardsmen entered my apartment. The officer in charge was one of my genial hosts of the morning, but now upon his face was no sign of friendship.

"Kulan Tith commands your presence before him," he said. "Come!"

NEW ALLIES

Surrounded by guardsmen I marched back along the corridors of the palace of Kulan Tith, Jeddak of Kaol, to the great audience chamber in the center of the massive structure.

As I entered the brilliantly lighted apartment, filled with the nobles of Kaol and the officers of the visiting jeddak, all eyes were turned upon me. Upon the great dais at the end of the chamber stood three thrones, upon which sat Kulan Tith and his two guests, Matai Shang, and the visiting jeddak.

Up the broad center aisle we marched beneath deadly silence, and at the foot of the thrones we halted.

"Prefer thy charge," said Kulan Tith, turning to one who stood among the nobles at his right; and then Thurid, the black dator of the First Born, stepped forward and faced me.

"Most noble Jeddak," he said, addressing Kulan Tith, "from the first I suspected this stranger within thy palace. Your description of his fiendish prowess tallied with that of the arch-enemy of truth upon Barsoom.

"But that there might be no mistake I despatched a priest of your own holy cult to make the test that should pierce his disguise and reveal the truth. Behold the result!" and Thurid pointed a rigid finger at my forehead.

All eyes followed the direction of that accusing digit—I alone seemed at a loss to guess what fatal sign rested upon my brow.

The officer beside me guessed my perplexity; and as the brows of Kulan Tith darkened in a menacing scowl as his eyes rested upon me, the noble drew a small mirror from his pocket-pouch and held it before my face.

One glance at the reflection it gave back to me was sufficient.

From my forehead the hand of the sneaking thern had reached out through the concealing darkness of my bed-chamber and wiped away a patch of the disguising red pigment as broad as my palm. Beneath showed the tanned texture of my own white skin.

For a moment Thurid ceased speaking, to enhance, I suspect, the dramatic effect of his disclosure. Then he resumed.

"Here, O Kulan Tith," he cried, "is he who has desecrated the temples of the Gods of Mars, who has violated the persons of the Holy Therns themselves and turned a world against its age-old religion. Before you, in your power, Jeddak of Kaol, Defender of the Holies, stands John Carter, Prince of Helium!"

Kulan Tith looked toward Matai Shang as though for corroboration of these charges. The Holy Thern nodded his head.

"It is indeed the arch-blasphemer," he said. "Even now he has followed me to the very heart of thy palace, Kulan Tith, for the sole purpose of assassinating me. He——"

"He lies!" I cried. "Kulan Tith, listen that you may know the truth. Listen while I tell you why John Carter has followed Matai Shang to the heart of thy palace. Listen to me as well as to them, and then judge if my acts be not more in accord with true Barsoomian chivalry and honor than those of these revengeful devotees of the spurious creeds from whose cruel bonds I have freed your planet."

"Silence!" roared the jeddak, leaping to his feet and laying his hand upon the hilt of his sword. "Silence, blasphemer! Kulan Tith need not permit the air of his audience chamber to be defiled by the heresies that issue from your polluted throat to judge you.

"You stand already self-condemned. It but remains to determine the manner of your death. Even the service that you rendered the arms of Kaol shall avail you naught; it was but a base subterfuge whereby you might win your way into my favor and reach the side of this holy man whose life you craved. To the pits with him!" he concluded, addressing the officer of my guard.

Here was a pretty pass, indeed! What chance had I against a whole nation? What hope for me of mercy at the hands of the fanatical Kulan Tith with such advisers as Matai Shang and Thurid. The black grinned malevolently in my face.

"You shall not escape this time, Earth man," he taunted.

The guards closed toward me. A red haze blurred my

vision. The fighting blood of my Virginian sires coursed hot through my veins. The lust of battle in all its mad fury was upon me.

With a leap I was beside Thurid, and ere the devilish smirk had faded from his handsome face I had caught him full upon the mouth with my clenched fist; and as the good, old American blow landed, the black dator shot back a dozen feet, to crumple in a broken heap at the foot of Kulan Tith's throne, spitting blood and teeth from his hurt mouth.

Then I drew my sword and swung round, on guard, to face a nation.

In an instant the guardsmen were upon me, but before a blow had been struck a mighty voice rose above the din of shouting warriors, and a giant figure leaped from the dais beside Kulan Tith and, with drawn long-sword, threw himself between me and my adversaries.

It was the visiting jeddak.

"Hold!" he cried. "If you value my friendship, Kulan Tith, and the age-old peace that has existed between our peoples, call off your swordsmen; for wherever or against whomsoever fights John Carter, Prince of Helium, there beside him and to the death fights Thuvan Dihn, Jeddak of Ptarth."

The shouting ceased and the menacing points were lowered as a thousand eyes turned first toward Thuvan Dihn in surprise and then toward Kulan Tith in question. At first the Jeddak of Kaol went white in rage, but before he spoke he had mastered himself, so that his tone was calm and even as befitted intercourse between two great jeddaks.

"Thuvan Dihn," he said slowly, "must have great provocation thus to desecrate the ancient customs which inspire the deportment of a guest within the palace of his host. Lest I, too, should forget myself as has my royal friend, I should prefer to remain silent until the Jeddak of Ptarth has won from me applause for his action by relating the causes which provoked it."

I could see that the Jeddak of Ptarth was of half a mind to throw his metal in Kulan Tith's face, but he controlled himself even as well as had his host.

"None knows better than Thuvan Dihn," he said, "the laws which govern the acts of men in the domains of their neighbors; but Thuvan Dihn owes allegiance to a higher law than these—the law of gratitude. Nor to any man upon Barsoom does he owe a greater debt of gratitude than to John Carter, Prince of Helium.

"Years ago, Kulan Tith," he continued, "upon the occasion of your last visit to me, you were greatly taken with the charms and graces of my only daughter, Thuvia. You saw how I adored her, and later you learned that, inspired by some unfathomable whim, she had taken the last, long, voluntary pilgrimage upon the cold bosom of the mysterious Iss, leaving me desolate.

"Some months ago I first heard of the expedition which John Carter had led against Issus and the Holy Therns. Faint rumors of the atrocities reported to have been committed by the therns upon those who for countless ages have floated down the mighty Iss came to my ears.

"I heard that thousands of prisoners had been released, few of whom dared to return to their own countries owing to the mandate of terrible death which rests against all who return from the Valley Dor.

"For a time I could not believe the heresies which I heard, and I prayed that my daughter Thuvia might have died before she ever committed the sacrilege of returning to the outer world. But then my father's love asserted itself, and I vowed that I would prefer eternal damnation to further separation from her if she could be found.

"So I sent emissaries to Helium, and to the court of Xodar, Jeddak of the First Born, and to him who now rules those of the thern nation that have renounced their religion; and from each and all I heard the same story of unspeakable cruelties and atrocities perpetrated upon the poor defenseless victims of their religion by the Holy Therns.

"Many there were who had seen or known my daughter, and from therns who had been close to Matai Shang I learned of the indignities that he personally heaped upon her; and I was glad when I came here to find that Matai Shang was also your guest, for I should have sought him out had it taken a lifetime.

"More, too, I heard, and that of the chivalrous kindness that John Carter had accorded my daughter. They told me how he fought for her and rescued her, and how he spurned escape from the savage Warhoons of the south, sending her to safety upon his own thoat and remaining upon foot to meet the green warriors.

"Can you wonder, Kulan Tith, that I am willing to jeopardize my life, the peace of my nation, or even your friendship, which I prize more than aught else, to champion the Prince of Helium?"

For a moment Kulan Tith was silent. I could see by the expression of his face that he was sore perplexed. Then he spoke.

"Thuvan Dihn," he said, and his tone was friendly though sad, "who am I to judge my fellow-man? In my eyes the Father of Therns is still holy, and the religion which he teaches the only true religion, but were I faced by the same problem that has vexed you I doubt not that I should feel and act precisely as you have.

"In so far as the Prince of Helium is concerned I may act, but between you and Matai Shang my only office can be one of conciliation. The Prince of Helium shall be escorted in safety to the boundary of my domain ere the sun has set again, where he shall be free to go whither he will; but upon pain of death must he never again enter the land of Kaol.

"If there be a quarrel between you and the Father of Therns, I need not ask that the settlement of it be deferred until both have passed beyond the limits of my power. Are you satisfied, Thuvan Dihn?"

The Jeddak of Ptarth nodded his assent, but the ugly scowl that he bent upon Matai Shang harbored ill for that pasty-faced godling.

"The Prince of Helium is far from satisfied," I cried, breaking rudely in upon the beginnings of peace, for I had no stomach for peace at the price that had been named.

"I have escaped death in a dozen forms to follow Matai Shang and overtake him, and I do not intend to be led, like a decrepit thoat to the slaughter, from the goal that I have won by the prowess of my sword arm and the might of my muscles.

"Nor will Thuvan Dihn, Jeddak of Ptarth, be satisfied when he has heard me through. Do you know why I have followed Matai Shang and Thurid, the black dator, from the forests of the Valley Dor across half a world through almost insurmountable difficulties?

"Think you that John Carter, Prince of Helium, would

72

stoop to assassination? Can Kulan Tith be such a fool as to believe that lie, whispered in his ear by the Holy Thern or Dator Thurid?

"I do not follow Matai Shang to kill him, though the God of mine own planet knows that my hands itch to be at his throat. I follow him, Thuvan Dihn, because with him are two prisoners—my wife, Dejah Thoris, Princess of Helium, and your daughter, Thuvia of Ptarth.

"Now think you that I shall permit myself to be led beyond the walls of Kaol unless the mother of my son accompanies me, and thy daughter be restored?"

Thuvan Dihn turned upon Kulan Tith. Rage flamed in his keen eyes; but by the masterfulness of his self-control he kept his tones level as he spoke.

"Knew you this thing, Kulan Tith?" he asked. "Knew you that my daughter lay a prisoner in your palace?"

"He could not know it," interrupted Matai Shang, white with what I am sure was more fear than rage. "He could not know it, for it is a lie."

I would have had his life for that upon the spot, but even as I sprang toward him Thuvan Dihn laid a heavy hand upon my shoulder.

"Wait," he said to me, and then to Kulan Tith. "It is not a lie. This much have I learned of the Prince of Helium—he does not lie. Answer me, Kulan Tith—I have asked you a question."

"Three women came with the Father of Therns," replied Kulan Tith. "Phaidor, his daughter, and two who were reported to be her slaves. If these be Thuvia of Ptarth and Dejah Thoris of Helium I did not know it—I have seen neither. But if they be, then shall they be returned to you on the morrow."

As he spoke he looked straight at Matai Shang, not as a devotee should look at a high priest, but as a ruler of men looks at one to whom he issues a command.

It must have been plain to the Father of Therns, as it was to me, that the recent disclosures of his true character had done much already to weaken the faith of Kulan Tith, and that it would require but little more to turn the powerful jeddak into an avowed enemy; but so strong are the seeds of superstition that even the great Kaolian still hesitated to cut the final strand that bound him to his ancient religion.

Matai Shang was wise enough to seem to accept the mandate of his follower, and promised to bring the two slave women to the audience chamber on the morrow.

"It is almost morning now," he said, "and I should dislike to break in upon the slumber of my daughter, or I would have them fetched at once that you might see that the Prince of Helium is mistaken," and he emphasized the last word in an effort to affront me so subtilely that I could not take open offense.

I was about to object to any delay, and demand that the Princess of Helium be brought to me forthwith, when Thuvan Dihn made such insistence seem unnecessary.

"I should like to see my daughter at once," he said, "but if Kulan Tith will give me his assurance that none will be permitted to leave the palace this night, and that no harm shall befall either Dejah Thoris or Thuvia of Ptarth between now and the moment that they are brought into our presence in this chamber at daylight I shall not insist."

"None shall leave the palace tonight," replied the Jeddak of Kaol, "and Matai Shang will give us assurance that no harm will come to the two women?"

The thern assented with a nod. A few moments later Kulan Tith indicated that the audience was at an end, and at Thuvan Dihn's invitation I accompanied the Jeddak of Ptarth to his own apartments, where we sat until daylight, while he listened to the account of my experiences upon his planet and to all that had befallen his daughter during the time that we had been together.

I found the father of Thuvia a man after my own heart, and that night saw the beginning of a friendship which has grown until it is second only to that which obtains between Tars Tarkas, the green Jeddak of Thark, and myself.

The first burst of Mars's sudden dawn brought messengers from Kulan Tith, summoning us to the audience chamber where Thuvan Dihn was to receive his daughter after years of separation, and I was to be reunited with the glorious daughter of Helium after an almost unbroken separation of twelve years.

My heart pounded within my bosom until I looked about me in embarrassment, so sure was I that all within the room must hear. My arms ached to enfold once more the divine form of her whose eternal youth and undying beauty were but outward manifestations of a perfect soul.

At last the messenger despatched to fetch Matai Shang returned. I craned my neck to catch the first glimpse of those who should be following, but the messenger was alone.

Halting before the throne he addressed his jeddak in a voice that was plainly audible to all within the chamber.

"O Kulan Tith, Mightiest of Jeddaks," he cried, after the fashion of the court, "your messenger returns alone, for when he reached the apartments of the Father of Therns he found them empty, as were those occupied by his suite."

Kulan Tith went white.

A low groan burst from the lips of Thuvan Dihn who stood next me, not having ascended the throne which awaited him beside his host. For a moment the silence of death reigned in the great audience chamber of Kulan Tith, Jeddak of Kaol. It was he who broke the spell.

Rising from his throne he stepped down from the dais to the side of Thuvan Dihn. Tears dimmed his eyes as he placed both his hands upon the shoulders of his friend.

"O Thuvan Dihn," he cried, "that this should have happened in the palace of thy best friend! With my own hands would I have wrung the neck of Matai Shang had I guessed what was in his foul heart. Last night my life-long faith was weakened—this morning it has been shattered; but too late, too late.

"To wrest your daughter and the wife of this royal warrior from the clutches of these archfiends you have but to command the resources of a mighty nation, for all Kaol is at your disposal. What may be done? Say the word!"

"First," I suggested, "let us find those of your people who be responsible for the escape of Matai Shang and his followers. Without assistance on the part of the palace guard this thing could not have come to pass. Seek the guilty, and from them force an explanation of the manner of their going and the direction they have taken."

Before Kulan Tith could issue the commands that would initiate the investigation a handsome young officer stepped forward and addressed his jeddak.

"O Kulan Tith, Mightiest of Jeddaks," he said, "I alone be responsible for this grievous error. Last night it was I who commanded the palace guard. I was on duty in other parts of the palace during the audience of the early morning, and knew nothing of what transpired then, so that when the Father of Therns summoned me and explained that it was your wish that his party be hastened from the city because of the presence here of a deadly enemy who sought the Holy Hekkador's life I did only what a lifetime of training has taught me was the proper thing to do—I obeyed him whom I believed to be the ruler of us all, mightier even than thou, mightiest of jeddaks.

"Let the consequences and the punishment fall on me alone, for I alone am guilty. Those others of the palace guard who assisted in the flight did so under my instructions."

Kulan Tith looked first at me and then at Thuvan Dihn, as though to ask our judgment upon the man, but the error was so evidently excusable that neither of us had any mind to see the young officer suffer for a mistake that any might readily have made.

"How left they," asked Thuvan Dihn, "and what direction did they take?"

"They left as they came," replied the officer, "upon their own flier. For some time after they had departed I watched the vessel's lights, which vanished finally due north."

"Where north could Matai Shang find an asylum?" asked Thuvan Dihn of Kulan Tith.

For some moments the Jeddak of Kaol stood with bowed head, apparently deep in thought. Then a sudden light brightened his countenance.

"I have it!" he cried. "Only yesterday Matai Shang let drop a hint of his destination, telling me of a race of people unlike ourselves who dwell far to the north. They, he said, had always been known to the Holy Therns and were devout and faithful followers of the ancient cult. Among them would he find a perpetual haven of refuge, where no 'lying heretics' might seek him out. It is there that Matai Shang has gone."

"And in all Kaol there be no flier wherein to follow," I cried.

"Nor nearer than Ptarth," replied Thuvan Dihn.

"Wait!" I exclaimed, "beyond the southern fringe of this great forest lies the wreck of the thern flier which brought me that far upon my way. If you will loan me men to fetch

76

it, and artificers to assist me, I can repair it in two days, Kulan Tith."

I had been more than half suspicious of the seeming sincerity of the Kaolian jeddak's sudden apostasy, but the alacrity with which he embraced my suggestion, and the despatch with which a force of officers and men were placed at my disposal entirely removed the last vestige of my doubts.

Two days later the flier rested upon the top of the watchtower, ready to depart. Thuvan Dihn and Kulan Tith had offered me the entire resources of two nations—millions of fighting men were at my disposal; but my flier could hold but one other than myself and Woola.

As I stepped aboard her, Thuvan Dihn took his place beside me. I cast a look of questioning surprise upon him. He turned to the highest of his own officers who had accompanied him to Kaol.

"To you I entrust the return of my retinue to Ptarth," he said. "There my son rules ably in my absence. The Prince of Helium shall not go alone into the land of his enemies. I have spoken. Farewell!"

THROUGH THE CARRION CAVES

STRAIGHT toward the north, day and night, our destination compass led us after the fleeing flier upon which it had remained set since I first attuned it after leaving the thern fortress.

Early in the second night we noticed the air becoming perceptibly colder, and from the distance we had come from the equator were assured that we were rapidly approaching the north arctic region.

My knowledge of the efforts that had been made by countless expeditions to explore that unknown land bade me to caution, for never had flier returned who had passed to any considerable distance beyond the mighty ice-barrier that fringes the southern hem of the frigid zone.

What became of them none knew—only that they passed forever out of the sight of man into that grim and mysterious country of the pole.

The distance from the barrier to the pole was no more than a swift flier should cover in a few hours, and so it was assumed that some frightful catastrophe awaited those who reached the "forbidden land," as it had come to be called by the Martians of the outer world.

Thus it was that I went more slowly as we approached the barrier, for it was my intention to move cautiously by day over the ice-pack that I might discover, before I had run into a trap, if there really lay an inhabited country at the north pole, for there only could I imagine a spot where Matai Shang might feel secure from John Carter, Prince of Helium.

We were flying at a snail's pace but a few feet above the ground—literally feeling our way along through the darkness, for both moons had set, and the night was black with the clouds that are to be found only at Mars's two extremities.

Suddenly a towering wall of white rose directly in our

path, and though I threw the helm hard over, and reversed our engine, I was too late to avoid collision.

With a sickening crash we struck the high looming obstacle three-quarters on.

The flier reeled half over; the engine stopped; as one, the patched buoyancy tanks burst, and we plunged, headforemost, to the ground twenty feet beneath.

Fortunately none of us was injured, and when we had disentangled ourselves from the wreckage, and the lesser moon had burst again from below the horizon, we found that we were at the foot of a mighty ice-barrier, from which outcropped great patches of the granite hills which hold it from encroaching farther toward the south.

What fate! With the journey all but completed to be thus wrecked upon the wrong side of that precipitous and unscalable wall of rock and ice!

I looked at Thuvan Dihn. He but shook his head dejectedly.

The balance of the night we spent shivering in our inadequate sleeping silks and furs upon the snow that lies at the foot of the ice-barrier.

With daylight my battered spirits regained something of their accustomed hopefulness, though I must admit that there was little enough for them to feed upon.

"What shall we do?" asked Thuvan Dihn. "How may we pass that which is impassable?"

"First we must disprove its impassability," I replied. "Nor shall I admit that it is impassable before I have followed its entire circle and stand again upon this spot, defeated. The sooner we start, the better, for I see no other way, and it will take us more than a month to travel the weary, frigid miles that lie before us."

For five days of cold and suffering and privation we traversed the rough and frozen way which lies at the foot of the ice-barrier. Fierce, fur-bearing creatures attacked us by daylight and by dark. Never for a moment were we safe from the sudden charge of some huge demon of the north.

The apt was our most consistent and dangerous foe.

It is a huge, white-furred creature with six limbs, four of which, short and heavy, carry it swiftly over the snow and ice; while the other two, growing forward from its shoulders on either side of its long, powerful neck, terminate in white, hairless hands, with which it seizes and holds its prey.

Its head and mouth are more similar in appearance to those of a hippopotamus than to any other earthly animal, except that from the sides of the lower jawbone two mighty horns curve slightly downward toward the front.

Its two huge eyes inspired my greatest curiosity. They extend in two vast, oval patches from the center of the top of the cranium down either side of the head to below the roots of the horns, so that these weapons really grow out from the lower part of the eyes, which are composed of several thousand ocelli each.

This eye structure seemed remarkable in a beast whose haunts were upon a glaring field of ice and snow, and though I found upon minute examination of several that we killed that each ocellus is furnished with its own lid, and that the animal can at will close as many of the facets of his huge eyes as he chooses, yet I was positive that nature had thus equipped him because much of his life was to be spent in dark, subterranean recesses.

Shortly after this we came upon the hugest apt that we had seen. The creature stood fully eight feet at the shoulder, and was so sleek and clean and glossy that I could have sworn that he had but recently been groomed.

He stood head-on eyeing us as we approached him, for we had found it a waste of time to attempt to escape the perpetual bestial rage which seems to possess these demon creatures, who rove the dismal north attacking every living thing that comes within the scope of their far-seeing eyes.

Even when their bellies are full and they can eat no more, they kill purely for the pleasure which they derive from taking life, and so when this particular apt failed to charge us, and instead wheeled and trotted away as we neared him, I should have been greatly surprised had I not chanced to glimpse the sheen of a golden collar about its neck.

Thuvan Dihn saw it, too, and it carried the same message of hope to us both. Only man could have placed that collar there, and as no race of Martians of which we knew aught ever had attempted to domesticate the ferocious apt, he must belong to a people of the north of whose very existence we were ignorant—possibly to the fabled yellow men of Barsoom; that once powerful race which was supposed to be extinct, though sometimes, by theorists, thought still to exist in the frozen north.

Simultaneously we started upon the trail of the great beast. Woola was quickly made to understand our desires, so that it was unnecessary to attempt to keep in sight of the animal whose swift flight over the rough ground soon put him beyond our vision.

For the better part of two hours the trail paralleled the barrier, and then suddenly turned toward it through the roughest and seemingly most impassable country I ever had beheld.

Enormous granite boulders blocked the way on every hand; deep rifts in the ice threatened to engulf us at the least misstep; and from the north a slight breeze wafted to our nostrils an unspeakable stench that almost choked us.

For another two hours we were occupied in traversing a few hundred yards to the foot of the barrier.

Then, turning about the corner of a wall-like outcropping of granite, we came upon a smooth area of two or three acres before the base of the towering pile of ice and rock that had baffled us for days, and before us beheld the dark and cavernous mouth of a cave.

From this repelling portal the horrid stench was emanating, and as Thuvan Dihn espied the place he halted with an exclamation of profound astonishment.

"By all my ancestors!" he ejaculated. "That I should have lived to witness the reality of the fabled Carrion Caves! If these indeed be they we have found a way beyond the ice-barrier.

"The ancient chronicles of the first historians of Barsoom —so ancient that we have for ages considered them mythology—record the passing of the yellow men from the ravages of the green hordes that overran Barsoom as the drying up of the great oceans drove the dominant races from their strongholds.

"They tell of the wanderings of the remnants of this once powerful race, harassed at every step, until at last they found a way through the ice-barrier of the north to a fertile valley at the pole.

"At the opening to the subterranean passage that led to their haven of refuge a mighty battle was fought in which the yellow men were victorious, and within the caves that gave ingress to their new home they piled the bodies of the dead, both yellow and green, that the stench might warn away their enemies from further pursuit.

"And ever since that long-gone day have the dead of this fabled land been carried to the Carrion Caves, that in death and decay they might serve their country and warn away invading enemies. Here, too, is brought, so the fable runs, all the waste stuff of the nation—everything that is subject to rot, and that can add to the foul stench that assails our nostrils.

"And death lurks at every step among rotting dead, for here the fierce apts lair, adding to the putrid accumulation with the fragments of their own prey which they cannot devour. It is a horrid avenue to our goal, but it is the only one."

"You are sure, then, that we have found the way to the land of the yellow men?" I cried.

"As sure as may be," he replied; "having only ancient legend to support my belief. But see how closely, so far, each detail tallies with the world-old story of the hegira of the yellow race. Yes, I am sure that we have discovered the way to their ancient hiding place."

"If it be true, and let us pray that such may be the case," I said, "then here may we solve the mystery of the disappearance of Tardos Mors, Jeddak of Helium, and Mors Kajak, his son, for no other spot upon Barsoom has remained unexplored by the many expeditions and the countless spies that have been searching for them for nearly two years. The last word that came from them was that they sought Carthoris, my own brave son, beyond the ice-barrier."

As we talked we had been approaching the entrance to the cave, and as we crossed the threshold I ceased to wonder that the ancient green enemies of the yellow men had been halted by the horrors of that awful way.

The bones of dead men lay man high upon the broad floor of the first cave, and over all was a putrid mush of decaying flesh, through which the apts had beaten a hideous trail toward the entrance to the second cave beyond.

The roof of this first apartment was low, like all that we traversed subsequently, so that the foul odors were confined and condensed to such an extent that they seemed to possess tangible substance. One was almost tempted to draw his short-sword and hew his way through in search of pure air beyond.

"Can man breathe this polluted air and live?" asked Thuvan Dihn, choking.

"Not for long, I imagine," I replied; "so let us make haste. I will go first, and you bring up the rear, with Woola between. Come," and with the words I dashed forward, across the fetid mass of putrefaction.

It was not until we had passed through seven caves of different sizes and varying but little in the power and quality of their stenches that we met with any physical opposition. Then, within the eighth cave, we came upon a lair of apts.

A full score of the mighty beasts were disposed about the chamber. Some were sleeping, while others tore at the fresh-killed carcasses of new-brought prey, or fought among themselves in their love-making.

Here in the dim light of their subterranean home the value of their great eyes was apparent, for these inner caves are shrouded in perpetual gloom that is but little less than utter darkness.

To attempt to pass through the midst of that fierce herd seemed, even to me, the height of folly, and so I proposed to Thuvan Dihn that he return to the outer world with Woola, that the two might find their way to civilization and come again with a sufficient force to overcome not only the apts, but any further obstacles that might lie between us and our goal.

"In the meantime," I continued, "I may discover some means of winning my way alone to the land of the yellow men, but if I am unsuccessful one life only will have been sacrificed. Should we all go on and perish, there will be none to guide a succoring party to Dejah Thoris and your daughter."

"I shall not return and leave you here alone, John Carter," replied Thuvan Dihn. "Whether you go on to victory or death, the Jeddak of Ptarth remains at your side. I have spoken."

I knew from his tone that it were useless to attempt to argue the question, and so I compromised by sending Woola back with a hastily penned note enclosed in a small metal case and fastened about his neck. I commanded the faithful creature to seek Carthoris at Helium, and though half a world and countless dangers lay between I knew that if the thing could be done Woola would do it.

Equipped as he was by nature with marvelous speed and endurance, and with frightful ferocity that made him a match for any single enemy of the way, his keen intelligence and wondrous instinct should easily furnish all else that was needed for the successful accomplishment of his mission.

It was with evident reluctance that the great beast turned to leave me in compliance with my command, and ere he had gone I could not resist the inclination to throw my arms about his great neck in a parting hug. He rubbed his cheek against mine in a final caress, and a moment later was speeding through the Carrion Caves toward the outer world.

In my note to Carthoris I had given explicit directions for locating the Carrion Caves, impressing upon him the necessity for making entrance to the country beyond through this avenue, and not to attempt under any circumstances to cross the ice-barrier with a fleet. I told him that what lay beyond the eighth cave I could not even guess; but I was sure that somewhere upon the other side of the ice-barrier his mother lay in the power of Matai Shang, and that possibly his grandfather and great-grandfather as well, if they lived.

Further, I advised him to call upon Kulan Tith and the son of Thuvan Dihn for warriors and ships that the expedition might be sufficiently strong to insure success at the first blow.

"And," I concluded, "if there be time bring Tars Tarkas with you, for if I live until you reach me I can think of few greater pleasures than to fight once more, shoulder to shoulder, with my old friend."

When Woola had left us Thuvan Dihn and I, hiding in the seventh cave, discussed and discarded many plans for crossing the eighth chamber. From where we stood we saw that the fighting among the apts was growing less, and that many that had been feeding had ceased and lain down to sleep.

Presently it became apparent that in a short time all the ferocious monsters might be peacefully slumbering, and thus a hazardous opportunity be presented to us to cross through their lair.

One by one the remaining brutes stretched themselves upon the bubbling decomposition that covered the mass of bones upon the floor of their den, until but a single apt remained awake. This huge fellow roamed restlessly about, nosing among his companions and the abhorrent litter of the cave.

Occasionally he would stop to peer intently toward first one of the exits from the chamber and then the other. His whole demeanor was as of one who acts as sentry.

We were at last forced to the belief that he would not sleep while the other occupants of the lair slept, and so cast about in our minds for some scheme whereby we might trick him. Finally I suggested a plan to Thuvan Dihn, and as it seemed as good as any that we had discussed we decided to put it to the test.

To this end Thuvan Dihn placed himself close against the cave's wall, beside the entrance to the eighth chamber, while I deliberately showed myself to the guardian apt as he looked toward our retreat. Then I sprang to the opposite side of the entrance, flattening my body close to the wall.

Without a sound the great beast moved rapidly toward the seventh cave to see what manner of intruder had thus rashly penetrated so far within the precincts of his habitation.

As he poked his head through the narrow aperture that connects the two caves a heavy long-sword was awaiting him upon either hand, and before he had an opportunity to emit even a single growl his severed head rolled at our feet.

Quickly we glanced into the eighth chamber—not an apt had moved. Crawling over the carcass of the huge beast that blocked the doorway Thuvan Dihn and I cautiously entered the forbidding and dangerous den.

Like snails we wound our silent and careful way among the huge, recumbent forms. The only sound above our breathing was the sucking noise of our feet as we lifted them from the ooze of decaying flesh through which we crept.

Halfway across the chamber and one of the mighty beasts directly before me moved restlessly at the very instant that my foot was poised above his head, over which I must step.

Breathlessly I waited, balancing upon one foot, for I did not dare move a muscle. In my right hand was my keen short-sword, the point hovering an inch above the thick fur beneath which beat the savage heart.

Finally the apt relaxed, sighing, as with the passing of a bad dream, and resumed the regular respiration of deep slumber. I planted my raised foot beyond the fierce head and an instant later had stepped over the beast.

Thuvan Dihn followed directly after me, and another moment found us at the further door, undetected.

The Carrion Caves consist of a series of twenty-seven connecting chambers, and present the appearance of having been eroded by running water in some far-gone age when a mighty river found its way to the south through this single breach in the barrier of rock and ice that hems the country of the pole.

Thuvan Dihn and I traversed the remaining nineteen caverns without adventure or mishap.

We were afterward to learn that but once a month is it possible to find all the apts of the Carrion Caves in a single chamber.

At other times they roam singly or in pairs in and out of the caves, so that it would have been practically impossible for two men to have passed through the entire twenty-seven chambers without encountering an apt in nearly every one of them. Once a month they sleep for a full day, and it was our good fortune to stumble by accident upon one of these occasions.

Beyond the last cave we emerged into a desolate country of snow and ice, but found a well-marked trail leading north. The way was boulder-strewn, as had been that south of the barrier, so that we could see but a short distance ahead of us at any time.

After a couple of hours we passed round a huge boulder to come to a steep declivity leading down into a valley.

Directly before us we saw a half dozen men—fierce, black-bearded fellows, with skins the color of a ripe lemon.

"The yellow men of Barsoom!" ejaculated Thuvan Dihn, as though even now that he saw them he found it scarce possible to believe that the very race we expected to find hidden in this remote and inaccessible land did really exist.

We withdrew behind an adjacent boulder to watch the actions of the little party, which stood huddled at the foot of another huge rock, their backs toward us.

One of them was peering round the edge of the granite mass as though watching one who approached from the opposite side.

Presently the object of his scrutiny came within the range

86

of my vision and I saw that it was another yellow man. All were clothed in magnificent furs—the six in the black and yellow striped hide of the orluk, while he who approached alone was resplendent in the pure white skin of an apt.

The yellow men were armed with two swords, and a short javelin was slung across the back of each, while from their left arms hung cuplike shields no larger than a dinner plate, the concave sides of which turned outward toward an antagonist.

They seemed puny and futile implements of safety against an even ordinary swordsman, but I was later to see the purpose of them and with what wondrous dexterity the yellow men manipulate them.

One of the swords which each of the warriors carried caught my immediate attention. I call it a sword, but really it was a sharp-edged blade with a complete hook at the far end.

The other sword was of about the same length as the hooked instrument, and somewhere between that of my longsword and my short-sword. It was straight and two-edged. In addition to the weapons I have innumerated each man carried a dagger in his harness.

As the white-furred one approached, the six grasped their swords more firmly—the hooked instrument in the left hand, the straight sword in the right, while above the left wrist the small shield was held rigid upon a metal bracelet.

As the lone warrior came opposite them the six rushed out upon him with fiendish yells that resembled nothing more closely than the savage war cry of the Apaches of the South-west.

Instantly the attacked drew both his swords, and as the six fell upon him I witnessed as pretty fighting as one might care to see.

With their sharp hooks the combatants attempted to take hold of an adversary, but like lightning the cupshaped shield would spring before the darting weapon and into its hollow the hook would plunge.

Once the lone warrior caught an antagonist in the side with his hook, and drawing him close ran his sword through him.

But the odds were too unequal, and, though he who fought alone was by far the best and bravest of them all, I saw that it was but a question of time before the remaining five would find an opening through his marvelous guard and bring him down.

Now my sympathies have ever been with the weaker side of an argument, and though I knew nothing of the cause of the trouble I could not stand idly by and see a brave man butchered by superior numbers.

As a matter of fact I presume I gave little attention to seeking an excuse, for I love a good fight too well to need any other reason for joining in when one is afoot.

So it was that before Thuvan Dihn knew what I was about he saw me standing by the side of the white-clad yellow man, battling like mad with his five adversaries.

WITH THE YELLOW MEN

THUVAN DIHN was not long in joining me; and, though we found the hooked weapon a strange and savage thing with which to deal, the three of us soon despatched the five black-bearded warriors who opposed us.

When the battle was over our new acquaintance turned to me, and removing the shield from his wrist, held it out. I did not know the significance of his act, but judged that it was but a form of expressing his gratitude to me.

I afterward learned that it symbolized the offering of a man's life in return for some great favor done him; and my act of refusing, which I had immediately done, was what was expected of me.

"Then accept from Talu, Prince of Marentina," said the yellow man, "this token of my gratitude," and reaching beneath one of his wide sleeves he withdrew a bracelet and placed it upon my arm. He then went through the same ceremony with Thuvan Dihn.

Next he asked our names, and from what land we hailed. He seemed quite familiar with the geography of the outerworld, and when I said I was from Helium he raised his brows.

"Ah," he said, "you seek your ruler and his company?"

"Know you of them?" I asked.

"But little more than that they were captured by my uncle, Salensus Oll, Jeddak of Jeddaks, Ruler of Okar, land of the yellow men of Barsoom. As to their fate I know nothing, for I am at war with my uncle, who would crush my power in the principality of Marentina.

"These from whom you have just saved me are warriors he has sent out to find and slay me, for they know that often I come alone to hunt and kill the sacred apt which Salensus Oll so much reveres. It is partly because I hate his religion that Salensus Oll hates me; but mostly does he fear my growing power and the great faction which has arisen throughout

Okar that would be glad to see me ruler of Okar and Jed-dak of Jeddaks in his place.

"He is a cruel and tyrannous master whom all hate, and were it not for the great fear they have of him I could raise an army overnight that would wipe out the few that might remain loyal to him. My own people are faith-ful to me, and the little valley of Marentina has paid no tribute to the court of Salensus Oll for a year.

"Nor can he force us, for a dozen men may hold the nar-row way to Marentina against a million. But now, as to thine own affairs. How may I aid you? My palace is at your disposal, if you wish to honor me by coming to Maren-tina."

"When our work is done we shall be glad to accept your in-vitation," I replied. "But now you can assist us most by di-recting us to the court of Salensus Oll, and suggesting some means by which we may gain admission to the city and the palace, or whatever other place we find our friends to be confined."

Talu gazed ruefully at our smooth faces and at Thuvan Dihn's red skin and my white one.

"First you must come to Marentina," he said, "for a great change must be wrought in your appearance before you can hope to enter any city in Okar. You must have yellow faces and black beards, and your apparel and trappings must be those least likely to arouse suspicion. In my palace is one who can make you appear as truly yellow men as does Salensus Oll himself."

His counsel seemed wise; and as there was apparently no other way to insure a successful entry to Kadabra, the capital city of Okar, we set out with Talu, Prince of Maren-tina, for his little, rock-bound country.

The way was over some of the worst traveling I have ever seen, and I do not wonder that in this land where there are neither thoats nor fliers that Marentina is in little fear of invasion; but at last we reached our destination, the first view of which I had from a slight elevation a half-mile from the city.

Nestled in a deep valley lay a city of Martian concrete, whose every street and plaza and open space was roofed with glass. All about lay snow and ice, but there was none

90

upon the rounded, domelike, crystal covering that enveloped the whole city.

Then I saw how these people combatted the rigors of the arctic, and lived in luxury and comfort in the midst of a land of perpetual ice. Their cities were veritable hothouses, and when I had come within this one my respect and admiration for the scientific and engineering skill of this buried nation was unbounded.

The moment we entered the city Talu threw off his outer garments of fur, as did we, and I saw that his apparel differed but little from that of the red races of Barsoom. Except for his leathern harness, covered thick with jewels and metal, he was naked, nor could one have comfortably worn apparel in that warm and humid atmosphere.

For three days we remained the guests of Prince Talu, and during that time he showered upon us every attention and courtesy within his power. He showed us all that was of interest in his great city.

The Marentina atmosphere plant will maintain life indefinitely in the cities of the north pole after all life upon the balance of dying Mars is extinct through the failure of the air supply, should the great central plant again cease functioning as it did upon that memorable occasion that gave me the opportunity of restoring life and happiness to the strange world that I had already learned to love so well.

He showed us the heating system that stores the sun's rays in great reservoirs beneath the city, and how little is necessary to maintain the perpetual summer heat of the glorious garden spot within this arctic paradise.

Broad avenues of sod sewn with the seed of the ocher vegetation of the dead sea bottoms carried the noiseless traffic of light and airy ground fliers that are the only form of artificial transportation used north of the gigantic ice-barrier.

The broad tires of these unique fliers are but rubber-like gas bags filled with the eighth Barsoomian ray, or ray of propulsion—that remarkable discovery of the Martians that has made possible the great fleets of mighty airships that render the red man of the outer world supreme. It is this ray which propels the inherent or reflected light of the planet off into space, and when confined gives to the Martian craft their airy buoyancy.

The ground fliers of Marentina contain just sufficient buoyancy in their automobile-like wheels to give the cars traction for steering purposes; and though the hind wheels are geared to the engine, and aid in driving the machine, the bulk of this work is carried by a small propeller at the stern.

I know of no more delightful sensation than that of riding in one of these luxuriously appointed cars which skim, light and airy as feathers, along the soft, mossy avenues of Marentina. They move with absolute noiselessness between borders of crimson sward and beneath arching trees gorgeous with the wondrous blooms that mark so many of the highly cultivated varieties of Barsoomian vegetation.

By the end of the third day the court barber—I can think of no other earthly appellation by which to describe him— had wrought so remarkable a transformation in both Thuvan Dihn and myself that our own wives would never have known us. Our skins were of the same lemon color as his own, and great, black beards and mustaches had been deftly affixed to our smooth faces. The trappings of warriors of Okar aided in the deception; and for wear beyond the hothouse cities we each had suits of the black- and yellowstriped orluk.

Talu gave us careful directions for the journey to Kadabra, the capital city of the Okar nation, which is the racial name of the yellow men. This good friend even accompanied us part way, and then, promising to aid us in any way that he found possible, bade us adieu.

On parting he slipped upon my finger a curiously wrought ring set with a dead-black, lusterless stone, which appeared more like a bit of bituminous coal than the priceless Barsoomian gem which in reality it is.

"There had been but three others cut from the mother stone," he said, "which is in my possession. These three are worn by nobles high in my confidence, all of whom have been sent on secret missions to the court of Salensus Oll.

"Should you come within fifty feet of any of these three you will feel a rapid, pricking sensation in the finger upon which you wear this ring. He who wears one of its mates will experience the same feeling; it is caused by an electrical action that takes place the moment two of these gems cut from the same mother stone come within the radius of each other's power. By it you will know that a friend is at hand upon whom you may depend for assistance in time of need.

"Should another wearer of one of these gems call upon you for aid do not deny him, and should death threaten you swallow the ring rather than let it fall into the hands of enemies. Guard it with your life, John Carter, for some day it may mean more than life to you."

With this parting admonition our good friend turned back toward Marentina, and we set our faces in the direction of the city of Kadabra and the court of Salensus Oll, Jeddak of Jeddaks.

That very evening we came within sight of the walled and glass-roofed city of Kadabra. It lies in a low depression near the pole, surrounded by rocky, snow-clad hills. From the pass through which we entered the valley we had a splendid view of this great city of the north. Its crystal domes sparkled in the brilliant sunlight gleaming above the frost-covered outer wall that circles the entire one hundred miles of its circumference.

At regular intervals great gates give entrance to the city; but even at the distance from which we looked upon the massive pile we could see that all were closed, and, in accordance with Talu's suggestion, we deferred attempting to enter the city until the following morning.

As he had said, we found numerous caves in the hillsides about us, and into one of these we crept for the night. Our warm orluk skins kept us perfectly comfortable, and it was only after a most refreshing sleep that we awoke shortly after daylight on the following morning.

Already the city was astir, and from several of the gates we saw parties of yellow men emerging. Following closely each detail of the instructions given us by our good friend of Marentina, we remained concealed for several hours until one party of some half dozen warriors had passed along the trail below our hiding place and entered the hills by way of the pass along which we had come the previous evening.

After giving them time to get well out of sight of our cave, Thuvan Dihn and I crept out and followed them, overtaking them when they were well into the hills.

When we had come almost to them I called aloud to their leader, when the whole party halted and turned toward us.

The crucial test had come. Could we but deceive these men the rest would be comparatively easy.

"Kaor!" I cried as I came closer to them.

"Kaor!" responded the officer in charge of the party.

"We be from Illall," I continued, giving the name of the most remote city of Okar, which has little or no intercourse with Kadabra. "Only yesterday we arrived, and this morning the captain of the gate told us that you were setting out to hunt orluks, which is a sport we do not find in our own neighborhood. We have hastened after you to pray that you allow us to accompany you."

The officer was entirely deceived, and graciously permitted us to go with them for the day. The chance guess that they were bound upon an orluk hunt proved correct, and Talu had said that the chances were ten to one that such would be the mission of any party leaving Kadabra by the pass through which we entered the valley, since that way leads directly to the vast plains frequented by this elephantine beast of prey.

In so far as the hunt was concerned, the day was a failure, for we did not see a single orluk; but this proved more than fortunate for us, since the yellow men were so chagrined by their misfortune that they would not enter the city by the same gate by which they had left it in the morning, as it seemed that they had made great boasts to the captain of that gate about their skill at this dangerous sport.

We, therefore, approached Kadabra at a point several miles from that at which the party had quitted it in the morning, and so were relieved of the danger of embarrassing questions and explanations on the part of the gate captain, whom we had said had directed us to this particular hunting party.

We had come quite close to the city when my attention was attracted toward a tall, black shaft that reared its head several hundred feet into the air from what appeared to be a tangled mass of junk or wreckage, now partially snow-covered.

I did not dare venture an inquiry for fear of arousing suspicion by evident ignorance of something which as a yellow man I should have known; but before we reached the city gate I was to learn the purpose of that grim shaft and the meaning of the mighty accumulation beneath it.

We had come almost to the gate when one of the party called to his fellows, at the same time pointing toward the distant southern horizon. Following the direction he indicated, my eyes descried the hull of a large flier approaching rapidly from above the crest of the encircling hills.

"Still other fools who would solve the mysteries of the forbidden north," said the officer, half to himself. "Will they never cease their fatal curiosity?"

"Let us hope not," answered one of the warriors, "for then what should we do for slaves and sport?"

"True; but what stupid beasts they are to continue to come to a region from whence none of them ever has returned."

"Let us tarry and watch the end of this one," suggested one of the men.

The officer looked toward the city.

"The watch has seen him," he said; "we may remain, for we may be needed."

I looked toward the city and saw several hundred warriors issuing from the nearest gate. They moved leisurely, as though there were no need for haste—nor was there, as I was presently to learn.

Then I turned my eyes once more toward the flier. She was moving rapidly toward the city, and when she had come close enough I was surprised to see that her propellers were idle.

Straight for that grim shaft she bore. At the last minute I saw the great blades move to reverse her, yet on she came as though drawn by some mighty, irresistible power.

Intense excitement prevailed upon her deck, where men were running hither and thither, manning the guns and preparing to launch the small, one-man fliers, a fleet of which is part of the equipment of every Martian war vessel. Closer and closer to the black shaft the ship sped. In another instant she must strike, and then I saw the familiar signal flown that sends the lesser boats in a great flock from the deck of the mother ship.

Instantly a hundred tiny fliers rose from her deck, like a swarm of huge dragon flies; but scarcely were they clear of the battleship than the nose of each turned toward the shaft, and they, too, rushed on at frightful speed toward the same now seemingly inevitable end that menaced the larger vessel.

A moment later the collision came. Men were hurled in every direction from the ship's deck, while she, bent and crumpled, took the last, long plunge to the scrap-heap at the shaft's base.

With her fell a shower of her own tiny fliers, for each of them had come in violent collision with the solid shaft.

I noticed that the wrecked fliers scraped down the shaft's side, and that their fall was not as rapid as might have been expected; and then suddenly the secret of the shaft burst upon me, and with it an explanation of the cause that prevented a flier that passed too far across the ice-barrier ever returning.

The shaft was a mighty magnet, and when once a vessel came within the radius of its powerful attraction for the aluminum steel that enters so largely into the construction of all Barsoomian craft, no power on earth could prevent such an end as we had just witnessed.

I afterward learned that the shaft rests directly over the magnetic pole of Mars, but whether this adds in any way to its incalculable power of attraction I do not know. I am a fighting man, not a scientist.

Here, at last, was an explanation of the long absence of Tardos Mors and Mors Kajak. These valiant and intrepid warriors had dared the mysteries and dangers of the frozen north to search for Carthoris, whose long absence had bowed in grief the head of his beautiful mother, Dejah Thoris, Princess of Helium.

The moment that the last of the fliers came to rest at the base of the shaft the black-bearded, yellow warriors swarmed over the mass of wreckage upon which they lay, making prisoners of those who were uninjured and occasionally despatching with a sword-thrust one of the wounded who seemed prone to resent their taunts and insults.

A few of the uninjured red men battled bravely against their cruel foes, but for the most part they seemed too overwhelmed by the horror of the catastrophe that had befallen them to do more than submit supinely to the golden chains with which they were menacled.

When the last of the prisoners had been confined, the party returned to the city, at the gate of which we met a pack of fierce, gold-collared apts, each of which marched between two warriors, who held them with strong chains of the same metal as their collars.

Just beyond the gate the attendants loosened the whole

terrible herd, and as they bounded off toward the grim, black shaft I did not need to ask to know their mission. Had there not been those within the cruel city of Kadabra who needed succor far worse than the poor unfortunate dead and dying out there in the cold upon the bent and broken carcasses of a thousand fliers I could not have restrained my desire to hasten back and do battle with those horrid creatures that had been despatched to rend and devour them.

As it was I could but follow the yellow warriors, with bowed head, and give thanks for the chance that had given Thuvan Dihn and me such easy ingress to the capital of Salensus Oll.

Once within the gates, we had no difficulty in eluding our friends of the morning, and presently found ourselves in a Martian hostelry.

IN DURANCE

THE public houses of Barsoom, I have found, vary but little. There is no privacy for other than married couples.

Men without their wives are escorted to a large chamber, the floor of which is usually of white marble or heavy glass, kept scrupulously clean. Here are many small, raised platforms for the guest's sleeping silks and furs, and if he have none of his own clean, fresh ones are furnished at a nominal charge.

Once a man's belongings have been deposited upon one of these platforms he is a guest of the house, and that platform his own until he leaves. No one will disturb or molest his belongings, as there are no thieves upon Mars.

As assassination is the one thing to be feared, the proprietors of the hostelries furnish armed guards, who pace back and forth through the sleeping-rooms day and night. The number of guards and gorgeousness of their trappings quite usually denote the status of the hotel.

No meals are served in these houses, but generally a public eating place adjoins them. Baths are connected with the sleeping chambers, and each guest is required to bathe daily or depart from the hotel.

Usually on a second or third floor there is a large sleeping-room for single women guests, but its appointments do not vary materially from the chamber occupied by men. The guards who watch the women remain in the corridor outside the sleeping chamber, while female slaves pace back and forth among the sleepers within, ready to notify the warriors should their presence be required.

I was surprised to note that all the guards with the hotel at which we stopped were red men, and on inquiring of one of them I learned that they were slaves purchased by the proprietors of the hotels from the government. The man whose post was past my sleeping platform had been commander of the navy of a great Martian nation; but fate had carried his flagship across the ice-barrier within the radius of power of the magnetic shaft, and now for many tedious years he had been a slave of the yellow men.

He told me that princes, jeds, and even jeddaks of the outer world, were among the menials who served the yellow race; but when I asked him if he had heard of the fate of Mors Kajak or Tardos Mors he shook his head, saying that he never had heard of their being prisoners here, though he was very familiar with the reputations and fame they bore in the outer world.

Neither had he heard any rumor of the coming of the Father of Therns and the black dator of the First Born, but he hastened to explain that he knew little of what took place within the palace. I could see that he wondered not a little that a yellow man should be so inquisitive about certain red prisoners from beyond the ice-barrier, and that I should be so ignorant of customs and conditions among my own race.

In fact, I had forgotten my disguise upon discovering a red man pacing before my sleeping platform; but his growing expression of surprise warned me in time, for I had no mind to reveal my identity to any unless some good could come of it, and I did not see how this poor fellow could serve me yet, though I had it in my mind that later I might be the means of serving him and all the other thousands of prisoners who do the bidding of their stern masters in Kadabra.

Thuvan Dihn and I discussed our plans as we sat together among our sleeping silks and furs that night in the midst of the hundreds of yellow men who occupied the apartment with us. We spoke in low whispers, but, as that is only what courtesy demands in a public sleeping place, we roused no suspicion.

At last, determining that all must be but idle speculation until after we had had a chance to explore the city and attempt to put into execution the plan Talu had suggested, we bade each other good night and turned to sleep.

After breakfasting the following morning we set out to see Kadabra, and as, through the generosity of the prince of Marentina, we were well supplied with the funds current in Okar we purchased a handsome ground flier. Having learned to drive them while in Marentina, we spent a delightful and profitable day exploring the city, and late in the afternoon at the hour Talu told us we would find government officials in their offices we stopped before a magnificent building on the plaza opposite the royal grounds and the palace.

Here we walked boldly in past the armed guard at the door, to be met by a red slave within who asked our wishes.

"Tell Sorav, your master, that two warriors from Illall wish to take service in the palace guard," I said.

Sorav, Talu had told us, was the commander of the forces of the palace, and as men from the further cities of Okar—and especially Illall—were less likely to be tainted with the germ of intrigue which had for years infected the household of Salensus Oll, he was sure that we would be welcomed and few questions asked us.

He had primed us with such general information as he thought would be necessary for us to pass muster before Sorav, after which we would have to undergo a further examination before Salensus Oll that he might determine our physical fitness and our ability as warriors.

The little experience we had had with the strange hooked sword of the yellow man and his cuplike shield made it seem rather unlikely that either of us could pass this final test, but there was the chance that we might be quartered in the palace of Salensus Oll for several days after being accepted by Sorav before the Jeddak of Jeddaks would find time to put us to the final test.

After a wait of several minutes in an ante-chamber we were summoned into the private office of Sorav, where we were courteously greeted by this ferocious-appearing, black-bearded officer. He asked us our names and stations in our own city, and having received replies that were evidently satisfactory to him, he put certain questions to us that Talu had foreseen and prepared us for.

The interview could not have lasted over ten minutes when Sorav summoned an aid whom he instructed to record us properly, and then escort us to the quarters in the palace which are set aside for aspirants to membership in the palace guard.

The aid took us to his own office first, where he measured and weighed and photographed us simultaneously with a machine ingeniously devised for that purpose, five copies being instantly reproduced in five different offices of the government, two of which are located in other cities miles distant. Then he led us through the palace grounds to the main guardroom of the palace, there turning us over to the officer in charge.

This individual again questioned us briefly, and finally despatched a soldier to guide us to our quarters. These we found located upon the second floor of the palace in a semidetached tower at the rear of the edifice.

When we asked our guide why we were quartered so far from the guardroom he replied that the custom of the older members of the guard of picking quarrels with aspirants to try their metal had resulted in so many deaths that it was found difficult to maintain the guard at its full strength while this custom prevailed. Salensus Oll had, therefore, set apart these quarters for aspirants, and here they were securely locked against the danger of attack by members of the guard.

This unwelcome information put a sudden check to all our well-laid plans, for it meant that we should virtually be prisoners in the palace of Salensus Oll until the time that he should see fit to give us the final examination for efficiency.

As it was this interval upon which we had banked to accomplish so much in our search for Dejah Thoris and Thuvia of Ptarth, our chagrin was unbounded when we heard the great lock click behind our guide as he had quitted us after ushering us into the chambers we were to occupy.

With a wry face I turned to Thuvan Dihn. My companion but shook his head disconsolately and walked to one of the windows upon the far side of the apartment.

Scarcely had he gazed beyond them than he called to me in a tone of suppressed excitement and surprise. In an instant I was by his side.

"Look!" said Thuvan Dihn, pointing toward the courtyard below.

As my eyes followed the direction indicated I saw two women pacing back and forth in an enclosed garden.

At the same moment I recognized them—they were Dejah Thoris and Thuvia of Ptarth!

There were they whom I had trailed from one pole to another, the length of a world. Only ten feet of space and a few metal bars separated me from them.

With a cry I attracted their attention, and as Dejah Thoris looked up full into my eyes I made the sign of love that the men of Barsoom make to their women.

101

To my astonishment and horror her head went high, and as a look of utter contempt touched her finely chiseled features she turned her back full upon me. My body is covered with the scars of a thousand conflicts, but never in all my long life have I suffered such anguish from a wound, for this time the steel of a woman's look had entered my heart.

With a groan I turned away and buried my face in my arms. I heard Thuvan Dihn call aloud to Thuvia, but an instant later his exclamation of surprise betokened that he, too, had been repulsed by his own daughter.

"They will not even listen," he cried to me. "They have put their hands over their ears and walked to the farther end of the garden. Ever heard you of such mad work, John Carter? The two must be bewitched."

Presently I mustered the courage to return to the window, for even though she spurned me I loved her, and could not keep my eyes from feasting upon her divine face and figure, but when she saw me looking she again turned away.

I was at my wit's end to account for her strange actions, and that Thuvia, too, had turned against her father seemed incredible. Could it be that my incomparable princess still clung to the hideous faith from which I had rescued her world? Could it be that she looked upon me with loathing and contempt because I had returned from the Valley Dor, or because I had desecrated the temples and persons of the Holy Therns?

To naught else could I ascribe her strange deportment, yet it seemed far from possible that such could be the case, for the love of Dejah Thoris for John Carter had been a great and wondrous love—far above racial distinctions, creed, or religion.

As I gazed ruefully at the back of her haughty, royal head a gate at the opposite end of the garden opened and a man entered. As he did so he turned and slipped something into the hand of the yellow guardsman beyond the gate, nor was the distance too great that I might not see that money had passed between them.

Instantly I knew that this newcomer had bribed his way within the garden. Then he turned in the direction of the two women, and I saw that he was none other than Thurid, the black dator of the First Born.

He approached quite close to them before he spoke, and as they turned at the sound of his voice I saw Dejah Thoris shrink from him.

There was a nasty leer upon his face as he stepped close to her and spoke again. I could not hear his words, but her answer came clearly.

"The granddaughter of Tardos Mors can always die," she said, "but she could never live at the price you name."

Then I saw the black scoundrel go upon his knees beside her, fairly groveling in the dirt, pleading with her. Only part of what he said came to me, for though he was evidently laboring under the stress of passion and excitement, it was equally apparent that he did not dare raise his voice for fear of detection.

"I would save you from Matai Shang," I heard him say. "You know the fate that awaits you at his hands. Would you not choose me rather than the other?"

"I would choose neither," replied Dejah Thoris, "even were I free to choose, as you know well I am not."

"You *are* free!" he cried. "John Carter, Prince of Helium, is dead."

"I know better than that; but even were he dead, and I must needs choose another mate, it should be a plant man or a great white ape in preference to either Matai Shang or you, black calot," she answered with a sneer of contempt.

Of a sudden the vicious beast lost all control of himself, as with a vile oath he leaped at the slender woman, gripping her tender throat in his brute clutch. Thuvia screamed and sprang to aid her fellow-prisoner, and at the same instant I, too, went mad, and tearing at the bars that spanned my window I ripped them from their sockets as they had been but copper wire.

Hurling myself through the aperture I reached the garden, but a hundred feet from where the black was choking the life from my Dejah Thoris, and with a single great bound I was upon him. I spoke no word as I tore his defiling fingers from that beautiful throat, nor did I utter a sound as I hurled him twenty feet from me.

Foaming with rage, Thurid regained his feet and charged me like a mad bull.

"Yellow man," he shrieked, "you knew not upon whom you had laid your vile hands, but ere I am done with you,

you will know well what it means to offend the person of a First Born."

Then he was upon me, reaching for my throat, and precisely as I had done that day in the courtyard of the Temple of Issus I did here in the garden of the palace of Salensus Oll. I ducked beneath his outstretched arms, and as he lunged past me I planted a terrific right upon the side of his jaw.

Just as he had done upon that other occasion he did now. Like a top he spun round, his knees gave beneath him, and he crumpled to the ground at my feet. Then I heard a voice behind me.

It was the deep voice of authority that marks the ruler of men, and when I turned to face the resplendent figure of a giant yellow man I did not need to ask to know that it was Salensus Oll. At his right stood Matai Shang, and behind them a score of guardsmen.

"Who are you," he cried, "and what means this intrusion within the precincts of the women's garden? I do not recall your face. How came you here?"

But for his last words I should have forgotten my disguise entirely and told him outright that I was John Carter, Prince of Helium; but his question recalled me to myself. I pointed to the dislodged bars of the window above.

"I am an aspirant to membership in the palace guard," I said, "and from yonder window in the tower where I was confined awaiting the final test for fitness I saw this brute attack the—this woman. I could not stand idly by, O Jeddak, and see this thing done within the very palace grounds, and yet feel that I was fit to serve and guard your royal person."

I had evidently made an impression upon the ruler of Okar by my fair words, and when he had turned to Dejah Thoris and Thuvia of Ptarth, and both had corroborated my statements it began to look pretty dark for Thurid.

I saw the ugly gleam in Matai Shang's evil eyes as Dejah Thoris narrated all that had passed between Thurid and herself, and when she came to that part which dealt with my interference with the dator of the First Born her gratitude was quite apparent, though I could see by her eyes that something puzzled her strangely.

I did not wonder at her attitude toward me while others

were present; but that she should have denied me while she and Thuvia were the only occupants of the garden still cut me sorely.

As the examination proceeded I cast a glance at Thurid and startled him looking wide-eyed and wonderingly at me, and then of a sudden he laughed full in my face.

A moment later Salensus Oll turned toward the black.

"What have you to say in explanation of these charges?" he asked in a deep and terrible voice. "Dare you aspire to one whom the Father of Therns has chosen—one who might even be a fit mate for the Jeddak of Jeddaks himself?"

And then the black-bearded tyrant turned and cast a sudden greedy look upon Dejah Thoris, as though with the words a new thought and a new desire had sprung up within his mind and breast.

Thurid had been about to reply and, with a malicious grin upon his face, was pointing an accusing finger at me, when Salensus Oll's words and the expression of his face cut him short.

A cunning look crept into his eyes, and I knew from the expression of his face that his next words were not the ones he had intended to speak.

"O Mightiest of Jeddaks," he said, "the man and the women do not speak the truth. The fellow had come into the garden to assist them to escape. I was beyond and overheard their conversation, and when I entered, the woman screamed and the man sprang upon me and would have killed me.

"What know you of this man? He is a stranger to you, and I dare say that you will find him an enemy and a spy. Let him be put on trial, Salensus Oll, rather than your friend and guest, Thurid, Dator of the First Born."

Salensus Oll looked puzzled. He turned again and looked upon Dejah Thoris, and then Thurid stepped quite close to him and whispered something in his ear—what, I know not.

Presently the yellow ruler turned to one of his officers.

"See that this man be securely confined until we have time to go deeper into this affair," he commanded, "and as bars alone seem inadequate to restrain him, let chains be added."

Then he turned and left the garden, taking Dejah Thoris with him—his hand upon her shoulder. Thurid and Matai

Shang went also, and as they reached the gateway the black turned and laughed again aloud in my face.

What could be the meaning of his sudden change toward me? Could he suspect my true identity? It must be that, and the thing that had betrayed me was the trick and blow that had laid him low for the second time.

As the guards dragged me away my heart was very sad and bitter indeed, for now to the two relentless enemies that had hounded her for so long another and a more powerful one had been added, for I would have been but a fool had I not recognized the sudden love for Dejah Thoris that had just been born in the terrible breast of Salensus Oll, Jeddak of Jeddaks, ruler of Okar.

THE PIT OF PLENTY

I DID not languish long within the prison of Salensus Oll. During the short time that I lay there, fettered with chains of gold, I often wondered as to the fate of Thuvan Dihn, Jeddak of Ptarth.

My brave companion had followed me into the garden as I attacked Thurid, and when Salensus Oll had left with Dejah Thoris and the others, leaving Thuvia of Ptarth behind, he, too, had remained in the garden with his daughter, apparently unnoticed, for he was appareled similarly to the guards.

The last I had seen of him he stood waiting for the warriors who escorted me to close the gate behind them, that he might be alone with Thuvia. Could it be possible that they had escaped? I doubted it, and yet with all my heart I hoped that it might be true.

The third day of my incarceration brought a dozen warriors to escort me to the audience chamber, where Salensus Oll himself was to try me. A great number of nobles crowded the room, and among them I saw Thurid, but Matai Shang was not there.

Dejah Thoris, as radiantly beautiful as ever, sat upon a small throne beside Salensus Oll. The expression of sad hopelessness upon her dear face cut deep into my heart.

Her position beside the Jeddak of Jeddaks boded ill for her and me, and on the instant that I saw her there, there sprang to my mind the firm intention never to leave that chamber alive if I must leave her in the clutches of this powerful tyrant.

I had killed better men than Salensus Oll, and killed them with my bare hands, and now I swore to myself that I should kill him if I found that the only way to save the Princess of Helium. That it would mean almost instant death for me I cared not, except that it would remove me from further efforts in behalf of Dejah Thoris, and for this reason alone I would have chosen another way, for even

107

though I should kill Salensus Oll that act would not restore my beloved wife to her own people. I determined to wait the final outcome of the trial, that I might learn all that I could of the Okarian ruler's intentions, and then act accordingly.

Scarcely had I come before him than Salensus Oll summoned Thurid also.

"Dator Thurid," he said, "you have made a strange request of me; but, in accordance with your wishes and your promise that it will result only to my interests, I have decided to accede.

"You tell me that a certain announcement will be the means of convicting this prisoner and, at the same time, open the way to the gratification of my dearest wish."

Thurid nodded.

"Then shall I make the announcement here before all my nobles," continued Salensus Oll. "For a year no queen has sat upon the throne beside me, and now it suits me to take to wife one who is reputed the most beautiful woman upon Barsoom. A statement which none may truthfully deny.

"Nobles of Okar, unsheath your swords and do homage to Dejah Thoris, Princess of Helium and future Queen of Okar, for at the end of the alloted ten days she shall become the wife of Salensus Oll."

As the nobles drew their blades and lifted them on high, in accordance with the ancient custom of Okar when a jeddak announces his intention to wed, Dejah Thoris sprang to her feet and, raising her hand aloft, cried in a loud voice that they desist.

"I may not be the wife of Salensus Oll," she pleaded, "for already I be a wife and mother. John Carter, Prince of Helium, still lives. I know it to be true, for I overheard Matai Shang tell his daughter Phaidor that he had seen him in Kaor, at the court of Kulan Tith, Jeddak. A jeddak does not wed a married woman, nor will Salensus Oll thus violate the bonds of matrimony."

Salensus Oll turned upon Thurid with an ugly look.

"Is this the surprise you held in store for me?" he cried. "You assured me that no obstacle which might not be easily overcome stood between me and this woman, and now I find that the one insuperable obstacle intervenes. What mean you, man? What have you to say?"

108

"And should I deliver John Carter into your hands, Salensus Oll, would you not feel that I had more than satisfied the promise that I made you?" answered Thurid.

"Talk not like a fool," cried the enraged jeddak. "I am no child to be thus played with."

"I am talking only as a man who knows," replied Thurid. "Knows that he can do all that he claims."

"Then turn John Carter over to me within ten days or yourself suffer the end that I should mete out to him were he in my power!" snapped the Jeddak of Jeddaks, with an ugly scowl.

"You need not wait ten days, Salensus Oll," replied Thurid; and then, turning suddenly upon me as he extended a pointing finger, he cried: "There stands John Carter, Prince of Helium!"

"Fool!" shrieked Salensus Oll. "Fool! John Carter is a white man. This fellow be as yellow as myself. John Carter's face is smooth—Matai Shang has described him to me. This prisoner has a beard and mustache as large and black as any in Okar. Quick, guardsmen, to the pits with the black maniac who wishes to throw his life away for a poor joke upon your ruler!"

"Hold!" cried Thurid, and springing forward before I could guess his intention, he had grasped my beard and ripped the whole false fabric from my face and head, revealing my smooth, tanned skin beneath and my close-cropped black hair.

Instantly pandemonium reigned in the audience chamber of Salensus Oll. Warriors pressed forward with drawn blades, thinking that I might be contemplating the assassination of the Jeddak of Jeddaks; while others, out of curiosity to see one whose name was familiar from pole to pole, crowded behind their fellows.

As my identity was revealed I saw Dejah Thoris spring to her feet—amazement writ large upon her face—and then through that jam of armed men she forced her way before any could prevent. A moment only and she was before me with outstretched arms and eyes filled with the light of her great love.

"John Carter! John Carter!" she cried as I folded her to my breast, and then of a sudden I knew why she had denied me in the garden beneath the tower.

What a fool I had been! Expecting that she would penetrate the marvelous disguise that had been wrought for me by the barber of Marentina! She had not known me, that was all; and when she saw the sign of love from a stranger she was offended and righteously indignant. Indeed, but I had been a fool.

"And it was you," she cried, "who spoke to me from the tower! How could I dream that my beloved Virginian lay behind that fierce beard and that yellow skin?"

She had been wont to call me her Virginian as a term of endearment, for she knew that I loved the sound of that beautiful name, made a thousand times more beautiful and hallowed by her dear lips, and as I heard it again after all those long years my eyes became dimmed with tears and my voice choked with emotion.

But an instant did I crush that dear form to me ere Salensus Oll, trembling with rage and jealousy, shouldered his way to us.

"Seize the man," he cried to his warriors, and a hundred ruthless hands tore us apart.

Well it was for the nobles of the court of Okar that John Carter had been disarmed. As it was, a dozen of them felt the weight of my clenched fists, and I had fought my way half up the steps before the throne to which Salensus Oll had carried Dejah Thoris ere ever they could stop me.

Then I went down, fighting, beneath a half-hundred warriors; but before they had battered me into unconsciousness I heard that from the lips of Dejah Thoris that made all my suffering well worth while.

Standing there beside the great tyrant, who clutched her by the arm, she pointed to where I fought alone against such awful odds.

"Think you, Salensus Oll, that the wife of such as he is," she cried, "would ever dishonor his memory, were he a thousand times dead, by mating with a lesser mortal? Lives there upon any world such another as John Carter, Prince of Helium? Lives there another man who could fight his way back and forth across a warlike planet, facing savage beasts and hordes of savage men, for the love of a woman?

"I, Dejah Thoris, Princess of Helium, am his. He fought for me and won me. If you be a brave man you will honor the bravery that is his, and you will not kill him. Make him a slave if you will, Salensus Oll; but spare his life. I would rather be a slave with such as he than be Queen of Okar."

"Neither slave nor queen dictates to Salensus Oll," replied the Jeddak of Jeddaks. "John Carter shall die a natural death in the Pit of Plenty, and the day he dies Dejah Thoris shall become my queen."

I did not hear her reply, for it was then that a blow upon my head brought unconsciousness, and when I recovered my senses only a handful of guardsmen remained in the audience chamber with me. As I opened my eyes they goaded me with the points of their swords and bade me rise.

Then they led me through long corridors to a court far toward the center of the palace.

In the center of the court was a deep pit, near the edge of which stood half a dozen other guardsmen, awaiting me. One of them carried a long rope in his hands, which he commenced to make ready as we approached.

We had come to within fifty feet of these men when I felt a sudden strange and rapid pricking sensation in one of my fingers.

For a moment I was nonplused by the odd feeling, and then there came to me recollection of that which in the stress of my adventure I had entirely forgotten—the gift ring of Prince Talu of Marentina.

Instantly I looked toward the group we were nearing, at at the same time raising my left hand to my forehead, that the ring might be visible to one who sought it. Simultaneously one of the waiting warriors raised his left hand, ostensibly to brush back his hair, and upon one of his fingers I saw the duplicate of my own ring.

A quick look of intelligence passed between us, after which I kept my eyes turned away from the warrior and did not look at him again, for fear that I might arouse the suspicion of the Okarians.

When we reached the edge of the pit I saw that it was very deep, and presently I realized I was soon to judge just how far it extended below the surface of the court, for he who held the rope passed it about my body in such a way that it could be released from above at any time; and then, as all the warriors grasped it, he pushed me forward, and I fell into the yawning abyss.

After the first jerk as I reached the end of the rope that

had been paid out to let me fall below the pit's edge they lowered me quickly but smoothly. The moment before the plunge, while two or three of the men had been assisting in adjusting the rope about me, one of them had brought his mouth close to my cheek, and in the brief interval before I was cast into the forbidding hole he breathed a single word into my ear:

"Courage!"

The pit, which my imagination had pictured as bottomless, proved to be not more than a hundred feet in depth; but as its walls were smoothly polished it might as well have been a thousand feet, for I could never hope to escape without outside assistance.

For a day I was left in darkness; and then, quite suddenly, a brilliant light illumined my strange cell. I was reasonably hungry and thirsty by this time, not having tasted food or drink since the day prior to my incarceration.

To my amazement I found the sides of the pit, that I had thought smooth, lined with shelves, upon which were the most delicious viands and liquid refreshments that Okar afforded.

With an exclamation of delight I sprang forward to partake of some of the welcome food, but ere ever I reached it the light was extinguished, and, though I groped my way about the chamber, my hands came in contact with nothing beside the smooth, hard wall that I had felt on my first examination of my prison.

Immediately the pangs of hunger and thirst began to assail me. Where before I had had but a mild craving for food and drink, I now actually suffered for want of it, and all because of the tantalizing sight that I had had of food almost within my grasp.

Once more darkness and silence enveloped me, a silence that was broken only by a single mocking laugh.

For another day nothing occurred to break the monotony of my imprisonment or relieve the suffering superinduced by hunger and thirst. Slowly the pangs became less keen, as suffering deaded the activity of certain nerves; and then the light flashed on once again, and before me stood an array of new and tempting dishes, with great bottles of clear water

112

and flagons of refreshing wine, upon the outside of which the cold sweat of condensation stood.

Again, with the hunger madness of a wild beast, I sprang forward to seize those tempting dishes; but, as before, the light went out and I came to a sudden stop against a hard wall.

Then the mocking laugh rang out for a second time.

The Pit of Plenty!

Ah, what a cruel mind must have devised this exquisite, hellish torture! Day after day was the thing repeated, until I was on the verge of madness; and then, as I had done in the pits of the Warhoons, I took a new, firm hold upon my reason and forced it back into the channels of sanity.

By sheer will-power I regained control over my tottering mentality, and so successful was I that the next time that the light came I sat quite still and looked indifferently at the fresh and tempting food almost within my reach. Glad I was that I had done so, for it gave me an opportunity to solve the seeming mystery of those vanishing banquets.

As I made no move to reach the food, the torturers left the light turned on in the hope that at last I could refrain no longer from giving them the delicious thrill of enjoyment that my former futile efforts to obtain it had caused.

And as I sat scrutinizing the laden shelves I presently saw how the thing was accomplished, and so simple was it that I wondered I had not guessed it before. The wall of my prison was of clearest glass—behind the glass were the tantalizing viands.

After nearly an hour the light went out, but this time there was no mocking laughter—at least not upon the part of my tormentors; but I, to be at quits with them, gave a low laugh that none might mistake for the cackle of a maniac.

Nine days passed, and I was weak from hunger and thirst, but no longer suffering—I was past that. Then, down through the darkness above, a little parcel fell to the floor at my side.

Indifferently I groped for it, thinking it but some new invention of my jailers to add to my sufferings.

At last I found it—a tiny package wrapped in paper, at the end of a strong and slender cord. As I opened it a few lozenges fell to the floor. As I gathered them up, feeling of them and smelling of them, I discovered that they were tablets of concentrated food such as are quite common in all parts of Barsoom.

Poison! I thought.

Well, what of it? Why not end my misery now rather than drag out a few more wretched days in this dark pit? Slowly I raised one of the little pellets to my lips.

"Good-bye, my Dejah Thoris!" I breathed. "I have lived for you and fought for you, and now my next dearest wish is to be realized, for I shall die for you," and, taking the morsel in my mouth, I devoured it.

One by one I ate them all, nor ever did anything taste better than those tiny bits of nourishment, within which I knew must lie the seeds of death—possibly of some hideous, torturing death.

As I sat quietly upon the floor of my prison, waiting for the end, my fingers by accident came in contact with the bit of paper in which the things had been wrapped; and as I idly played with it, my mind roaming far back into the past, that I might live again for a few brief moments before I died some of the many happy moments of a long and happy life, I became aware of strange protuberances upon the smooth surface of the parchment-like substance in my hands.

For a time they carried no special significance to my mind—I merely was mildly wondrous that they were there; but at last they seemed to take form, and then I realized that there was but a single line of them, like writing.

Now, more interestedly, my fingers traced and retraced them. There were four separate and distinct combinations of raised lines. Could it be that these were four words, and that they were intended to carry a message to me?

The more I thought of it the more excited I became, until my fingers raced madly back and forth over those bewildering little hills and valleys upon that bit of paper.

But I could make nothing of them, and at last I decided that my very haste was preventing me from solving the mystery. Then I took it more slowly. Again and again my forefinger traced the first of those four combinations.

Martian writing is rather difficult to explain to an Earth man—it is something of a cross between shorthand and picture-writing, and is an entirely different language from the spoken language of Mars.

Upon Barsoom there is but a single oral language.

114

It is spoken today by every race and nation, just as it was at the beginning of human life upon Barsoom. It has grown with the growth of the planet's learning and scientific achievements, but so ingenious a thing it is that new words to express new thoughts or describe new conditions or discoveries form themselves—no other word could explain the thing that a new word is required for other than the word that naturally falls to it, and so, no matter how far removed two nations or races, their spoken languages are identical.

Not so their written languages, however. No two nations have the same written language, and often cities of the same nation have a written language that differs greatly from that of the nation to which they belong.

Thus it was that the signs upon the paper, if in reality they were words, baffled me for some time; but at last I made out the first one.

It was "courage," and it was written in the letters of Marentina.

Courage!

That was the word the yellow guardsman had whispered in my ear as I stood upon the verge of the Pit of Plenty.

The message must be from him, and he I knew was a friend.

With renewed hope I bent my every energy to the deciphering of the balance of the message, and at last success rewarded my endeavor—I had read the four words:

"Courage! Follow the rope."

"FOLLOW THE ROPE!"

WHAT could it mean?

"Follow the rope." What rope?

Presently I recalled the cord that had been attached to the parcel when it fell at my side, and after a little groping my hand came in contact with it again. It depended from above, and when I pulled upon it I discovered that it was rigidly fastened, possibly at the pit's mouth.

Upon examination I found that the cord, though small, was amply able to sustain the weight of several men. Then I made another discovery—there was a second message knotted in the rope at about the height of my head. This I deciphered more easily, now that the key was mine.

"Bring the rope with you. Beyond the knots lies danger."

That was all there was to this message. It was evidently hastily formed—an afterthought.

I did not pause longer than to learn the contents of the second message, and, though I was none too sure of the meaning of the final admonition, "Beyond the knots lies danger," yet I was sure that here before me lay an avenue of escape, and that the sooner I took advantage of it the more likely was I to win to liberty.

At least, I could be but little worse off than I had been in the Pit of Plenty.

I was to find, however, ere I was well out of that damnable hole that I might have been very much worse off had I been compelled to remain there another two minutes.

It had taken me about that length of time to ascend some fifty feet above the bottom when a noise above attracted my attention. To my chagrin I saw that the covering of the pit was being removed far above me, and in the light of the courtyard beyond I saw a number of yellow warriors.

Could it be that I was laboriously working my way into some new trap? Were the messages spurious, after all? And then, just as my hope and courage had ebbed to their lowest, I saw two things.

One was the body of a huge, struggling, snarling apt being lowered over the side of the pit toward me, and the other was an aperture in the side of the shaft—an aperture larger than a man's body, into which my rope led.

Just as I scrambled into the dark hole before me the apt passed me, reaching out with his mighty hands to clutch me, and snapping, growling, and roaring in a most frightful manner.

Plainly now I saw the end for which Salensus Oll had destined me. After first torturing me with starvation he had caused this fierce beast to be lowered into my prison to finish the work that the jeddak's hellish imagination had conceived.

And then another truth flashed upon me—I had lived nine days of the allotted ten which must intervene before Salensus Oll could make Dejah Thoris his queen. The purpose of the apt was to insure my death before the tenth day.

I almost laughed aloud as I thought how Salensus Oll's measure of safety was to aid in defeating the very end he sought, for when they discovered that the apt was alone in the Pit of Plenty they could not know but that he had completely devoured me, and so no suspicion of my escape would cause a search to be made for me.

Coiling the rope that had carried me thus far upon my strange journey, I sought for the other end, but found that as I followed it forward it extended always before me. So this was the meaning of the words: "Follow the rope."

The tunnel through which I crawled was low and dark. I had followed it for several hundred yards when I felt a knot beneath my fingers. "Beyond the knots lies danger."

Now I went with the utmost caution, and a moment later a sharp turn in the tunnel brought me to an opening into a large, brilliantly lighted chamber.

The trend of the tunnel I had been traversing had been slightly upward, and from this I judged that the chamber into which I now found myself looking must be either on the first floor of the palace or directly beneath the first floor.

Upon the opposite wall were many strange instruments and devices, and in the center of the room stood a long table, at which two men were seated in earnest conversation.

He who faced me was a yellow man—a little, wizened-

117

up, pasty-faced old fellow with great eyes that showed the white round the entire circumference of the iris.

His companion was a black man, and I did not need to see his face to know that it was Thurid, for there was no other of the First Born north of the ice-barrier.

Thurid was speaking as I came within hearing of the men's voices.

"Solan," he was saying, "there is no risk and the reward is great. You know that you hate Salensus Oll and that nothing would please you more than to thwart him in some cherished plan. There be nothing that he more cherishes today than the idea of wedding the beautiful Princess of Helium; but I, too, want her, and with your help I may win her.

"You need not more than step from this room for an instant when I give you the signal. I will do the rest, and then, when I am gone, you may come and throw the great switch back into its place, and all will be as before. I need but an hour's start to be safe beyond the devilish power that you control in this hidden chamber beneath the palace of your master. See how easy," and with the words the black dator rose from his seat and, crossing the room, laid his hand upon a large, burnished lever that protruded from the opposite wall.

"No! No!" cried the little old man, springing after him, with a wild shriek. "Not that one! Not that one! That controls the sunray tanks, and should you pull it too far down, all Kadabra would be consumed by heat before I could replace it. Come away! Come away! You know not with what mighty powers you play. This is the lever that you seek. Note well the symbol inlaid in white upon its ebon surface."

Thurid approached and examined the handle of the lever.

"Ah, a magnet," he said. "I will remember. It is settled than I take it," he continued.

The old man hesitated. A look of combined greed and apprehension overspread his none too beautiful features.

"Double the figure," he said. "Even that were all too small an amount for the service you ask. Why, I risk my life by even entertaining you here within the forbidden precincts of my station. Should Salensus Oll learn of it he would have me thrown to the apts before the day was done."

"He dare not do that, and you know it full well, Solan,"

118

contradicted the black. "Too great a power of life and death you hold over the people of Kadabra for Salensus Oll ever to risk threatening you with death. Before ever his minions could lay their hands upon you, you might seize this very lever from which you have just warned me and wipe out the entire city."

"And myself into the bargain," said Solan, with a shudder.

"But if you were to die, anyway, you would find the nerve to do it," replied Thurid.

"Yes," muttered Solan, "I have often thought upon that very thing. Well, First Born, is your red princess worth the price I ask for my services, or will you go without her and see her in the arms of Salensus Oll tomorrow night?"

"Take your price, yellow man," replied Thurid, with an oath. "Half now and the balance when you have fulfilled your contract."

With that the dator threw a well-filled money-pouch upon the table.

Solan opened the pouch and with trembling fingers counted its contents. His weird eyes assumed a greedy expression, and his unkempt beard and mustache twitched with the muscles of his mouth and chin. It was quite evident from his very mannerism that Thurid had keenly guessed the man's weakness—even the clawlike, clutching movement of the fingers betokened the avariciousness of the miser.

Having satisfied himself that the amount was correct, Solan replaced the money in the pouch and rose from the table.

"Now," he said, "are you quite sure that you know the way to your destination? You must travel quickly to cover the ground to the cave and from thence beyond the Great Power, all within a brief hour, for no more dare I spare you."

"Let me repeat it to you," said Thurid, "that you may see if I be letter-perfect."

"Proceed," replied Solan.

"Through yonder door," he commenced, pointing to a door at the far end of the apartment, "I follow a corridor, passing three diverging corridors upon my right; then into the fourth right-hand corridor straight to where three corridors meet; here again I follow to the right, hugging the left wall closely to avoid the pit.

"At the end of this corridor I shall come to a spiral

runway, which I must follow down instead of up; after that the way is along but a single branchless corridor. Am I right?"

"Quite right, Dator," answered Solan; "and now begone. Already have you tempted fate too long within this forbidden place."

"Tonight, or tomorrow, then, you may expect the signal," said Thurid, rising to go.

"Tonight, or tomorrow," repeated Solan, and as the door closed behind his guest the old man continued to mutter as he turned back to the table, where he again dumped the contents of the money-pouch, running his fingers through the heap of shining metal; piling the coins into little towers; counting, recounting, and fondling the wealth the while he muttered on and on in a crooning undertone.

Presently his fingers ceased their play; his eyes popped wider than ever as they fastened upon the door through which Thurid had disappeared. The croon changed to a querulous muttering, and finally to an ugly growl.

Then the old man rose from the table, shaking his fist at the closed door. Now he raised his voice, and his words came distinctly.

"Fool!" he muttered. "Think you that for your happiness Solan will give up his life? If you escaped, Salensus Oll would know that only through my connivance could you have succeeded. Then would he send for me. What would you have me do? Reduce the city and myself to ashes? No, fool, there is a better way—a better way for Solan to keep thy money and be revenged upon Salensus Oll."

He laughed in a nasty, cackling note.

"Poor fool! You may throw the great switch that will give you the freedom of the air of Okar, and then, in fatuous security, go on with thy red princess to the freedom of—death. When you have passed beyond this chamber in your flight, what can prevent Solan replacing the switch as it was before your vile hand touched it? Nothing; and then the Guardian of the North will claim you and your woman, and Salensus Oll, when he sees your dead bodies, will never dream that the hand of Solan had aught to do with the thing."

Then his voice dropped once more into mutterings that I could not translate, but I had heard enough to cause me to guess a great deal more, and I thanked the kind Providence that had led me to this chamber at a time so filled with importance to Dejah Thoris and myself as this.

But how to pass the old man now! The cord, almost invisible upon the floor, stretched straight across the apartment to a door upon the far side.

There was no other way of which I knew, nor could I afford to ignore the advice to "follow the rope." I must cross this room, but however I should accomplish it undetected with that old man in the very center of it baffled me.

Of course I might have sprung in upon him and with my bare hands silenced him forever, but I had heard enough to convince me that with him alive the knowledge that I had gained might serve me at some future moment, while should I kill him and another be stationed in his place Thurid would not come hither with Dejah Thoris, as was quite evidently his intention.

As I stood in the dark shadow of the tunnel's end racking my brain for a feasible plan the while I watched, catlike, the old man's every move, he took up the money-pouch and crossed to one end of the apartment, where, bending to his knees, he fumbled with a panel in the wall.

Instantly I guessed that here was the hiding place in which he hoarded his wealth, and while he bent there, his back toward me, I entered the chamber upon tiptoe, and with the utmost stealth essayed to reach the opposite side before he should complete his task and turn again toward the room's center.

Scarcely thirty steps, all told, must I take, and yet it seemed to my overwrought imagination that that farther wall was miles away; but at last I reached it, nor once had I taken my eyes from the back of the old miser's head.

He did not turn until my hand was upon the button that controlled the door through which my way led, and then he turned away from me as I passed through and gently closed the door.

For an instant I paused, my ear close to the panel, to learn if he had suspected aught, but as no sound of pursuit came from within I wheeled and made my way along the new corridor, following the rope, which I coiled and brought with me as I advanced.

But a short distance farther on I came to the rope's end

at a point where five corridors met. What was I to do? Which way should I turn? I was nonplused.

A careful examination of the end of the rope revealed the fact that it had been cleanly cut with some sharp instrument. This fact and the words that had cautioned me that danger lay beyond the *knots* convinced me that the rope had been severed since my friend had placed it as my guide, for I had but passed a single knot, whereas there had evidently been two or more in the entire length of the cord.

Now, indeed, was I in a pretty fix, for neither did I know which avenue to follow nor when danger lay directly in my path; but there was nothing else to be done than follow one of the corridors, for I could gain nothing by remaining where I was.

So I chose the central opening, and passed on into its gloomy depths with a prayer upon my lips.

The floor of the tunnel rose rapidly as I advanced, and a moment later the way came to an abrupt end before a heavy door.

I could hear nothing beyond, and, with my accustomed rashness, pushed the portal wide to step into a room filled with yellow warriors.

The first to see me opened his eyes wide in astonishment, and at the same instant I felt the tingling sensation in my finger that denoted the presence of a friend of the ring.

Then others saw me, and there was a concerted rush to lay hands upon me, for these were all members of the palace guard—men familiar with my face.

The first to reach me was the wearer of the mate to my strange ring, and as he came close he whispered: "Surrender to me!" then in a loud voice shouted: "You are my prisoner, white man," and menaced me with his two weapons.

And so John Carter, Prince of Helium, meekly surrendered to a single antagonist. The others now swarmed about us, asking many questions, but I would not talk to them, and finally my captor announced that he would lead me back to my cell.

An officer ordered several other warriors to accompany him, and a moment later we were retracing the way I had just come. My friend walked close beside me, asking many silly questions about the country from which I had come, until finally his fellows paid no further attention to him or his gabbling.

Gradually, as he spoke, he lowered his voice, so that presently he was able to converse with me in a low tone without attracting attention. His ruse was a clever one, and showed that Talu had not misjudged the man's fitness for the dangerous duty upon which he was detailed.

When he had fully assured himself that the other guardsmen were not listening, he asked me why I had not followed the rope, and when I told him that it had ended at the five corridors he said that it must have been cut by someone in need of a piece of rope, for he was sure that "the stupid Kadabrans would never have guessed its purpose."

Before we had reached the spot from which the five corridors diverge my Marentinian friend had managed to drop to the rear of the little column with me, and when we came in sight of the branching ways he whispered:

"Run up the first upon the right. It leads to the watchtower upon the south wall. I will direct the pursuit up the next corridor," and with that he gave me a great shove into the dark mouth of the tunnel, at the same time crying out in simulated pain and alarm as he threw himself upon the floor as though I had felled him with a blow.

From behind the voices of the excited guardsmen came reverberating along the corridor, suddenly growing fainter as Talu's spy led them up the wrong passageway in fancied pursuit.

As I ran for my life through the dark galleries beneath the palace of Salensus Oll I must indeed have presented a remarkable appearance had there been any to note it, for though death loomed large about me, my face was split by a broad grin as I thought of the resourcefulness of the nameless hero of Marentina to whom I owed my life.

Of such stuff are the men of my beloved Helium, and when I meet another of their kind, of whatever race or color, my heart goes out to him as it did now to my new friend who had risked his life for me simply because I wore the mate to the ring his ruler had put upon his finger.

The corridor along which I ran led almost straight for a considerable distance, terminating at the foot of a spiral runway, up which I proceeded to emerge presently into a circular chamber upon the first floor of a tower.

In this apartment a dozen red slaves were employed polishing or repairing the weapons of the yellow men. The walls of the room were lined with racks in which were hundreds of straight and hooked swords, javelins, and daggers. It was evidently an armory. There were but three warriors guarding the workers.

My eyes took in the entire scene at a glance. Here were weapons in plenty! Here were sinewy red warriors to wield them!

And here now was John Carter, Prince of Helium, in need both of weapons and warriors!

As I stepped into the apartment, guards and prisoners saw me simultaneously.

Close to the entrance where I stood was a rack of straight swords, and as my hand closed upon the hilt of one of them my eyes fell upon the faces of two of the prisoners who worked side by side.

One of the guards started toward me. "Who are you?" he demanded. "What do you here?"

"I come for Tardos Mors, Jeddak of Helium, and his son, Mors Kajak," I cried, pointing to the two red prisoners, who had now sprung to their feet, wide-eyed in astonished recognition.

"Rise, red men! Before we die let us leave a memorial in the palace of Okar's tyrant that will stand forever in the annals of Kadabra to the honor and glory of Helium," for I had seen that all the prisoners there were men of Tardos Mors's navy.

Then the first guardsman was upon me and the fight was on, but scarce did we engage ere, to my horrow, I saw that the red slaves were shackled to the floor.

THE MAGNET SWITCH

THE guardsmen paid not the slightest attention to their wards, for the red men could not move over two feet from the great rings to which they were padlocked, though each had seized a weapon upon which he had been engaged when I entered the room, and stood ready to join me could they have but done so.

The yellow men devoted all their attention to me, nor were they long in discovering that the three of them were none too many to defend the armory against John Carter. Would that I had had my own good long-sword in my hand that day; but, as it was, I rendered a satisfactory account of myself with the unfamiliar weapon of the yellow man.

At first I had a time of it dodging their villainous hook-swords, but after a minute or two I had succeeded in wresting a second straight sword from one of the racks along the wall, and thereafter, using it to parry the hooks of my antagonists, I felt more evenly equipped.

The three of them were on me at once, and but for a lucky circumstance my end might have come quickly. The foremost guardsman made a vicious lunge for my side with his hook after the three of them had backed me against the wall, but as I sidestepped and raised my arm his weapon but grazed my side, passing into a rack of javelins, where it became entangled.

Before he could release it I had run him through, and then, falling back upon the tactics that have saved me a hundred times in tight pinches, I rushed the two remaining warriors, forcing them back with a perfect torrent of cuts and thrusts, weaving my sword in and out about their guards until I had the fear of death upon them.

Then one of them commenced calling for help, but it was too late to save them.

They were as putty in my hands now, and I backed them about the armory as I would until I had them where I wanted them—within reach of the swords of the shackled slaves. In an instant both lay dead upon the floor. But their cries had not been entirely fruitless, for now I heard answering shouts and the footfalls of many men running and the clank of accouterments and the commands of officers.

"The door! Quick, John Carter, bar the door!" cried Tardos Mors.

Already the guard was in sight, charging across the open court that was visible through the doorway.

A dozen seconds would bring them into the tower. A single leap carried me to the heavy portal. With a resounding bang I slammed it shut.

"The bar!" shouted Tardos Mors.

I tried to slip the huge fastening into place, but it defied my every attempt.

"Raise it a little to release the catch," cried one of the red men.

I could hear the yellow warriors leaping along the flagging just beyond the door. I raised the bar and shot it to the right just as the foremost of the guardsmen threw himself against the opposite side of the massive panels.

The barrier held—I had been in time, but by the fraction of a second only.

Now I turned my attention to the prisoners. To Tardos Mors I went first, asking where the keys might be which would unfasten their fetters.

"The officer of the guard has them," replied the Jeddak of Helium, "and he is among those without who seek entrance. You will have to force them."

Most of the prisoners were already hacking at their bonds with the swords in their hands. The yellow men were battering at the door with javelins and axes.

I turned my attention to the chains that held Tardos Mors. Again and again I cut deep into the metal with my sharp blade, but ever faster and faster fell the torrent of blows upon the portal.

At last a link parted beneath my efforts, and a moment later Tardos Mors was free, though a few inches of trailing chain still dangled from his ankle.

A splinter of wood falling inward from the door announced the headway that our enemies were making toward us.

The mighty panels trembled and bent beneath the furious onslaught of the enraged yellow men.

What with the battering upon the door and the hacking of the red men at their chains the din within the armory was appalling. No sooner was Tardos Mors free than he turned his attention to another of the prisoners, while I set to work to liberate Mors Kajak.

We must work fast if we would have all those fetters cut before the door gave way. Now a panel crashed inward upon the floor, and Mors Kajak sprang to the opening to defend the way until we should have time to release the others.

With javelins snatched from the wall he wrought havoc among the foremost of the Okarians while we battled with the insensate metal that stood between our fellows and freedom.

At length all but one of the prisoners were freed, and then the door fell with a mighty crash before a hastily improvised battering-ram, and the yellow horde was upon us.

"To the upper chambers!" shouted the red man who was still fettered to the floor. "To the upper chambers! There you may defend the tower against all Kadabra. Do not delay because of me, who could pray for no better death than in the service of Tardos Mors and the Prince of Helium."

But I would have sacrificed the life of every man of us rather than desert a single red man, much less the lion-hearted hero who begged us to leave him.

"Cut his chains," I cried to two of the red men, "while the balance of us hold off the foe."

There were ten of us now to do battle with the Okarian guard, and I warrant that that ancient watchtower never looked down upon a more hotly contested battle than took place that day within its own grim walls.

The first inrushing wave of yellow warriors recoiled from the slashing blades of ten of Helium's veteran fighting men. A dozen Okarian corpses blocked the doorway, but over the gruesome barrier a score more of their fellows dashed, shouting their hoarse and hideous war-cry.

Upon the bloody mound we met them, hand to hand, stabbing where the quarters were too close to cut, thrusting when we could push a foeman to arm's length; and mingled with the wild cry of the Okarian there rose and fell the glorious words: "For Helium! For Helium!" that for countless ages have spurred on the bravest of the brave to

127

those deeds of valor that have sent the fame of Helium's heroes broadcast throughout the length and breadth of a world.

Now were the fetters struck from the last of the red men, and thirteen strong we met each new charge of the soldiers of Salensus Oll. Scarce one of us but bled from a score of wounds, yet none had fallen.

From without we saw hundreds of guardsmen pouring into the courtyard, and along the lower corridor from which I had found my way to the armory we could hear the clank of metal and the shouting of men.

In a moment we should be attacked from two sides, and with all our prowess we could not hope to withstand the unequal odds which would thus divide our attention and our small numbers.

"To the upper chambers!" cried Tardos Mors, and a moment later we fell back toward the runway that led to the floors above.

Here another bloody battle was waged with the force of yellow men who charged into the armory as we fell back from the doorway. Here we lost our first man, a noble fellow whom we could ill spare; but at length all had backed into the runway except myself, who remained to hold back the Okarians until the others were safe above.

In the mouth of the narrow spiral but a single warrior could attack me at a time, so that I had little difficulty in holding them all back for the brief moment that was necessary. Then, backing slowly before them, I commenced the ascent of the spiral.

All the long way to the tower's top the guardsmen pressed me closely. When one went down before my sword another scrambled over the dead man to take his place; and thus, taking an awful toll with each few feet gained, I came to the spacious glass-walled watchtower of Kadabra.

Here my companions clustered ready to take my place, and for a moment's respite I stepped to one side while they held the enemy off.

From the lofty perch a view could be had for miles in every direction. Toward the south stretched the rugged, ice-clad waste to the edge of the mighty barrier. Toward the east and west, and dimly toward the north I descried other Okarian cities, while in the immediate foreground, just beyond the walls of Kadabra, the grim guardian shaft reared its somber head.

Then I cast my eyes down into the streets of Kadabra, from which a sudden tumult had arisen, and there I saw a battle raging, and beyond the city's walls I saw armed men marching in great columns toward a near-by gate.

Eagerly I pressed forward against the glass wall of the observatory, scarce daring to credit the testimony of my own eyes. But at last I could doubt no longer, and with a shout of joy that rose strangely in the midst of the cursing and groaning of the battling men at the entrance to the chamber, I called to Tardos Mors.

As he joined me I pointed down into the streets of Kadabra and to the advancing columns beyond, above which floated bravely in the arctic air the flags and banners of Helium.

An instant later every red man in the lofty chamber had seen the inspiring sight, and such a shout of thanksgiving arose as I warrant never before echoed through that age-old pile of stone.

But still we must fight on, for though our troops had entered Kadabra, the city was yet far from capitulation, nor had the palace been even assaulted. Turn and turn about we held the top of the runway while the others feasted their eyes upon the sight of our valiant countrymen battling far beneath us.

Now they have rushed the palace gate! Great battering-rams are dashed against its formidable surface. Now they are repulsed by a deadly shower of javelins from the wall's top!

Once again they charge, but a sortie by a large force of Okarians from an intersecting avenue crumples the head of the column, and the men of Helium go down, fighting, beneath an overwhelming force.

The palace gate flies open and a force of the jeddak's own guard, picked men from the flower of the Okarian army, sallies forth to shatter the broken regiments. For a moment it looks as though nothing could avert defeat, and then I see a noble figure upon a mighty thoat—not the tiny thoat of the red man, but one of his huge cousins of the dead sea bottoms.

The warrior hews his way to the front, and behind him rally the disorganized soldiers of Helium. As he raises his head aloft to fling a challenge at the men upon the palace walls I see his face, and my heart swells in pride and happiness as the red warriors leap to the side of their leader and win back the ground that they had but just lost—the face of him upon the mighty thoat is the face of my son—Carthoris of Helium.

At his side fights a huge Martian war-hound, nor did I need a second look to know that it was Woola—my faithful Woola who had thus well performed his arduous task and brought the succoring legions in the nick of time.

"In the nick of time?"

Who yet might say that they were not too late to save, but surely they could avenge! And such retribution as that unconquered army would deal out to the hateful Okarians! I sighed to think that I might not be alive to witness it.

Again I turned to the windows. The red men had not yet forced the outer palace wall, but they were fighting nobly against the best that Okar afforded—valiant warriors who contested every inch of the way.

Now my attention was caught by a new element without the city wall—a great body of mounted warriors looming large above the red men. They were the huge green allies of Helium—the savage hordes from the dead sea bottoms of the far south.

In grim and terrible silence they sped on toward the gate, the padded hoofs of their frightful mounts giving forth no sound. Into the doomed city they charged, and as they wheeled across the wide plaza before the palace of the Jeddak of Jeddaks I saw, riding at their head, the mighty figure of their mighty leader—Tars Tarkas, Jeddak of Thark.

My wish, then, was to be gratified, for I was to see my old friend battling once again, and though not shoulder to shoulder with him, I, too, would be fighting in the same cause here in the high tower of Okar.

Nor did it seem that our foes would ever cease their stubborn attacks, for still they came, though the way to our chamber was often clogged with the bodies of their dead. At times they would pause long enough to drag back the impeding corpses, and then fresh warriors would forge upward to taste the cup of death.

I had been taking my turn with the others in defending the approach to our lofty retreat when Mors Kajak, who had been watching the battle in the street below, called aloud in sudden excitement. There was a note of apprehension in his voice that brought me to his side the instant that I could turn my place over to another, and as I reached him he pointed far out across the waste of snow and ice toward the southern horizon.

"Alas!" he cried, "that I should be forced to witness cruel fate betray them without power to warn or aid; but they be past either now."

As I looked in the direction he indicated I saw the cause of his perturbation. A mighty fleet of fliers was approaching majestically toward Kadabra from the direction of the ice-barrier. On and on they came with ever increasing velocity.

"The grim shaft that they call the Guardian of the North is beckoning to them," said Mors Kajak sadly, "just as it beckoned to Tardos Mors and his great fleet; see where they lie, crumpled and broken, a grim and terrible monument to the mighty force of destruction which naught can resist."

I, too, saw; but something else I saw that Mors Kajak did not; in my mind's eye I saw a buried chamber whose walls were lined with strange instruments and devices.

In the center of the chamber was a long table, and before it sat a little, pop-eyed old man counting his money; but, plainest of all, I saw upon the wall a great switch with a small magnet inlaid within the surface of its black handle.

Then I glanced out at the fast-approaching fleet. In five minutes that mighty armada of the skies would be bent and worthless scrap, lying at the base of the shaft beyond the city's wall, and yellow hordes would be loosed from another gate to rush out upon the few survivors stumbling blindly down through the mass of wreckage; then the apts would come. I shuddered at the thought, for I could vividly picture the whole horrible scene.

Quick have I always been to decide and act. The impulse that moves me and the doing of the thing seem simultaneous; for if my mind goes through the tedious formality of reasoning, it must be a subconscious act of which I am not objectively aware. Psychologists tell me that, as the subconscious does not reason, too close a scrutiny of my mental activities might prove anything but flattering; but be that as it may, I have often won success while the thinker would have been still at the endless task of comparing various judgments.

131

And now celerity of action was the prime essential to the success of the thing that I had decided upon.

Grasping my sword more firmly in my hand, I called to the red man at the opening to the runway to stand aside.

"Way for the Prince of Helium!" I shouted; and before the astonished yellow man whose misfortune it was to be at the fighting end of the line at that particular moment could gather his wits together my sword had decapitated him, and I was rushing like a mad bull down upon those behind him.

"Way for the Prince of Helium!" I shouted as I cut a path through the astonished guardsmen of Salensus Oll.

Hewing to right and left, I beat my way down that warrior-choked spiral until, near the bottom, those below, thinking that an army was descending upon them, turned and fled.

The armory at the first floor was vacant when I entered it, the last of the Okarians having fled into the courtyard, so none saw me continue down the spiral toward the corridor beneath.

Here I ran as rapidly as my legs would carry me toward the five corners, and there plunged into the passageway that led to the station of the old miser.

Without the formality of a knock, I burst into the room. There sat the old man at his table; but as he saw me he sprang to his feet, drawing his sword.

With scarce more than a glance toward him I leaped for the great switch; but, quick as I was, that wiry old fellow was there before me.

How he did it I shall never know, nor does it seem credible that any Martian-born creature could approximate the marvelous speed of my earthly muscles.

Like a tiger he turned upon me, and I was quick to see why Solan had been chosen for this important duty.

Never in all my life have I seen such wondrous swordsmanship and such uncanny agility as that ancient bag of bones displayed. He was in forty places at the same time, and before I had half a chance to awaken to my danger he was like to have made a monkey of me, and a dead monkey at that.

It is strange how new and unexpected conditions bring out unguessed ability to meet them.

That day in the buried chamber beneath the palace of Salensus Oll I learned what swordsmanship meant, and to what heights of sword mastery I could achieve when pitted against such a wizard of the blade as Solan.

For a time he liked to have bested me; but presently the latent possibilities that must have been lying dormant within me for a lifetime came to the fore, and I fought as I had never dreamed a human being could fight.

That that duel-royal should have taken place in the dark recesses of a cellar, without a single appreciative eye to witness it has always seemed to me almost a world calamity—at least from the viewpoint Barsoomian, where bloody strife is the first and greatest consideration of individuals, nations, and races.

I was fighting to reach the switch, Solan to prevent me; and, though we stood not three feet from it, I could not win an inch toward it, nor he force me back an inch for the first five minutes of our battle.

I knew that if I were to throw it in time to save the on-coming fleet it must be done in the next few seconds, and so I tried my old rushing tactics; but I might as well have rushed a brick wall for all that Solan gave way.

In fact, I came near to impaling myself upon his point for my pains; but right was on my side, and I think that that must give a man greater confidence than though he knew himself to be battling in a wicked cause.

At least, I did not want in confidence; and when I next rushed Solan it was to one side with implicit confidence that he must turn to meet my new line of attack, and turn he did, so that now we fought with our sides towards the coveted goal—the great switch stood within my reach upon my right hand.

To uncover my breast for an instant would have been to court sudden death, but I saw no other way than to chance it, if by so doing I might rescue that oncoming, succoring fleet; and so, in the face of a wicked sword-thrust, I reached out my point and caught the great switch a sudden blow that released it from its seating.

So surprised and horrified was Solan that he forgot to finish his thrust; instead, he wheeled toward the switch with a loud shriek—a shriek which was his last, for before his hand could touch the lever it sought, my sword's point had passed through his heart.

THE TIDE OF BATTLE

But Solan's last loud cry had not been without effect, for a moment later a dozen guardsmen burst into the chamber, though not before I had so bent and demolished the great switch that it could not be again used to turn the powerful current into the mighty magnet of destruction it controlled.

The result of the sudden coming of the guardsmen had been to compel me to seek seclusion in the first passageway that I could find, and that to my disappointment proved to be not the one with which I was familiar, but another upon its left.

They must have either heard or guessed which way I went, for I had proceeded but a short distance when I heard the sound of pursuit. I had no mind to stop and fight these men here when there was fighting aplenty elsewhere in the city of Kadabra—fighting that could be of much more avail to me and mine than useless life-taking far below the palace.

But the fellows were pressing me; and as I did not know the way at all, I soon saw that they would overtake me unless I found a place to conceal myself until they had passed, which would then give me an opportunity to return the way I had come and regain the tower, or possibly find a way to reach the city streets.

The passageway had risen rapidly since leaving the apartment of the switch, and now ran level and well lighted straight into the distance as far as I could see. The moment that my pursuers reached this straight stretch I would be in plain sight of them, with no chance to escape from the corridor undetected.

Presently I saw a series of doors opening from either side of the corridor, and as they all looked alike to me I tried the first one that I reached. It opened into a small chamber, luxuriously furnished, and was evidently an ante-chamber off some office or audience chamber of the palace.

On the far side was a heavily curtained doorway beyond which I heard the hum of voices. Instantly I crossed the small chamber, and, parting the curtains, looked within the larger apartment.

Before me were a party of perhaps fifty gorgeously clad nobles of the court, standing before a throne upon which sat Salensus Oll. The Jeddak of Jeddaks was addressing them.

"The allotted hour has come," he was saying as I entered the apartment; "and though the enemies of Okar be within her gates, naught may stay the will of Salensus Oll. The great ceremony must be omitted that no single man may be kept from his place in the defenses other than the fifty that custom demands shall witness the creation of a new queen in Okar.

"In a moment the thing shall have been done and we may return to the battle, while she who is now the Princess of Helium looks down from the queen's tower upon the annihilation of her former countrymen and witnesses the greatness which is her husband's."

Then, turning to a courtier, he issued some command in a low voice.

The addressed hastened to a small door at the far end of the chamber and, swinging it wide, cried: "Way for Dejah Thoris, future Queen of Okar!"

Immediately two guardsmen appeared dragging the unwilling bride toward the altar. Her hands were still manacled behind her, evidently to prevent suicide.

Her disheveled hair and panting bosom betokened that, chained though she was, still had she fought against the thing that they would do to her.

At sight of her Salensus Oll rose and drew his sword, and the sword of each of the fifty nobles was raised on high to form an arch, beneath which the poor, beautiful creature was dragged toward her doom.

A grim smile forced itself to my lips as I thought of the rude awakening that lay in store for the ruler of Okar, and my itching fingers fondled the hilt of my bloody sword.

As I watched the procession that moved slowly toward the throne—a procession which consisted of but a handful of priests, who followed Dejah Thoris and the two guardsmen—I caught a fleeting glimpse of a black face peering from behind the draperies that covered the wall back of the dais upon which stood Salensus Oll awaiting his bride.

Now the guardsmen were forcing the Princess of Helium up the few steps to the side of the tyrant of Okar, and I had no eyes and no thoughts for aught else. A priest opened a book and, raising his hand, commenced to drone out a sing-song ritual. Salensus Oll reached for the hand of his bride.

I had intended waiting until some circumstance should give me a reasonable hope of success; for, even though the entire ceremony should be completed, there could be no valid marriage while I lived. What I was most concerned in, of course, was the rescuing of Dejah Thoris—I wished to take her from the palace of Salensus Oll, if such a thing were possible; but whether it were accomplished before or after the mock marriage was a matter of secondary import.

When, however, I saw the vile hand of Salensus Oll reach out for the hand of my beloved princess I could restrain myself no longer, and before the nobles of Okar knew that aught had happened I had leaped through their thin line and was upon the dais beside Dejah Thoris and Salensus Oll.

With the flat of my sword I struck down his polluting hand; and grasping Dejah Thoris round the waist, I swung her behind me as, with my back against the draperies of the dais, I faced the tyrant of the north and his roomful of noble warriors.

The Jeddak of Jeddaks was a great mountain of a man—a coarse, brutal beast of a man—and as he towered above me there, his fierce black whiskers and mustache bristling in rage, I can well imagine that a less seasoned warrior might have trembled before him.

With a snarl he sprang toward me with naked sword, but whether Salensus Oll was a good swordsman or a poor I never learned; for with Dejah Thoris at my back I was no longer human—I was a superman, and no man could have withstood me then.

With a single, low: "For the Princess of Helium!" I ran my blade straight through the rotten heart of Okar's rotten ruler, and before the white, drawn faces of his nobles Salensus Oll rolled, grinning in horrible death, to the foot of the steps below his marriage throne.

For a moment tense silence reigned in the nuptial-room. Then the fifty nobles rushed upon me. Furiously we fought, but the advantage was mine, for I stood upon a raised platform above them, and I fought for the most glorious woman

136

of a glorious race, and I fought for a great love and for the mother of my boy.

And from behind my shoulder, in the silvery cadence of that dear voice, rose the brave battle anthem of Helium which the nation's women sing as their men march out to victory.

That alone was enough to inspire me to victory over even greater odds, and I verily believe that I should have bested the entire roomful of yellow warriors that day in the nuptial chamber of the palace at Kadabra had not interruption come to my aid.

Fast and furious was the fighting as the nobles of Salensus Oll sprang, time and again, up the steps before the throne only to fall back before a sword hand that seemed to have gained a new wizardry from its experience with the cunning Solan.

Two were pressing me so closely that I could not turn when I heard a movement behind me, and noted that the sound of the battle anthem had ceased. Was Dejah Thoris preparing to take her place beside me?

Heroic daughter of a heroic world! It would not be unlike her to have seized a sword and fought at my side, for, though the women of Mars are not trained in the arts of war, the spirit is theirs, and they have been known to do that very thing upon countless occasions.

But she did not come, and glad I was, for it would have doubled my burden in protecting her before I should have been able to force her back again out of harm's way. She must be contemplating some cunning strategy, I thought, and so I fought on secure in the belief that my divine princess stood close behind me.

For half an hour at least I must have fought there against the nobles of Okar ere ever a one placed a foot upon the dais where I stood, and then of a sudden all that remained of them formed below me for a last, mad, desperate charge; but even as they advanced the door at the far end of the chamber swung wide and a wild-eyed messenger sprang into the room.

"The Jeddak of Jeddaks!" he cried. "Where is the Jeddak of Jeddaks? The city has fallen before the hordes from beyond the barrier, and but now the great gate of the palace itself has been forced and the warriors of the south are pouring into its sacred precincts.

"Where is Salensus Oll? He alone may revive the flagging

courage of our warriors. He alone may save the day for Okar. Where is Salensus Oll?"

The nobles stepped back from about the dead body of their ruler, and one of them pointed to the grinning corpse.

The messenger staggered back in horror as though from a blow in the face.

"Then fly, nobles of Okar!" he cried, "for naught can save you. Hark! They come!"

As he spoke we heard the deep roar of angry men from the corridor without, and the clank of metal and the clang of swords.

Without another glance toward me, who had stood a spectator of the tragic scene, the nobles wheeled and fled from the apartment through another exit.

Almost immediately a force of yellow warriors appeared in the doorway through which the messenger had come. They were backing toward the apartment, stubbornly resisting the advance of a handful of red men who faced them and forced them slowly but inevitably back.

Above the heads of the contestants I could see from my elevated station upon the dais the face of my old friend Kantos Kan. He was leading the little party that had won its way into the very heart of the palace of Salensus Oll.

In an instant I saw that by attacking the Okarians from the rear I could so quickly disorganize them that their further resistance would be short-lived, and with this idea in mind I sprang from the dais, casting a word of explanation to Dejah Thoris over my shoulder, though I did not turn to look at her.

With myself ever between her enemies and herself, and with Kantos Kan and his warriors winning to the apartment, there could be no danger to Dejah Thoris standing there alone beside the throne.

I wanted the men of Helium to see me and to know that their beloved princess was here, too, for I knew that this knowledge would inspire them to even greater deeds of valor than they had performed in the past, though great indeed must have been those which won for them a way into the almost impregnable palace of the tyrant of the north.

As I crossed the chamber to attack the Kadabrans from the rear a small doorway at my left opened, and, to my surprise, revealed the figures of Matai Shang, Father of Thern and Phaidor, his daughter, peering into the room.

A quick glance about they took. Their eyes rested for a moment, wide in horror, upon the dead body of Salensus Oll, upon the blood that crimsoned the floor, upon the corpses of the nobles who had fallen thick before the throne, upon me, and upon the battling warriors at the other door.

They did not essay to enter the apartment, but scanned its every corner from where they stood, and then, when their eyes had sought its entire area, a look of fierce rage overspread the features of Matai Shang, and a cold and cunning smile touched the lips of Phaidor.

Then they were gone, but not before a taunting laugh was thrown directly in my face by the woman.

I did not understand then the meaning of Matai Shang's rage or Phaidor's pleasure, but I knew that neither boded good for me.

A moment later I was upon the backs of the yellow men, and as the red men of Helium saw me above the shoulders of their antagonists a great shout rang through the corridor, and for a moment drowned the noise of battle.

"For the Prince of Helium!" they cried. "For the Prince of Helium!" and, like hungry lions upon their prey, they fell once more upon the weakening warriors of the north.

The yellow men, cornered between two enemies, fought with the desperation that utter hopelessness often induces. Fought as I should have fought had I been in their stead, with the determination to take as many of my enemies with me when I died as lay within the power of my sword arm.

It was a glorious battle, but the end seemed inevitable, when presently from down the corridor behind the red men came a great body of reenforcing yellow warriors.

Now were the tables turned, and it was the men of Helium who seemed doomed to be ground between two millstones. All were compelled to turn to meet this new assault by a greatly superior force, so that to me was left the remnants of the yellow men within the throneroom.

They kept me busy, too; so busy that I began to wonder if indeed I should ever be done with them. Slowly they pressed me back into the room, and when they had all passed in after me, one of them closed and bolted the door, effectually barring the way against the men of Kantos Kan.

It was a clever move, for it put me at the mercy of a dozen men within a chamber from which assistance was locked out, and it gave the red men in the corridor beyond no avenue of escape should their new antagonists press them too closely.

But I have faced heavier odds myself than were pitted against me that day, and I knew that Kantos Kan had battled his way from a hundred more dangerous traps than that in which he now was. So it was with no feelings of despair that I turned my attention to the business of the moment.

Constantly my thoughts reverted to Dejah Thoris, and I longed for the moment when, the fighting done, I could fold her in my arms, and hear once more the words of love which had been denied me for so many years.

During the fighting in the chamber I had not even a single chance to so much as steal a glance at her where she stood behind me beside the throne of the dead ruler. I wondered why she no longer urged me on with the strains of the martial hymn of Helium; but I did not need more than the knowledge that I was battling for her to bring out the best that is in me.

It would be wearisome to narrate the details of that bloody struggle; of how we fought from the doorway, the full length of the room to the very foot of the throne before the last of my antagonists fell with my blade piercing his heart.

And then, with a glad cry, I turned with outstretched arms to seize my princess, and as my lips smothered hers to reap the reward that would be thrice ample payment for the bloody encounters through which I had passed for her dear sake from the south pole to the north.

The glad cry died, frozen upon my lips; my arms dropped limp and lifeless to my sides; as one who reels beneath the burden of a mortal wound I staggered up the steps before the throne.

Dejah Thoris was gone.

REWARDS

WITH the realization that Dejah Thoris was no longer within the throneroom came the belated recollection of the dark face that I had glimpsed peering from behind the draperies that backed the throne of Salensus Oll at the moment that I had first come so unexpectedly upon the strange scene being enacted within the chamber.

Why had the sight of that evil countenance not warned me to greater caution? Why had I permitted the rapid development of new situations to efface the recollection of that menacing danger? But, alas, vain regret would not erase the calamity that had befallen.

Once again had Dejah Thoris fallen into the clutches of that archfiend, Thurid, the black dator of the First Born. Again was all my arduous labor gone for naught. Now I realized the cause of the rage that had been writ so large upon the features of Matai Shang and the cruel pleasure that I had seen upon the face of Phaidor.

They had known or guessed the truth, and the hekkador of the Holy Therns, who had evidently come to the chamber in the hope of thwarting Salensus Oll in his contemplated perfidy against the high priest who coveted Dejah Thoris for himself, realized that Thurid had stolen the prize from beneath his very nose.

Phaidor's pleasure had been due to her realization of what this last cruel blow would mean to me, as well as to a partial satisfaction of her jealous hatred for the Princess of Helium.

My first thought was to look beyond the draperies at the back of the throne, for there it was that I had seen Thurid. With a single jerk I tore the priceless stuff from its fastenings, and there before me was revealed a narrow doorway behind the throne.

No question entered my mind but that here lay the opening of the avenue of escape which Thurid had followed, and had there been it would have been dissipated by the sight of a tiny, jeweled ornament which lay a few steps within the corridor beyond.

As I snatched up the bauble I saw that it bore the device of the Princess of Helium, and then pressing it to my lips I dashed madly along the winding way that led gently downward toward the lower galleries of the palace.

I had followed but a short distance when I came upon the room in which Solan formerly had held sway. His dead body still lay where I had left it, nor was there any sign that another had passed through the room since I had been there; but I knew that two had done so—Thurid, the black dator, and Dejah Thoris.

For a moment I paused uncertain as to which of the several exits from the apartment would lead me upon the right path. I tried to recollect the directions which I had heard Thurid repeat to Solan, and at last, slowly, as though through a heavy fog, the memory of the words of the First Born came to me:

"Follow a corridor, passing three diverging corridors upon the right; then into the fourth right-hand corridor to where three corridors meet; here again follow to the right, hugging the left wall closely to avoid the pit. At the end of this corridor I shall come to a spiral runway which I must follow down instead of up; after that the way is along but a single branchless corridor."

And I recalled the exit at which he had pointed as he spoke.

It did not take me long to start upon that unknown way, nor did I go with caution, although I knew that there might be grave dangers before me.

Part of the way was black as sin, but for the most it was fairly well lighted. The stretch where I must hug the left wall to avoid the pits was darkest of them all, and I was nearly over the edge of the abyss before I knew that I was near the danger spot.

A narrow ledge, scarce a foot wide, was all that had been left to carry the initiated past that frightful cavity into which the unknowing must surely have toppled at the first step. But at last I had won safely beyond it, and then a feeble light made the balance of the way plain, until, at the end of the last corridor, I came suddenly out into the glare of day upon a field of snow and ice.

Clad for the warm atmosphere of the hothouse city of Kadabra, the sudden change to arctic frigidity was anything but pleasant; but the worst of it was that I knew I could not endure the bitter cold, almost naked as I was, and that I would perish before ever I could overtake Thurid and Dejah Thoris.

To be thus blocked by nature, who had had all the arts and wiles of cunning man pitted against him, seemed a cruel fate, and as I staggered back into the warmth of the tunnel's end I was as near hopelessness as I ever have been.

I had by no means given up my intention of continuing the pursuit, for if needs be I would go ahead though I perished ere ever I reached my goal, but if there were a safer way it were well worth the delay to attempt to discover it, that I might come again to the side of Dejah Thoris in fit condition to do battle for her.

Scarce had I returned to the tunnel than I stumbled over a portion of a fur garment that seemed fastened to the floor of the corridor close to the wall. In the darkness I could not see what held it, but by groping with my hands I discovered that it was wedged beneath the bottom of a closed door.

Pushing the portal aside, I found myself upon the threshold of a small chamber, the walls of which were lined with hooks from which depended suits of the complete outdoor apparel of the yellow men.

Situated as it was at the mouth of a tunnel leading from the palace, it was quite evident that this was the dressing-room used by the nobles leaving and entering the hothouse city, and that Thurid, having knowledge of it, had stopped here to outfit himself and Dejah Thoris before venturing into the bitter cold of the arctic world beyond.

In his haste he had dropped several garments upon the floor, and the telltale fur that had fallen partly within the corridor had proved the means of guiding me to the very spot he would least have wished me to have knowledge of.

It required but the matter of a few seconds to don the necessary orluk-skin clothing, with the heavy, fur-lined boots that are so essential a part of the garmenture of one who would successfully contend with the frozen trails and the icy winds of the bleak northland.

Once more I stepped beyond the tunnel's mouth to find the fresh tracks of Thurid and Dejah Thoris in the new-fallen snow. Now, at last, was my task an easy one, for though the going was rough in the extreme, I was no longer vexed by doubts as to the direction I should follow, or harassed by darkness or hidden dangers.

Through a snow-covered cañon the way led up toward the summit of low hills. Beyond these it dipped again into another cañon, only to rise a quarter-mile farther on toward a pass which skirted the flank of a rocky hill.

I could see by the signs of those who had gone before that when Dejah Thoris had walked she had been continually holding back, and that the black man had been compelled to drag her. For other stretches only his foot-prints were visible, deep and close together in the heavy snow, and I knew from these signs that then he had been forced to carry her, and I could well imagine that she had fought him fiercely every step of the way.

As I came round the jutting promontory of the hill's shoulder I saw that which quickened my pulses and set my heart to beating high, for within a tiny basin between the crest of this hill and the next stood four people before the mouth of a great cave, and beside them upon the gleaming snow rested a flier which had evidently but just been dragged from its hiding place.

The four were Dejah Thoris, Phaidor, Thurid, and Matai Shang. The two men were engaged in a heated argument —the Father of Therns threatening, while the black scoffed at him as he went about the work at which he was engaged.

As I crept toward them cautiously that I might come as near as possible before being discovered, I saw that finally the men appeared to have reached some sort of a compromise, for with Phaidor's assistance they both set about dragging the resisting Dejah Thoris to the flier's deck.

Here they made her fast, and then both again descended to the ground to complete the preparations for departure. Phaidor entered the small cabin upon the vessel's deck.

I had come to within a quarter of a mile of them when Matai Shang espied me. I saw him seize Thurid by the shoulder, wheeling him around in my direction as he pointed to where I was now plainly visible, for the moment that I knew I had been perceived I cast aside every attempt at stealth and broke into a mad race for the flier.

The two redoubled their efforts at the propeller at which

144

they were working, and which very evidently was being replaced after having been removed for some purpose of repair.

They had the thing completed before I had covered half the distance that lay between me and them, and then both made a rush for the boarding-ladder.

Thurid was the first to reach it, and with the agility of a monkey clambered swiftly to the boat's deck, where a touch of the button controlling the buoyancy tanks sent the craft slowly upward, though not with the speed that marks the well-conditioned flier.

I was still some hundred yards away as I saw them rising from my grasp.

Back by the city of Kadabra lay a great fleet of mighty fliers —the ships of Helium and Ptarth that I had saved from destruction earlier in the day; but before ever I could reach them Thurid could easily make good his escape.

As I ran I saw Matai Shang clambering up the swaying, swinging ladder toward the deck, while above him leaned the evil face of the First Born. A trailing rope from the vessel's stern put new hope in me, for if I could but reach it before it whipped too high above my head there was yet a chance to gain the deck by its slender aid.

That there was something radically wrong with the flier was evident from its lack of buoyancy, and the further fact that though Thurid had turned twice to the starting lever the boat still hung motionless in the air, except for a slight drifting with a low breeze from the north.

Now Matai Shang was close to the gunwale. A long, claw-like hand was reaching up to grasp the metal rail.

Thurid leaned farther down toward his co-conspirator.

Suddenly a raised dagger gleamed in the upflung hand of the black. Down it drove toward the white face of the Father of Therns. With a loud shriek of fear the Holy Hekkador grasped frantically at that menacing arm.

I was almost to the trailing rope by now. The craft was still rising slowly, the while it drifted from me. Then I stumbled on the icy way, striking my head upon a rock as I fell sprawling but an arm's length from the rope, the end of which was now just leaving the ground.

With the blow upon my head came unconsciousness.

It could not have been more than a few seconds that I lay

senseless there upon the northern ice, while all that was dearest to me drifted farther from my reach in the clutches of that black fiend, for when I opened my eyes Thurid and Matai Shang yet battled at the ladder's top, and the flier drifted but a hundred yards farther to the south—but the end of the trailing rope was now a good thirty feet above the ground.

Goaded to madness by the cruel misfortune that had tripped me when success was almost within my grasp, I tore frantically across the intervening space, and just beneath the rope's dangling end I put my earthly muscles to the supreme test.

With a mighty, catlike bound I sprang upward toward that slender strand—the only avenue which yet remained that could carry me to my vanishing love.

A foot above its lowest end my fingers closed. Tightly as I clung I felt the rope slipping, slipping through my grasp. I tried to raise my free hand to take a second hold above my first, but the change of position that resulted caused me to slip more rapidly toward the end of the rope.

Slowly I felt the tantalizing thing escaping me. In a moment all that I had gained would be lost—then my fingers reached a knot at the very end of the rope and slipped no more.

With a prayer of gratitude upon my lips I scrambled upward toward the boat's deck. I could not see Thurid and Matai Shang now, but I heard the sounds of conflict and thus knew that they still fought—the thern for his life and the black for the incrased buoyancy that relief from the weight of even a single body would give the craft.

Should Matai Shang die before I reached the deck my chances of ever reaching it would be slender indeed, for the black dator need but cut the rope above me to be freed from me forever, for the vessel had drifted across the brink of a chasm into whose yawning depths my body would drop to be crushed to a shapeless pulp should Thurid reach the rope now.

At last my hand closed upon the ship's rail and that very instant a horrid shriek rang out below me that sent my blood cold and turned my horrified eyes downward to a shrieking, hurtling, twisting thing that shot downward into the awful chasm beneath me.

It was Matai Shang, Holy Hekkador, Father of Therns, gone to his last accounting.

Then my head came above the deck and I saw Thurid, dagger in hand, leaping toward me. He was opposite the forward end of the cabin, while I was attempting to clamber aboard near the vessel's stern. But a few paces lay between us. No power on earth could raise me to that deck before the infuriated black would be upon me.

My end had come. I knew it; but had there been a doubt in my mind the nasty leer of triumph upon that wicked face would have convinced me. Beyond Thurid I could see my Dejah Thoris, wide-eyed and horrified, struggling at her bonds. That she should be forced to witness my awful death made my bitter fate seem doubly cruel.

I ceased my efforts to climb across the gunwale. Instead I took a firm grasp upon the rail with my left hand and drew my dagger.

I should at least die as I had lived—fighting.

As Thurid came opposite the cabin's doorway a new element projected itself into the grim tragedy of the air that was being enacted upon the deck of Matai Shang's disabled flier.

It was Phaidor.

With flushed face and disheveled hair, and eyes that betrayed the recent presence of mortal tears—above which this proud goddess had always held herself—she leaped to the deck directly before me.

In her hand was a long, slim dagger. I cast a last look upon my beloved princess, smiling, as men should who are about to die. Then I turned my face up toward Phaidor —waiting for the blow.

Never have I seen that beautiful face more beautiful than it was at that moment. It seemed incredible that one so lovely could yet harbor within her fair bosom a heart so cruel and relentless, and today there was a new expression in her wondrous eyes that I never before had seen there—an unfamiliar softness, and a look of suffering.

Thurid was beside her now—pushing past to reach me first, and then what happened happened so quickly that it was all over before I could realize the truth of it.

Phaidor's slim hand shot out to close upon the black's dagger wrist. Her right hand went high with its gleaming blade.

147

"That for Matai Shang!" she cried, and she buried her blade deep in the dator's breast. "That for the wrong you would have done Dejah Thoris!" and again the sharp steel sank into the bloody flesh.

"And that, and that, and that!" she shrieked, "for John Carter, Prince of Helium," and with each word her sharp point pierced the vile heart of the great villain. Then, with a vindictive shove she cast the carcass of the First Born from the deck to fall in awful silence after the body of his victim.

I had been so paralyzed by surprise that I had made no move to reach the deck during the awe-inspiring scene which I had just witnessed, and now I was to be still further amazed by her next act, for Phaidor extended her hand to me and assisted me to the deck, where I stood gazing at her in unconcealed and stupefied wonderment.

A wan smile touched her lips—it was not the cruel and haughty smile of the goddess with which I was familiar. "You wonder, John Carter," she said, "what strange thing has wrought this change in me? I will tell you. It is love —love of you," and when I darkened my brows in disapproval of her words she raised an appealing hand.

"Wait," she said. "It is a different love from mine—it is the love of your princess, Dejah Thoris, for you that has taught me what true love may be—what it should be, and how far from real love was my selfish and jealous passion for you.

"Now am I different. Now could I love as Dejah Thoris loves, and so my only happiness can be to know that you and she are once more united, for in her alone can you find true happiness.

"But I am unhappy because of the wickedness that I have wrought. I have many sins to expiate, and though I be deathless, life is all too short for the atonement.

"But there is another way, and if Phaidor, daughter of the Holy Hekkador of the Holy Therns, has sinned she has this day already made partial reparation, and lest you doubt the sincerity of her protestations and her avowal of a new love that embraces Dejah Thoris also, she will prove her sincerity in the only way that lies open—having saved you for another, Phaidor leaves you to her embraces."

With her last word she turned and leaped from the vessel's deck into the abyss below.

With a cry of horror I sprang forward in a vain attempt to save the life that for two years I would so gladly have seen extinguished. I was too late.

With tear-dimmed eyes I turned away that I might not see the awful sight beneath.

A moment later I had struck the bonds from Dejah Thoris, and as her dear arms went about my neck and her perfect lips pressed to mine I forgot the horrors that I had witnessed and the suffering that I had endured in the rapture of my reward.

THE NEW RULER

THE flier upon whose deck Dejah Thoris and I found ourselves after twelve long years of separation proved entirely
useless. Her buoyancy tanks leaked badly. Her engine would
not start. We were helpless there in mid air above the
arctic ice.

The craft had drifted across the chasm which held the
corpses of Matai Shang, Thurid, and Phaidor, and now hung
above a low hill. Opening the buoyancy escape valves I permitted her to come slowly to the ground, and as she touched,
Dejah Thoris and I stepped from her deck and, hand in
hand, turned back across the frozen waste toward the city of
Kadabra.

Through the tunnel that had led me in pursuit of them we
passed, walking slowly, for we had much to say to each
other.

She told me of that last terrible moment months before
when the door of her prison cell within the Temple of the
Sun was slowly closing between us. Of how Phaidor had
sprung upon her with uplifted dagger, and of Thuvia's
shriek as she had realized the foul intention of the thern
goddess.

It had been that cry that had rung in my ears all the long,
weary months that I had been left in cruel doubt as to my
princess' fate; for I had not known that Thuvia had wrested
the blade from the daughter of Matai Shang before it had
touched either Dejah Thoris or herself.

She told me, too, of the awful eternity of her imprisonment.
Of the cruel hatred of Phaidor, and the tender love of
Thuvia, and of how even when despair was the darkest those
two red girls had clung to the same hope and belief—that
John Carter would find a way to release them.

Presently we came to the chamber of Solan. I had
been proceeding without thought of caution, for I was sure
that the city and the palace were both in the hands of my
friends by this time.

And so it was that I bolted into the chamber full into the midst of a dozen nobles of the court of Salensus Oll. They were passing through on their way to the outside world along the corridors we had just traversed.

At sight of us they halted in their tracks, and then an ugly smile overspread the features of their leader.

"The author of all our misfortunes!" he cried, pointing at me. "We shall have the satisfaction of a partial vengeance at least when we leave behind us here the dead and mutilated corpses of the Prince and Princess of Helium.

"When they find them," he went on, jerking his thumb upward toward the palace above, "they will realize that the vengeance of the yellow man costs his enemies dear. Prepare to die, John Carter, but that your end may be the more bitter, know that I may change my intention as to meting a merciful death to your princess—possibly she shall be preserved as a plaything for my nobles."

I stood close to the instrument-covered wall—Dejah Thoris at my side. She looked up at me wonderingly as the warriors advanced upon us with drawn swords, for mine still hung within its scabbard at my side, and there was a smile upon my lips.

The yellow nobles, too, looked in surprise, and then as I made no move to draw they hesitated, fearing a ruse; but their leader urged them on. When they had come almost within sword's reach of me I raised my hand and laid it upon the polished surface of a great lever, and then, still smiling grimly, I looked my enemies full in the face.

As one they came to a sudden stop, casting affrighted glances at me and at one another.

"Stop!" shrieked their leader. "You dream not what you do!"

"Right you are," I replied. "John Carter does not dream. He knows—knows that should one of you take another step toward Dejah Thoris, Princess of Helium, I pull this lever wide, and she and I shall die together; but we shall not die alone."

The nobles shrank back, whispering together for a few moments. At last their leader turned to me.

"Go your way, John Carter," he said, "and we shall go ours."

"Prisoners do not go their own way," I answered, "and you are prisoners—prisoners of the Prince of Helium."

Before they could make answer a door upon the opposite side of the apartment opened and a score of yellow men poured into the apartment. For an instant the nobles looked relieved, and then as their eyes fell upon the leader of the new party their faces fell, for he was Talu, rebel Prince of Marentina, and they knew that they could look for neither aid nor mercy at his hands.

Talu took in the situation at a glance, smiling.

"Well done, John Carter," he cried. "You turn their own mighty power against them. Fortunate for Okar is it that you were here to prevent their escape, for these be the greatest villains north of the ice-barrier, and this one"—pointing to the leader of the party—"would have made himself Jeddak of Jeddaks in the place of the dead Salensus Oll. Then indeed would we have had a more villainous ruler than the hated tyrant who fell before your sword."

The Okarian nobles now submitted to arrest, since nothing but death faced them should they resist, and, escorted by the warriors of Talu, we made our way to the great audience chamber that had been Salensus Oll's. Here was a vast concourse of warriors.

Red men from Helium and Ptarth, yellow men of the north, rubbing elbows with the blacks of the First Born who had come under my friend Xodar to help in the search for me and my princess. There were savage, green warriors from the dead sea bottoms of the south, and a handful of white-skinned therns who had renounced their religion and sworn allegiance to Xodar.

There was Tardos Mors and Mors Kajak, and tall and mighty in his gorgeous warrior trappings, Carthoris, my son. These three fell upon Dejah Thoris as we entered the apartment, and though the lives and training of royal Martians tend not toward vulgar demonstration, I thought that they would suffocate her with their embraces.

And there were Tars Tarkas, Jeddak of Thark, and Kantos Kan, my old-time friends, and leaping and tearing at my harness in the exuberance of his great love was dear old Woola—frantic mad with happiness.

Long and loud was the cheering that burst forth at sight of us; deafening was the din of ringing metal as the veteran

152

warriors of every Martian clime clashed their blades together on high in token of success and victory, but as I passed among the throng of saluting nobles and warriors, jeds and jeddaks, my heart still was heavy, for there were two faces missing that I would have given much to have seen there—Thuvan Dihn and Thuvia of Ptarth were not to be found in the great chamber.

I made inquiries concerning them among men of every nation, and at last from one of the yellow prisoners of war I learned that they had been apprehended by an officer of the palace as they sought to reach the Pit of Plenty while I lay imprisoned there.

I did not need to ask to know what had sent them thither —the courageous jeddak and his loyal daughter. My informer said that they lay now in one of the many buried dungeons of the palace where they had been placed pending a decision as to their fate by the tyrant of the north.

A moment later searching parties were scouring the ancient pile in search of them, and my cup of happiness was full when I saw them being escorted into the room by a cheering guard of honor.

Thuvia's first act was to rush to the side of Dejah Thoris, and I needed no better proof of the love these two bore for each other than the sincerity with which they embraced.

Looking down upon that crowded chamber stood the silent and empty throne of Okar.

Of all the strange scenes it must have witnessed since that long-dead age that had first seen a Jeddak of Jeddaks take his seat upon it, none might compare with that upon which it now looked down, and as I pondered the past and future of that long-buried race of black-bearded yellow men I thought that I saw a brighter and more useful existence for them among the great family of friendly nations that now stretched from the south pole almost to their very doors.

Twenty-two years before I had been cast, naked and a stranger, into this strange and savage world. The hand of every race and nation was raised in continual strife and warring against the men of every other land and color. Today, by the might of my sword and the loyalty of the friends my sword had made for me, black man and white, red man and green, rubbed shoulders in peace and good-fellowship. All the nations of Barsoom were not yet as one, but a great stride forward toward that goal had been taken, and now if I could but cement the fierce yellow race into this sodality of nations I should feel that I had rounded out a great life-work, and repaid to Mars at least a portion of the immense debt of gratitude I owed her for having given me my Dejah Thoris.

And as I thought, I saw but one way, and a single man who could insure the success of my hopes. As is ever the way with me, I acted then as I always act—without deliberation and without consultation.

Those who do not like my plans and my ways of promoting them have always their swords at their sides wherewith to back up their disapproval; but now there seemed to be no dissenting voice, as, grasping Talu by the arm, I sprang to the throne that had once been Salensus Oll's.

"Warriors of Barsoom," I cried, "Kadabra has fallen, and with her the hateful tyrant of the north; but the integrity of Okar must be preserved. The red men are ruled by red jeddaks, the green warriors of the ancient seas acknowledge none but a green ruler, the First Born of the south pole take their law from black Xodar; nor would it be to the interests of either yellow or red man were a red jeddak to sit upon the throne of Okar.

"There be but one warrior best fitted for the ancient and mighty title of Jeddak of Jeddaks of the North. Men of Okar, raise your swords to your new ruler—Talu, the rebel Prince of Marentina!"

And then a great cry of rejoicing rose among the free men of Marentina and the Kadabran prisoners, for all had thought that the red men would retain that which they had taken by force of arms, for such had been the way upon Barsoom, and that they should be ruled henceforth by an alien Jeddak.

The victorious warriors who had followed Carthoris joined in the mad demonstration, and amidst the wild confusion and the tumult and the cheering, Dejah Thoris and I passed out into the gorgeous garden of the jeddaks that graces the inner courtyard of the palace of Kadabra.

At our heels walked Woola, and upon a carved seat of wondrous beauty beneath a bower of purple blooms we saw two who had preceded us—Thuvia of Ptarth and Carthoris of Helium.

The handsome head of the handsome youth was bent low above the beautiful face of his companion. I looked at Dejah Thoris, smiling, and as I drew her close to me I whispered: "Why not?"

Indeed, why not? What matter ages in this world of perpetual youth?

We remained at Kadabra, the guests of Talu, until after his formal induction into office, and then, upon the great fleet which I had been so fortunate to preserve from destruction, we sailed south across the ice-barrier; but not before we had witnessed the total demolition of the grim Guardian of the North under orders of the new Jeddak of Jeddaks.

"Henceforth," he said, as the work was completed, "the fleets of the red men and the black are free to come and go across the ice-barrier as over their own lands.

"The Carrion Caves shall be cleansed, that the green men may find an easy way to the land of the yellow, and the hunting of the sacred apt shall be the sport of my nobles until no single specimen of that hideous creature roams the frozen north."

We bade our yellow friends farewell with real regret, as we set sail for Ptarth. There we remained, the guest of Thuvan Dihn, for a month; and I could see that Carthoris would have remained forever had he not been a Prince of Helium.

Above the mighty forests of Kaol we hovered until word from Kulan Tith brought us to his single landing-tower, where all day and half a night the vessels disembarked their crews. At the city of Kaol we visited, cementing the new ties that had been formed between Kaol and Helium, and then one long-to-be-remembered day we sighted the tall, thin towers of the twin cities of Helium.

The people had long been preparing for our coming. The sky was gorgeous with gaily trimmed fliers. Every roof within both cities was spread with costly silks and tapestries.

Gold and jewels were scattered over roof and street and plaza, so that the two cities seemed ablaze with the fires of the hearts of the magnificent stones and burnished metal that reflected the brilliant sunlight, changing it into countless glorious hues.

At last, after twelve years, the royal family of Helium was reunited in their own mighty city, surrounded by joy-mad millions before the palace gates. Women and children and mighty warriors wept in gratitude for the fate that had restored their beloved Tardos Mors and the divine princess whom the whole nation idolized. Nor did any of us who had been upon that expedition of indescribable danger and glory lack for plaudits.

That night a messenger came to me as I sat with Dejah Thoris and Carthoris upon the roof of my city palace, where we had long since caused a lovely garden to be made that we three might find seclusion and quiet happiness among ourselves, far from the pomp and ceremony of court, to summon us to the Temple of Reward—"where one is to be judged this night," the summons concluded.

I racked my brain to try and determine what important case there might be pending which could call the royal family from their palaces on the eve of their return to Helium after years of absence; but when the jeddak summons no man delays.

As our flier touched the landing stage at the temple's top we saw countless other craft arriving and departing. In the streets below a great multitude surged toward the great gates of the temple.

Slowly there came to me the recollection of the deferred doom that awaited me since that time I had been tried here in the Temple by Zat Arrras for the sin of returning from the Valley Dor and the Lost Sea of Korus.

Could it be possible that the strict sense of justice which dominates the men of Mars had caused them to overlook the great good that had come out of my heresy? Had they so soon forgotten the debt they owed me in releasing them from the bondage of their horrid belief? Could they ignore the fact that to me, and me alone, was due the rescue of Carthoris, of Dejah Thoris, of Mors Kajak, of Tardos Mors?

I could not believe it, and yet for what other purpose could I have been summoned to the Temple of Reward immediately upon the return of Tardos Mors to his throne?

My first surprise as I entered the temple and approached the Throne of Righteousness was to note the men who sat there as judges. There was Kulan Tith, Jeddak of Kaol, whom we had but just left within his own palace a few days since; there was Thuvan Dihn, Jeddak of Ptarth—how came he to Helium as soon as we?

There was Tar Tarkas, Jeddak of Thark, and Xodar, Jeddak of the First Born; there was Talu, Jeddak of Jeddaks of the North, whom I could have sworn was still in his ice-bound hothouse city beyond the northern barrier, and among them sat Tardos Mors and Mors Kajak, with enough lesser jeds and jeddaks to make up the thirty-one who must sit in judgment upon their fellow-man.

A right royal tribunal indeed, and such a one, I warrant, as never before sat together during all the history of ancient Mars.

As I entered, silence fell upon the great concourse of people that packed the auditorium. Then Tardos Mors arose.

"John Carter," he said in his deep, martial voice, "take your place upon the Pedestal of Truth, for you are to be tried by a fair and impartial tribunal of your fellow-men."

With level eye and high-held head I did as he bade, and as I glanced about that circle of faces that a moment before I could have sworn contained the best friends I had upon Barsoom, I saw no single friendly glance—only stern, uncompromising judges, there to do their duty.

A clerk rose and from a great book read a long list of the more notable deeds that I had thought to my credit, covering a long period of twenty-two years since first I had stepped the ocher sea bottom beside the incubator of the Tharks. With the others he read of all that I had done within the circle of the Otz Mountains where the Holy Therns and the First Born had held sway.

It is the way upon Barsoom to recite a man's virtues with his sins when he is come to trial, and so I was not surprised that all that was to my credit should be read there to my judges—who knew it all by heart—even down to the present moment. When the reading had ceased Tardos Mors arose.

"Most righteous judges," he exclaimed, "you have heard recited all that is known of John Carter, Prince of Helium—the good with the bad. What is your judgment?"

Then Tars Tarkas came slowly to his feet, unfolding all his mighty, towering height until he loomed, a green-bronze statue, far above us all. He turned a baleful eye upon me—he, Tars Tarkas, with whom I had fought through countless battles; whom I loved as a brother.

I could have wept had I not been so mad with rage that I

157

almost whipped my sword out and had at them all upon the spot.

"Judges," he said, "there can be but one verdict. No longer may John Carter be Prince of Helium"—he paused—"but instead let him be Jeddak of Jeddaks, Warlord of Barsoom!"

As the thirty-one judges sprang to their feet with drawn and upraised swords in unanimous concurrence in the verdict, the storm broke throughout the length and breadth and height of that mighty building until I thought the roof would fall from the thunder of the mad shouting.

Now, at last, I saw the grim humor of the method they had adopted to do me this great honor, but that there was any hoax in the reality of the title they had conferred upon me was readily disproved by the sincerity of the congratulations that were heaped upon me by the judges first and then the nobles.

Presently fifty of the mightiest nobles of the greatest courts of Mars marched down the broad Aisle of Hope bearing a splendid car upon their shoulders, and as the people saw who sat within, the cheers that had rung out for me paled into insignficance beside those which thundered through the vast edifice now, for she whom the nobles carried was Dejah Thoris, beloved Princess of Helium.

Straight to the Throne of Righteousness they bore her, and there Tardos Mors assisted her from the car, leading her forward to my side.

"Let a world's most beautiful woman share the honor of her husband," he said.

Before them all I drew my wife close to me and kissed her upon the lips.

ABOUT EDGAR RICE BURROUGHS

Edgar Rice Burroughs is one of the world's most popular authors. With no previous experience as an author, he wrote and sold his first novel—*A Princess of Mars*—in 1912. In the ensuing thirty-eight years until his death in 1950, Burroughs wrote 91 books and a host of short stories and articles. Although best known as the creator of the classic *Tarzan of the Apes* and *John Carter of Mars,* his restless imagination knew few bounds. Burroughs' prolific pen ranged from the American West to primitive Africa and on to romantic adventure on the moon, the planets, and even beyond the farthest star.

No one knows how many copies of ERB books have been published throughout the world. It is conservative to say, however, that of the translations into 32 known languages, including Braille, the number must run into the hundreds of millions. When one considers the additional world-wide following of the Tarzan newspaper feature, radio programs, comic magazines, motion pictures and television, Burroughs must have been known and loved by literally a thousand million or more.